REMEMBERING HYPATIA

REMEMBERING HYPATIA

a novel of ancient Egypt

Brian Trent

iUniverse, Inc.

New York Lincoln Shanghai

"In Alexandria there was a woman named Hypatia, daughter of the philosopher Theon, who made such attainments in literature and science as to far surpass all others of her own time."

—Socrates Scholasticus, Ecclesiastical History

"And in those days there appeared in Alexandria a female philosopher, a pagan named Hypatia, and she was devoted at all times to magic, and she beguiled many people through her Satanic wiles."

—Bishop John of Nikiu, Chronicle 84.87-103

Before he was taken from the cell, Thasos sat in complete darkness.

He could feel a wooden bench beneath him, and a cold stone floor under his sandaled feet. Two hours earlier when his captors pushed him inside, he got a glimpse of his four-walled prison. Now he was blind in its blackness. Iron shackles weighed heavily on his wrists, but he found that if he sat still he could almost forget about them. Wrapped in shadow, Thasos felt incorporeal, more a ghost than a prisoner of flesh.

Yet the din of the crowd beyond the cell's thick wooden door made his heart stutter.

Thasos breathed deeply. He tried imagining that he was not in a dark cell but rather in a boundless cavern, or even above the clouds where the bright planets wheeled in silent revolutions. *That's it!* he thought, instantly warmed. *Think of the stars, and let them comfort you before you die.*

Then the door burst open, jarring his entranced senses. Two men wearing mud-brown robes that covered them from neck to ankles entered, seized his nineteen-year-old body, and hauled him out into the chill night air. He stumbled on his blistered feet. His tunic was ragged, no longer white but dirtied by miles of travel through Egyptian country.

When he had first returned to Alexandria, when the Archbishop's men arrested him, only a small mob had been present. Now, the Kinaron courtyard swarmed with nearly two hundred eager, bustling bodies and, when they saw him, their yells exploded.

"*You returned to peddle your witchcraft?*" a burly, balding man accused. "We'll return you to *hell!*"

Thasos, hands shackled in front of him, was pushed ahead of his robed captors. At the end of the courtyard, he saw the execution pyre—a mound of chopped wood, with a wooden stake like an upright needle rising from its center. Wood was expensive; it had to be imported to Egypt. Perversely, he imagined the Archbishop's expenditure note: *A few hundred pounds of Lebanese wood for the execution of the last heretic!* Beyond the pyre, the stone courtyard ended abruptly at the dark expanse of the River Nile. The sky was clouded and Thasos could see neither stars nor moon, and so the beloved river appeared like a moving sheet of black silk, less like a giver of life than a stream through the bowels of the underworld.

"Burn her last disciple!" a woman shrieked, and Thasos recoiled as she tried to claw at him from the crowd. His guards led him onto the pyre's uneven slope. There, they spun him around so he faced away from the Nile. His wrists were unshackled, only to be bound to the stake behind him.

Not even allowed to face the Nile, he thought, closing his eyes and trying desperately to concentrate on his breathing. *Moon or no moon, I should be allowed to see the great river in my final moments.*

Suddenly a new cry lifted from the crowd. Thasos opened his eyes to see two wheelbarrows, piled tall with linen-jacketed scrolls and books, pushed toward the pyre by more robed men.

"The witch's books!" someone yelled. "Burn them with her apprentice!" At that, a man sprang at one of the wheelbarrows and grabbed a fistful of scrolls. He threw them at Thasos' feet.

"Take these back to hell, pagan! They have no place here!"

With the frenetic energy of imitative monkeys, the crowd surged to the wheelbarrows, boldly pushing aside the guards' swords to scoop the books into their arms in a grotesque parody of embrace. Eyes glittering, mouths twisted in primitive glee, they pelted the prisoner. The bound volumes rained on his defenseless body. Scrolls popped free of their sheaths and unraveled, fluttering to his feet. There, they collected like crumpled souls discarded from heaven.

Thasos' heart sank at the sight. *I will not despair*, he pleaded, though his hands fisted impotently behind him. With horror he read the scroll covers and book jackets, the Greek and Latin titles faintly visible by nearby torchlight. *Eratosthenes!* he thought. *And Archimedes, and Thales and Democritus! And there, a volume of Heron?* There was even a moldy grey book with Egyptian hieroglyphics pressed into the spine, and this Thasos could not read, but he railed in silent agony at the sight of it, desperate to know what those strange symbols said. Long ago, some native scholar labored to write that volume, inscribing some thought or discovery to papyrus, his oil-lamp burning softly, his fingers trembling with excitement at the notion that his ideas would survive him. And through deep centuries the work *had* survived, a beloved heirloom circulating across generations while Alexander lived and died, while Rome rose like a budding flower, while Carthage vanished in fiery cataclysm, while Cleopatra pressed a cobra to her breast, while Egypt became a province of the Empire...and *here*, now, this sacred book is to meet its end? *No! My friends, I would eagerly burn to spare you this fate! I am nothing, and you are everything that matters.*

Another book landed on the littered heap. Something fell out of its pages, slid down the slope of parchment, and stopped to rest a few inches from his toes.

An envelope. Yellowed about the edges. Sealed with red candle-wax.

Thasos blinked in surprise. He stared at the envelope with growing anxiety.

Black Latin lettering was clearly visible on the envelope's papyrus. Thasos felt his heart stammer. He blinked sweat from his eyes and finally, ending the untold hours of self-control, his face twisted in anguish.

TO THASOS, the lettering said. **FROM THE PHILOSOPHER.**

Breathing hard, Thasos rubbed his shackles into the wooden stake behind him. The shouts continued, parchments rained upon him. Thasos cried out at last, fighting against his bonds to the crowd's enjoyment. A new scroll struck him above his left eye and drew blood. The wound leaked into his eyebrow and spilled like a crimson tear onto his face. Oblivious, he tried to touch the envelope with his feet. His toes knocked it closer, but the hands he needed to open it were imprisoned.

TO THASOS, FROM THE PHILOSOPHER.

Four robed monks drew near with lit torches in their hands.

"*Burn him!*" the crowd pleaded. "*Burn him now!*"

Thasos' vision became blurred by tears, and when he looked back to the envelope it warbled as if seen through misshapen glass. The torchbearers approached, their shadows like animated skeletons behind them.

Again Thasos shut his eyes. His heart wailed silently in the cavity of his chest yet he tried, as he had in his prison moments ago, to relax his thoughts. The words burned behind his eyelids:

TO THASOS, FROM THE PHILOSOPHER.

Time, he thought, *is a merciless ocean, forever pounding on our shores of accomplishment. What man builds at sunrise may crumble by nightfall. I will not weep at that, for there is nothing in the world that doesn't change. My quarrel is not with time.*

Behind his eyelids he could feel the bright torches.

I will not utter a single cry, Thasos promised. *For you, my love, no sound will escape me.*

The monks raised their torches to the sky, as if aping the irreverence of Prometheus on the night he stole fire from the gods. The crowd screamed their approval. The torches fell onto the pyre and the flames ignited like four separate creatures. They wriggled and blackened the scrolls. The ancient words folded and collapsed in sizzling death throes.

TO THASOS…

The fire climbed steadily towards him, eating parchment and expelling a flurry of glowing embers that drifted off on the river breeze. Thasos breathed deep of the disintegrating manuscripts and took their burning incense into his lungs. The heat roared closer.

Thasos looked away from the crowd, the flames, the scrolls.

He turned his gaze upwards to the sky.

PART I

▼

Two years earlier in the city of Alexandria, Egypt,
Province of the Eastern Roman Empire

Late October, 414 A.D.

CHAPTER 1

▼

On his seventeenth birthday—by Roman law the day he was now declared a man—Thasos met Hypatia of Alexandria.

He had left his home that morning and walked the stone-cobbled road that ran alongside the River Nile. Autumn was descending on Alexandria and turning the nights cold, but the heat of the Egyptian day never waned and Thasos breathed in the sweet, moist air as he went. It was the flood season of Egypt, when the Nile swelled like a fat serpent from the heavy rains of Africa's interior. The early sun brightened the limestone homes that cluttered the riverside avenue, and Thasos squinted under their painful glare.

Mighty Alexandria sat in Lower Egypt, where the Nile fanned out and emptied into the Mediterranean Sea. This time of year, the canals were brimming, and the Delta became a green, flowering blanket of new life. The local Christians did not fail to see this season as a metaphor for the Christ-king's resurrection, just as the old pagans had likened it to Osiris' return from the dead. With little else in common, all Alexandrians cherished the immortal river which gave them everything from fresh water to lucrative fishing and, when it receded in the spring, black silt that made for rich harvests. For fifteen miles Alexandria stretched. A passing bird could spy a sweeping vista of stone fountains, coliseum-style theaters, craft-shops, and the densely populated residential districts.

It was the only world Thasos knew, the only one he wanted to. Beyond Egypt, all was dark and hideous. The year before his birth, the Roman Empire had been split by the two sons of Emperor Theodosios into Western and Eastern halves, to be ruled by Rome and Constantinople, respectively. It had been a desperate measure to rescue civilization. Barbarian tribes were overrunning the cities of the

West, burning the countryside, and straining an ailing economy. Five years ago Rome itself fell to the Visigoths, worst of the bearded invaders, and the total disintegration of the West seemed inevitable. This tragedy had sent shockwaves through the remainder of the civilized world. *The West has fallen!* people cried. *The barbarians have taken Italy! But at least here, in the warm south of the Eastern Empire, we are safe. May the Lord preserve and protect us!*

At seventeen, Thasos was of medium height and possessed a lean, spare frame. His eyes were deep-set, brown, and a shade darker than his hair, which he wore short in the Roman style. He had a cleft chin and his nose was well-sculpted, neither too big nor too small for his face. He had friendly, generous lips and a healthy flush to his skin. His face was clean-shaven. The sky-blue tunic he wore was tied at his waist with a dark blue sash.

From his home in the poorer, plebeian quarters of the city, it was a thirty minute walk to the Great Library; his appointment with the Librarian was, judging by the faultless clock of the sun, in fifteen minutes. Irritated by his slipshod management of time that morning, Thasos broke into a light run, passing West Harbor where merchant vessels from other nations had arrived, their colorful banners flapping in the sea-breeze.

I won't be late, he prayed, though a crease of anxiety marred his warm, open face.

Within minutes he could see the building on the hill above the city's royal district. The Great Library was long and rectangular, with a porch shaded by a row of ionic columns. A gabled roof topped it, bronze and bright in the sun. The front courtyard was enclosed by a peristyle, rows of marble columns that formed a decorative perimeter. Leading up to this courtyard was an aisle of stone steps, hewn delicately into the emerald hillside.

Thasos had never been inside the Library. It was a strange irony, given that his father Admetus had worked there. Thasos had been very young then, a boy whose only interest was in playing with the other children of his neighborhood…pretending to be gladiators or legionnaires or Persian magicians. Then his father died and going to the Library was impossible; Thasos' mother had forbid it.

But not today, he thought. Today I am a man.

At the feet of the hill was a wall of shrubbery with a circular entrance carved into it. Beyond this green portal, Thasos could see the start of the hill stairs.

Three minutes left, Thasos guessed. He increased his pace, his slender legs propelling him like an Olympic athlete through the entrance. He was in mid-leap up the first few stairs when he realized someone was coming *down*, and it was too late to avoid the inevitable collision. He heard a girl's scream, then felt the impact that sent him and his victim sprawling into the steps.

"I'm so sorry!" Thasos sputtered.

A young Egyptian woman wearing a white cotton tunica stood up and shot him a Medusa-like glare. "Lunatic!"

"I'm sorry, truly, truly sorry. Forgive me."

She gathered herself, brushed off her clothes. "Are you at the Library to learn how to *walk?*"

"It might be better than trying to fly, no?"

"Perhaps!" the woman laughed, disarmed by his levity. When he had apologized again she said, "You're a new student?"

"If my appointment goes well. I mean, yes, this will be my first day at the Library." *And the Library is the heart of Alexandria,* he thought, remembering his father's deathbed words. *It is the soul of the civilized world, Thasos.* For a moment, Thasos was overpowered by a haunted memory. His father, dying in a bed soaked with sweat. Thasos' mother, wailing and begging her husband not to leave her. A physician at the bedside, cloaked in shadows like a bird of prey.

The memory flickered away. Thasos felt the onset of an awkward silence between him and the woman. He offered a smile. "A friend is waiting for me. Impatiently I fear."

"Then you must fly again, I fear," she replied. By her tone she clearly wanted to extend the encounter. Her hazel eyes shimmered with interest.

Thasos sighed, torn by choices. "Perhaps we'll collide again if Fortune is kind?"

"Perhaps."

For a moment Thasos stalled. But he knew he was already late, and he did have a friend, Arion, awaiting his arrival. Thasos bid her farewell and, with a cautious look at the stairs ahead of him, scrambled up the hill without further accident.

"Now here's something to see!" Arion exclaimed from atop the stairs. "Thasos the glass-worker at the Great Library! One of us has gone mad!"

Sweating lightly, Thasos grinned at his friend. "To justify this climb, there had better be ambrosia, not just books!"

Arion smirked. Two years older than Thasos, shorter by several inches, Arion was round about the waist and had stringy, shoulder-length black hair. "No ambrosia. Just every book from the four corners of the Earth!" The two friends embraced warmly and Arion bid him a cheerful birthday.

"Seventeen," Thasos repeated, gazing past Arion at the pale courtyard and the colonnaded porch of the Library. A set of double doors, ornate and inlaid with lapis lazuli and gold, glinted in that shade. "I pledged to my father that this place would possess me for one year, beginning today. Now, shall we enter?"

In the deepest chamber of the Library, the teacher named Hypatia sat by the steady burn of a lantern and desperately regarded the half-written scroll in front of her.

Though a lengthy cedar desk lay nearby, she sat on the red-carpeted floor with her bare feet drawn under her. Her lantern was a lonely illumination. The surrounding chamber was shadow-drenched...the walls lined with shelves, and each shelf straining under the weight of oak scroll cases and piled leather-bound volumes. The air was mildewy sweet.

Standing over her, Professor Apollonius peered down at her writing with distaste. "*Latin?*" he cried. "Every book should be written in Greek! We *think* in Greek, we speak in Greek! Don't give the future this guttural language of dogs when you could be giving them *art!*"

Hypatia sighed. She glanced at her red ceramic ink jar as if it could summon a genie to dispel her unwelcome visitor.

"You don't agree?" Apollonius roared.

"I agree that Greek is the most musical language. Yet the world is embracing Latin."

Apollonius snorted, not so much at this prophecy but at Hypatia's unwillingness to really argue. He was a figure burned away by time to a wiry, white-haired stalk. His eyes were immense, too large, it seemed, for his sagging face, and fixed in a permanent scowl. In his hand he clutched a tightly-wound scroll and with it he batted the air as if striking an invisible opponent. "Every time you indulge Latin, you put our own music deeper in the grave!"

Hypatia finally looked at him.

At the age of forty-five, she was still beautiful, still tall and slender like an idealized statue. Her face was oval, with a narrow nose and full lips. Her eyes were dark blue, piercing and mesmerizing, framed under the black arches of her eyebrows. Her skin, darkened to the color of honey by the Egyptian sun, showed the gentle beginning of creases across her forehead and at the corners of her mouth. Her chestnut hair retained all the thickness of her youth, giving her an untamed look. When she scowled, this look bordered on savage.

"Latin is the language people will read in tomorrow's books—"

"Because we're *writing* those books in Latin! The West has fallen and we can make the world Greek again! The world doesn't have to change!"

Hypatia fluidly switched languages to make her point: "*Nihil est quod perstet in orbe.*" *There is nothing in the world that doesn't change.*

"Indeed," Apollonius said, recoiling from the Latin syllables like a demon from sunlight. "Not even Hypatia is immune to that law. Do I see another silver hair sprouting on the Philosopher's head?"

"Apollonius—"

"I'm leaving," he said, contenting himself with this parting shot. Then he seemed to remember the scroll he had in his hand. "Oh…this is for you." He placed it on her desk and withdrew into the hallway.

"So glad I could quicken you this morning," Hypatia muttered. She felt swept up by sudden anger and frustration. The blank page of her newest book lay wanting, like rough stone set before a sculptor who couldn't think what to chisel.

My seventh book, she thought. Assuming I ever finish writing it. Seven books in forty-five years.

Her earlier books had already made her famous…or infamous, depending on who was speaking of them. Her first, written at seventeen and published the next year, had proposed a prime number theorem that instantly became a staple of the world's three libraries—Persia's Antioch Library, Greece's University of Athens, and the Great Library of Alexandria. But her next two books she considered her best—written at the darkest time of her life, the death of her father. *Variation and Independent Variables*, and *Quantifying Disorder: a Study of Given and Eventual States.* They were bold works, brilliant and frightening to many of her peers. Twenty years after their publication, Hypatia could still tip-toe through the Library dormitories and hear resident scholars arguing them, her detractors calling *Quantifying Disorder* "lunacy in ink" while others declared it was the "new science, one day to have its own Hall in the Library." Her last three books—two of astronomy and one of philosophy, had received quieter reactions.

And what will they say of this book? Hypatia wondered, scowling darkly at her seventh manuscript-in-progress. Each morning she awoke possessed by the need to work on it, driven as if gods were urging her on. She'd struggle, twist her feather-pen, scribble ink onto papyrus and watch her work take slow, agonizing shape. But that was the reality of the scientist. Playwrights could pen a dozen works each year, but scientists needed time to craft a single volume.

And it is time I'm exactly short on! She lifted the lantern and turned its light onto the *clepsydra*, the water-clock. Its steady drip of water from the upper to lower vessel turned a wheel marked with each hour on its spokes. Morning's seventh hour was already past. She was late for an appointment with a new student.

The day's schedule flashed through her mind like an unwelcome equation— appointments, classes and meetings. Hypatia grumbled, seeing how her day had already been stolen from her.

She stood at last, her white teacher's robe covering her from neck to ankles like a monastic garment tied at the waist by a thin gold sash. Quite suddenly, she recognized the waxen seal on the scroll Apollonius had brought her and, with surging eagerness, she broke the letter's seal and read:

Hypatia,

There will be a gathering at the palace tonight that you will attend. I will not accept a refusal. It is a formal affair, and I am quite certain you will find the other guests to your liking. They will begin arriving at sundown. I trust you will as well.

Governor Orestes

Orestes? Hypatia frowned, puzzled. She knew the Governor was currently in Constantinople holding audience with the Royal Court. Was he returning sooner? Why?

She folded the parchment and thrust it into the pocket of her robe. Then she regarded the blank scroll again.

"Tomorrow, then," she told it, and pushed aside her thoughts of writing to better concentrate on her impending appointment. She had seen the student's name on the Library roster—*Thasos, son of Admetus the Scholar.*

Ah! Admetus! she thought, saddened by Time's thieving hands. Admetus had been a beloved part of the Library staff, his early death tragic. A friendly man with a remarkable talent for memorization. Hypatia recalled how often she would discover his lonely lamplight in a hidden aisle, him not far from it, crouching by a scroll bin, searching for another work to use in his research. "Admetus?" she would say patiently. "Were you intending on sleeping here tonight? The Library is closed!" And then he would smile at her, laugh agreeably, and say, "Sorry, Philosopher. Never enough hours in a day!"

That was ten years ago he left us! Hypatia was startled by the decade's rapid passage. Now his son is of age to study here! It was a bittersweet thought.

Leaning over the desk, the cuffs of her robe dangling, she extinguished the lantern and the room went dark as if it had never existed at all.

"All right," Arion said, grinning. "Step forward and open your eyes."

Feeling sheepish, Thasos walked through the Library's double doors and did as he was told. "My God," he said at once, and the rest of his breath was snatched away.

The Great Library's Main Hall was an airy, square chamber. Its floor shone with mosaics of grey tiles, interrupted by straight paths of darker grey like an arabesque. At the center of the room was a flowering garden, nourished by sunlight which streamed in through the long windows that faced east. Thin, grey pillars lined the room like sentries and supported a second level balcony, from which another tier of pillars supported a third level. The roof had coffers, or indentations, shaped like five-pointed stars, and an *oculus*, the sky-light, pierced the center. Nine hallways branched off of the Main Hall, three per level, leading to separate corridors. Tunic-clad students and robed professors roamed about as if in an enclosed metropolis. From where Thasos stood on the bottom floor, he could see an information kiosk manned by two elderly bearded men at the far end of the room. Above them towered a giant mosaic of the Library's founder, Alexander the Great, in full Egyptian regalia like a pharaoh. The conqueror's arms were crossed, a crook in one hand, a flail in the other, his fierce eyes set with determination.

Thasos gasped, "Tremendous!"

"It is," Arion agreed. "I've been here three years and the sight never loses luster. Nine halls, one dedicated to each of the Muses. And the entire Library dedicated to Urania, muse of astronomy." As Thasos looked around in open-mouthed astonishment, Arion chuckled and added, "It's a rare thing to see you humbled. I'm enjoying this!"

Thasos turned his attention to the people who wandered in and out of the branching hallways. He remembered his father telling him that the Great Library lured travelers from all lands. Now at last, he could appreciate those words. He saw bearded Persians, toga-clad Greeks, dark-skinned Egyptians, a strutting black man in an orange toga, and even two fair-haired Celts mingling and conversing. It was as if the world's continents had joined at this juncture of the Earth.

"I'm speechless," Thasos admitted.

"Good. Now when's your appointment?"

"Five minutes ago."

"Naturally!" Arion snapped. "Do you know which Librarian was to interview you?" When Thasos shook his head Arion said, "Then stay here and wait for me!"

As he watched Arion sprint away, Thasos felt a childish spirit of adventure bubble in his stomach. He imagined running through the Main Hall watching the patterns of the floor rush under his feet. He could feel the building's history like a veil brushing his face. Seven hundred years earlier, Egypt had been brutally oppressed by Persia, the largest power in the world at that time. Native beliefs were trampled, the Egyptians enslaved to their new masters. Then the young Macedonian Alexander had swept down the coast of Asia Minor like a whirlwind. He had smashed through every Persian army in his way; by the time he reached Egypt, Persia had no spirit to oppose him. They fled the country while Egypt received Alexander as the god everyone, particularly himself, believed him to be. This city of Alexandria—one of *sixteen* namesake cities—was built to commemorate that liberation, and the Great Library conceived as its crowning jewel.

Thasos looked warmly to the long-dead king's mosaic. He offered a small but reverent bow. Then he turned, quite by chance, to examine the gardens again.

It was only a glance in the direction of the flowering stalks and ferns, to openly wonder at this collection of exotic vegetation. How ironic, he would wonder in months to come, that his sideways glance would change the course of his life forever.

CHAPTER 2

▼

"The poets are wrong to say the world is losing its wonders," Thasos told the woman who stood near the gardens.

Hypatia looked at him and instantly realized this was the son of Admetus. The similarity was unsettling…the lost scholar's features resurrected here in the softness of new youth. Even Admetus' cheerful optimism shone from this boy's eyes.

Thasos noticed the glimmer of recognition in the woman's blue gaze, though he was certain they had never met before.

"And why do you say that?" she asked.

Thasos smiled pleasantly, instantly intrigued by her mature and natural beauty. Not a hint of makeup blemished her honeyed skin. No jewelry sparkled on her fingers or at the lobes of her ears. Without a shred of enhancement, she was stunning. Her pale robe refused to hide her well-bosomed figure, the flare of her hips, the length of legs.

"I think our wonders are intact while this Library stands. I regret I've let so much of my life pass without ever setting foot inside."

Hypatia nodded amicably. Thasos knew that female students were a rarity at the Great Library. They were a rarity at any school, actually. Few families wasted money on educating their daughters—a woman's duty as wife and mother hardly required expensive scholarly training—and thus the hall bustled with men. It made Thasos wonder about the girl he had met at the bottom of the hill. He reflected on her air of confidence and the gold thread that brocaded the seams of her tunic. Probably a nobleman's daughter, he thought, simultaneously amused and disturbed by the way she had been flirting with him. Amused, because he was only a plebeian and a craftsman by trade—the brazen girl's rich parents would not approve of such a dalliance. Disturbed, for the same reason.

But what was the story with *this* woman? He was moved by the unaccountable independence in her eyes and poise. It was the independence of a spirit who belonged to no husband. Thasos felt his confidence blossom.

She was looking at him in a curious way. "Are you a student here?"

"I am. Forgive me, but you are as entrancing a muse as any poet could desire, My Lady."

"Really? And are you a poet?"

"Of sorts. My name is Thasos. Greek by heritage, Alexandrian by country."

The woman's face changed subtly. "Thasos? What brings you here, to the Great Library?"

"The desire for a new experience. And you? Have you studied here long?" When she nodded, he added, "Then may I request your company on a tour of this building? I would be indebted to you."

"Have you been approved?"

Thasos glanced at the kiosk, where Arion was speaking to the bearded men who sat across from him. "I was supposed to meet one of the Librarians here. But if his answer is no, then I consider your company more than fair compensation."

He had intended the remark as a flattering compliment and was unprepared for her reaction. A cold glint came to her eyes. He had never seen such a savage light in a woman's face before. "Then I regret your compensation is over, Thasos! You should seek something more substantial!" She strode for one of the hallways.

"Such as?" he called after her.

Without looking back she said, "Room Three, in the Hall of Astronomy."

He watched her go, aroused by the sight of her legs scissoring within her robe. Moody, he thought. But she's secretly flattered, too. What was the old Persian expression? *Flattery fells dragons and women.*

Running footsteps came up behind him. Thasos turned and saw Arion's outraged face.

"What just happened?!"

"I was socializing."

Arion reddened in irritation. "I abandoned you for a *sliver* of time! That this could happen, on your *first day here*, is beyond explanation! Even for you!"

"What did those men say?"

"That your father had set funds aside for you for the study of astronomy…" Arion stayed his tongue, wondering if Thasos had received Hypatia's approval.

Judging from the way she had stormed off, things didn't look optimistic. "What did she say to you?"

"Does it matter? Did I break some rule that...Astronomy? When?"

"That depends. Tell me what she said."

"Why?"

"*Just tell me, Thasos!*"

Wonderingly, Thasos recounted his conversation with the woman. When he finished he said, "What's wrong with you? When is my class?"

"*Right now!*"

"Why are you so angry?" Thasos snapped, finally upset at his friend's strange line of questioning and wondering if jealousy lay at the root of it. "If you like that girl, just tell me and I'll treat her like plague! Otherwise, show me where my damn class is taught!"

Arion sighed. They had been friends for three years and Arion was conscious of Thasos' obsession for female flesh. It was embarrassing, actually, the way Thasos was steered by that passion. Last year, he had almost gotten himself murdered by planting his flag with an Egyptian girl named Baketemon who was betrothed to an ill-tempered, massive Egyptian man named Kapta. The husband's inevitable discovery that his wife was not pure had sent Kapta insane. Baketemon (whose lips were as loose as her legs) coughed up Thasos' name, and Kapta had gathered two friends to hunt half the city for Thasos. Arion still feared that one day he would see Kapta's bald head in a crowd.

Part of it *was* jealousy, too. Arion had never been comfortable around women and would watch his friend's inexplicable confidence with respect and smoldering envy. Every February 14th, Alexandria celebrated the Festival of Lupercalia, when maidens would write their names on slips of paper and drop them into jars to be later matched up with a young boy. Arion had never participated.

But this time there was nothing to be jealous about. Arion was mortified by Thasos' behavior.

"Follow me," Arion said finally, leading the way into the Hall of Astronomy. Thasos tailed him into the inner hive of the building where scroll-bins honeycombed the walls and overhead swinging lamps (open candles were forbidden in the Library) threw enough light to illuminate the Greek lettering burned into the soft wood. HIPPARCHUS, said one. ARISTARCHUS was another. The hallway broke into deeper corridors and study chambers where shelves reached to the marble ceiling. There were tables, too, and men huddled by them reading quietly or arguing ferociously.

Then Arion and Thasos passed a small room that opened up from the corridor. Inside were low, wooden stools arranged in a half-circle. A chalkboard erected on a tripod stand stood in the center, unattended and blank. A bronze plaque with Roman numerals hung on the archway of this chamber: **II**.

"Your classroom is the next one on the right," Arion sighed.

"I was just having a conversation with her, Arion."

"The Library of Alexandria is not a marketplace for flesh, Thasos. You've got to change your habits here! You're a man today! Act like it!"

Before Thasos could reply, a memory pierced his thoughts like an arrow and took him back to his childhood. He remembered his father standing out in the yard, neck craned to the evening sky. Thasos had gone to him and asked what he was doing. *See all those little lights?* his father had asked. *They move, Thasos. See this parchment? This describes the movement of those lights.* It was a decade ago, but Thasos could still hear his father's excited voice listing the constellations.

And he realized what had triggered this memory so suddenly.

This Library smells like my father, he thought, moved and saddened by this truth. The smell of candle-wax and scented oils, of papyrus and leather. This is the smell that permeated him. This is the perfume that was forever on his clothes.

Abruptly, Thasos halted. He had reached another classroom chamber. On its archway hung a "**III**".

He hesitated. "I am here to honor my father's wishes, Arion. As such I'll observe the rules here…as soon as I learn them." Thasos raised an eyebrow. "Now is there a rule prohibiting relations between students?"

"No. But not—"

"Then I'll wager you that woman spends a night of her own free will in my embrace."

"Wager me the Nile…I am in need of a bigger pool."

Thasos rested his hand on Arion's shoulder and squeezed gently. "Good day, Arion."

Arion felt his anger leave at once, reminded that Thasos for all his faults was a loyal companion. "Good luck, Thasos."

Thasos entered the classroom.

For a few seconds longer, he remained ignorant of the mistake he'd made. Within the square-shaped room he saw his classmates already seated on stools. There were five besides himself. Closest to the archway were two young men who appeared to be brothers. They were both in their early twenties, had curly brown hair, identical aquiline noses, and were dressed in brocaded white tunics. Separated from them by an empty stool was an old man, his head crowned in thin wisps of white hair, with silver stubble dotting his chin. Next was a man near Thasos' age, lean and swarthy, a black goatee shaped to his mouth. Last was another young man the same age. Unlike the others, he had thick golden hair and strong, prominent features on his wide face. After him was another empty stool.

"Thasos, native to Alexandria!"

The voice was sudden and belligerent…and *female*. Startled, he shot a look to the far end of the chamber where an unnoticed sixth occupant of the room was standing.

"I am," he replied to her challenging tone. He felt his palms grow slippery with sweat; he fought the urge to bolt from the room. The other students looked at him, sensing his anxiety and not understanding it.

"I am Hypatia, instructor of this class," the woman teacher said. "There are two stools. Seat yourself quickly…you are late."

He forced his legs to work, taking the spare stool between the old man and one of the brother-types. The teacher approached the half-ring of seats.

"As I was about to say, astronomy begins *right here*," Hypatia told the students, "on Earth, which passes around the sun with four other worlds. Tell me about Earth, Thasos!"

"It has three oceans and three continents," he responded, his face flush with shame but refusing to be cowed. *I made a mistake*, he thought. *In my defense, it was an easy one to make and I don't deserve being humiliated for it.*

"What's it's shape?"

"My eyes tell me it's flat, but I know many scholars argue it's round."

"What's it's size?"

"I don't know."

Hypatia kept her adversarial gaze trained on him, seeing the blood fill his face. She pressed him further. "If I told you that your first lesson in my class was to figure out the exact shape and size of the Earth, would this be a fair challenge?"

"If I had winged sandals," he replied. The two brothers chuckled; the others smiled slightly but looked to their teacher for approval.

Her stare abandoned him at last. It singled out the goateed student. "Karam, I offer *you* the challenge. Tell me the size of the Earth or, if you can't, tell me the tools I should provide you with to find the answer!"

"A fleet of ships to map the oceans," replied the student, unintimidated and eager. "And legions to pace off the breadth of Africa, Europe, and Asia. Then by the end of my lifetime I might be able to tell you."

"Instead of a fleet I'll give you two sticks," Hypatia told him. "Instead of a legion, you get one healthy soldier, but he's not allowed to wander beyond Egypt.

And I don't have the patience to wait until the end of your lifetime: I want your answer in exactly eight months. Am I being unreasonable?"

Yes, Thasos thought. Is this your way of controlling a class? By giving them impossible paradoxes so you'll seem clever by comparison?

As if she'd heard his thoughts Hypatia's eyes found him again. "Six centuries ago, the task I've described was accomplished with the same tools I gave you, right here in Alexandria. The man who did it was the Great Library's curator, Eratosthenes." Her eyes softened. "So relax, Thasos and Karam. Eratosthenes did your work for you." Karam gave Thasos a conspiratorial grin, but Thasos, annoyed by her showmanship, did not return the friendliness and gradually Karam looked away.

Hypatia continued with the practiced speech she delivered at the beginning of every class, and her voice was strong. "I notice none of you even twitched at my earlier heresy. Remember what it was? I stated that the Earth and the four planets circled the sun, even though the Church and the Library's first patron thought otherwise. But before you lift a stone against me, tell me how I'm wrong...and then I'll show you how I'm correct."

The blonde student, the one who looked like a Visigoth despite his civilized toga, piped up. His words were thickly accented, at times difficult to understand, but he spoke them with energetic enthusiasm. "I won't argue, Teacher. I'll agree. During a lunar eclipse, an astronomer noticed that the size of the Earth's shadow was being produced by the sun. But he figured that the sun had to be immense to make that shadow, especially since it's so far away. So he thought it strange that a giant object like the sun should revolve around a small object like the Earth. He invented the helios...heli..." He struggled to form the proper word, his face blushing with shame. "Helio-centeric model of the cosmos," he said at last. "I don't remember the man's name."

Hypatia did not let her pleasure show on her face. "Aristarchus. That was the astronomer's name, and if you want to start a battle, just go two rooms down on the left and repeat that name to Professor Apollonius...a man who disagrees with the heliocentric model of our universe. Apollonius' trouble is that he can't find mathematical errors with it; his opposition is ideological. Since mankind is the crowning glory of the Earth, he will tell you, then all the cosmic bodies *must* revolve around that glory. The idea that we live on the *third* planet, ignobly swinging around the sun, drives him mad."

They were a good crop of students, she decided at last. A healthy mix, which would throw them off-guard and force them to cooperate. Already, too, Hypatia had received a pleasant surprise: the Celtic boy was the last one she had expected to know Aristarchus' work. How had he known it? Had word-of-mouth reached the icy northern frontiers of Europe? Or were the Celts somehow in possession of a copy of the astronomer's work? This latter possibility was unlikely; copies were few, laboriously made by the hand of Library resident scholars. Three, maybe four copies of Aristarchus' text might exist in all the world, and half of those would be in Egypt.

Hypatia laced her hands behind her back. "We're beginning a voyage of thought together. You see, I *do* agree with Apollonius on one point. Mankind *is* glorious. He is capable of *anything*. From our little corner of Egypt men have measured the size of the Earth, the position of the sun and all planets, and determined the *life and death of stars*." This time she saw the older student cringe at her heresy. The stars, after all, were believed to be immortal, affixed by God to sparkle like diamonds on the black silk of the firmament for all time. *Fixed stars*, they were called, because they never moved. The idea that stars lived and died was not Hypatia's invention—earlier scientists had suggested it—but it was another notion that would get Apollonius frothing at the mouth.

"There is nothing we can't do," Hypatia continued, unconcerned. "Over the course of this year I shall prove this above all else to you. You will learn to see the world in sharper colors. You will learn the value of asking, of thinking...even to think wrongly is better than not to think at all. The method of science is to grow knowledge out of the facts you accumulate." She looked into each face as she spoke. At her last words, she held Thasos in her steady gaze. He reddened and sweated beneath her attention, but didn't look away.

"You may have heard through the halls of rumor that I expect much of my students. It is true. My expectations are that you think as individuals. I do not tolerate a student who is a puppet; we have enough of those in this city. Do not be afraid to be Socrates."

Thasos felt laughter bubbling in his stomach. Sure! Be Socrates! he thought. Live a life that ends with persecution and one mighty drink of hemlock!

Every school child from Rome to Egypt to Persia knew the story of the Athenian named Socrates, who eight hundred years ago distinguished himself as a pest, a haunt, an asker of ridiculous questions. He would approach city officials in taverns and challenge them. What is justice? Government? Religion? Whose right was it to rule a people? It was a great historical irony that the same Athens which had executed Socrates now hailed him as an idol.

Hypatia's voice broke his humor: "Today, our class is short. Your first lesson is one you will do alone: Read. Go to the bins in the corridor. Use the catalogues.

Find one treatise that describes the movement of stars and planets and read as much as you can."

Karam, unable to contain himself any longer, said, "But Teacher? Forgive me…how *do* you measure the size of the earth with two sticks, one soldier, and only eight months to do it?"

Hypatia smiled. It lit her face like a beam of sunlight. Thasos' heart quickened as he saw the reason he had first talked to her at the garden.

"I'll give you that answer tomorrow, Karam. Today, read."

They were silent, attentive, unblinking.

"We can now begin," she said. "Good day, class."

Only when the other students had filed out of the room did Thasos approach her, heavy with anxiety.

Hypatia waited for him, expecting his confrontation. "Did you forget something, oh poet? Your muse, perhaps?"

Thasos bowed in genuine humility. "I offer you an apology, Teacher. I had…today marks my first visit here…I did not know—"

Hypatia nodded. "I understand the confusion. You are approved for my class. Good day."

"Good day," Thasos said, shuffling out the doorway. It *is* a good day, he thought as he went. *I am a man now, treading in my father's footsteps. It was important to him that I come here. I will make it important to myself as well.*

It was Tuesday, October 26.

CHAPTER 3

▼

Twelve hours later the Lady Marina, wife to Governor Orestes, paused in mid-sentence and lifted her goblet to her lips. Night had arrived. The Great Library was silent on its hill, while the palace below it swarmed with light and bodies. Over the gilded rim of her cup Marina gazed at the party that had invaded her palace when suddenly her eyes spotted the Philosopher Hypatia, robed in green silk, joining the fray.

The palace lay seven miles inland from the harbor on the northwest side of the city in the Royal District of Alexandria. Like much of the city's architecture, it was an endearing blend of Egyptian and Greek elements built by Alexander's general and friend Ptolemy. Since then it had been the ruling seat of the Ptolemaic Dynasty until Cleopatra ended the bloodline with a cobra's kiss when the Romans came in 30 B.C. Now it was merely the home of Egypt's prefect and his wife—though an opulent home it remained. An outdoor patio shot out from the rear of the building and hugged a deep swimming pool. Tall shrubbery enclosed the grounds and afforded complete privacy from the rest of the city. Tonight, however, a deluge of visitors filled the patio, sitting or standing by tables, drinking from goblets and eating from platters borne by the servants. The gathering was composed of the city's patrician elite; men of law and commerce and trade, happily fraternizing.

Marina, seated at the largest of the outdoor tables, tilted her goblet and let the wine trickle into her mouth. She was twenty-five, daughter of a Greek nobleman, and had been living in Alexandria for two years. Her pale skin was splashed with freckles. Her black hair was lengthy, but she wore it piled atop her head, secured with tiny dove-shaped barrettes. Her slight, lithe body added to a pubescent appearance which had inspired many whispered jokes among the city's officials during Orestes' inaugural ceremony. He's marrying a child! people said when Orestes was well out of ear-shot. She looks like a tiny doll beside him!

Yet the illusion of immaturity was shattered by Marina's startling blue eyes. She had a fierce sapphire gaze which seemed possessed of their own light. They were not the eyes of a child. When they registered rage or displeasure, men had been known to sweat uneasily, feeling probed by both flame and ice.

Still holding Hypatia in her gaze Marina swallowed the sip, lowered her goblet, and finished her statement to her table guests. "I would be the last one to know. If Orestes had gone to China, he would still find time to send letters dictating how the palace is to run in his absence. I don't ask, Heliodorus. His letter commanded me to host a party, just as his letters to you commanded you to attend. He has us all on a leash." Orestes had also sent a letter to Head Servant Neith, entrusting her with the responsibility of organizing the gala. Neith, the sixty-year-old Persian lady who oversaw all palace servants, had dutifully monitored the night's cooking, wine flow, and contentment of guests. Marina looked to the far side of the pool and saw the old hag verbally lashing one of the younger servants who had taken too long in bringing another plate of oysters to the long, rectangular buffet table.

Three men shared Marina's table. Her left saw Heliodorus, the forty-two-year-old Egyptian lawyer for the city's native quarter. He was like a gentle shadow, his brown body clad in a sleek black tunic that hugged his spidery frame. His face was smooth, shaved, and unremarkable if not for his deceptively innocent eyes. Almost directly across from Marina sat Synesius of Cyrene. At seventy-one he was the group elder, a man of winter whose white hair and bushy eyebrows matched his toga. Time had cracked his face like a mud-mask yet it was a face that exuded agreeable, silent humility. Last at the table, to Synesius' left, sat the brooding military general Simplicius. Forty years old, he had a face that looked ten years younger; unblemished, rounded, framed by sandy-colored hair. He was the most elaborately dressed of the group, with a white tunic, red sash, and red stola slung across one shoulder and tied at his waist. He was also the quietest. Despite the group's diverse backgrounds and choice of careers, they were a closely-bonded company of cherished friends and graduates of the Great Library. All except Marina.

Heliodorus looked to his friends and shrugged. "Perhaps this party is no mystery at all. Orestes knows we haven't seen each other in some time. It may be a glimmer of nostalgia on his part, to have us reunited while he's away."

Marina spun around at the comment and laughed bitterly. "Nostalgia? My, my, Heliodorus! My husband is incapable of that emotion. Parties like this are strategies for him! Remember when he was campaigning for prefect? In the first four months of our marriage we made *three* trips to Egypt. Never missed a party or debate. Why? Because people can be shaped like wet clay when there's wine and food around!"

"But he's not even here."

"Isn't he?" she challenged sharply. "Remember what was said about Alexander? 'When Alexander dies, the whole world will stink of his corpse.' Even when Orestes is away, you can smell him. And every servant here is a pair of my husband's eyes."

Heliodorus smiled politely in the face of Marina's undisguised hostility. How many drinks has she had? he wondered, trying to remember. And can it be that she doesn't know the *real* reason for this party? Orestes *is* here, secretly back from Constantinople ahead of schedule. It was the kind of thing Heliodorus had seen Orestes do before. But who else realizes it?

Synesius spoke, his voice a smooth instrument despite his withered throat. "And yet we are *not* reunited. I notice one missing piece."

The men at the table murmured in agreement, and Heliodorus smiled slightly.

"I don't know if Hypatia was invited," he admitted.

Marina's eyes flickered, amused that the men had not noticed their former teacher in the crowd. It would be a mistake to badmouth the famed Lady Philosopher among her present company, but Marina was feeling petulant and the words rose in her throat. Then she stopped, spying the party guest she had been wanting all evening—Darius, standing at the buffet table near fruit-cluttered plates. Tall and handsome, he was chatting happily with two other men, but his eyes were trained on Marina. Across the distance, his grin deepened.

Marina's venomous words dissolved before she could speak them. To her table guests she said with newly-discovered sweetness, "I plead my guests excuse me for a few moments. My husband will never forgive me if I ignore his other associates." With that, she seized her goblet and escaped the table.

Heliodorus, Synesius, Simplicius. They were Orestes' friends, not hers. She was not part of their circle, had no wish to be. In fact, their closeness only reminded her of how much she hated Alexandria and didn't belong.

It hadn't always been that way. Two years ago the city had seemed a promised Paradise, replete with adventure and luxury. The palace alone made her father's Athenian villa seem a hovel by comparison. Daily, Marina bathed in hot baths, perfumed herself with the finest scented oils in the Empire, wore silken garments

that hugged her body like lovers' hands. And Orestes! What an incredible speci-
men of man he was! How delighted she'd been upon learning of the marriage
arrangement to the ruggedly attractive statesman from Olympia! She recalled
their first voyage to Egypt when he was campaigning for the governorship.
They'd taken a trireme up the golden Nile into deep, heathen country! They were
received at every port like royalty! It was the dream of every noblewoman—a
meteoric ascension in social status, a powerful husband, and the *land of pharaohs*
beneath her feet! She had often fantasized, during those first few months, that she
was the legendary Cleopatra strolling through her vast palace halls, eager to
seduce her Mark Antony when he returned from business.

And that was the first problem. Orestes never returned from business. In body
perhaps, but never in mind. He hadn't married her; he had married Egypt.

The night air chilled her through her thin, white tunica as she crossed the
patio to the table where Darius awaited her. The wine burned in the pit of her
stomach and her face was flush. How much *did* I drink tonight? she wondered as
she reached the table and, without meeting Darius' stare, plucked a grape off a
silver tray. Do I trust myself in keeping this charade?

"Is the food to your liking, Darius?" she asked casually.

"It is well prepared, My Lady," he said. He watched as she sliced the grape in
half with her teeth. "I've eaten my fill."

"Have you?" Marina started, but before she could continue the crowd parted
like a mist sundered by wind, and Hypatia passed by only a meter away. Marina
noticed the green silk tunica she wore. A darker green stola draped from shoulder
clasp to her ankles. Her long hair dangled in ringlets. A chorus of cheerful greetings rose to meet her.

Marina looked at Darius. "Could we ask for better distraction? Follow me."
With that, she walked into the foyer of the palace. Darius lingered a moment to
be sure no one was watching him, and joined her.

Hypatia crossed the patio to reach her table of friends and smiled delightedly
when she saw Synesius' wrinkled countenance fill with vigor.

"The Philosopher herself, come to make our circle complete!" he cried, standing. Yet before she could reach them she was intercepted by a drunken guest:
Ciro the councilman, and he thrust a goblet toward her.

"Hypatia!" He grinned like a jackal. "I hoped you would be here tonight!"

Ciro was stocky, robust, and pale, but with bright red cheeks. Dressed in a
white toga and heavy red stola, the bald crown of his head visible like a fleshy

mountain above his remaining hair, he seemed the very caricature of a Roman senator. He had also been one of her most ardent pursuers.

"It is good to see you, Ciro," she said with a forced smile. "How is your wife?"

"She is well!" he declared. "And I would inquire as to the health of your own husband, yet I assume such a man continues to not exist!"

"And you would be right," Hypatia said, and bid him goodnight to forestall a more protracted encounter. She went hurriedly to her friends and embraced Synesius where he stood.

"I missed you dearly," he said in her ear.

"And I you," Hypatia asserted. She regarded her other friends and her heart swelled with joy. "All of you together again! Do we know what the occasion is?"

General Simplicius sighed, drumming his fingers on the table. "None of us can guess, Teacher. But enough of that! I understand your classes have begun at the Library. How are you finding the newest crop of students?"

"Too early to tell," Hypatia replied crisply, and quickly changed the subject. She wanted to hear about *them*, their lives, their careers. And for the next few minutes they indulged her happily.

They talked; she listened and privately rejoiced in the simple pleasure of their company. In fact, her smile never left her lips while they bantered around her. Too many times in the life of a teacher, faces would come and go and never be seen again. But her friends were a special breed. They were former students— having begun as an eager crew little different from the class she had taught that morning. Quickly they had blossomed into major players in Alexandria's politics and machinations. Their correspondence with her was constant, their visits as frequent as time allowed, and their loyalty unquestionable.

Sensing her nostalgia, Synesius suddenly grabbed his goblet and held it up, declaring, "A toast to the Philosopher! My friend, *our* friend, across these years. You have been the guiding light in our pursuits, and I thank you."

"Nonsense," Hypatia said, denying the proposed toast. "None of you need guidance! You're the leaders of Egypt, not me."

From the meshed wooden latticework of the palace foyer, Marina watched as Hypatia's friends lifted their cups in honor of their former teacher. The foyer offered the privacy Marina wanted. *She* could see *out*, but none could see in through the ivy and flowering bramble. Darius swiftly entered this pocket of privacy, and Marina snatched his hand.

"Would the whole evening go by before you approached me?" she demanded.

Darius chuckled and slipped his arms around her waist. "I was helping maintain the illusion of indifference. Would you have it any other way?"

Darius worked as representative of the Persian-Arabic population of the city, just as Heliodorus represented the interests of the native Egyptians. Marina had met him upon her arrival in Egypt. The affair had begun a year later.

He had barely finished talking when Marina grasped the back of his neck and kissed him so savagely that he tasted blood in his mouth. His body responded to the ferocity at once. No other woman could excite him faster than Lady Marina. As always he found himself helplessly controlled, slipping into a trance of kissing and groping her. When his head cleared for a moment, he realized that he had already gotten down on his knees and was hiking her tunica up to reveal the sleek luster of her unblemished thighs. Then she took hold of his hand and placed it between her legs, and his fingers slipped across her. His lucid moment passed like a freak blast of cool air during a hot desert afternoon.

Marina smiled and leaned her head back, surrendering to his needful kisses. Yet when she opened her eyes and caught another view of Hypatia through the lattice-work, her mood faltered.

Look how they flock, she thought. Like enamored birds, they huddle close to hear whatever comes from her mouth.

"No gathering is complete without the seductress' presence," Marina quipped.

Darius glanced up, his face blushing. "What?"

"The seductress," Marina repeated.

Darius followed her eyes. "Hypatia? I prefer the sight of you, My Lady." He promptly returned to kissing her thighs, lavishing helpless attention on her warm flesh and reveling in the feel of it against his face. But Marina couldn't look away from Hypatia flanked by her adoring circle. She had met Hypatia two years ago while Orestes was campaigning. A brief meeting, little impression. Now the mere thought of her could sour Marina's mood.

"Four hundred years ago she would have been the main bait at an Egyptian Pleasure House. And yet she touts herself as a virgin to men!" And tonight, Marina thought, she looks more feminine than I've ever seen her before.

Darius sighed, feeling the passion splintering. "I don't care if she touts herself as Hera, wife to Zeus. Are we to talk all night when we can be indulging other sport?"

Marina stared fiercely at him. "*Now* I have your interest?"

"You've had it all evening, My Lady." Darius exhaled sharply, his head clearing as if from a witch's spell. The moment of clarity shattered as he smelled Marina's arousal.

Darius' voice thickened with urgency. "I cannot wait until the others are drunk or departed. I need you, Marina!"

"Then indulge," Marina said, and watched his head disappear under her tunica.

"I wonder how the governor's journey is going," Hypatia said at the table. "He hasn't even written, except to order me to this gala with his customary tact."

An amused smirk formed on Heliodorus' lips. "He invited me with the same courtesy. But you should know he thinks quite highly of you. Before he left, he said he regretted that he would have to miss your recent lecture."

"Lecture!" Synesius exclaimed. "On what subject? My hometown never has lectures! My neighbors gossip. Never a stimulating dialogue, ever! Just seasons and trinkets and who's sleeping with who!"

"If you're so unhappy," Heliodorus exclaimed, "then leave, fool! With all your friends here, I should think that securing a residence in Alexandria would be easy." Synesius had been born in Cyrene, lived in Pentapolis, but made no secret that Alexandria was his love.

"Returning to my original inquiry," Synesius continued playfully, "I was asking Hypatia what the subject was of her recent lecture...one that I had not been invited to, apparently."

"Teleology," Hypatia answered.

"Ah! Then it must have been a tranquil crowd!" They all laughed at his sarcasm.

Teleology was one of the fiercest, most argued subjects in Alexandria's philosophical circles. Friendships had ended over it. Peaceful mobs had been known to explode into bloody frays when the subject was broached. Teleology was the view that all earthly things contained a purpose. An acorn, for example, had the purpose of taking root and sprouting into an oak. When it did this, it had succeeded. If it didn't, then the acorn had failed. At first glance, such a philosophy seemed too basic to give rise to contention. At first glance.

From this fundamental premise, however, a dozen different schools of thought had splintered off and went for each other's throats. Was an acorn's potential instilled by God? If so, then do some acorns fail because they have displeased God? Are failed acorns a part of His plan, or are they proof of His absence? Or do all acorns begin with the dream of succeeding, yet are sometimes thwarted by earthly chaos...which suggests that either God allows chaos to interfere or is incapable of lending a helping hand? Or were failed acorns the very best proof of a Plan, since if every acorn produced a tree then the resulting forest would strangle itself? But if that was the case, then why start with an acorn surplus? If God wanted a forest of seventy thousand trees, why not just make seventy thousand acorns?

"I'm sure you didn't confine the lecture to acorns," said Synesius, pushing away his goblet of wine, not caring for the additional sip which would shove him into gluttony.

"I discussed the purpose of civilization. I suggested that our own choices, not interference from God, is what sees the success or failure of our purpose." Hypatia smiled. "And yes, it was a lively crowd."

Hers was a point which, in Alexandria and the rest of the Christianized Empire, had resulted in violence so many times in the past. What was mankind's purpose? Surely a species which built roads, aqueducts, and irrigation canals had demonstrated the ability to remake the Earth as it saw fit! Why accept the existence of a desert when the hand of man could divert rivers and turn the land bountiful? The more fanatical elements of the Christian community would scream that God had made the Earth and all that lived on it, and so mankind's purpose was to serve that God. The question over how to serve Him was even more incendiary. Must we deny all earthly pleasures like the ascetic monks of southern Nitria, living in caves, eating only bread and water, renouncing women and spending each day in penitent prayer? Was it to embrace the teachings of the Savior Jesus Christ...or could *any* religious path lead to God?

For Hypatia, the questions of God were irrelevant. It was a position that had always made her lectures fiery arenas for verbal gladiators.

"Did anyone have to be carried out?" Heliodorus asked. He had seen it happen: red-faced men cursing at her with spit flying from their teeth, dragged out of the forum because of their unmanageable tempers.

"Not this time."

"But still rousing?"

"There was a visiting professor from Athens who challenged me."

Her friends gasped. They knew what few did...the volatile relationship between Hypatia of Alexandria and the men of Athens.

Synesius winced. "And?"

"It was spirited," Hypatia replied. In actual fact it had been disastrous for the Athenian professor. Words had flown back and forth like a barrage of arrows. Their defending points were their shields. The audience had watched breathlessly as the battle waged, Hypatia like a female Achilles and her opponent as outmatched as Hector outside the walls of Troy. With the precision of Olympic javelins, she had drilled her points through his defenses until, beaten, he had withdrawn to lick his wounds.

Synesius squeezed her hand affectionately. "How is your writing?"

Hypatia smiled. "If I can hunt down the right Muse, I'll have a new manuscript for you to read by the dry season."

"And what subject are you wrestling?"

"The future."

Ciro, who had not wandered far despite Hypatia's gentle dismissal, overheard the comment. "The future is set ahead of us like glyphs in wet clay. It waits for us to arrive."

Hypatia bristled. For a moment she thought last week's teleology debate was going to repeat itself here. *Fate was for fools*, she thought savagely. People who believed their future was already decided were cowards before the responsibility of choice. For her, who had spent three decades attacking laziness of thought as if it were a life-choking weed, Ciro's words flayed her raw.

"I must oppose that sentiment," she said sharply. "The future isn't something we stumble into like an ox, Ciro. We must engineer it like a bridge or city."

"Agreed," Synesius said. "And what must we engineer?"

Hypatia saw Orestes emerging from the crowd like a man parting a sea of bodies. Before the others were aware of him or even that he had heard Synesius' question, he walked to them and said, "A fleet of ships more suitable than the one I just sailed in, I should hope."

The company spun around.

"Governor!" They rose to their feet. Heliodorus made a motion to surrender his chair.

"Keep your seat, Heliodorus," Orestes assured him. "I prefer to feel the steady earth beneath me at the moment...and I don't wish to interrupt our Philosopher."

Governor Orestes was a well-muscled man with broad shoulders and a strong, imposing frame. He was taller than most men by a head, his body noticeably in proportion to that height. It was an athletic build though he had never competed in sports. His face was roughly-hewn, attractive the way a sandstone carving of an ancient warrior is attractive. His alert, dark eyes were deep-set and unsettling. In his purple tunic and black overcloak, he seemed even larger, a titan.

From the foyer, Marina, her head leaned back in the throes of passion, glanced absently toward the patio and saw her husband. She involuntarily cried out and jumped back, forcing Darius to fall face-forward to the floor. He grunted loudly in pain.

"Shh!"

"What?"

Shooting him a horrid glare, she hissed, "Shut up!"

What was he doing back? The considerations ran through her head. Another two weeks he was scheduled to be in Constantinople. How could that estimate have been miscalculated so badly? And by Orestes, of all men?

Marina was sure it could be no accident. He had returned to Alexandria early *for a reason*, and she wondered if he suspected her and Darius. But that was impossible: Darius was such a stickler about anonymity that she felt confident not a single official suspected anything. Darius even went so far as to make public, off-hand comments at her expense to some of his friends, calling her "Orestes' child-wife" as others had done in the past.

Darius was standing far back in the foyer, his face transfixed with fear as if a hidden cobra slithered at his feet. He, too, had just noticed Orestes.

"You went into the house to get more wine," Marina told him.

Darius shook his head. "You have a servant for that, Marina. He'll see through a feeble lie like that."

"Let me go out first, then," she said, and straightened her tunica. "And don't be foolish! Orestes is passionate in words, but that is all."

At the table Orestes greeted his guests briefly and repeated his request.

Synesius beamed. "The Philosopher was telling us the subject matter of a new manuscript."

A new manuscript? Orestes wanted to smile and profess the genuine pleasure that her earlier works had brought him. He had read all six books written by Hypatia of Alexandria, and the promise of a new work excited him. But he allowed none of that sentiment to show on his face, and in a low voice that did not betray his intrigue he said, "What is your new work about?"

"Days to come," she replied, flushing. "Rather, days to achieve."

"You mean like a calendar?"

"A calendar that promises things, instead of being a series of blank tablets."

"And what does it promise?"

"Good health from medicine," she said, trying to collect her thoughts while they whirled in a tempest of surging emotion. Alexandrian medicine was improving yearly, largely due to old Egyptian science being translated into Greek and Latin. "Maps of the world."

Orestes nodded. "Indeed…"

"Faster ships to reach every part of the Earth, connecting all people."

"Faster ships need faster winds."

Hypatia gasped. "Shame on you! Ever read Heron's *Automata?* He declares that machinery is an infinite power. One day it will give us ships that move through the air, and…" She smiled suddenly, her cheeks reddened as if exposed to the fires of a secret sun.

Orestes' eyebrows raised. "Yes? And…what?"

"Artificial people," she finished, earning his immediate laughter.

"You mean like Galatea? Statues that walk around and try to pass for fellow Alexandrians?"

"And above those statues, Governor, we'll see ships to the stars."

"There were moments on my return voyage when I felt I was on just that sort of ship," Orestes replied soberly. The ground seemed to sway beneath him, as if he were still aboard his storm-besieged vessel. Then he brushed away the thought and fixed Hypatia with a friendly gaze. "Still, you amaze me. Your dreams are so vivid."

She noticed the intensity in his eyes. She chanced a smile, though his sudden attention made her feel awkward. Nonetheless, she was glad that she'd plucked the silver hair Apollonius had found earlier that day.

Orestes started to say something more, but then noticed new movement from the corner of his vision. "Marina," he uttered, as if pronouncing the name of a city that held no fascination for him. "I was just about to ask of your where-abouts!"

Marina's lips were tightly pursed, and no more than a playful smirk appeared on them. She embraced him, withdrew. "Another two weeks in Constantinople?"

"I requested leave of the Regent early. I've discovered matters at home deserving of my attention."

Marina's heart jumped in terror. "This entire gathering is speculating on what those matters are. As the architect of this mystery, you must be pleased."

Orestes scowled at her words. "Pleased? There is nothing in the story I've heard that pleases me, Marina. Particularly since it concerns this city. News found me as far away as Regent Pulcheria's courts, and *that* is why I sent all of you letters. *That* is why I am here early."

Orestes turned and commanded all the attendees to gather round. Then he spoke of what he had heard. While in Constantinople, he had been approached by a pretty woman who begged to speak to him in private. Perhaps it had been the desperation in her voice and pleading eyes that had convinced him to oblige. Once alone with her, the woman peeled out of her dress. Orestes recoiled at the sight of the black contusions over her body. Her breasts had been cruelly clawed by fingernails, her ribs were dark stripes, her legs riddled with lumpish injuries. Orestes saw defensive lashes on her arms. The contusions were weeks old, and some were still hard with clotted blood.

"She told me that she had been seized in the streets of Alexandria while on her way to worship," Orestes said. "Dragged into a house. Raped by five men. Beaten. Accused of defiling the son of God. Beaten again, into unconsciousness. When she came to, she limped back to her husband. He demanded they go to Constantinople to find me." Orestes hesitated, examining each face in the gathering. "Have any of you heard this tale before it came to me?"

Some nodded, others shook their heads and regarded him with pale expressions. Heliodorus was the only one who spoke:

"She was a Hebrew?"

"She was."

Heliodorus nodded. "Then that explains it, Governor. There have been beatings, and abuses, between Christian and Jew for several months now."

Orestes' nostrils flared. "I am aware of the strained relations. Now, everyone here is aware of them. Now...you will all personally see about ending it."

There was a murmur of dissent in the crowd. Orestes sprang to the nearest malcontent and roared, "Ciro, what city do you serve?"

Ciro's face darkened at being singled out. "Alexandria, Governor."

"Founded as a place for all people to coexist under a single banner!" Orestes hissed, the tension he had suppressed from his voyage now bursting out through this vein of rage. "All of you here are Christians." He stopped and cast an imperceptible glance at Hypatia. "Nearly all of you, anyway. You are also subjects of the Empire. Thus, you are subject to *me*. As of tomorrow I will hold each of you responsible for any violence that erupts between people of varying faiths within your spheres of influence. Ciro here owns a shipping industry, one of the largest in Egypt. He employs a thousand people from Alexandria to Karnak. Tomorrow he will mandate that any conflicts will result in the permanent dismissal of all who are guilty. District representatives will circulate word that this kind of sedition will have immediate legal consequences."

Sedition, Heliodorus repeated inwardly. It was a well-selected word. Who here will argue now, for fear of being labeled a seditionist?

The gathering was as silent as a collection of stone idols. No one dared move or speak.

"I thank all of you," Orestes said easily. The color in his face slowly returned to normal. "There are barbarians in the West; see that they stay there. Goodnight." When no one moved, Orestes thanked them again. When still they didn't move, he ordered them away and turned back to Hypatia and her company. "You are all clear on your orders?"

"We are, Governor," Heliodorus replied.

Orestes sighed and his entire frame seemed to shrink as he did, as if a vast weight was melting off his bones. "Then I bid you goodnight as well." He retired into the palace foyer, Marina trailing him like a shadow.

Orestes passed through the foyer and removed his overcloak as he did. One of the palace servants rushed to take it from him. Marina flew in behind him.

"Not welcome in Constantinople?" she asked.

"I told you why I returned early."

"And I wasn't convinced that was your only reason."

"It was," he retorted. "I'm glad you're so concerned over the strife in our city."

"Whether the Hebrews are here or not doesn't change my life," she snapped. "And you know Archbishop Cyril is behind it all. You want to war with him? May God be with you!"

Orestes grinned coldly. "Don't tell me *you've* converted! You love jewelry and dresses, not any god I know of."

Marina smiled with sweet irony. "No, my dear, my love is still of you, and you alone."

"Sweet relief!" He turned his back on her to signal that their interview was over and made for the stairs. "Losing your love would be tragic indeed."

Marina watched him vanish into the gloom of the upper balcony. Could he be telling the truth? she wondered. Could the word of a Jew have brought him home so early?

For the second time that night, Marina wondered if Orestes actually suspected her affair with Darius. She wondered what he would have done if he had discovered Darius burying his face between her thighs. Nothing, she concluded bitterly. Orestes always has something else on his mind.

CHAPTER 4

▼

Thasos left the Library and was astonished to see that evening had fallen like a black pall over the city. The past hours had been a blurry tapestry of exploring the great building behind him. Now Alexandria was dark and he ran swiftly home.

His home was an unassuming, mud-brick structure in the lower merchant quarter of the city by the main canal. The location afforded residents the smell of the sea, a view of the Nile, and the benefits of meeting foreign traders before any-one else in Alexandria. Yet a riverside home had its drawbacks, too, in the form of the unsavory sailors who came ashore hungry for food, females, and fights.

Thasos ascended the clay-brick steps of his house and stepped into the tiny rectangular foyer where he removed his sandals. A glowing incense bowl burned in the darkness, it's floral odor protecting the doorway from evil spirits.

He found his mother Demetria making bread at the cutting board, a large pot boiling and the kiln red-hot beside her. Thasos gently closed the front door and hesitated in the doorway, watching her by the lambent glow of the chamber's candles.

Demetria had once been an attractive woman with a reed-thin figure and smooth, unmarred skin. If painters were to be believed, then the painting of her as a young woman—the one hanging on the wall of her bedroom—depicted her as a dainty sprite possessing a glowing smile and warm, expressive eyes. Now forty, she had maintained her light body but had a tendency to stoop. Lines were carved on her face as if by channels of running water. The light-brown hair she had in the portrait had transformed into a brittle mass of greying weeds.

It hurt him to see her so aged. There was an ancient Sumerian saying that old age was wisdom in a silver basket, but his mother seemed a victim of time rather than priestess of its secrets. For a moment, Thasos drew forth memories of her as a younger woman. His recollection wasn't old. She had been full of vitality only ten years ago. Could a decade transform a woman, as if by vile sorcery, into the twilight figure he now looked upon?

Demetria hadn't looked away from her task of kneading bread, but she sensed his presence. "The soup is ready," she said.

Thasos approached the pot. Stirred it once. Removed it from the bed of coals. He poured two bowls and brought them to the table. When he turned he saw his mother placing the bread into the kiln and then coming to join him at the table.

"You're late tonight," she observed, seating herself.

"No later than usual," he said, still waiting for her to look at him. Since entering the house she hadn't met his eyes.

Demetria hoisted a jug of wine from the floor and poured two glasses, draining it. "Today you went to the Library, not to the shop. I was expecting you earlier."

Thasos stirred his soup and felt the hot vapors moisten his face. "I spent some time exploring the Library."

Demetria sipped to wet her palate. "You could have been tending to the yard like I've been asking you. You will tend the yard tomorrow, Thasos."

Don't you want to ask me about the Library? he thought, watching her concentrate on her next sip. "My teacher warned us to expect many taxing months of study. She said…"

Demetria finally glanced up with hard eyes. "She?"

"Hypatia," he said. The name rolled off his tongue like an Egyptian prayer.

"The Library employs women as its teachers?"

"Not just any woman. The daughter of Theon, the great scientist. You've heard of him?"

"From your father."

"Hypatia is said to exceed him."

"I want the weeds cleared from the yard by morning."

Thasos sighed quietly. "I'll take care of it."

And that would be it.

The rest of the dinner would be held in relative silence. Thasos knew the pattern by now. Like hieroglyphics engraved in stone, the ritual of his family's day-to-day existence seemed unalterable. Thasos remembered that when his father was alive meals were warm moments of laughter and conversation. No fights. No awkward silences.

But then his father died and the change had started. The following months had been difficult. Neighbors brought gifts to the household and made dinner for Thasos and his mother. Hardly a day went by when there wasn't a visitor bearing consolation and Demetria took obvious comfort in their sympathy. Yet over the next year, she had begun to withdraw. Meals became quiet, wintry affairs. Daily conversation calcified into functional necessities. Finally a young and grieving Thasos had brought it to his mother's attention, asking her, "Why don't you like to talk anymore, Mother?"

The innocent question had wrought a spectacular effect. Demetria's eyes had welled up with tears, and she had embraced him and sobbed against his neck. For one week life returned to as it had once been. It seemed as if Admetus' death would find acceptance and that the family would move on. Then the week passed, and she had reverted like a plant withering for lack of water.

Thasos' memories were broken by a sudden knock at the foyer. The door swung in. Arion peered into the chamber, smiling affably.

"Arion!" Demetria brightened. "Come in and have some soup."

Arion shook his head politely, but closed the door behind him and approached. "Thank you but no, I've just finished dinner. It does smell good, though!" He embraced Demetria and then slapped Thasos on the back in greeting.

"Thasos!" he said. "Doing well today, I hope? First day of class wasn't too straining, distracting?"

Thasos stirred his soup. "Arion, tend to my yards, won't you?"

Demetria left the table to fetch another amphora of wine. As soon as she was out of range Arion stooped to whisper to his friend.

"I'm sorry for yelling earlier. Others have made your mistake, you know. Hypatia's beauty is famous throughout Egypt. In Greece, too! If this was an earlier age, they might have launched a thousand ships for a glimpse of her face...or ten thousand for a glimpse—"

"And are your instructors as captivating?"

"My instructor is a great architect," Arion said, grinning, "as comely as the Minotaur. But I'm not here to seduce my teachers...like other people I know."

Thasos grasped his friend's tunic and pulled him close in parody of threat. "A miscalculation, based on a lack of information...and the lack of a proper guide."

Arion gasped. "You have but one guide in your life, Thasos. One that commands you without needing a voice." He laughed heartily, saw Demetria returning, and added hastily, "And don't think I've forgotten our bargain. I do believe you owe me a rather large body of water?"

"The year isn't over."

Arion lost his smile. "What?"

"The laws of attraction are without border."

Arion searched Thasos's face, trying to decide whether or not he was serious or simply covering for his pride. "She's older than you."

"So are the fig trees. That doesn't prevent me from plucking their fruit, does it?"

Demetria set the amphora on the table, and went to the kiln to fetch an earlier loaf of bread she had baked. When she brought it to the table she insisted that Arion partake.

"As I am a veteran of the Library," Arion told Thasos while he chewed, "I should hope you would abide by my wisdom there." His eyes said the rest: *Do not paint yourself a fool with Hypatia any more than you have done already!*

"Of course," Thasos said, but his eyes retorted playfully: *I have always enjoyed a challenge, friend.*

Arion was not amused, but he pursued the matter no further in Demetria's presence. He finished his bread in silence and then bid them farewell. "I will see you tomorrow, Thasos. May it be a better day!"

"You are always welcome, Arion," Demetria said. "Go carefully."

As the rest of the dinner passed quietly, Thasos wondered just how serious his own remarks were. Absently stirring his soup, he found himself smiling, so immersed in the memory of Hypatia that he didn't notice Demetria watching him, sharp-eyed as a hawk, over her wine.

Egyptian nights are bitter cold—the haunted twelve-hour journey through which the sun god Ra braves the netherworld pursued by dark creatures seeking to kill his radiance—and thus few people wander when the sun is gone. Heliodorus, though, was awake an hour before dawn. The streets were chill and deserted as he went to the Governor's palace. A rosy blush of sunrise was breaking the dark by the time he knocked upon the ornate copper palace doors.

In a few moments the doors swung open and head servant Neith bowed politely to him.

"Good morning, Heliodorus," she said, her round sun-dried face turning friendly.

"Good morning to you, my dear." He had been coming to the palace for twenty years to meet with Egypt's governors; from that first day, Neith had always been the one to greet him at the door to show him in. He was amused at how little she had changed in all that time. She still had the same stocky body, was still overbearing to the servants who worked under her, still proud despite her lowly station in life. How fascinating the ironies of history are! he thought. Neith was a Persian, descended from the brutal conquerors of Egypt. Heliodorus, a full-blooded Egyptian, had frequently wondered if one of his own ancestors had been servant to one of *hers* seven centuries earlier.

The thought generated neither hostility nor smugness. Heliodorus smiled congenially at her, feeling the kind of kinship that two people develop when they see so much else change around them. "Is the governor awake?"

"He is by the pool, Heliodorus."

He thanked her, and crossed the audience hall to the corridor that led to the lattice-work foyer. Quietly, he stepped onto the patio.

Orestes was standing by the pool, silently staring into the black water. Unmoving.

What was *this?* Heliodorus waited with growing intrigue, privy to this rare instance of catching the governor in a moment of uninterrupted honesty. No posturing, no threatening. Just Orestes standing by the pool, thinking…

Heliodorus hardly dared to breathe.

He had worked with three Egyptian governors before Orestes. After two years of knowing him, however, he still couldn't decide if he liked him or not. Orestes was a bull in public. But what lay at his core? Heliodorus knew he'd been a states-men in Olympia, Greece, and had married Marina while campaigning for the governorship. But of parents, education, history? Heliodorus didn't know. With effort, he could imagine Orestes had been a child long ago…perhaps an athletic youth given to wrestling or javelin-throwing like most Greek boys. And he recalled how at Orestes' induction ceremony, some merchants comprising a for-midable economic coalition had approached the new prefect to request a tax break for Alexandrian businesses. Orestes had listened to their request, nodded, and said he would look into it immediately. As the merchants turned away, one of them had chanced to mutter, "He'll look into it as surely as the others did." Orestes heard the remark. Fiercely, he demanded they explain themselves in full public view. Red-faced and ashamed, the men reported that the previous prefect, Pentadius, was notorious for promises never kept. "I am not Pentadius," the gov-ernor had declared. Two weeks later he decreed the sought-after tax break.

Privately, Heliodorus wondered what Orestes' motives were. The man seemed a true loyalist to Alexandria. Twice a week, he held audience with city officials to learn the state of health, attitude, food surpluses, shipping, trade, agriculture, and education throughout Egypt. But was it patriotism or power that ruled him? After all, how could anyone not be tempted to think of himself as pharaoh while living in the palace that Ptolemy had built, Julius Caesar and Mark Antony visited, and Cleopatra threw her legendary parties?

By the pool-side, Orestes exhaled sharply as if in pain. His shoulders sagged as if bearing the weight of massive, invisible things.

Not wishing to be caught intruding, Heliodorus finally took a noisy step onto the patio's stonework. Orestes' back sprang upright.

"Governor," Heliodorus said affably. "Are you well-rested?"

"You are punctual, Heliodorus."

The lawyer glanced around the pool-side. "Where is the Lady Marina?"

"Asleep," Orestes said in a dismissive tone. "But not for long. I am taking her to the theater tonight, so soon she'll wake and rush to market, looking for another addition to her wardrobe. One that will impress the attendees."

Not sure what to say to that, Heliodorus waited awkwardly.

"Tell me of the events leading up to the rape of that Hebrew woman," Orestes said suddenly. "We both know it isn't an isolated matter."

Heliodorus spoke on the soaring tensions between Christian and Jew during the past few weeks, mostly while Orestes had been away. The full story went back much further than that, however, and both men knew it well.

The martyrdom of Jesus of Nazareth in 33 A.D. had been a small event, barely noticed by the population-at-large. After all, Rome executed many people each year. Eventually a quiet cult sprouted over this particular crucifixion. Even then few noticed, since a garden of religious beliefs blossomed within the Empire's borders. Nowhere was this more striking than in Alexandria, where a visitor could meet worshipers of the Greek Apollo, Rome's belligerent Mars, Babylon's frightening Ishtar, or Egypt's beloved Isis all in the same crowd. Only the faith of Judea had caused problems. The Jews insisted only a single God existed, a notion which divided them from the rest of the Roman nation where even a devout priestess of Dionysus would acknowledge other gods.

The years grew and the cult of Christ gained some momentum among the plebeians, who were enamored of its promise for a glorious afterlife. Still it might have vanished altogether had it not been for Constantine. The victor in an Empire-wide civil war, Constantine declared that the Christian god had delivered him success. In 311 with the Empire firmly under his control, Constantine established Christianity as the state religion of the Empire. It was the start of many problems.

Constantine raided the treasuries of other faiths and gave the gold to his favored religion, funding the construction of churches in every province. With royal and financial support, the religion gained tremendous ground. Other faiths continued, however, until June of 391 when Emperor Theodosios was persuaded by Egypt's foremost Christian leader, the Patriarch Theophilus, to outlaw competing religions. In a flash, the old temples and shrines were obliterated, their priests executed or, ironically, crucified. In Egypt, land of harmonious religious coexistence for seven centuries, Theodosios' edict was particularly abhorred for fracturing the peace.

But as in the early days of the Roman Empire, the Jews still presented a problem. Although the Emperor's edict had been eagerly applied to the beast-gods of Egypt or the Olympian deities of the Greeks, the Jewish religion was strangely left alone...to the outrage of the more zealous Christian leaders. Many merchants, artisans, craftsmen, and bankers were Jewish; as they refused to convert to Christianity, they also refused to see their own temples destroyed. The Emperor did not press the issue. Had not Jesus been born a Jew? More importantly, was not half of Alexandria's businesses owned by Hebrew coalitions, including the granaries that supplied the Empire's bread? The Jews were let be.

Yet tension remained. And though Theophilus had been dead five years now, his nephew and successor had taken up the cause.

"Archbishop Cyril," Orestes said softly.

Heliodorus nodded. "I've attended his Masses. Cyril isn't subtle; he thinks the Jews are traitors to Christ."

"Then you believe these instances will continue."

"I believe you might consider holding a summit meeting with leaders of both religious communities," Heliodorus replied.

"That wasn't an answer to my question," Orestes snapped.

Rather than apologize, Heliodorus clarified his meaning: "As long as one man continues to shout and stir hatred, these attacks will continue. Lay down secular law so the words of the archbishop are held in check by civic fear."

Orestes scoffed, "I was under the impression that Alexandrians were educated enough to understand secular law." He sighed, his furrowed frown so deep it looked like a battle-scar in his flesh. He glanced back to the quivering surface of the pool and his eyes became distant. Once again Heliodorus found himself privy to a rare moment of seeing this private side of the prefect.

After a few seconds of silence, Orestes asked, "How are other matters?"

"What matters are those, Governor?"

"How is your wife?"

"She is well," Heliodorus replied cautiously. "She asked of you."

"How is Hypatia?"

Don't you know? Heliodorus wanted to say. "You missed a very great series of lectures she gave. I hear her next one will be on ideals of government."

"To remind men such as we that we have failed in forging paradise on Earth," Orestes said, yet for a statement which could have been caustic he softened it with a reverence that belied his apparent affection for the Philosopher. He added, "After listening to the ramble of senators, the words of our Philosopher would be soothing music!"

The governor's levity was disarming. For a moment Heliodorus entertained the fantasy that Orestes would suddenly smile, tell a joke, and invite him and his wife over for an evening dinner in the palace dining hall.

"When I was her student," Heliodorus said, "I wrote a dissertation on government and politics for her class."

Orestes raised an eyebrow. "And?"

"I proposed that an educated population might be a peaceful population."

"And what did Hypatia think of it?"

"She said it was a piece of unadulterated idealism," Heliodorus said. "In other words, she loved it."

Orestes shook his head. "A peaceful population is only possible when people are united in pride or fear." He folded his arms across his chest and his mood changed like a violent shift of the wind. "Thank you, Heliodorus. That is all for today."

C H A P T E R 5

▼

"This is how he did it," Hypatia said smoothly. She turned to the chalk-board-stand and drew a flat horizon, then two vertical sticks standing up from it. Directly above the sticks, she made a circle to signify the sun. Then she turned back to her students. "Any ideas now?"

It was the second day of class, and Hypatia had begun by asking the students what astronomy texts they had read the day before. When it was Karam's turn he had said "Eratosthenes," but complained that the selected work did not explain how to measure Earth's size using two sticks.

Now the students were gazing at the simple chalk drawing. "Shadows, Teacher," said Karam thoughtfully.

Hypatia nodded. "Eratosthenes had stumbled across an astronomical journal from Syene. It reported that on June 21 at the noon hour, a vertical stick lost its shadow." She tapped the board to make her point. "You can see why...the sun is directly overhead. Eratosthenes marked his calendar and waited for the next time June 21 arrived. When it did, he drilled a stick into the soil and watched as the noon hour approached...and *a shadow was still being cast.* Remember that he lived here in Alexandria, eight hundred kilometers north of Syene. There were only two possibilities. Either the Syene journal was wrong, or..."

The oldest student, shoulders hunched as he leaned forward to peer at the chalkboard, said, "Or the surface of the Earth is curved."

With a dirtied cloth, Hypatia erased everything on the chalkboard except for the sun. She then redrew the horizon as a semi-circle that filled the bottom half of slate. Then she drew the sticks again, so that they were standing out from the curved ground. The result was that one stick was exactly below the sun, but the other tilted.

"On a curved Earth, the rays of the sun impact the two sticks at different angles," Hypatia explained, her enthusiasm for the discovery making her talk rapidly. "The Syene journal is not inaccurate. There *is* a curvature to the surface of this world that can be measured from here to Syene. And Eratosthenes measured it by hiring a soldier to pace out the distance between the two cities. That distance is seven degrees, or one-fiftieth of a circle's circumference. Eight hundred kilometers multiplied by fifty is a circle measuring forty thousand kilometers. That's the size, and shape, of our world."

Thasos breathed out sharply, astonished at the simplicity of the solution. Yesterday he had considered the example to be an intentional riddle designed to confuse them. Now the complexity vanished. He saw what his teacher plainly intended them to see: Great questions could be solved by one questing mind.

"And *that* is my point," Hypatia said, placing the chalk on her desk and rubbing her hands clean. "Astronomy, like every science, is about observation. How many people flipped through that Syene journal unaware that it held the key to understanding the nature of our planet? Any one of you can make a discovery as monumental. But you must be an observer of this world first. Based on what you see, formulate some opinions. Then, test those opinions. Build on the work of others and expand our understanding of the universe."

Because that's our purpose, *our* teleology, she thought.

There were so many views on mankind's purpose. But Hypatia couldn't conceive of philosophies which told people not to question the world. An ox doesn't formulate theories because it *cannot*, she had argued with the visiting Athenian professor yesterday. Who among you would advocate a world-view that turns us into oxen? We have minds powerful enough to measure the distance of the stars themselves! Isn't our purpose, then, to tap that power? Why would God or Fate imbue man with thinking minds and demand he reject the gift?

She said none of this to her class. Let them come to their own conclusions, she thought. But let them be informed enough to make such a decision!

Hypatia decided that Karam had selected a worthy author to merit discussion for the remainder of the class. She spoke, they listened, and her words held them spellbound. Eratosthenes lived again because of Hypatia's talent for explanation. Thasos could almost see the great man's ghost, almost feel it drift through them all like a cool autumn breeze. When Hypatia stopped talking, Thasos felt the spell shatter. Eratosthenes, he thought, has just died once more.

His fellow students let out a collective sigh of awe.

"Continue your reading," Hypatia said. "And tonight, I ask that you look at the stars. Watch them, note the wandering planets. Wrap your mind around the fact that those planets are spheres like this Earth, so distant to us that they appear as flecks of light. Good day."

The spell broke again. The students stood. Karam grinned at Thasos, who remained sitting.

"What do you think of the second day?" Karam asked him.

Thasos leaned back on his stool, indulging a carefree stretch of his muscles. "Illuminating," he said.

"A choice word," Karam agreed, and bid Thasos good day as he left.

Hypatia watched them go. Then her eyes fell on Thasos.

"You were angry at me yesterday," he started. "I had compared the pleasure of your company to the joy of studying in the Great Library."

"Well I remember," Hypatia replied crisply.

"I was right."

"How so?"

"Your gift of teaching is not dependent on this place, Teacher," Thasos said, and felt an affectionate stirring in his heart as he looked at her. "I've never heard anyone talk like that before. The sun, the stars…they're items for priests and poets to gape at. But you imply that we might measure their distances some day. That we might even reach them."

We might even reach them. Hypatia sighed, moved by the image of setting sail on some mechanical bird and soaring into the firmament.

To reach the stars. What would that be like?

The question had been a source of her fascination since childhood. Her father had taught her the basic mystery of the heavens: Each night there were some stars which remained fixed in the black sky, while others would travel—with varying degrees of speed—over the course of a year. Like celestial boats driven by divine winds, the fastest moving points of light were the planets. But why? And *how* were they driven through those celestial waters? Finally, since the planets were sisters of Earth did it follow that nations had arisen on them as surely as Egyptian culture had sprouted by the side of the Nile?

Her thoughts and passion flowed quickly through her mind and her eyes glinted softly at the passage of dreams. "Yes."

Thasos stood at last. "That's either brilliance or lunacy. With respect, Teacher."

"Good day, Thasos. With respect, you will be the first one I call on next time we meet."

Thasos flashed his smile. "I look forward to it."

He's such a *boy*, Hypatia thought. Like the mass of male students she had met in Greece thirty years ago when she attended the University of Athens. Still, she recognized more playfulness in Thasos than in the students who had been her peers in Greece.

"You say that now," she said.

"I'll say it next class as well."

"Good day, Thasos."

There ends the conversation, Thasos thought, and he resigned himself to his role as student as he moved to the doorway. But once there, he couldn't bring himself to pass through its portal without a parting comment. "You remind me of Socrates."

Hypatia puzzled over the statement. "I didn't realize you had known him. You look good for a boy of eight hundred years."

"My father studied Socrates," Thasos clarified. "He said that Socrates could bring a subject so alive that when he was finished talking his words and images stayed with you, like glowing embers from a fire."

"People say he was a great teacher," Hypatia agreed.

"You admire him?"

Hypatia nodded. She leaned against the desk in an unexpectedly casual pose. "He was a man worth admiring."

"My father said so as well."

"And you?"

Nervous by his sudden seizure of conversation with her, Thasos assumed a stance of mild bravado. "I have an argument with Socrates."

Hypatia saw through the veil. She felt a sudden need to shred it and show him the tattered pieces. "Really? And how does he give you offense?"

"I hear that when the Athenian state had him arrested, he was given the chance to escape. I hear his admirers and followers came to his cell in the dead of night, and offered to break him free. I hear he refused."

"Such has history recorded."

"So morning came," Thasos continued, feeling himself grow hot as he tried not to look at her sleek body, "And he was led from his cell, shackled, and given a cup of hemlock to drink! Without complaint! He poured it down his throat to the last drop."

"You have yet to state your argument, student."

"Why not escape and go on living?"

Hypatia nodded in understanding. It was a heavily-debated matter. What if Socrates had escaped? Would the world be different? Would his reputation have suffered injury?

"'Won't society fail if laws are ignored?'" Hypatia said, quoting the philosopher's words from memory. "That was his answer, student. The state found him guilty of corrupting the youth of Greece. He didn't agree, but felt that the law had to be obeyed or anarchy would result. His convictions were very strong."

"And yet his convictions were his murderers."

"His fellow men were his murderers," Hypatia admonished. "Understand that distinction."

Thasos stepped aside as Hypatia moved past, but he joined her in the hallway. Together they trekked past scroll-filled bins that honeycombed the walls to the Main Hall.

Walking abreast with her Thasos said, "And what of today? There are people in the city who claim this very Library is a force of corruption to youth. They say it's heathen. Pagan. The devil's work."

Hypatia turned on him with controlled anger. "Everything is the devil's work to the ignorant. The sun sets and night is to be feared! The sun rises and people thank God! When you commit yourself to learning, you start to see the mechanics of how the universe works. The sun will rise, it will set, and no prayer will change that motion of solar reality."

Thasos held his ground. "I never looked at it that way."

Voice softening, Hypatia said, "How did you look at it before?"

Crossing one of the pillars of sunlight which streamed down from the skylight into the Hall, Thasos said, "To be honest I never really looked at it at all. It's the sun. It's there. Whether it was hung in the sky by God or formed as an apple on the tree of the universe."

Hypatia crossed the illuminated square of floor and reached the double doors of the Library entrance, propped open to allow the breeze to circulate into the cavernous interior. There she stopped in the shade of the archway's overhang. Thasos came to her side.

Hypatia's blue tunic was not transparent, yet Thasos could see the shadow of her body within the material like a pearl encased in translucent armor. The silhouette of one breast became visible like a ripe fruit beneath the cloth. Where the neckline ended, his eyes rested hungrily on the sight of her tanned skin and he swayed, transfixed by the overpowering urge to plant delicate kisses along the base of her throat. The blowing wind carried scented oils like jasmine off her body, and he felt his loins stirring.

"You don't have the same attitude as the other students here, Thasos."

He almost failed to respond, as he was prisoner to her sweet smell and closeness of her body. But then he caught himself and hazarded a reply. "And how would you describe my attitude?"

Hypatia noticed his hesitation and guessed the cause. "Apathetic," she said. "Reluctant. Lost."

Her editorial stung him. He lifted his gaze from the swells of her bosom and said in a wounded tone, "Well...apathetic?"

"There's wonder all around you and you've told me you don't notice it."

He felt tricked and trapped, and could offer no reply to her comment.

"I notice some things," Thasos said.

I'm sure you do, she thought. "Close your eyes."

"My eyes?"

"The two portals on your face which you use to see, yes."

"Oh," Thasos said, feeling nervous once again with her undivided attention. "Those."

Hypatia drew nearer. "Now slow your breathing and listen to the world around you. Once you've listened, open your eyes as a new child does."

Thasos did as he was told. "I hear lots of people..."

"That's society you hear. Listen beyond it."

He did. At first it was difficult because there were a good deal of people coming and going, so much chatter and so many sandaled footsteps on the marble courtyard. People dominated the day, and each one brandished their own activity like hornets constructing a hive. They talked to fill silence, they walked in groups because to stand alone was uncomfortable.

Soon, however, his ears picked up the gentle lapping of water breaking on the jagged shoreline. It was an immeasurably relaxing sound, and Thasos found himself swaying as if being lulled to sleep by its rhythm.

Deeply, Thasos said, "I hear water."

Hypatia nodded, her lips by his ear as she looked out into the distance. "What's the water doing?"

"I hear...waves lapping the shore, I think." His words came as if from a dream, still clinging to half-remembered islands of fancy.

"Is that all?"

"I don't know, I...hear the patterns of the water, I think." The heartbeat of the water, the timeless flow of pattern that connected him to all other eras. Mark Antony and Cleopatra might have closed their eyes on their final night together and heard the same rhythm. The great Alexander, exhausted and bloody from battle, might have rested his eyes and listened to the ocean's calming and word-less chant.

Hypatia spoke again: "Now open your eyes and look."

Thasos obeyed. The blue-gold light of the world came rushing in and struck his vision with new strength. From the hill's vantage point, he saw where the Nile joined the Mediterranean Sea.

"The Nile," he breathed.

"And reflected in its water?"

"The sun, like melted gold."

"People wander this way and that, but the Nile flows on and the sun rises each day. This is a bigger world than society. Most people are afraid to realize that; it's too big a task on them to ask big questions. Other people are apathetic. They don't care to ask those questions. Learn to see, Thasos. Only then can you begin asking."

She touched his shoulder and walked off, leaving him standing alone in the doorway.

Thasos watched her go. His heart returned to its normal pace only when she had disappeared around the corner of the peristyle.

One hour later, Thasos and Arion entered the Restless Jackal tavern.

It was a popular if disreputable place. Along the tops of each red wall were frescos of nymphs exposing their breasts, centaurs galloping through forests, and satyrs plucking the strings of harps to seduce pale-skinned women reclining on palm fronds. With morning trade finished, the tavern was slowly enlivening with its usual lot: traders and merchants from India, Greece, Persia, and Crete gathering for the catharsis the Restless Jackal was known to provide. There were even dusky back rooms offering services beyond beer or wine.

Thasos seated himself at a spare table near the tavern's entrance, while Arion bought two beers from the massive, shaved Egyptian bartender who owned the place. As he returned with the drinks, Arion took a look at his friend and sighed.

"Will you stop obsessing over her? Here, drink up."

Thasos cradled his mug absently. "What do you know about her?"

"Hypatia is…" Arion searched for the correct words, drumming his fingers on the tabletop. "She's the celebrity of the Great Library. Everyone knows her, everyone respects her. I know she's a good friend with the Governor. And…I know she doesn't tolerate amorous students." Arion wiped his brow of sweat and took a long gulp of the thick, sepia-colored drink.

Thasos leaned forward, intrigued. "How do you know that?"

Scowling, Arion said, "If I relate this story to you, will you promise me that for the sun's duration in the sky today you will stop talking about her?"

"I give you my oath upon the River Styx. Now speak."

Arion leaned back in his chair and held the mug in his lap. "I heard that a few years ago there was a student who fell in love with her. He persisted in following her everywhere, constantly professing his feelings. She...discouraged him from continuing the pursuit." He took another sip of his beer.

Thasos blinked. "Will you finish the story, or am I to guess?"

His voice tinny as he spoke into his mug Arion said, "I don't think you want the details."

"I certainly do."

"Let's just say," Arion said, chin dripping with foam, "that she set the young man straight with a vivid lesson he never forgot."

"Unless you want the rest of that beer in your face," Thasos warned, "talk to me."

"Fine. I heard that—" He froze as three men entered the tavern, passed behind Thasos, and approached the bar.

"Arion?"

Arion lowered his mug. "Keep your voice down."

Thasos pushed the beer away from himself. "I have never felt so moved by anyone, Arion. The sun follows this woman wherever she goes."

Arion stared in growing horror at the three men who had arrived. He watched as they received their drinks and then looked about for available seating in the crowded, noisy room.

Oblivious, Thasos continued. "For years you've roasted me on my indulgences, so let me put this into perspective. I would trade my experiences with any other woman for a single hour with Hypatia. Granted, it would an hour of my choosing, but—"

Arion placed his drink on the table and leaned close. "Do you remember Baketemon?"

Thasos blinked. "You think I forgot that episode? Are you mad?"

The three men at the bar approached. Arion's heart stuttered as he watched them seat themselves at the table directly behind Thasos. Ignorant of the new arrivals, Thasos persisted. "You want to compare *her* with Hypatia? Baketemon's greatest qualities were under her dress!"

Arion's eyes grew wild with fear as he saw the name register in the ears of the three men behind Thasos. They turned.

I'm going to die today, Arion thought, and he watched as the men stood.

"Thasos of Alexandria?"

The voice was like a bellowing trumpet, and Thasos paled as he instantly recognized its owner. Before he could react, the man seized the back of Thasos' chair and, with one hand, twisted it around so the two were facing.

Kapta looked even bigger than when Arion first saw him a year ago, his muscular body bursting out of his tunic. His arms rippled, his bald head glittered in sweat. Thasos stared helplessly at him. All he managed to say was, "Do I know you, sir?" He had only met Kapta twice before, and never formally.

But Kapta seemed to remember, and his face was dark with wrath. He turned to his friends who stood on either side of Kapta like ceremonial jackals. "This is the boy who disgraced my Baketemon!"

Arion had stopped breathing. He peripherally noted that the entire bar had suddenly fallen into silence, conversations evaporating at the potential fight.

"It is a common name!" Thasos challenged. "And unless your Baketemon is a sixteen-year-old girl, then I don't—"

Kapta lunged forward, his thick hands intent on grabbing Thasos by the throat. It was Arion who saved him. Anticipating the attack, he pitched his beer mug straight into the Egyptian's nose. The man recoiled, yelling in pain. Thasos jumped up, grabbed his friend by the arm, and bolted from the tavern.

Arion imagined his life transcribed on his future tomb as he ran, depicted in colorful wall frescoes. In the first frame would be painted his birth to proud and happy parents. Next would be his fine education at a young age, his training in music, a trip to India with his father, and his enlistment as a student in the Great Library. Then in the final panel would be a scene depicting his broken body, held in one of Kapta's iron hands as Thasos dangled in the other.

With fear flooding his brain Arion dashed with Thasos around a street corner as six footsteps trailed them like wolves on their scent. "*Kapta is going to kill us because you can't control yourself!*" he screamed.

Thasos' face twisted in desperation. As he shot a look back to see their pursuers he nearly collided with two camels on the road ahead. Both animals reared back in fright, spilling their carry-load onto the cobbled road. Beyond the beasts was the familiar crowd of the marketplace. Thasos dared to hope. Kapta and his friends cleared the corner and bore down on them.

Wrenching Arion by the sleeve once more, Thasos sprang into the thick of the marketplace like an arrow fired into a bustling herd. With feline agility, he slid beneath a table of northern cloth. Arion scrambled behind him.

"That man is going to kill us!" Arion spat.

Squatting behind the cloth merchants, Thasos saw Kapta and his friends enter the marketplace. They paused and surveyed the crowd, red-faced and cursing.

"How did Hypatia discourage him?" Thasos whispered.

"Who? Kapta?"

"No. The student who fell in love with her."

Kapta strode into the crowd. His two friends shot off in different directions to thoroughly search the area.

Thasos ducked low and pulled Arion close. "Arion?"

Still thinking of his funeral frescoes, Arion snapped, "Your loins got us into this trouble and now you are *still* thinking with them! Make peace with Kapta. Apologize. Tell him you never did more than put your lips to Baketemon!"

"She was supposed to be a virgin when they married. My lips are not that talented."

"I'm not dying over this!"

Thasos was about to retort when he saw from beneath the table Kapta's swollen, deeply-tanned legs. The man had stopped directly in front of the table to survey the crowd again.

Thasos' heart jumped painfully. "Run to the ferry. Now."

Arion's eyes bulged. "He'll see us! He's right there!"

"I know," Thasos hissed. "Run."

"No."

"Run!"

Cursing, Arion stood up and rose directly into Kapta's gaze. The man's scowl deepened. His eyes were simmering coals. The table with two Phoenician merchants haggling with an elderly woman over cloth were all that separated them.

"Where's your friend?" Kapta belted out.

"He's not my friend," Arion said as he steadied himself. "I met him drinking. Let's talk about this, I'll buy you a—"

In a blur of motion Kapta leapt forward and tossed the table aside, and Arion shrieked and jumped into the crowd. Thasos had vanished and Arion didn't bother looking for him. All he noticed was the stone wall guarding the riverside perimeter of the market, and in a wild surge of strength Arion clambered over it and rolled down an earthy slope into the shallow edge of the canal.

Thasos, having seen the action from behind a cart being pulled by two oxen, ducked low behind the wooden wheel of the vehicle as Kapta stopped at the stone wall and turned back to the crowd. Through the spinning spokes he watched the

Egyptian look directly at the cart and then look away, dismissing it as a potential hiding place.

Using the cart as a shield, Thasos waited until it came within a short range of the stone wall. Then he chanced to break from cover and sprinted to the wall. Below it, Arion was knee-deep in the golden canal.

His friend glared up at him.

"Grab the ferry!" Thasos called down to him, and slipped across the wall to drop down the slope.

A heavy hand suddenly grasped him by the tunic and he jerked like a hooked fish. With unnatural ease, Thasos was hauled backwards and thrown to the street. Kapta glowered over him, approaching steadily so that his shadow fell upon him.

Thasos, on his back, crawled away and let his terror show. "I didn't know she was engaged to you, Kapta! I swear on my father's soul I didn't know!"

Kapta continued to advance.

Desperately Thasos said, "*She* knew she was engaged, and yet she gave herself to me! Had I known, I would have taken any other woman!"

Kapta pulled a bronze dagger from his tunic. Thasos turned grey.

"I decided I'm not going to kill you, Thasos," Kapta said, still advancing. His face had calmed and now a malevolent excitement radiated from his eyes. He knew he had his quarry. His confidence was demonic.

"No," he continued, "I think it fitting that since you love women so much, you should become a woman."

Thasos struck a table suddenly, ending his retreat. He glanced up and saw two sun-burnt men, dressed in blue-gold tunics, talking amongst themselves. Thasos looked them up and down.

"Don't worry," Kapta said, the dagger glinting in the sunlight. "It won't go to waste. The fish will enjoy it."

And then Thasos shouted, "Crete is *not* a country of beggars and thieves! It's a beautiful land, with beautiful women!" The two merchants were jolted by his words.

Kapta lunged forward and suddenly was halted in mid-leap by the two merchants, who barricaded Thasos behind them.

"Have you a problem, Egyptian, with Crete?" one of the men challenged.

The second merchant nodded vigorously. "Beggars and thieves? Say that to us!"

"I said no such thing!" Kapta declared, spit flying from his mouth. "Step away!"

Thasos rose to his feet behind the merchants as they erupted into a yelling match with Kapta.

"—what would a man of a stinking, filthy desert know of real beauty—"

"—I've seen monkeys more attractive than some of your wives—"

Thasos raced by the merchants, avoiding a desperate grasp from Kapta. He sailed over the stone wall, striking the slope and rolling down into the shallows as the ferry pulled away from the harbor and began rowing out.

"Wait!" Thasos cried out to the ferryman. "Two more wish to cross!"

From behind him Arion stumbled forward. Thasos grasped his sleeve once again and the two friends splashed through the water to the ferry. Handing two copper coins to the ferryman, they climbed aboard and Arion, panting, slunk into an available seat.

Thasos heard yelling, and turned back to see Kapta from atop the stone wall, dagger outstretched with murderous intent.

"I will serve you to the crocodiles!" he screamed. "The fish will enjoy you I promise!"

Thasos bellowed back, "Not as much as Baketemon did!"

The ferry rowed out through the gleaming canal waters.

"Has Hypatia ever taken a lover?"

Arion sighed. His legs were soaked up to his thighs, and his heart was still thundering at a frightful gallop.

"Not that I know of," he said finally. "They say she's a virgin wedded to science and philosophy. I hear that many suitors have approached her, but that she declined marrying on every occasion."

The ferry held nine people, including Thasos and Arion. Thasos looked them over with disinterest. A young couple holding hands, an aged old woman with a little boy who may have been her grandchild, and three middle-aged women, holding baskets full of newly-purchased goods, constituted the rest of the passengers. The ferryman was dark-skinned and muscular with arms that looked built for the act of rowing. The oars made delicate splashes alongside the boat.

Thasos turned back to Arion. "Where did you hear these things?"

"You are not the only man who notices Hypatia. Many speak of her. Stories perpetrate." Arion squeezed out the bottom hem of his tunic.

"And what of the student who pursued her?"

"We almost died today, and Kapta would have been within his cultural rights to do it. I'm not discussing Hypatia with you for the rest of the day as punishment."

Thasos leaned to the side of the ferry and stared across the water to the walkways lined with palm trees and reeds. The recent pursuit faded from his mind.

Arion's edgy voice interrupted his thoughts. "You are a glass-blower, Thasos. She is the head of the Library and the most esteemed lecturer in the city! Look to other women or do us both a great service and become a eunuch!"

"That choice was almost made for me."

"If you want a touch of philosophy then dwell on this," Arion persisted. "We are people of the earth, Thasos. You and I. You work with *sand*. I use bricks and stone. We both dig our hands into the very flesh of the earth."

"What's your point?"

"That she is of other elements," he persisted. "She's a philosopher, Thasos. A woman of incredible learning. Even if she does have sexual thoughts, she wouldn't waste them on us. Forget her."

"She is the most beautiful woman I have ever seen," Thasos whispered, and continued in his head: I could never forget her. Each time I look at the sun now, it will be wearing her face.

CHAPTER 6

▼

Hypatia liked to lecture to the common, plebeian crowd.

Twice a week she flew on her silver chariot like a Messenger of the gods, yelling for more speed from Thoth, her black Arabian stallion, and Minerva, the grey mare tethered beside him. Now with the sun dying in the grisly western sky, she brought her chariot to a halt by a green riverbank where the smiling crowd awaited her.

They consisted of the lower brackets of society: the plebeians—peasants, craftsmen, and merchants, clustered beneath the shade of palm trees that sprouted from the damp earth. The highest point of the embankment had been reserved for her, with the tallest palm shooting up like a pillar behind it.

Hypatia was not the first Librarian to lecture to commoners, but the practice was rare and not encouraged by the intellectual elite. Most in the city's academic circles considered it a pointless excursion. Her predecessor in the post had told her not to sacrifice her precious time in "preaching to oxen." *The common man is a beast of burden, Hypatia,* he had said with a dismissive wave of his hand when she expressed her thoughts on the matter. *Naturally they do much for the city, as an ox does much in dragging the plough. Yet though I will marvel at the strength of an ox, I would never presume to teach it Pythagoras! Leave the merchants to their wares. Even if they were capable of understanding us, what good could it possibly do for them?*

Now Hypatia climbed the slope and faced a group fifty-strong. She felt a swell of pleasure as she viewed their expectant faces in the blush of the setting sun. *These people are as willing to learn as any who can afford study at the Library,* she thought. *Their station in life has nothing to do with their appetite for learning.*

She began at once, taking advantage of the remaining daylight. And she employed a tactic that forged an instant intimacy with her listeners. Rather than address them as a collective crowd, she singled out men and women with her stare, drawing their attention into a tight beam of focus. When she locked gazes with her listeners, they were forced into a quiet kind of confrontation. *Why is she looking at me?* they would ask themselves. *Am I the sole recipient of her words today?* In this way Hypatia collected their stares as she spoke, and wove them into a web of unblinking concentration.

"Treasure your right to think," she said at the mid-point of her discourse on philosophy, reciting the core theme of all her teachings. "To think is a precious ability and yet so many throw it away! If you let it burn out, others will fill that darkness for you! They will tell you what to believe and insist you never question them! Should you dwell in this darkness, you will one day forget you were ever capable of thinking on your own!"

Were they thinking on their own?

She hesitated, her next words gelling in her mouth. Suddenly she recalled something else her predecessor had stated: *The common mob does not possess the strength of mind that we do, Hypatia; they are quite intimidated by the prospect of independent thought. That is why they will always be sheep, eager to be herded…even by you, Hypatia! They do not understand what you teach them. They come to you because the commoner needs something to worship. They need to surrender their own wills in something more powerful than they! Anything will fit that need! A storm, a golden calf, a god…whatever it is, they need something to bow down to. You are preaching strength to people who don't want such a thing! Your common-mob students will end up erecting you on their altar!*

Hypatia glanced surreptitiously at the baskets and bundled gifts the people had piled at the base of the embankment. Offerings of fruit, perfumes, and honey candies. Her smile faltered. *Are these gifts to thank me…or to worship me?* Suddenly she was concerned about the glittering pairs of reverent eyes watching her.

She decided to attack the subject directly in their presence.

"Long ago, people found fire and worshiped it as a god," she said. "But some people studied it, learned that fire can be manufactured, that it could warm their cold skin, cook their meat, light their caves, keep at bay the dangerous animals. It became a tool, not a god, for us to use! Today that same fire crowns Alexandria's Lighthouse!"

Her listeners murmured contentedly, pleased with the episodic example. She looked into their faces and thought: They *are* listening, not idolizing.

She concluded her lecture with a brief insistence that they come to the Library. Its scrolls, after all, were not reserved for students. Anyone could come in and read them without needing to pay for classes, a small yearly fee being all that was required for membership. But Hypatia had been telling the common crowd that for ten years! How many took the offer? A dozen maybe, through that whole decade? *Why was that?* Why wait for me to come to *them?*

She sighed. The last sliver of sun winked out behind her, and the horizon took on the color of a sickly bruise growing yellow at the ragged edges of a swelling.

And it was by this dying light that she came to the attention of Archbishop Cyril, the Patriarch of Alexandria.

Overlooking the riverbank from a high road, Archbishop Cyril brought his horses to a halt and stared down at the inexplicable gathering. He counted fifty people gathered on the grassy embankment, sitting like children at the feet of a woman dressed in a pale blue tunic.

He had nearly missed the sight as he careened his chariot around the high road that wound to the Kinaron District of Alexandria. After all, the sun had been glaring at him from the direction of the west, and he had been looking away from it to shield his eyes. A minute earlier and he might never have seen this secret congregation. At the bend in the road, however, the sun had slipped low enough that its wrathful glare subsided, and he had chanced to steal a look at the canal.

What he saw startled him. He strained to hear the woman but she was too far away. Cyril was forced to content himself with watching her gestures and trying to glean some understanding.

Archbishop Cyril had never been a handsome man. Even in his youth there had been a sharp quality to his features invariably off-putting, and his face had not softened with age. His high forehead was creased with more lines than his forty years of age should naturally have boasted. He had an aquiline nose set above thin lips. His chin was a jagged point. Two lines ran from his nose to the corners of his mouth, etching a permanent scowl. Grey eyes peered brightly from their sockets, framed by thick black eyebrows.

People who had met Archbishop Cyril, when asked their impression, always remembered his eyes above other details. As the soft compromise between extremes, grey would have been a serene color in another's face. In Cyril, the color was pale like sun-burnt stone. As if to compensate for their anemic hue, they appeared luminous; a stark gaze, bleached into severity.

He now fixed this gaze at the canal-side gathering. He did not recognize the woman. Her tunic was simple. She could be a noblewoman. Certainly her poise was regal and self-assured. But what nobleman would permit his wife to draw such attention? And for what reason? Was it a marriage party?

That was certainly possible.

One of the black stallions tethered to his chariot snorted impatiently, distressed at the narrow road overlooking the sharp slope. The creature stamped one hoof and looked at its master, but Cyril barely noticed. I should go down to meet her, he thought. There's something wrong in all this.

Suddenly the last shard of daylight vanished. The crowd dispersed. Cyril knew that by the time he reached the lower avenue, she and her followers would be gone.

Followers?

Was that what they were? Cyril settled back into his chariot and pressed his fingernails into his palms—a nervous habit he had developed long ago. He knew that paganism was not dead in Egypt. Rumors persisted of bloody Anubis cults or Dionysian orgies in the ancient cities of southern Egypt. Even in Alexandria…the natives stubbornly clung to their falcon-headed idols; that was no secret. But since the Edict of 391, what cult would dare be so open?

Just then Cyril saw the gift baskets and he almost laughed. It's a wedding party! he thought. And that woman is probably the bride! May the Lord bless you, lady, with many fine children!

Then Cyril stared a moment longer. At last he decided it was *not* a wedding party. Her undecorated clothes were not befitting a bride. There was no ceremony in what he was seeing. And the quiet dispersion of the crowd…what was *that* about? The whole thing seemed like a grotesque parody of Christ's own sermons. The thought inflamed him.

Unable to sit still any longer, Cyril seized his reigns and shook them. The horses jumped into their trot. Now that Cyril had stopped digging into his palms, he began to chew his lip—another habit that replaced the earlier. The Archbishop felt a swell of hunger, born not from his stomach but from tension, to discover what mysterious preacher had blown into Alexandria like an unwanted insect driven by desert winds.

"That is all," Hypatia told the crowd, and they gradually disintegrated until she was alone in the deep shadow of the palm tree.

Nearly alone, she realized. One person remained on the grass, looking at her with merry eyes. The evening had grown dark but she could see him nonetheless: Simplicius, dressed in a loose-fitting black tunic.

"An eavesdropper in my midst!" said Hypatia. "Simplicius the Spy?"

Simplicius went to her, embraced her. "Just reliving my memories of when I sat enthralled, listening to your lectures. It is always good to hear you speak, Hypatia."

"And I thought soldiers shunned philosophy!"

She had meant it as a joke, but Simplicius' smile fizzled at the remark and he looked to the ground.

Hypatia inwardly cursed herself. She touched his shoulder. "I didn't mean that."

"I know."

"Forgive me, it was a misplaced joke," she insisted, having forgotten how sensitive he was. "You were a tremendous student, Simplicius. Always know that."

"One who has read *Automata*, anyway."

She laughed. "And I wonder how our Governor would have reacted, had you flaunted the fact to shame him."

Simplicius was the *generalissimo* of Egypt, appointed by the royal court to protect this most important province of the Eastern Empire. His father had held the same post and risen to great prestige during military campaigns against raiders harassing the country's trade routes. By the end of his life, Simplicius' father had earned the nickname "Wraith of the Desert."

Simplicius began his own career as a mirror of his father's. He soared through the military ranks. Then after five years of service he had startled his superiors by requesting a sabbatical. "For what purpose, Simplicius?" he had been asked by his puzzled commander. "I'm happy to grant it to you…you've earned it. But why?" Simplicius had explained that he wished to enlist in a somewhat different institution: the Great Library. The announcement, predictably, sparked taunts of disbelief.

"The new Wraith of the Desert seeks to be a student of *books?*" they had cried. "He'll come back to us in a dress, singing Sappho's sonnets!" Simplicius bore their teasing in silence. They knew him as a warrior stained in enemy blood. But they never saw him at night in his tent, reading every play by Aeschylus. They didn't know that he quoted Homer to his soldiers to inspire them with passages of glory. And they didn't realize he was gifted with an intellect of remarkable proportions. He read…everything. By day he studied enemy troop formations; by the glow of the moon, he studied Euclid and Archimedes. All commanders were expected to know chess and Senet—the Egyptian strategy game—to make them effective tacticians, yet Simplicius regularly bested masters of both games at the yearly New Year festival in Persia which he discreetly attended.

Thus it was he came to the Great Library, enlisting in courses on philosophy taught by Hypatia and others. She had immediately perceived his brilliance. As a student, he had been gentle-mannered to the point of being shy. Hypatia had encouraged him—the Wraith of the Desert—to feel at home in the Library's scholarly halls. Few other professors had cared to bother, seeing Simplicius as a mere attack dog for the Empire.

"What did you think of Orestes' decree last night?" she asked.

"He's right. The city officials should be held accountable if these attacks are commonplace."

"I agree. Now that it's come to his attention, he'll handle it. He is tremendously concerned by Alexandria's affairs."

"Is it concern?" Simplicius asked, his voice cool and measured.

"Yes, it is. I know how he appears, Simplicius, but he has an honest heart. He and I have spoken on too many occasions for me not to know that."

Simplicius said nothing, not wishing to offend Hypatia. He thought Orestes a pompous, arrogant, egotistical bully. He knew, though, that Hypatia was his good friend.

Finally he asked, "*Are* these religious attacks commonplace?"

She nodded grimly.

"Why now? What's happening?"

Hypatia leaned against the tall palm tree. "Theophilus' nephew, the Archbishop Cyril. When he was first appointed I went to hear him speak at a gathering of his supporters. I stood in the back and listened as he promised to crack the 'heathen heart of Egypt.' The spirit of his uncle was in him even then. But then I heard no more of him. Sometimes, when I'm in the city square, I hear edges of conversation making reference to a speech he gave. Yet it has been so quiet." She sighed. "No more. The whispers have exploded to angry shouts, and..." She stopped, seeing that Simplicius was barely paying attention to her. He was staring, listlessly, at the water of the canal.

"Simplicius?"

He looked back to her. "My apologies, Hypatia. I was just thinking...tomorrow I'm off to Pentapolis again." Pentapolis was a southern city, several days journey from Alexandria.

Hypatia sensed his sadness. She touched his arm. "The Empire's borders need protection. More than ever now, with the fall of the West."

"Yes, they do."

"What troubles you?"

He gave her with a weary grin, reminded as always that there was no use in trying to hide his feelings around her. She had the eyes of a falcon and a perception like the aim of a cobra.

"This assignment will be my last. By my choice. I will write to Regent Pulcheria and request one closer to home, or else I will retire."

"Closer to home?"

"Closer to Alexandria," he clarified. "Unlike you, I've traveled a great deal. I know how rare and wonderful a city this is. It's a place I could die in, not on some haunted sand dune with scorpions as my final company. Away from here, there is only bitter desert and empty winds. I have lived my life as a soldier, but I will not age and die like one, too."

Hypatia was silent at the forcefulness in his voice. She knew by his tone that he had just sworn an oath. It elated her. Over the years she had watched friends disappear. With difficulty, she had come to grips with this inevitable loss, but now could it be that her favorite companions were retiring to the city where they had first met? Hadn't Synesius, who also lived in Pentapolis, expressed a desire to relocate here too?

Good things, she thought. There were good things coming.

Simplicius sighed and stared at the water again. He decided not to share with her the real reason for his wanting to move closer to Alexandria. Even as far as Pentapolis, he had been hearing reports of the city's growing religious conflict. The gossip was poisonous and disturbing.

I'm guardian against barbarism, he thought. But what if the barbarians aren't on Egypt's borders? What if they're already inside?

CHAPTER 7

▼

The palace chariot wheeled leisurely down the Canopic Way and pedestrians stepped aside to let it pass. From where he sat behind the driver, Governor Orestes studied the road with simmering nostalgia. Ahead of him, fires danced atop the high copper lampposts that lined both sides of the Way, and by their light he observed the vast crowd of nobles who, like him, were heading to the city's theater district. His first night in Egypt three years ago when he was only a statesman had included a chariot ride down the Canopic. That October night had been chilly, too, fragrant with lotuses and young grapevines. Now Orestes breathed deeply of their aroma, and found it easy to imagine that he was reliving the past. His heart swelled desperately for that to be true.

Orestes was dressed in a black breastplate as smooth as the shell of a scarab beetle, and a purple cloak hung like folded wings over his shoulders. Seated next to him, Marina wore the tunica she had bought that afternoon: red, studded with precious stones, with a low-cut neckline that drew attention to her pale throat and shoulders. Looped earrings glittered at her ears, and a pearl medallion bordered by lapis lazuli stared like a milky eye between her collarbones.

The couple was silent as their chariot pulled in front of the main amphitheater, built according to classical Greek design. It was airy and open with ringed stone seating for the general masses. The arena at the center was encircled by more lampposts, but these were unlit...keeping the set and actors shrouded in mystery until the play began.

Orestes and Marina were led inside by the guards to the high balcony that overlooked the arena pit. It was reserved for city officials—twelve empty cedar chairs stood behind a slender table. Only two centuries ago, balconies such as these had hovered over Roman gladiator matches and other grisly sports.

"It's a cold evening," Marina said finally, enjoying the stares of the half-filled amphitheater as she took her seat. "What is showing here tonight?"

"The Prometheus Saga," Orestes replied quietly.

Marina rolled her eyes, thinking ahead to the hours of sitting still and pretending to be fascinated by men in large masks. "I am well aware of how it ends."

"I wouldn't have married an uncultured woman," Orestes snapped. "You're Greek, you should know."

She grinned at the challenge. "I forgot that was one of your marital requirements. The wife of Orestes must be highly cultured!"

"Now you are reminded."

How did this happen? Orestes wondered. Why am I always fighting a battle with her? It didn't begin this way, did it? He pretended to be concentrating on the shadowy arena as he considered these questions. With an effort, he dredged up the memory of his first meeting with her at her father's home in Athens. Three years ago, only a month before he visited Egypt the first time. Her father had thrown a party in honor of a nephew's engagement and had invited influential people…the custom of self-important men. Orestes had already earned a reputation as an ambitious, successful statesman for Greece. He had made important friends in the Roman Senate. Everyone suspected he would soon ascend to greater rank.

At that party, Orestes had met Marina. He remembered how she had approached him brazenly and asked him to dance. How surprising, how bold! It had impressed him immediately. She was confidant, strong-willed, fearless. Rather than shy from conversation the way most women did, Marina had willfully encouraged it, asking him of his past and inviting him to share his thoughts of the future. Orestes remembered how, happily indulging her, he had felt intoxicated by the speed his life was changing. His youth in Olympia had been dark and difficult, marred by too much anger and sorrow. Now those meager beginnings seemed like someone else's life. Here's my life now! he had mused. I am a *statesman*, a guest of the wealthy, and now the object of interest for a powerful nobleman's daughter! Can it be that this is *not* a dream?

There was a burst of fire from the stadium pit. Orestes was torn from his pained contemplations. The arena lampposts were now ablaze with blue fire. By this melancholy glow the play's set emerged. A long slab of volcanic stone was the centerpiece with one up-thrusting rock in the center, tilted so that all could see the cruel iron cuffs nailed into the ore. Sparse weeds and thorn bushes sprouted from the rock's crevices. Pale blue linens blanketed the rest of the arena, creating the illusion of sky. The result was that the rock appeared to be a cliff-top jutting up through the center of the amphitheater, an azure sky all around it.

A bare-chested man with long curls was forcibly dragged onto the stage by two other men who wore masks. It was the famous opening—the imprisoning of the newly-captured Prometheus by the henchmen of gods, Strength and Violence. Strength had a mask made to resemble granite stone, with hard features befitting the embodiment of raw physical power. Dressed in a rough tunic of the same grey color, he bound Prometheus' left hand to the shackles. Violence wore a red mask visible even in the gloom, and his tunic was likewise stained to the bloody hue of Mars. He bound Prometheus' right hand.

Boys dressed up in preposterous costumes, Marina thought tiredly. The actors bellowed their lines, informing the audience of Prometheus' unforgivable crime of stealing fire from the gods. Marina saw movement from the left side of the balcony. Darius and his wife Kipa appeared at the top of the balcony stairs.

"Good evening, My Lady," Darius said. He was clutching his wife's hand but his lascivious eyes were shackled to Marina.

"Darius! You've brought your wife out for the evening!"

Kipa was a hybrid. Half-Egyptian, half-Persian, and half the weight of a normal person. She was frail and silent, given to smiles and polite talk. In truth, polite talk was all she was capable of, for her knowledge of Greek was like a child's. She had been raised in a remote Egyptian villa in Upper Egypt outside of Memphis, where Roman rule was more symbolic than actual and Roman culture had yet to penetrate. Darius had met her while on official business in the region, fell helplessly in love with the brown-skinned girl, and decided to marry her. In Marina's opinion, he must have been running a high fever that day. If ever there was a couple more ill-fit than herself and Orestes, it was Kipa and Darius.

Kipa now smiled at Marina, her pretty face lighting. "Greetings, My Lady. I sorry, I know I not see you in long time. I not go to theater in long time." She peeked at the arena's setting and gasped. "I have always loved theater, ever since I was child!"

Marina nodded. "Ever since you were child, yes."

The couple took the seats to Marina's left, with Kipa separating Darius from her. Darius leaned over and greeted Orestes.

"Are you fully recovered from your voyage?" he asked, but his voice betrayed his anxiety. Marina's ears bristled, and she thought: Be careful. Be *careful*.

Orestes didn't look away from the three actors below. "Fully recovered and desiring to watch this play, yes."

"Prometheus!" Kipa whispered happily to her husband. "I know this play!"

"You do?" Marina said with an undercurrent of cruelty in her voice. "Apparently, Darius, you too hold it as a marital requirement for your wife to be cultured!"

Below, Strength and Violence finished fastening the god's legs to the rock so that he was a helpless prisoner. They drew back and admired their handiwork while Prometheus, dressed only in a tattered loincloth, pleaded with them. His unmasked face was anguished as he sucked in a gulp of air and cried out to the universe, but before any words could leave his lips a cacophony of angry voices erupted from the crowd. Visibly shaken, the actor started in the direction of the disturbance. Orestes looked as well, and his eyes despaired at what they saw.

Two separate groups of people had become a yelling, roaring fray. They congested one of the arena's middle steps. Curses rose from the din, a tenuous battle-line drawn, dividing the vocal melee into a group of five and a group of six. The surrounding crowd cleared to give them room.

Orestes' eyes blazed coldly as he watched the commotion. "Is there no authority to ensure peace at the theater?"

Darius shook his head. "I see theater guards near the entrance, yet they stand like statues!"

Then a voice distinguished itself from the storm of chatter: "—not our fault that your wife's slit begs for so many men!"

A nearly imperceptible silence followed. Then as if the trumpets of Ares had sounded, the group of five dove into their opponents' ranks. Fists flew, legs kicked. The surrounding crowd screamed. A glint of bronze flashed in the maelstrom like a flicker of lightning.

At that, Orestes flew up from his seat. He sprang to the balcony stairs when suddenly he recognized one of the men in the fight.

He was the fellow who had spoken those last words. He was thin-bodied, and his sunken face had alert black eyes and a flat nose owing to an untreated break. He belonged to the group of six men. He was the only one lingering back from the fight, though he surveyed it with an air of triumph. His arms were folded across his chest, and there was something awkward about his stance…Orestes recognized a subtle deformity to his spine.

Seeing that, the pieces fell into place.

Hierax.

Orestes had met him only once before, just weeks after arriving in Alexandria as governor. Hierax had begged for an audience with him. On the day of the appointment, the man had entered the audience chamber slowly, his awkward gait betraying a malformed spine. Hierax had greeted Orestes with a sad smile, relating how he had been unfairly dismissed from his teaching post during the past administration. "My academic peers consider me an embarrassment, perhaps even a monster," Hierax had pined, "and they convinced your predecessor that I was unfit to teach our city's children! Please, great Governor! Allow an ill-born man the chance to earn an honest pay, without ridicule!"

The speech had been delivered with wet eyes and a broken voice. It had been designed to elicit pity. Yet Orestes knew more than Hierax suspected. Yes, Hierax had worked as a schoolteacher. And it was true he had been dismissed, but not for the reasons he professed. Hierax had been teaching his students that the Jewish race was a rot that had destroyed mighty Rome and would fell Alexandria next "unless the might of our Savior struck back."

The matter had been a scandal for the school; Jewish leaders had demanded Hierax's removal. Forearmed with this information, Orestes had confronted the estranged teacher with it, had seen the truth in the man's eyes, and had terminated the interview.

Now here was Hierax again at the heart of another racial riot. Orestes descended the balcony to the seats below.

As Orestes came into view the theater guards sprang to action. The bronze dagger had succeeded in cutting two men, neither severely. The groups were wrenched apart. The shouting continued, unabated. Orestes neared swiftly. Hierax saw him. They beheld each other. And then it happened: Orestes remembered the battered, sobbing woman he had met in Constantinople. The sight of her black bruises, the abrasions that encircled her belly and thighs. The cruel gouges near her womanhood. The purplish-yellow blotches of clotted blood. Suddenly he remembered her description of one of her attackers. "He was the only one I saw clearly," the woman had said. "There was something bent about his body...I can't explain...just an impression that he was crooked, misshaped. And his nose was flattened, too, as if in an old fight."

"Silence! *Silence!*" Orestes stopped before the two groups and their babble evaporated. "What kind of animals are you? This is a theater, a place for the civilized! I will be informed of how this brawl began!"

The explanations exploded with fervor until Orestes silenced them again and singled out the men, one at a time. The group of five men included the husband of the violated woman; he was a stocky, red-faced man. Apparently, he had embarked on his own investigation into the attack on his wife. That search had led him and his four friends to the theater when they heard Hierax would be in attendance.

Hierax paled in Orestes' presence. His eyes flickered at the recollection of their initial meeting two years ago. Then he recovered swiftly and denied all knowledge of the woman. "*I* was attacked tonight without provocation, great Governor!" he said, face changing to the crestfallen visage he had worn two years ago. "We are all fortunate that it happened before your own eyes, so that your wisdom on this matter will not be swayed."

"It won't be swayed," Orestes assured him. "My eyes are quite healthy. As are my ears, Hierax, though I admit I caught only part of your words. Please finish the story about his wife's hungry slit!"

Hierax's face did not change this time, but his eyes did. They clouded over in unconcealed fear.

Orestes addressed the crowd. "There are eleven men here who have disturbed the peace of your night and mine! They fought openly! One brandished a dagger," he lifted the unburnished blade from the steps and held it out for them to see. "By law, what should happen to them?"

A calamitous shout piped up from the crowded theater: "Imprisonment for five days!"

Orestes looked at Hierax. In a much quieter tone that only the closest could hear, he said, "We also have a man accused of beating and violating a woman. For that, an entirely different punishment is levied."

"Will I be allowed to speak at my trial, Governor?" Hierax asked in defiance, dropping all pretense of injury and naivety.

Orestes nodded and offered a smile he did not feel. "Most certainly, Hierax. As will your accuser..." His smile melted from his face. "And his wife."

He motioned to the guards to take the eleven men to the magistrate. Then, with barely-controlled fury, he looked back to the audience.

"This is the city of tolerance!" he called out, thinking: *Calm yourself. Calm yourself, Orestes!* "After seven hundred years I will *not* let two populations destroy all that we have created! If you cannot tolerate each other, at least pretend!" As he spoke, he noticed as with new eyes the fantastic mix of cultures that stood listening to him. Egyptians and Christians and Jews and Persians, lithe children and adults as old as withered trees.

"When you go home tonight tell your neighbors and families what I am telling you. Keep peace in this city, or be assured that no God's wrath will equal mine!"

Orestes turned to Prometheus, who stared at him behind an unruly beard.

"I don't recall that the Fire-Bearer was ever so silent," Orestes said. Like the crack of a whip, the actor resumed his anguished cry to the heavens.

Orestes returned to the balcony. Kipa, Darius, and Marina had their heads turned in his direction. As he sat down, they looked away one by one.

"The mighty Governor has spoken," Marina whispered scornfully.

Orestes folded his hands across his lap. "Yes, Marina, he has."

The trial came as dawn blushed across the Nile, turning the sky the color of iron plucked from a glowing forge. The proceedings did not last long, and by the time the sun was perched on the horizon word of the sentencing was flying through the city as if borne by the Four Winds themselves.

Archbishop Cyril was among the very first to hear it. He was awake and bathing when he heard the demanding knock upon his wooden rectory door. He wrapped himself in a thick robe and discovered Peter the Reader, his attendant during Mass, shivering at the door.

Cyril's chambers lay in the Kinaron quarter of Alexandria. The rectory was a small stone hovel attached leech-like to the Caesarion Church. The church itself was a grand, handsome structure built along the same concept as the Pantheon of Rome, though far smaller in scale. A rectangular building with a massive dome supported by Corinthian pillars, it was the first Christian Church built in Egypt by Emperor Constantine. Two oak doors allowed the public to enter the church for Mass. There were no seats inside; parishioners were expected to sit or kneel. The stained-glass windows were shaped like long teardrops. The pulpit was plated with silver, and swinging lamps hung from the ceiling over an interior that could hold six hundred souls.

The rectory boasted none of that splendor, much to Cyril's pleasure. He didn't like or want riches. His monastic quarters contained only books, water jugs, an amphora of wine, and two oil lanterns as well as his bed. In fact, the only object of value in the rectory was an engraved stone plaque affixed to the wall above his study desk. The plaque, a gift to the church from Constantine, had the words: "Offer them the Hope of Salvation." Above it was an engraving of a fish, the Empire-wide symbol for the Christian religion because the Greek word for fish—*ichthus*—was an anagram for *Ieous Christos Theou Uios Soter*—"Jesus Christ, God's Son, Savior."

The Archbishop saw the distress in Peter's face at once. He ushered the boy inside and made him sit below the stone engraving. There, by the glow of three candles as slender as knives, the boy related the arrest of Hierax and five other Christian men at the theater last night. He described the trial, the charges, the result.

"And so Orestes ordered the man's torture," Peter said, still shuddering with frustration. At sixteen years old, he retained a very boyish appearance. His bony frame seemed frozen in the thrall of puberty. He had bright, cedar-colored eyes and large lips. Like many in the church he dressed in a brown robe, though his was untailored; it was felt he would eventually grow into it. He was also a ward of the church—born out of wedlock, abandoned by his mother when he was only four, Peter now lived with a host family in the Kinaron community.

"Tortured for brawling?" Cyril snapped, incredulous.

"For the rape of a Jew. The little slut accused Hierax, and the Governor was captured by her pretty web." There was lascivious urgency in Peter's voice when he spoke of the woman, and his face congested with blood. Cyril noted it but said nothing. The boy was not as shy of puberty as he appeared.

"Is this blasphemy to go unpunished?" Peter cried.

Cyril's thoughts wandered uncertainly as he came to grips with this unexpected news. He knew Hierax. He didn't care for him at all. Hierax had approached him two years ago, protesting his dismissal from his teaching post. When Cyril first heard the reason for the dismissal, he had felt a brimming respect for the deformed man. After all, Cyril had spent twenty of his forty years making fellow Christians aware that Jews were an affront to Christ. Hadn't it been Jews who, awaiting their Messiah, had fed Him to Roman wolves when He came at last?

But though Cyril had agreed ideologically with Hierax, he had no love for him. In fact, he found the mere presence of the man disturbing. No beloved child of God would have that hideous malformation: a spine which undulated like a knobby tree root between his shoulder blades. A man like that could only be as crooked spiritually as he was physically.

And I was right! Cyril thought, hearing Peter describe the crime Hierax was convicted of. God did not smile upon a violator of women. Certainly the courts had been correct in punishing Hierax, who already bore the physical sign of the wicked. Cyril did not doubt it. But would five other Christian men have participated in such a sin? It was possible—God was perfect, but men were far from it.

Cyril grumbled angrily, sweating. There was a war on, and the future of Alexandria hung on a delicate thread. *Alexandria is a battleground*, his uncle Theophilus had told him. *It's steeped in sin, in blood-drinking paganism, in Jewish coalitions.* Cyril held his uncle in great reverence for cracking the pagan heart of the city after Theodosios' Edict of 391. Theophilus had personally led the charge against the city's pagan temples. But the Jews were far worse than some deluded cult of Isis. Pagans were divided, lost, relics of the old era, hopeless. Jews were tightly-knit and organized, united in belief and tradition. It was no secret that they had infiltrated Alexandria's grain trade and guilds for the purpose of ruling the city behind a veil...

Cyril bristled at a new thought. The Jews are always meeting, planning, making new grabs at power...they see all events in the city as things to exploit for their own ends. So, this Jewish woman gets raped by Hierax, she tells her husband, and her husband tells his friends...who decide to implicate as many Christian men as possible. To be sure, Hierax is likely guilty. But to charge five others with the crime?

"Who were these five others, the ones accused with Hierax?"

Peter rattled off their names. Cyril listened, unfamiliar with them.

"I know that three of them work in the granaries," Peter said. At this, Cyril stiffened with fear.

For months, he had been maneuvering good Christians into guilds and industries dominated by Jews. Was it possible the Jews realized what he was doing? And if they knew, wouldn't they try to get rid of them in ways that weren't obvious? To fire them outright would raise eyebrows. But if five were convicted of rape...

"What happened to the men with Hierax? Were they tortured as well?"

"They were given five days of imprisonment for disturbing the peace."

"And the Jewish men who started this entire 'disturbance?'"

"Five days as well, Archbishop. There are ten men in chains, and one limping home from brutal, bloody punishment."

Orestes is no fool then, Cyril thought. He had met Orestes once when the man was campaigning in Egypt. It had been a short meeting and entirely political; Cyril had instantly seen that Orestes was trying to stroke the right people to gain popular support. Cyril had made inquiries on Orestes' background and was pleased with what was uncovered. The man was reportedly a fair, somewhat fiery statesman from Olympia, Greece. He attended Christian Mass. He had crafted friendships with many Jewish leaders, but these were necessary political friendships. In the end, Cyril had lent some quiet support for Orestes, writing favorable words to the then-Emperor.

Another thought flashed through Cyril's mind. *Hierax's conviction will be used by Jewish leaders.* That the man disgusts me is irrelevant; in this war, every man is a soldier whether he realizes it or not. In fact, was it so unlikely that the Jewish woman didn't know who raped her, but was coerced into accusing Christian men—three innocent granary workers, and an unsavory creature like Hierax to give the accusation weight? Cyril felt his anger rising. What better way, he reasoned, to sway a man than to use a woman's tears?

A woman…

Cyril suddenly remembered the woman he had seen by the riverbank. The one who had gathered fifty disciples to her feet. Was she a part of this war too?

"I saw a woman last evening near the greater canal," Cyril said suddenly, emerging from his meditation. "A crowd had gathered around to listen to her speak. Who might she be?"

Peter blinked, confused by the change in subject. "I can only guess it is Hypatia of whom you speak."

The name jolted him. It seemed familiar, with the distant ring of recognition just out of reach. "Hypatia? Who is she?"

"Daughter of the pagan Theon," Peter said, and noticing Cyril's blatant puzzlement, he added with incredulity, "You've never heard of her, *not once* since your ascension to Patriarch?"

Cyril was annoyed at the challenge. "If I had heard of her, I would not be asking you. I have been busy protecting our faith!"

Peter talked and Cyril felt a slithering unease take possession of his thoughts. His uncle had achieved the glorious triumph over the pagans. Cyril felt the need to strike a similar blow for the faith and the Jews were a deserving target. Yet what was this now? A pagan, a *prominent* pagan, who continued to flaunt her feathers as if the Edict of Theodosius had never been?

Pagans were, of course, an affront to the One God. They were the midnight revelers, drinkers of blood and conjurers of demons. They believed in witchery of all kinds, and had as many gods as there were stars in the firmament. The Church now knew that all other gods were false or, more insidiously, were different avatars of Lucifer. Anyone who danced the bonfires of hell had no place in Creation; Theophilus had been right to target their festering evil…and yet the late Patriarch's triumph had been incomplete. Alexandria had not lost its pagan influences. The Great Library was nothing more than a temple to that bygone era. And now…Hypatia?

He remembered the blue-shadowed woman, the sun setting behind her. The crowds. The *crowds*.

"Had I seen so many people at a Christian sermon I would have thought our Lord was returning from Paradise," Cyril said.

Peter licked his lips out of habit. "What of the Jews, Archbishop?"

Cyril nodded in acknowledgment of the more blatant problem facing the city. "This entire situation may work to our benefit, Peter."

"How?"

"Six Christian men have been imprisoned. One was tortured. This is enough to make a complaint to the Regent. I had warned her that no spider could ever weave a web like the Jews have done in Alexandria. They have their pincers hooked into everything. The grain business, the trade routes…" He sighed irritably, his fingernails pushing themselves into his palms in a fit of frustration. "Now they're trying to corrupt Orestes' judgment."

"I hear Orestes has already dispatched a letter to Pulcheria regarding this incident."

Cyril was silent, surprised by that news. *Why would Orestes do that? Does he feel he needs to justify his actions? Why? Who is he afraid of…the Jews or me?* Cyril quietly mulled over the questions for several minutes, forgetting that Peter was even there. The boy, however, only saw that he was being ignored. His soft face flushed, and at last he could take no more.

"Your action was so swift with the Novations! Why do you stall now?"

The Novations were a heretical sect of Christianity which Cyril, only months into his patriarchy, had driven from Alexandria. The *Cathari*, they called themselves—the Pure Ones, for they were descended from families who had not renounced Jesus Christ during the days of pagan Rome's Christian persecutions. They wore this genealogical distinction proudly, garbing themselves only in white robes and refusing to accept parishioners who had previously sinned. All that Cyril could have accepted, but their real heresy was that they denied the authority of the Catholic Church, considering it corrupt and fallible. They went so far as to perform a Second Baptism on a new initiate who had been originally baptized a Catholic. This audacious blasphemy could not go unaddressed. Cyril, famed in theological circles for his unmatched debating prowess, challenged the Novations to a debate at the Emperor's court in Constantinople. He had accused them of dividing the Church, of corrupting true Christians. He had argued them into red-faced silence. The Emperor was impressed by Cyril's arguments and instantly signed an edict outlawing the practice of the Second Baptism on penalty of death. This early victory for Alexandria's new Patriarch gave him the influence under Governor Pentadius' administration to drive the Novations out of the city entirely.

His success had been swift and devastating to his opponents. It had also convinced Cyril that God had blessed him with a special gift: He was an invulnerable debater, with verbal tactics akin to the swordplay of a seasoned warrior. He knew how to parry. To lunge. To lure. And to deliver the killing blow at precisely the right moment.

"Why can't we simply close the Jewish temples?" Peter continued, in the voice of a mean-spirited adolescent who whined to get his way. Cyril did not respond to the foolish query.

"Go home, Peter."

"Archbishop, one century ago we were being persecuted! Now we have numbers! We have influence! We can stamp out the enemies to the faith. You must—"

Cyril advanced on him with dreadful speed. "Enough! Go home! And put your impulses to good use by summoning all my parishioners to a Mass at sundown."

Peter slipped out of his chair and knelt. He grabbed the Archbishop's hand in a fervent act of apology. Cyril's explosive anger subsided and he patted the boy's head affectionately.

"Forgive me, Archbishop!" Peter was eager to please again. "I will tell our people. A sundown Mass." He made for the door, stepped into the morning, and hesitated.

"Something wrong, Peter?"

"There is no Mass scheduled for tonight."

Cyril felt a renewed surge of rage, and for a moment he thought he was going to throttle the boy. The urge passed. "There is now, Peter. There is now."

Peter detected the hostility. He scurried off like a cub that realized it had strayed into the den of an ill-tempered male. Cyril watched him go.

He's right, he thought. Swift action is required. Tonight it will be done.

CHAPTER 8

▼

"Enough!" Hypatia yelled to herself, throwing her feather pen to the floor in disgust. She had awakened at dawn, bathed, dressed in her white robe, and set herself the task of finishing the draft of her book's newest chapter. But after two hours she had managed to write three pages of crossed-out beginnings. *Walk away*, Hypatia told herself. Give yourself something else to do.

And so it was she found herself crouching in her yard, a sponge in hand and a wooden bucket by her feet, scrubbing the old sundial that stood on her father's grassy estate. The instrument had been a gift from the Great Library Council, presented for Theon's outstanding contributions to mathematics. Its base stood a meter tall, was white marble, and had a brass face inlaid with the hours of the day.

Most Library scholars lived in the ancient building's dormitories where Hypatia too had a room. But her father's house was still her home.

"That's better," she told herself, seeing the glossy luster of the sundial's face returning under her tireless scrubbing. She glanced at the house—an aging, limestone rectangular home with two ionic columns supporting the porch's archway. She imagined Theon standing there, half-visible in the shade, smiling at her.

Theon had been tall, heavy in the belly, and balding when Hypatia knew him. Her mother had died giving birth to her—the woman not even a shade in her daughter's mind. Many times growing up, Hypatia had crept into her father's room to stare at the wall fresco of the mother she'd never known. It was a portrait made of small, colored tiles. It showed the profile of a beautiful Greek lady, eyes lowered, head tilted slightly as if in sorrow. Like Hypatia, she had splendid curls of chestnut hair, worn wreathed about her head as was the style of the day.

Theon had been all the family Hypatia had known. He died when she was twenty, a year after her return from the University of Athens. *I don't even have a fresco of him to gaze at,* she thought sorrowfully. *No portraits at all…just a house with empty rooms. And a sundial.*

She remembered with perfect clarity the day he had brought the sundial home. In the Library's chariot it had arrived, with three men to help erect it on the lawn.

To help us make appointments on time? a seven-year-old Hypatia had asked him. Even at that young age, she had seen the Great Library's spectacular observatory. A sundial was a meager thing by comparison.

To learn to appreciate small details, Theon had replied. *Most people have no idea how important little details are. A shadow, for instance, seems a terribly ordinary spectacle. Yet, two little shadows once helped a man deduce the size of our world!*

"I miss you," Hypatia told his imagined phantom on the porch. Her eyes moistened.

Sudden footsteps approached, jarring her. The yard was protected by rows of shrubbery, a figure moving swiftly behind this floral barrier. The flowering bramble quivered as a shape came into view.

Hypatia sighed.

"Good day, Thasos."

Thasos, flanked on both sides by the short flowery bushes, chanced a slight smile and held his hands out as if in peace offering. He was dressed in a yellow tunic, and his hair was wet, either from sweat or, more likely, a very recent bathing.

"Am I disturbing you, Philosopher?"

Hypatia forged a smile. "A good teacher is not disturbed by her students, so long as they conduct themselves as students."

"Then I, Thasos the student, approach you if I may."

"You may, of course."

Thasos took a step into her yard and halted. He squinted at her in the sun. "By the laws of good etiquette, I must inform you of an impending accusation."

Hypatia stared at him, fishing for purpose in his words aside from the obvious. "Accusation? Am I to presume that you are my would-be accuser?"

"Correct, Teacher. I accuse you with all respect of great selfishness."

Was his father ever so entrenched in the urges of youth? Hypatia wondered. "State your case, student Thasos."

"Were you to keep to yourself the fact that in ten days there shall be a storm in the heavens so violent that the stars will shake loose and drop into the desert?"

Hypatia was too stunned to speak. Her face betrayed her astonishment.

"I leave you speechless! Were I not so modest, I'd be pleased!"

Impressed in spite of herself, Hypatia said, "How did you come by this information, student? Surely not in a dream."

Smiling proudly, Thasos continued, "Modesty aside, I *am* pleased with myself!"

Hypatia dropped her scrubbing sponge to the bucket and crossed the distance to him. "There is no one at the Library who knows that prediction."

Thasos held his ground. "Pardon my brashness, Teacher, but I know."

"Yes," she said coyly. "You do."

It was a ploy of course, but she couldn't fathom how he had learned it. In 401, her father had completed a five-year-study of Sumerian astronomical texts. He then cross-referenced them with a rare manuscript from the Far East, and made a prediction for the beginning of November, 414. His forecast was that a shower of shooting stars would fill the skies over Alexandria. This he had written on a scrap of papyrus, keeping it in a little book of unfinished notes and scribbles. He had told *no one*, save his daughter.

Showers of stars were one of the rare gems of the night sky. Few in the history of civilization had ever accurately predicted them.

Hypatia drew close and Thasos felt his pride fleeing him as if he were a water-skin being drained of every drop. He smelled her perfume and lovingly held it in his lungs like an exotic incense. Don't let your eyes wander, he warned himself. The desire to gaze and appreciate the voluptuous landscape of her body was nearly overpowering.

Don't, don't, *don't*. He strove to overcome his fluster. "I made a flourish of discoveries last night. Do you remember I told you my father had studied Socrates?"

"I do," she said. "Among many, many other philosophical works, Thasos."

"Well, I learned that my father was friendly with Theon the scientist. Theon, *your* father! My father kept notes on conversations they enjoyed. And in one of those notes, he remarks that Theon had confided a prediction to him. 'The rare phenomenon of falling stars for the end of November's first week, 414.' Those were the exact words. I believe Theon would have confided this in his daughter as well?"

Hypatia's eyes glimmered. So her father *had* told another. Interesting!

"It is only a prediction," she said, "and may be proven fallible."

"Why didn't he publish it?"

"If wrong, he didn't want to be a public spectacle."

Thasos chuckled. "Yet he shared his poetry with that same public."

Again Hypatia was temporarily speechless by this disclosure of little-known knowledge. Theon had been an astronomer, mathematician, and philosopher—few Library scholars confined themselves to a single field of study. In his private time, he also dabbled in poetry.

"You seem a scholar on my father's work, suddenly," she said. "It is not commonly known that he tried to write poetry."

"Tried," Thasos said.

"Have you read my father's poems?"

Too far, Thasos thought. *I'm going to far.* "Yes. A few."

Hypatia looked at him expectantly. "And your assessment?"

"Dearest Teacher, your father was a miserable poet."

Hypatia burst into laughter. Every muscle in Thasos' body relaxed.

It was the first time he had seen her laugh, and his heart swelled unexpectedly at the sight. Her face was red with mirth and she seemed to grow younger with the delighted expression. It was as if her laughter had sloughed off decades of her life, and she was suddenly a young woman as old as he, rejuvenated by joy. His eyes strayed to her body…he lifted them at once. *Don't be a leering jackal!*

"Poetry," Hypatia said, grinning, "was not his strong suit."

"Yet his enlightened lyrics aside, his reputation dominates the Library."

Hypatia recovered from her laughter. Thasos would not have thought it possible for her to look more beautiful, but with her face flushed from merriment and her eyes sparkling, he couldn't imagine that Helen of Troy had been more radiant.

Hypatia saw his worshipful stare. It sobered her delight. Thasos, detecting the shift in her mood, figured she was mourning her father's memory.

"Pardon me, Teacher, but when did he die?"

"Twenty-five years ago."

"Forgive me if I've depressed you. That wasn't my intention."

"You haven't," she said truthfully. *Just don't make yourself a fool again, Thasos.*

"Do you intend to tell other students about his prediction? If he's right, I really think others should know."

Hypatia shook her head, her dark curls dangling down the supple flank of her neck. "With respect to my father I don't believe he'd want others to know…should the stars *not* fall."

"And if they *do* fill the sky on the calculated night?"

"I believe his reasoning and research are sound."

"Shouldn't others know of it, then?" Thasos persisted. "It would be a great testament to him."

"Others *will* know. I have written letters to some friends of mine, instructing them to watch the skies ten days from now. I didn't tell them what to look for, but they know I do not make idle requests. And my father's work won't be forgotten. If the stars fall, I'll publish his paper on that prediction. Future generations can then use it to predict future star showers."

"I would honor you by keeping it to myself then."

Hypatia was moved by his gesture. "You flatter me."

Again, Thasos felt a rise of heat pouring up from his chest. "You are worthy of more than flattery, Philosopher."

"Thasos…"

"I also learned that you had studied in Athens," Thasos said quickly, realizing he had gone too far, trying to recover. As soon as the words left his lips, however, he saw that perhaps he had made a worse mistake. At the mention of Athens, Hypatia's face changed. The pleasant gleam in her blue eyes darkened with displeasure.

"Is there a class being taught of which I am the subject?" Hypatia asked with a sternness she didn't feel. "How do you know these things, student?"

Thasos felt several lies suggest themselves in response to her directness. They writhed in his mind like the bobbing heads of a hydra, but Hypatia's imperious gaze seemed to lay all his devices bare. Feeling as transparent as glass, he silenced the hydra and said, "Someone told me that a student must commit himself to learning. That he must notice and study the world around him. Surely the person who uttered these advices is not above being studied and investigated herself?"

Hypatia softened a little. "Yes, student. I have been to Athens."

The memory was as dark and lonely as the voyage she had taken to get there. She had been eighteen. She had never left Alexandria before. She had not wanted to go.

But the journey could not be refused. Hypatia had already completed all of the Great Library's courses on mathematics…at the age of thirteen. At fifteen she had written a commentary on Aristarchus' supposition that stars had a life-cycle—they were birthed in the womb of distant space, matured, and eventually died. At seventeen, she had written her first work—her prime number theorem that, even before publication, was creating a stir among Theon's contemporaries. A month later—as the work was copied for publication—Hypatia had written a letter at her father's urging to the University of Athens. She had not wanted to write the letter, but he had insisted her education be crowned with a degree from Greece. His obstinacy that she make an academic pilgrimage to the birthplace of philosophy had been nearly religious. "It is the world of our ancestors, Hypatia!" he had told her. "Think of it as visiting your ancestral home. The spirit of the ancients still walk there! Their essence lingers like jasmine in the breeze." She remembered biting her tongue at his words, tempted to reply, "Father, you are indeed making progress on your poetry!"

Her letter, however, was soundly rejected by the University. When she received the reply, Theon had flown into a fury the likes of which she had never seen. Red-faced and cursing, he had penned a letter to their Schoolmaster challenging them to accept his daughter on his own reputation.

Hypatia's acceptance letter came four weeks later. For the sake of honor, her own and her father's, she dared not refuse. She found herself on a royal transport to Greece the very next day.

And the afternoon she arrived on the green shores of Greece, she had marveled at the fabled University. It was a house befitting a god, a colonnaded building with an arena-like atrium and several floors for study. The architecture was towering, made as if by giants. Craning her neck to stare, Hypatia had read its unwritten message: *I dwarf you, mere mortal! You are an ant that crawls in my mighty shadow!* Hypatia had responded to the silent challenge with one of her own: *Ants like me create you, mighty building! Never forget that!*

Inside the gaping structure she had sought the Schoolmaster. His name was Tyndarus, the latest in a family of prestigious Athenian scholars. He was tall, gaunt, and had silver hair that hung from his head like a metallic wig.

"Hypatia? Ah! Daughter of the indefatigable Theon! I received his letter myself!" His eyes glimmered like coals. "I hold him in high regard. I would never offend him by denying his pretty daughter her fair try at the University."

The first thing Hypatia learned about the University of Athens was that academia was a fierce battle pitting students against their peers like a cockfight. Classes were fiery sessions as students warred for the love of their professors. They argued, they clashed like bronze sabers, they ranted and spewed classical arguments with the gusto of titans besieging heaven. Hypatia found herself listening—not participating—to these whirlwind affairs. And the more she listened the more she became impressed...with their idiocy.

With few exceptions, the students of Athens were not at the University to learn. They were there to fulfill a role like actors searching for the right mask to don. Whereas Plato had been a student of Socrates but then went off to found his own schools of thought, Hypatia's peers seemed eager to be exact replicas of their chosen heros. As a result, when she went for walks in the rolling countryside she would run into dozens of Platos and Diogenes and Aristotles. The "trail of the ancients" proved not so ancient. Yet these walking copies possessed an engulfing absence of independent thought. Each student was so obsessed with recreating a legendary orator that they were sacrificing their own minds to the recreation! It was eerie, discouraging, and at the end of the day immensely laughable.

It was not Alexandria. The soil of Athens might still be healthy, but no one was planting in it.

Gradually, a more insidious problem had crept into her life. As the only girl in an all-male school, Hypatia felt as if her skin were truly made of honey and every ant in the region was scuttling towards her for a taste. It didn't start right away. At first every boy she met professed friendship, invited her to join him at meals, asked for her on evening walks. But when each "friend" tried to seduce her, tried to make her tumble into his bed, she grew wary and cynical. She politely refused their advances...and that made everything change. Their smiles disappeared. Their pleasantries became caustic. Suddenly she was unwelcome to sit with them. Suddenly she heard cruel whispers as she passed them in the great dining hall. Suddenly she was very conscious of her gender and her danger.

Boys started filling the corridor that led to her bedroom. She felt like a hare filing by rows of wolves. The anxiety was constant. She started propping a chair against her door while she slept. Then one night a crashing sound awoke her. She sprang up in bed to see that the chair had toppled over, the door was now wide open, and black shapes slithered in the corridor beyond. She screamed...and they went away.

The next day she decided to do something. That evening she went to see Tyndarus the Schoolmaster. It was February, 383 A.D.

"The boys here act as if they have never seen a woman before!" she had told him in his private chamber, on the top floor of the University's dormitory "And now they're breaking into my room!"

"Did you see any faces?"

"It was dark. I saw shapes."

"Hypatia, you might have forgotten to close the door yourself. Or a student tried the wrong door. Your conclusion is premature."

Controlling her anger, Hypatia had retorted thickly, "My conclusion is reasonable. Your students leer at me incessantly. They follow me in packs."

"Packs?" the Schoolmaster had repeated, appalled. He was sitting on a luxuriant blue couch, an opened scroll in his lap. "That is hardly an appropriate word to use when describing University students."

Hypatia glanced at the scroll, then looked back to Tyndarus. "It is a metaphor, Schoolmaster."

"*Packs* is a term applied to animals. We are not animals. We are men of learning. Not packs. We use *packs* to describe wolves. Not people."

"I am only explaining, Schoolmaster, that I—"

"It is an inappropriate statement, Hypatia. Groups, perhaps. A *number* of boys. But not packs."

"Not packs," she said, new anxiety fluttering in her chest.

"Man is Creation's ultimate result. I find it personally insulting when you do not address him as such. The fact that you're tolerated here speaks for the civilized nature we engender in our students."

"I apologize for…What did you say, Schoolmaster?"

An amused smirk then appeared on his face. "Hypatia, who exactly do you think you are? Lysistrata? Sappho? No, no, no, no, no, no, no, no, no, no, no." He shook his head and suddenly she smelled the stale wine on his breath. There was a goblet on the counter near the couch. It was empty.

"You are a woman," the Schoolmaster said in a thickening voice. "Which is to be an animal to breed, to please her owner, and to raise her owner's children. That is the difference between men and women. Theon, Theon." Tyndarus had shaken his head in disapproval. "God did not grant him a son so he raised his daughter as one!"

It was too much for her to take, and she forgot her fear in a flash of murderous anger. "You dare to speak of my father, of *me*, in such a way!"

"A woman is only a warm envelope for a man's contents. Go back to Egypt, Hypatia, if this truth is hard to take."

Hypatia was shaking so much she knew it must be visible. "A man is judged on how well he can master his own elements, Schoolmaster. By day your students may chatter like admiring monkeys eager to please you, but I've seen them at night! I've seen them in the shadows. They're not the risen angels you pretend, but lusty beasts who run in *packs!*"

With feral agility the Schoolmaster leapt up from his sofa. He grasped her by her tunic, shoving her to the wall with remarkable force. Again, she smelled the acrid wine on his breath and beard.

"Such a bull-headed girl," he said, eyes narrowing mischievously. "But such a pretty girl too. Such a very pretty thing." He pushed his body up against hers, and she felt something large and stiff rubbing against her covered belly. One of his spidery hands crawled into the narrow opening of her toga and seized one of her breasts, pinching the large nipple.

There had been no way to fight him off. But Hypatia's mind raced amid her terror, thinking of a way out of this.

"You were reading the work of Paramenides, Schoolmaster."

Her words visibly jolted him. "What?"

"On the couch," Hypatia continued quickly. "That scroll, that was Paramenides."

"Yes it is. How did—"

"Are you an admirer of his work?"

Her question seemed to snap him out of a trance. Though he continued to hold her nipple between his thumb and first finger, he was no longer grinding his rigid manhood against her. "Yes actually."

Knowing she had earned only a momentary reprieve, she pressed her clandestine offensive. "You must be familiar with his philosophies, then?"

Tyndarus finally released her breast and pulled his hand from her toga. "Paramenides is underestimated by contemporary scholars. He said the world never changed, that change is impossible because in order for something to change, it must become something else. In order to do that, it must shed its earlier form into nothingness—"

"—and nothingness in unthinkable and unreal," Hypatia finished the quote from the ancient philosopher. "Therefore the world must be static and non-changing."

Tyndarus became aware that the round pink head of his softening erection was visible through his toga's folds. He released Hypatia's garment and tucked his organ inside.

Run! she thought. He's released you! Run! But then she recalled an observation made by a student of Aristotle. Once while studying the behavior of jungle beasts, the student had witnessed a lion stumble across a sleeping gazelle in the tall grass of the Savannah. Perhaps testing to see if the animal was dead, the lion had pawed the creature. The gazelle awoke and jumped to its feet…but was so transfixed by fear that it stood, frozen. The lion, only inches away, made no attack. Perhaps accustomed to the chase, it couldn't think how to manage a prey animal being so unresponsive. Both animals remained paralyzed by uncertainty. Then the gazelle tried to run. The lion attacked. The kill was made. Hypatia considered her own situation a mirror of that one; any outright flight would trigger his impulses to attack her again.

Therefore Hypatia planted her feet, fixed her toga, and said, "Paramenides was a bright man."

"He was brilliant," Tyndarus snapped.

"He was wrong."

If there had been any remaining lustful intentions in Tyndarus, they were snuffed out by her stinging comment. His mouth opened as if trying to force words which wouldn't form. "And you are an adept critic of his work, to be sure! What passage did you memorize, so you could parade yourself as a philosopher?"

"The passages from his fifty-three treatises."

That silenced him for a moment. He looked at her as if trying to ascertain her honesty. "Paramenides is one of the most brilliant philosophers in history. It is a bold statement to make for one so young, to criticize someone who will forever be greater than you or I."

"He was a great man," Hypatia agreed. "But great men still make errors. I challenge that Paramenides' philosophy of an unchanging universe is completely wrong."

The sense of authority in her voice affected him. He glanced to the open scroll on the couch as if for support.

"You are aware that I am the University's honorary professor of philosophy, not just the Schoolmaster?"

"I was not aware of that," Hypatia admitted.

"Of course not, Hypatia. So you see that to challenge me on this subject is, while not as intimidating as challenging Paramenides, nonetheless a daunting task?"

"Perhaps," Hypatia said, and seeing her opportunity she headed for the door.

"Wait," he called after her. "In one month the University will host its Dialogues. I will be one of the lecturers, and it is within my power to choose any subject I like. I fancy that I will choose Paramenides."

Hypatia hesitated in the doorway. "I fancy that I may attend, Schoolmaster," she said, and left.

The memory was twenty-seven years old yet it still throbbed like a living creature in her skull. Hypatia remembered every detail of the Schoolmaster in his dimly-lit room. She could still smell the alcohol on his breath, though little more than a flicker of gloom passed across her face.

"I have been to Athens, Thasos."

Thasos sensed a mountain of tension behind her sparse words. Tactfully, he steered the subject back to its earlier course. "Your father's prediction is soon. May I inquire where you intend to watch the skies on that night?"

Hypatia looked at her yard with a sweeping glance, where the sundial stood like a memorial stone to Theon. "I should expect to watch the heavens from the comfort of my own yard."

"Would that comfort be spoiled if I happened to be walking by?"

I was waiting for that, Hypatia thought. Perhaps with a little research, *I* could predict the precise moments when he will launch yet another attempt at bedding me.

"If your eyes remain on the sky," she said slowly, "my comfort will be intact."

Thasos was glowing. "Ten days is an eternity." He turned away and made for the perimeter of her yard when suddenly he looked back, flashed a grin, and added, "You haven't gotten around to asking me what astronomy works I've been reading."

Hypatia nodded. "I haven't yet."

"I challenge you to ask me tomorrow!" He bowed with flourish. In that instant the sun caught him just the right way, and Hypatia saw Admetus in him. The resemblance was strong, and even Thasos' tone sounded like his father...a willful, playful boom to his voice. Then Thasos straightened, bid her good day, and vanished through her shrubbery again.

Hypatia continued to stare at where he had been. A minute passed before she realized she was smiling.

This one's inventive, she thought. But he's also coming along more than he realizes. I think his father will soon be very proud.

CHAPTER 9

▼

It was evening when Heliodorus, returning home from work, glanced up and saw a crested lapwing soar across the crimson sky. The bird was a foreigner to Egypt. It migrated from Europe every winter to make nest on the Egyptian flood-plain. Heliodorus stopped mid-stride to watch it circle once, the small hooked beak and upturned head-crest unmistakable. It glided carelessly, as if surveying the city it had not seen in a year. Then it passed out of sight over a ridge of limestone homes, seeking the green swamps on the eastern edge of Alexandria.

It's a good sign, Heliodorus thought. When Rome had been captured five years ago by the Visigoths, many Alexandrians came to see the arrival of the lapwing as an ill omen suggesting Europe's barbarians would also migrate to the warm south of the world. This view, however, was not shared by native Egyptians. The lapwing, like the grey heron that also turned up in the flood season, was a symbol of joy and hope.

I could use both right now, Heliodorus thought anxiously.

He had prosecuted Hierax that morning before the city council. The man was ruled guilty of rape and given twenty lashes. Heliodorus didn't know which was worse: the plaintive mewling of the convicted man as his back was carved up by the whip, or the outrage of his supporters. In particular, Heliodorus had noticed a boy no older than sixteen watching Hierax's punishment with unconcealed, almost mindless, rage.

The lawyer breathed a sigh of comfort when he reached his quiet neighborhood, in the Egyptian District of the city. He was intensely proud of his heritage, and the sight of rows of mud-brick homes in the red-orange light of sunset smoothed out his wrinkles of tension. He stared at yards which sported obsidian statues of cats and falcons, and the sandstone walls that displayed bas reliefs of pharaohs, chariots, women carrying reed baskets, and crocodiles basking alongside the Nile.

The road opened up into a wide intersection. At the center of the four-way was a large bubbling fountain carved from ebony. A troop of children played at its basin. Five in all, three boys and two girls, each with brown skin and dressed in pale-colored tunics. The fountain was a favored place for them to play with their toys.

Heliodorus shouted to them, "Who is winning the war?"

The children jumped up, grabbed their toys, and ran to meet him.

"Helios! Helios!" they sang in unison. In a flash, he was surrounded.

"It's getting late," he said. "You should be home with your families!"

"Look!" one of the boys said, handing him a palm-sized chariot carved from cedar wood. In the cart stood a miniature charioteer wielding a tiny spear. The paint was fresh, the artistry of the piece impressive.

Heliodorus held it aloft, making a show of appraising it. "Very nice. This is new, isn't it?"

"He's a Hittite," the boy said. "My father bought him at the market today."

Heliodorus knew the ritual by now. He was to inspect each of their new toys and ask about them. He never tired of it. He enjoyed their laughter, as well as the curious repertoire that he, an Egyptian lawyer of the royal court, had with children no older than seven.

And they loved him for the attention. Several times a week, his solitary walks would be assaulted by these little smiling children. Inexplicably, he was friends to them all.

"Did you bring anything for me?" one of the Egyptian girls asked shyly, half-hiding behind her brother.

Pastries is what she meant, as pastries had much to do with the children liking him. Every so often, Heliodorus made a detour on his homeward trek to buy a basket of Greek sweet-breads or rare honey-candies.

"No candy today. Your parents would not be endeared to me if I fed you sweetened dates at this late hour."

"We won't tell!"

"You won't have to. They'll know when they see you running around like madmen, unable to sleep!"

They laughed, repeating his words in a teasing chorus.

"Run along now," Heliodorus told them. He felt a familiar sadness welling up inside him. "The sun has almost set, and you can't be on the streets after it does."

"Why?"

Stories, he thought. They wanted him to tell them stories…creepy stories of river spirits or tomb guardians. Perhaps more than his gifts of candy, the children adored him for the tales he would share with them. Sometimes classics from Homer, sometimes originals he would conceive on the spot. Above all, they wanted scary stories to shriek at in delight.

"Because," he told them, "I am very tired. And…storm demons come out at night."

The little girl who had asked for the pastries—her name was Astarte—hid again behind her brother, and her voice was a peep: "What do storm demons look like?"

Before Heliodorus could reply, he saw a shaft of warm light spill from the house on the intersection's corner. Its door had opened, and the slim figure of his wife Nephthys stood in the doorway. He saw her fold her arms across her chest and laugh at the sight of him ringed by children.

Heliodorus waved to her, then turned back to the children. "Storm demons look very scary. In fact…" He turned his back on them, made his face into a twisted grin, lips curled back from his teeth, eyes wide, hands gnarled, and then spun around. The children screamed and giggled and ran away. Heliodorus called after them. "Now go home! Don't be out after dark!"

"Good night Helios!" they said, sprinting away. In a moment they had vanished. It was as if they had never been there at all.

Anguish set in the moment they were gone. Heliodorus pushed back the rise of bile in his throat. He took a deep breath. He exhaled, tried to exorcize his sadness for Nephthys' sake. However, he knew his efforts would likely prove futile; she had the uncanny ability to see right into his heart, no matter how hard he tried to deceive her.

Approaching her, he was moved as always by her beauty. Outlined in light, she looked like an upright feline statuette, thin but well-shaped. She buried her face in his chest as he reached her. He embraced her tightly.

"I always know when you're near," she whispered.

"My welcoming committee does give me away," he admitted.

"No," Nephthys said, pulling back to stare deeply into his eyes. She had almond-shaped, liquid brown eyes. Under their gaze Heliodorus felt himself laid bare. "I just know when you're near. I always know."

Heliodorus said nothing. He was afraid that if he spoke further she would hear the sorrow that throbbed in his chest.

They had lost their only child two years ago, but time was subjective in that tragedy. A week could pass and all would be well. Then like a sandstorm the sorrow would hit, crippling, and it would seem as if beloved Khonsu had perished only one night ago. Two years ago the boy had gone to sleep but never awoke. Physicians called it the sleeping-death. There was no way to predict it. It could strike a young child at any time. Usually it reserved its lethal bite for infants. But Khonsu had been three years old. He should have been spared.

Heliodorus and Nephthys had been devastated. With terrible clarity Heliodorus could recall every detail of the boy's last evening. *"Daddy!" The boy's ear-to-ear smile and delighted kiss. Dinner with wife and son by candlelight. Laughter at the table. Khonsu giving his father a kiss and hug before bed-time. That little embrace...*

The memory of *that* hurt worse than anything. There were times when Heliodorus could still feel the ghostly impression of his boy's hugging arms. For a long time when that happened, he would excuse himself from wherever he was, find a private chamber, and weep uncontrollably.

Since then Heliodorus had discovered a catharsis in talking with the neighborhood children. When he brought them gifts and told them stories meant for Khonsu's ears, there was a pang of comfort. Usually. Other times it only reopened the wound. He could never tell how it would affect him. There was no way to win; there were only ways to cope.

"Were you scaring the children again?" Nephthys asked teasingly, leading him into the house.

"Only dressing up a moral about staying indoors at night."

"Terrifying them with demons will do the trick."

He laughed and closed the door behind him. A clear lamp-bowl, its twisted wick like a white serpent curled inside, burned steadily on the kitchen counter.

"How was work?" she asked. She extinguished the lamp with a brass snuffer. He slipped his arms around her waist. Nephthys rotated in his embrace so that she was facing him, feeling the warmth of their bodies through their garments.

"You are preoccupied," she whispered.

"Affairs of state have a tendency to preoccupy." He thought again of the wrathful crowd at Hierax's punishment. Their flashing eyes, hate-twisted grimaces. That young boy, full of monstrous venom...

Mankind was not separated by skin color or religion, Heliodorus thought, clutching his wife. At least not in Alexandria, where there was such a mix of mankind. Celtic visitors the color of milk or Nubian merchants as dark as sable. No. The real division was not of culture or color, but of natures. He recalled the city council on which an array of different men sat, united in their concern for the city. Their natures were of peacekeepers and progressives.

Men like Hierax, however, possessed a different nature altogether. They were predators. They thirsted to dominate, control, subjugate. *That* was real division. Heliodorus raged at this thought. There is so much evil in the world without mankind adding to it! There were lions in the brush and sharks in the seas. There were sandstorms of the desert and a blistering sun in the sky. There were invisible ills that could infect children in their cribs...

Heliodorus felt the tears rise. He shut his eyes to prevent them from escaping. Nephthys caressed his face.

"Let's go to bed," she said in a whisper as velvety as the brush of a silken scarf. Without a word, he followed her. His inner debate became a vault of silence as they disrobed and slipped beneath the cool bed-sheets.

Heliodorus made love to his wife in a slow, dream-like rhythm. It was always wondrous with her. In the pitch black of the bedroom they became like spirits, and the sexual act seemed elevated to a coupling of the soul. As her hot whisper breathed in his ear, he imagined that tonight the old gods were with them again. What else could the sight of the lapwing mean?

Tonight they would make another child.

The sun god Ra plunged into the underworld and night took the city hostage. Beneath the lampposts of the main roads, shadows moved like black obelisks cris-crossing the avenues.

An owl shrieked a single, bloodcurdling note.

The shadows uncoiled like a black serpent, shuffling through back-alleys that led to the Hebrew District. They twisted, gyrated, crouched beneath glowing windows and avoided the main roads. At the unguarded perimeter of the district they poured into the open courtyard where the Jewish synagogue waited. The moon was a white scythe in the sky, revealing the invading shadows for what they were: A hundred dark-robed people, with Peter the Reader at the head of their column.

The men had hitherto been silent, but at the sight of the synagogue they murmured. Peter silenced them with a hiss. He sprinted to the nearest main avenue and, with graceful agility, climbed the ridged spine of one of the lampposts. Into its flame he thrust a torch dipped in black oil. The glistening head immolated at once.

With the firebrand in hand he rejoined the crowd. They clustered around him, shoving unlit torches to his fire. Once each was lit, Peter raced to the steps of the synagogue. He leapt onto its stone stairs, turned to face the undulating crowd.

"All other faith are false!" he yelled. "Do you believe that in your heart?"

"All other faiths are false!" cried the men.

"In the year of our Lord shall we tolerate the blasphemers?"

Shouting together, they replied: "No!"

Peter felt wild, his heart galloping like a racing steed. "Do we honor Hierax? Tortured by a man who thinks himself God!"

"Yes!"

"Do we remember the holy destruction of the pagan temple at Serapis?"

"Yes!"

Peter delivered Cyril's command with an intensity that seized him like an orgasm. "Then strike down with holy wrath those who oppose us!"

The crowd fell upon the synagogue and the force of so many bodies caved in the ornate wooden doors. They lit the tapestries, the wooden benches, and lastly the curtains that hung across the entrance.

Next, the men descended on the nearest homes, smashing the latticework windows and breaking down doors. The silent courtyard became a chorus of madness. Men and women were dragged from their homes, half-clothed and unready for the assault. The crowd swarmed over them. Torches were pitched into the interior of residences.

"Do not burn the homes!" Peter cried, remembering Cyril's words to him after the Mass at sundown. *If we start a fire, it'll spread to the rest of the city! Keep them in control, Peter! Direct their strength into driving off the Jews.* "Do not burn the homes!"

Trampled residents were forcibly hauled to their feet and pushed ahead of the surging mass. In moments the alleys were crammed with bloodied Hebrews, struggling to find each other amid the chaos. Women and children wailed.

"*Do not burn the homes!*" Peter screamed.

More doors were kicked in, families pulled from their beds, herded, wrenched, pushed into the shadows where they joined the rest of the screaming fray.

Peter stood with the blazing synagogue behind him, his shadow dancing before him in the freakish light. He stared, unbelieving, at the ease of the battle.

No. Not a battle. This was a rout.

In batches, the Jews were being fished from their homes, and those that emerged of their own accord only expedited the process. Grouped together. Driven like oxen. Pushed. Out of the district, sobbing, screaming in the night...

Seven hundred years! Peter thought numbly. The heathen Jews had been here for seven *hundred* years! But now…is this how history ends? Dazed, Peter looked to the synagogue. It was billowing fire. For a moment, he feared that the airborne cinders of the blaze might catch elsewhere, but the night was windless and the embers that did fall landed in the empty courtyard.

The attacking mob pursued the fleeing families. Peter saw this and shouted for them to regroup and retreat. Cyril didn't want anyone captured. Drive them off, he had told Peter. Ruin their homes, but leave before the city guards come!

At one street corner, a group of Jews had barricaded themselves behind some push-carts and were holding off the invasion. Peter saw this. He called to the crowd and directed their efforts there. It was as if he had held out his hands and conjured a midnight sea, the way Cyril's parishioners fell upon the barricade with united strength. The resistance was broken, the defenders pummeled to the cobblestone.

"Don't kill them!" Peter screamed, fearful that this rout would turn into slaughter. Cyril would go berserk if that happened. The royal court would not side with a murdering mob.

We're attacking in self-defense, Cyril had told them. For months now our people have been assaulted, our churches vandalized. The torture of Hierax tips the scales. Tonight we deliver a blow of revenge, but we mustn't become the vermin we oppose. Kill no one. Burn not a single house. Fall upon them, show them our united strength!

Won't the governor respond? Peter had asked. Won't he go mad and condemn us all?

Cyril had responded at once: Leave that part to me.

CHAPTER 10

▼

Two hours before sunrise the furnaces at Thasos' glass shop were lit, fed, and stoked. News had not yet reached them of the horror in the Hebrew District. By morning the entire city would hear of it, and in two week's time every province of the Empire would be condemning or praising the incident. In the purple pre-dawn, however, Thasos and his fellow workers had only their assignments to con-sider as they filed into the shop. With six, maybe seven hours before the heat of the day made the shop's temperature unbearable, every moment counted.

Thasos had been a glass-worker for three years, the third job of his young life. Two years after his father's death, he had been apprenticed to a carpenter for a year. Then he went to work with his mother at the linen shop. That had lasted two years until Thasos decided that although he loved women he didn't love working with them, and so he sought employment elsewhere.

He enjoyed his latest profession. Four days a week he toiled in the hot-house of the shop, plucking the molten glass from red furnaces, clasping the liquid gather to the end of his blowpipe, and breathing shape into the protean substance with skill and speed. Yet this morning, Thasos found his work lagging. He kept drifting off, struggling with thoughts as amorphous as the material with which he worked.

Hypatia dominated his mind. With unending obsession he found himself replaying every conversation he had enjoyed with her. He imagined a good deal of fictional ones. He remembered the tickle of her whisper in his ear. Suddenly he felt himself swelling with fierce desire. The hellish heat of the furnaces could not faze his fantasy.

Nor could it faze his pride. As he removed globs of glass from the furnace's maw and rotated his blowpipe to prevent it from dripping off the swivel, he caught himself grinning. *She was so surprised when I told her of the falling stars! She probably thought about me the rest of the day! And when she asks me what I've been studying I'll be ready to impress her.*

Knowledge was the way to her heart. Thasos was certain. After talking with Arion on the ferry after the terrifying encounter with Kapta, he realized that Hypatia was no different from any other woman he'd known. More beautiful, yes. More intelligent, absolutely! But she was *not* intangible. A knowledgeable mind was what she had, and so a knowledgeable mind was what would attract her. After visiting her at her home he had gone straight to the Library to study several hours' worth of astronomy texts.

Preparing. For class today.

He snapped out of his daydream when he realized that he had forgotten about the incandescent bulk of glass fastened to the end of his pipe. It dropped like the sappy residue of a magical plant, and hit the shop's floor with a *splat!*

His mishap caught the attention of others in the shop. Thasos cleaned up the mess with a trowel and cast it back into the furnace, waiting until it was ready again.

Could Hypatia love me?

The questioned haunted him. It was followed by another: Is that what I'm after? Her body, *and* her heart?

He had loved many girls. And though young, he was not inexperienced in matters of the bed. He had pleasured five women in his life. It had astonished him, actually, the ease in which they came to him. At a very young age he started noticing their attentions. He seemed to collect their smiles. He learned quickly how to make them giggle, blush, flirt. As he came of age, he discovered an obsession for them. The way they moved, talked, smelled...oh! the sweet smell of a woman! The feel of their legs entwined around him! Thasos had never written a single verse of poetry, but could think of no inspiration grander than a female's touch. Wasn't that why all Greek Muses were depicted as women?

No woman was immune to love. Not even Hypatia. And yes, he thought, I want her body *and* her heart. She distracts me like nothing else in life. She is—

"Do you need a break?" a sharp voice asked behind him.

"No," Thasos said, and hastily re-clasped the gather to his blowpipe, rotating it as he plucked it from the fire. He recognized the owner of the voice, a Greek named Zeno who had been at the shop for as long as Thasos had.

"You look like you do," Zeno persisted, antagonizing.

"I don't," Thasos repeated, and blew gently into the blowpipe causing the gather to balloon slightly as he worked it. "What's wrong, Zeno? I won't believe you've finished your quota!" Each day at the shop, the workers had a daily quota of products to make. The shop was noted for its wide assortment of products, from perfume bottles sold up-river to Thebes, to vases and mirrors sold to Rome and Greece, to colored beads and bowls sold within the limits of Alexandria. There were also four major shipments overseas each year, a source of tremendous income—and thus of anxiety—to the shop-owners. Thasos had been assigned to produce a series of vases.

Zeno frowned darkly, watching him work. "We won't ship lop-sided vases, Thasos."

"Actually, it isn't a vase," Thasos answered, bringing the blowpipe over to the marvering table to roll and shape the bottom of the vessel.

"What is it, then?"

"A mask of your wife's face, Zeno," Thasos said. The other workers in the shop laughed heartily, looking up from their work-benches and furnaces to watch this latest confrontation.

Zeno, short and with a mass of black curly hair tied back into a pony-tail, frowned as he debated a come-back. Thasos got along with everyone at the shop except for Zeno, who was ill-tempered and insulting. Thus, the two became partners in consistent bickering which had quickly evolved into a roasting contest to the amusement of the rest of the shop.

"I think Thasos has fallen in love again!" Zeno challenged. "He's been smiling like a simpleton all morning! A man only grins like that when his mind is stuck in some woman's portals!"

Thasos said nothing, offended that Zeno had read so easily into his heart. Thasos didn't discuss his affairs with his coworkers, but his girlfriends had frequently visited him at the shop.

"Who is it this time?" Zeno continued, and without waiting for an answer, said, "I hope that I outlive you, Thasos, for I have a divine idea of what to put on your tomb. A statue of Min. What could be more accurate than that?"

Renewed laughter filled the shop. Min was the Egyptian god of fertility, invariably depicted with a fully-erect phallus protruding from his body.

"Come now," Zeno persisted, growing in confidence. "Share her with your good friend Zeno!"

"To give you fantasies your marriage hasn't sustained?"

"Oh!" the men in the shop began hooting and clapping. Zeno bristled, striving for a verbal counter-punch.

"You really wish to know who I am thinking of, Zeno?" He leaned close to the man. In a quiet whisper he said, "I was thinking about Seneca."

Zeno's grin froze. His eyes blinked in befuddlement. Similarly, the laughter silenced, waiting for a punch-line. When Thasos provided none the awkward quiet began to fill with the sounds of familiar toiling. Thasos focused on his glass-working again.

"Seneca?" Zeno asked finally. "Who the hell is that?"

"Someone who lived four hundred years ago," Thasos responded. "He wrote about astronomy, Zeno, something you wouldn't know about."

Before Zeno could counter-attack, one of the shop-owners entered the room. Zeno finally returned to his own work as the owner spent a few moments rallying them to work harder so that the shop's reputation wouldn't be spoiled "from here to the Indus," the man said. Thasos barely heard him. He stared at the glass at the end of his blowpipe, and imagined that it was a falling star he had caught to offer the Philosopher.

I want her, he thought desperately. *And I'll have her soon enough.*

The news reached Orestes at first light, and he flew into a rage like his servants had never seen before. Neith was terrified, and ordered all the servants to stay away from him until he had calmed down. She alone followed at his heels while he paced around the palace like a demon, cursing.

At last, Orestes ordered her to dispatch a messenger. "Bring Heliodorus here!" he said. "I don't care what he's doing. I want him here in *one hour!*" Then he retreated to his study where he drew up a letter to Regent Pulcheria, describing what had taken place. He was so angry that his Latin scribbling flowed effortlessly. He finished it inside of ten minutes.

Neith returned while he was waiting for the ink to dry. "Heliodorus is here, Governor."

Orestes looked at her. "How? Did the messenger *fly?*"

"He was already on his way to see you."

"Send him to the patio. And mail this…" He jabbed a finger at the letter. "The very instant it dries!"

Marina was awake and on the patio, sitting at the little reed table she often used for breakfast. When she heard Orestes coming she glanced up from her meal of robin's eggs and fish. She saw his fury.

"Good morning, Orestes," she said carefully.

Heliodorus sat across from her. He too stiffened when he observed Orestes' thinly-constrained anger. "I needn't ask the source of your anger."

Orestes nostrils flared. "You needn't."

The news was all over the city. As morning caravans departed like bees on a quest to pollinate, they would carry word of the attack until all the Empire knew of the civil strife within the proud city of Alexandria.

Heliodorus had seen the destruction for himself. Hearing the babble in the streets, he had passed the Hebrew District and stared in horrific amazement at the toppled synagogue, charred and still smoking from the previous night's fire. Homes, too, showed signs of burning and destruction, their doors caved in, their windows conspicuously dark.

Now he related all this while the governor listened.

"Many of the Jews were routed during the night," Heliodorus said. "A great many have fled the city limits entirely."

"Where did they go?"

"There are seven hundred years of Jewish families in Egypt. They're probably settling in with relatives up-river. But I think this is just the start. With their synagogue destroyed, many Jewish families will flee Alexandria altogether."

"Does their faith rest on a *building?*" Orestes snapped. Control yourself! he thought. Don't lose the strength you've been building all these years! He lowered his voice, though his jaw muscles still clenched as he said, "I can have a hundred masons and carpenters at the ruined site in two hours."

Heliodorus held the governor's stare. "Why rebuild if the foundation is so shaky? The Jews won't trust to stay in a city—" He was going to say "dominated by Cyril's thugs" but he caught the words before they came out. Recovering swiftly, he said, "—with so much strife."

Orestes frowned darkly. He had sensed the lawyer's unspoken words. "Why haven't the Jewish leaders come to see me?"

Heliodorus had no answer.

"Maybe their god sent them into exile again," Marina offered after a sip of her wine. "It isn't our concern."

The remark had a visible effect on Orestes' incendiary mood. His cheeks flushed and he turned on her with vehemence. Heliodorus stood at once to intercept the impending argument: "Governor, perhaps we should talk in private?"

Heliodorus excused himself from the table and waited by the pool-side, where they could steal some privacy by the flowering shrubbery.

"This whole affair is Cyril's statement against my punishment of Hierax," Orestes said.

Heliodorus nodded. "Partly. And partly it is the solidification of his plan to rid the city of many Jews."

Orestes fixed Heliodorus with a stare. "It was also a political, not solely a religious strike. Ninety percent of grain trading with Constantinople had been under Hebrew control. If Cyril's Christians control that…"

Heliodorus nodded in understanding. "The grain has to be traded. In the end no one will care who does the trading. Hebrews who don't show up for work will be replaced by Cyril's parishioners. I've made inquiries; he seems to have placed people well in the industry. They could make a grab at power if the Jews pull out. And then a percentage of their money will go to his church."

"Freeze those positions. No one will be hired until an investigation is completed."

"And let Alexandria suffer an economic drought?"

Orestes ground his teeth, realizing the foolishness of his own statement. "Cyril led the mob?"

"I don't know if he was with them in body."

"Arrest him."

Heliodorus stiffened. "Governor, if you have Cyril arrested without due investigation his supporters will raise a rallying cry and have you removed. Regent Pulcheria will back the Church before secular authority. Since Constantine, there has never been an exception."

Orestes folded his arms across his chest. "Since the days of Hammurabi in Babylon there have been laws forbidding wanton rioting. There is no legal way Cyril can protect himself. The Jews will be brought back—"

"The Jews won't want to come back," Heliodorus said finally. "At least, not with the situation the way it is. What will they come back to? More persecutions? More riots? Christian Rome will not support a Jewish cause."

"This is the blackest stain on the city since the days of Caracalla," Orestes declared, thinking briefly of the Emperor who, incensed over an Alexandrian play which had mocked his arrogance, had ordered the butcher of thousands of Alexandrians youths in retribution two centuries earlier.

Heliodorus is right, he thought. *There are no witnesses to the attack who can verify who was there or not. Everyone knows it was Cyril's parishioners, but he's the Archbishop of the city! Arresting Cyril will impel Pulcheria to send military reinforcements and declare Alexandria under martial law. To preserve the "peace," I'll find himself reassigned to another prefecture.*

But there are still things I can do…

Heliodorus noticed Orestes' sudden introspectiveness. "May I ask what you're thinking of doing?"

"I am calling an emergency council meeting for sundown. Only city officials. The magistrate. The city guard. Yourself. But no one else. You will spread the word and have everyone meet here."

While he spoke, he pictured the Jewish synagogues burned and bleeding black smoke. He pictured men and women running from the flames and from the assault of Cyril's followers. Somewhere, the ghosts of Caracalla's victims were watching. Somewhere, they were seeing history repeat itself.

The Jews, crying for help. Hauled out into cold and fire, assault and wickedness. Who could have seen it coming? In *one* night? The images whirled like fireflies through his head.

He pushed out the gruesome images. He looked to the Heliodorus and said quietly, "Do you understand?"

Heliodorus nodded, withholding a sigh. "I do, Orestes. I do."

CHAPTER 11

▼

An hour later Orestes returned to his bedroom to change into an appropriate attire for the evening's meeting. Twice, he found his hands clenching into white-knuckled fists as if of their own accord. His body shivered in helpless impotence. It was a feeling he had not known in a long time.

Orestes had been the second child of his parent's marriage. His older sister had died when he was two. He did not remember her, except for a vague recollection of her peering down at him in his crib...a faceless, voiceless memory. His father Hesperos had been a record-keeper. For such a man—large, strong, and quick to temper—the vocation was ill-suited. Hesperos had once served in the Roman army but had torn his knee during a climb. The injury had terminated his military aspirations, turning the legionnaire into a grudging dabbler of ink and parchment.

How different might things have been if the knee had not been injured? Orestes had often wondered. Was it the injury that gave Hesperos his violent temper or streak of cruelty? Or had he always been like that? Each night when Hesperos would return home from work he would find reason to fly into an incredible rage. Orestes' mother was his favorite target. By the time Orestes was twelve, Hesperos had shattered her nose so often that it was as fragile as glass and shapeless as a lump of clay. When Orestes tried defending her, he too would earn abuses that kept him hobbling for days.

Helpless. That was the feeling Orestes had been most accustomed to as a child. It was a welcome relief when Orestes was of age to go away to school in Athens.

And there he had quickly discovered how life in Olympia had ill-prepared him for the challenge of academia. Athens was a proud city, the birthplace of Socrates and the wellspring from which Greek culture flowed. Orestes was a boy of no money and little education.

He also came to realize that he wasn't that smart.

Perhaps it was because his peers had grown up on works of literature and philosophy that he had never been exposed to. They talked of things he didn't understand. They referenced anecdotes which were gibberish to his ears. Orestes was a stranger in that city, and the loneliness he felt was as acute as his sense of inferiority.

So it was that he had made a decision to defeat this, because he *could* defeat it. His father would always be stronger than him, always fiercer and more savage. But his fellow students were *not* his father. They were young, physically weak, and spoiled by privileged lives. Though their words might intimidate him, he soon found ways to intimidate *them*. He resolved to memorize one book at a time. Every night, he trudged through classic works at the school's library. In time, when one of his peers would taunt him into a debate on some lofty metaphysical subject, Orestes would counter the argument using quotes from whatever he had been reading the night before. At first it was just one book. Then two. But Orestes quickly learned that it wasn't so much *what* he quoted, but *how* he conducted himself when quoting it. Fierce eyes. A strong, confident voice. An imposing posture. A practiced readiness of speech, so that he could never be taken off-guard by some nobleman's aloof son. All this was helped by his blossoming body, which proved a mold of his father's. Strong. Imposing. Muscular.

Soon he had memorized hundreds of volumes—a cornucopia of plays, philosophical treatises, and legal doctrines. What he couldn't accomplish in abstract argument he accomplished through sheer force of confidence. He won many an instructor over simply because he presented himself as a person built to succeed. "You would make a terrific statesmen, Orestes," one instructor told him, and a year later he fulfilled this off-hand prophecy.

With these newfound powers, Orestes had returned home with the lofty intention of making peace with his father. Years had passed, and Orestes had become a man. From Athens, he had walked the long road to Olympia, to his old neighborhood, to his house, and discovered his bloodied mother on the floor of the kitchen.

Hesperos must have beaten her a minute earlier. She was trying to lift herself up, blood spilling from a nose broken for the fortieth time. Orestes still remembered how frail she looked as she gripped the counter. When she saw him in the doorway, she looked miserable and ashamed.

"Orestes," she had whispered with a bruised, toothless smile. "You've come home."

"Don't move mother," he had told her. "Lie still and wait for me to return."

He found Hesperos in the den. The rest was a blur of images. There had been a fight. There had been blood. There had been the sound of his father's bones crunching under Orestes' manic, feral attack. And parading through his head, one thought had glittered like a lightning strobe that wouldn't fade: I could crack his neck so easily! He's *nothing!* He was powerful to a woman and a child! Now he's *nothing!* End him, Orestes!

Instead, Orestes had thrown Hesperos out of the house into a street gutter. He then had used his friends in Athens to get a divorce for his mother. She didn't live much longer...four years was all. But they were years of overwhelming joy for her. Orestes had helped her relocate to Athens. In her new home she toiled happily at sewing and cooking. Always thankful for the new life he had given her. Four years into her rebirth she died in her sleep. Orestes found her the next morning. It was the last time in his life he had cried.

Hesperos had outlived her. On a state visit to Olympia, Orestes had walked into a tavern and seen the grey, withered, limping figure of the man that had been his father. He had walked out before Hesperos could see him.

As a statesman for Greece Orestes quickly became known as a strong-willed orator. When news of Governor Pentadius' impending retirement reached Athens, Orestes memorized volumes on Alexandrian society. He wrote letters to all dignitaries in Alexandria, introducing himself to the leaders of the Jewish, Persian, Arabic, Greco-Roman, and Egyptian populations. He visited them, was guest at their dinners and rallies. His eagerness puzzled even himself. Why be so obsessively determined to win over Egypt? Did he not have a respectable, well-paying job in the capital of Greece? Did he truly wish to have the headaches and stresses of governing one of the greatest provinces in the Roman Empire?

Such questions failed to mire his intentions. His campaigning was typical of all else in his life: direct, strict, severe. In the end, the support he accumulated convinced the royal court to appoint him over all competition.

Four months earlier he had met Marina. Like a living embodiment of how much his life had changed, Marina was high-born, attractive, and interested in him. Women had been strangers to him in his youth; there had simply been no time for dalliance. As statesman, he had bedded three women. None had turned into relationships because none intrigued him beyond a night of pleasure. Marina was different. She happily invited him to share his ambitions. She was supportive. As he scurried from appointment to appointment all across the Empire, she came to haunt his thoughts. She became a destination he anticipated returning to.

If I'm to be Governor of Egypt, he had thought during one voyage, could I ask for a wife more intoxicating? What was she, but perfect?

Four months later Orestes had found himself standing on the deck of a royal trireme pulling into the Alexandrian harbor as prefect. And that's when everything had changed.

The thumping of footsteps on the staircase jarred his meditations. Orestes came to his senses, realizing that he had been standing at the closet motionless for several minutes, fingers touching the sleeve of his folded blue tunic.

Behind him, Marina entered the bedroom.

She still looks lovely, he thought. An orange tunica with one strap, the exposed shoulder smooth and enticing. A necklace of pearls clasped at her throat with an Egyptian medallion showing a bird with wings and claws stretched.

"Pretending you're Cleopatra again?" he said.

There was only one window in the bedroom, covered by a blue curtain. The afternoon sun filtered through and washed the room as if in seawater. Marina walked to the window and her hair, worn up and clasped so that a few curls trailed down the back of her neck, shimmered pleasantly in the aquatic glow. There, she rested against the sill so the soft breeze could cool her back. Her pose was suggestive; her elbows on the sill, her thin legs slightly parted. The tunica accentuated her body.

"I fancied you'd be donning armor and a helmet to go charging into battle," she said.

"That *is* what I am doing," he quipped. He stripped off his tunic and dressed into the blue one.

Marina was strangely reserved. After a moment while Orestes dug in a drawer for his tunic clasp, she said, "I am going out this evening. To the Forum."

"I'll be sure to inform everyone at the council tonight."

Marina let the comment glance off her. "When are they arriving?"

"At sundown."

"I'm sure I won't be needed."

"You're not."

Marina said nothing for a long moment. Then her lips curled into a smirk out of habit. "This whole incident has really riled you, hasn't it? The great Orestes, confronted with someone who defies him! What will history say?"

"I'll answer that inquiry by the end of the week." He turned to leave when he realized he had nowhere to go. *Until the meeting, what have I to do? Walk around the pool? Sit and read in the palace study?*

"It really gives you great pleasure, doesn't it?" he asked her. "On one side is Cyril, the other is me, and there you are perched on a branch like a vulture, watching with morbid curiosity."

Marina laughed and threw herself onto the bed, her legs up behind her in a mock display of seductiveness. *She really does look like a young girl*, Orestes thought. *An adolescent, cynical and spoiled, judging me as I stand before her.*

"Should I choose a side?" Marina asked. "I don't really care, Orestes, and I think the whole business is foolish. But then you don't listen to me. There's always something else on your mind."

Orestes fought the urge to leave again. *Why do I want to go? If this is a battle, don't flee it!*

"The whole city is on my mind," Orestes countered. "That's my job, Marina. I rule the city of Alexandria and the whole of Egypt. I am responsible for its citizens."

"That," Marina hissed, feeling angry suddenly, "must be it."

"It is," Orestes insisted, hearing the defensiveness in his own voice.

"Must be." Marina stared hard at him.

"Something on your mind, Marina?" *Something is on her mind, but the Nile will dry up before she tells me. And why do I really care?*

Marina tried to think of a sarcastic retort. She propped herself up on her elbows and rolled her head back to stare up at the ceiling.

Orestes took a hesitant step towards her. He waited for her to look at him again. "We used to walk together, you and I. In your father's villa."

Marina said nothing. She watched him with a seemingly blank gaze.

What are you doing? Orestes asked himself, horrified at the way he was opening himself up to her. When a long silence intervened, he forced a humorless grin and said, "As always, you're an adept at conversation! Enjoy your evening at the Forum." He headed for the stairs.

"The age of the conquerors is over, Orestes."

"What?"

Marina sat up, drew her legs under her. "Cyrus the Persian, Alexander the Great, Julius Caesar...they're all dead and this world has no more place for their kind. You are governor of *one* province in the Empire. You're not a king, or a pharaoh, or a Caesar!"

Orestes nodded slowly. "So very relevant, Marina. Thank you for your perspective. I see it was worth my time to listen to it."

"Whatever you're planning against this archbishop is just the continuation of your fantasy, Orestes," she said. "You think I'm the one who pretends? Yes, I like to think of Cleopatra. Who do you think you are, Orestes? What part are you playing? If you challenge the Archbishop, all you'll accomplish is getting yourself hurt."

"Be careful, Marina. It almost sounds like you really care."

"I don't," she countered. *I don't. At all.*

He held her gaze. "What *do* you care about?"

Marina glared at him, her eyes more blue and brilliant than the glowing curtains. "When have my cares ever mattered to you?"

"I'm asking now." *How could this person be the one I used to seek as a confidant, a comfort, a consoler? Were those the real reasons I married her?*

The question reverberated like distant thunder through his mind.

Why did I marry you, Marina?

"What happened with us?" Orestes said, and then stiffened as he heard himself speak words which he had intended not to share.

Marina visibly stiffened, also, the muscles of her back tensing beneath her tunica. A cruel smile formed. "The thrill wore off, Orestes."

It occurred to him that he should have been hurt, stung by her words. Instead, he had the most peculiar feeling of wrongness.

It was all wrong.

Him in the bedroom with Marina, with her as his wife, was wrong. A mistake.

"You know," Orestes heard himself say, "I wonder if there ever *was* a thrill."

Then he left.

Too swiftly, too quickly. He was nearly running. He scurried down the stairs like a swimmer dashing for air. He stumbled through the shadowy palace chambers, brushing by two servants who were dusting the archways. His chest tightened with burning anxiety pains. Suddenly he was outside. By the pool. The feel of fresh air on his face was a welcome relief.

He looked down to the pool and regarded his reflection.

"It was a mistake," he said to his watery doppelganger. For long moments, he neither moved nor spoke further, as if awaiting a response.

CHAPTER 12

▼

At the end of his shift at the glass shop, Thasos rinsed his sweaty body in the public baths, changed into a fresh tunic, and hurried to the Great Library. He kept reviewing what he'd studied the night before, anxious to impress Hypatia. When he had reached the green hill on which the Library perched, he realized in his eagerness that he was an hour early for class.

Good, he thought. That gives me time to conduct a little search. An hour should be plenty.

He reached the zenith of the stairs and gazed delightedly upon the Library grounds. Several classes were being held outside, the students sitting comfortably in the shade of the peristyle, listening to their professors lecture on this sun-drenched afternoon. Thasos crossed the grassy expanse, glancing at the groups he passed as if they were islands on a green sea. Suddenly as he was nearing the corner of the peristyle, a shape jumped out from behind one of the columns and blocked his path.

Thasos froze, mid-stride. In the bright sun he squinted at the person in front of him.

"I had started to think the entire year would pass before I saw you again," the young, Egyptian female student told him. As when he had first met her, she was clad in a white tunic with a gold brocade. Her almond-shaped eyes chastised him.

Thasos grinned. "I beg your forgiveness."

His words brightened her demeanor. In the luminous afternoon, she was an extraordinarily sleek, supple creature. Her breasts were shadowy plumes, faintly visible through the fabric of her clothing. "A little begging might get you far," she retorted, seeing how his eyes had wandered.

"Might I beg an answer to a question then, dearest Aphrodite?"

"You may."

And so this game emerges once again, he thought. The moves and counter-moves, the tactics of delicious language, the strategy to a familiar fleshy finish.

"I was wondering," he said, "if you had been a student of the Library for long?"

"I have," she replied. "For two years I've studied here."

"You know the Library well?"

"I do."

"I hear rumor of secret chambers. Places a new student might not be aware of."

The girl's smile grew. "Maybe."

Thasos flashed his smile. "Could I trouble you for the location of one such chamber?"

"Of course."

"Hypatia's laboratory," Thasos said. "I've heard rumor of it. A secret place where she does most of her work."

The woman's smile vanished as if in a puff of magician's smoke. Her eyes turned threatening. "Is that what you want? Is that what you were hoping I'd tell you?"

Innocently he said, "I was hoping you would."

She stormed away, dismissing him with a wave of her hand. "Invest your hopes in someone else!" Thasos watched her go with barely a sigh of regret. Then he straightened his tunic, cracked his knuckles, and made for the Library doors again.

"Nine halls," he whispered to himself as he stood in the Main Hall, studying the options for exploration. In Greek mythology there were Nine Muses. They held dominion over specific areas of human inspiration, from love poems to comedy, choral dance to tragedy. In being assigned to the Great Library, their fields were expanded somewhat. Thus, there was a Hall of Astronomy, History, Literature, Philosophy, Mathematics, Natural Science and Medicine, Theology, Invention, and Music. And as with the hall he was already familiar with, each choice branched into deeper corridors like the tunnel-work of ants.

One of them protected a secret chamber. Thasos had first heard mention of it while exploring the Astronomy Hall. Two old scholars had been talking. One of them was complaining that he couldn't find a particular volume in the Library's bins. The other had suggested that perhaps Hypatia was borrowing it for her research, and that it "was likely in her secret little laboratory."

Since then Thasos had cautiously asked other students about the legendary place. Most had heard of it, but couldn't (or wouldn't) tell him where it was. From them, he learned only that it was reserved for the Chief Librarian. Which meant that if ever there was a place where Hypatia stored her secrets, it was there.

One thing he knew. The laboratory wasn't in the Hall of Astronomy. He had combed that twisting labyrinth like a Minotaur, discovering nothing but books and scholars and tables and lamps. He wondered if, since Hypatia was a mathematician, physicist, astronomer, and philosopher, he might do well to confine his quest to those respective halls. But the Great Library was seven centuries old, and thus its secret chamber wouldn't have been built according to Hypatia's tastes. It could be anywhere.

True, he debated, chewing his lip. But the man who actually built the Library was Ptolemy I, Alexander's friend and general. That man became an astronomer and *philosopher*...

Oh hell.

Thasos headed for Hall of Philosophy. He abruptly lost himself in its depths that smelled of scented lanterns and aging parchment. As he wound through its honeycombed corridors, he thought again of how he would impress his teacher when class began.

The astronomy text he had been studying was written by Seneca, a Roman writer and politician who lived in 40 A.D. Seneca had penned a fantastic statement: "To assume that the Earth is the only inhabited world in infinite space is as absurd as to assert that on a vast plain only one stalk of grain will grow." Thasos had been astonished by the announcement, and spent that night pondering the stars above his home. If each star is a sun, as Seneca had said, then there *were* likely planets that passed around those suns. And if planets, then inhabitants. Which suggested more than a universe filled with life. It suggested the future of the Earth's own residents.

"Think about it," Thasos planned on telling Hypatia. "What do we know of our own history on Earth? Civilizations cropped up around rivers. The Nile gave birth to Egypt, the Tigris and Euphrates to Babylon, the Indus to the Indians, the Tiber to the Romans...we don't know much about Far-Distant China, but I'll wager they too were born by a river. So, all these separate civilizations were like worlds, and their rivers were like suns. Over time, they branched out and contacted each other."

He could imagine Hypatia's probable response: "And what is your point, student?"

"My point," he would tell her, "is that if Seneca is right, then humanity will one day branch out and contact these other civilizations. That will answer teleology." He had heard of the subject of her recent lecture. "Think of it as a knitting together of cosmic intelligences! Just as Alexander went forth and wove different cultures together into a united banner, then Seneca seems to be suggesting that this will happen again. That it is our duty. Our purpose. Like Ra's sun-boat crossing the sky in the old religion, perhaps one day we'll create our own sun-boats and visit those other worlds! Isn't that why you always refer to this class as a voyage, dear Teacher? Aren't we explorers in the truest sense of the word?"

Thasos realized he was grinning proudly. He laughed in anxious anticipation as he rounded yet another book-lined corner. Then he stopped. He looked back the way he had come. He looked ahead. He followed the corridor to its end. He stopped again as he saw that his path forked into two different directions. His heart skipped a nervous beat.

I'm lost.

That's ridiculous! he thought. But he felt the books closing in on him and nothing looked familiar. Thasos chose the path that followed the right of the fork. More honeycombs, reading rooms, empty classrooms. The corridor ran ahead of him and vanished into unlit shadow. The scholars he had seen in the Main Hall were nowhere to be found here, and Thasos, finally afraid, broke into a sprint.

The damn building is playing tricks on me! Worse, it's swallowed me!

He followed the dark aisle until he came to an intersection, equally unlit. He felt like a man faced with four roads in an empty city. Up ahead, all was black.

Thasos staved off his rising panic and considered his situation logically. The Great Library has finite dimensions! I went straight through the last intersection, and I'll continue straight until, eventually, this path links with the next Hall. All the Nine Halls seem to be connected, that's why they don't seem to ever end. But they *do* end. Already, he could see lamplight ahead. Like a moth, he dashed to this source of illumination.

The path opened up into a huge room filled a large mechanism. Thasos saw iron wheels and gears and grooved tracks on the floor. What the hell? There were no books in here, just metallic materials and wooden work-benches…

Ah! This must be Invention. He had heard gossip of the machines that brilliant engineers created in the deep chambers of the Library. In fact…

Thasos scampered across the room until he found another corridor of scrolls. Anxiously, he snatched one and read its casing: Heat and Motion, by Lucius Amedio. Yes! he breathed a happy sigh. I've found my way into the Hall of Invention. This isn't a nightmare…it's just a really complex repository of knowledge…or being lost in the skull of a god!

His relief made him realize just how panicked his disorientation had made him. He felt feverish. Is that what happened to my father? he wondered. Is this where and how he caught the fever that killed him? Indeed, his father Admetus had been at the Library all day when he caught some airborne ill. He had come home looking flushed, ravenously hungry.

What had the meal been that night? Thasos strained to recall.

Seasoned bread. Soup. Roasted lamb. Wine. The memory was as vibrant as the steam from those moist dishes. After dinner, Admetus had kissed Thasos goodnight and sent him to bed. Thasos had been sleeping a few hours when he had been awakened by strange sounds. Rapid footsteps. Furniture moving. His mother's edgy voice, muffled through the mud-brick walls. Thasos had peeled back the linens of his bed and walked nervously down the short hallway to his parents' bedroom. The door had been ajar, and in the haunted candlelight he had seen a strange man lurking by his father's bedside: the physician, sent for in the middle of the night.

Father? Thasos remembered crying, seeing Admetus' sweat-drenched face and glazed eyes. *Mother, what's wrong with him?*

Demetria had been unable to disguise her anguish when she replied in five terrible words: *Your father has a fever.*

Will he die?

No! Demetria had exclaimed angrily. *Your father is a strong man! He just has a fever!*

The following night, however, Demetria had brought Thasos in to say goodbye. Admetus had been awake, burning up, breathing rapidly like a man who had run several miles.

You will be such a great young man! Admetus had panted, managing a weak smile. *I can see it in you, Thasos. You will make me very proud. Promise me that you will follow in my footsteps…*Demetria brought more water to his lips. *The Library, Thasos. It justifies us. It is the gem of the earth, more precious than any metal or kingdom or jewel. Give of yourself one year, Thasos. Taste its fruit. Promise me you will, when you are seventeen and old enough to make your own choice of fate.*

I promise. I promise, just please don't die…

Then his mother's piercing scream: *Admetus! Don't leave me! Don't leave me here, I beg you! Admetus, please, please, PLEASE...*

Thasos remembered how his father had died with open eyes, as if straining to see the stars through his bedroom ceiling.

Now, ten years later Thasos shivered and pushed himself to keep moving. He hungered for the free air of the Main Hall. I'm in the Hall of Medicine now, he thought, seeing the names of famous physicians on the bins as he went. Suddenly he heard voices ahead. He saw light and knew the Main Hall wasn't far.

Then he glanced left, to what seemed a dead-end corridor. He stopped so abruptly that he nearly tripped over his feet.

Upon closer inspection, Thasos realized that the "dead-end" was in fact the start of a staircase that went down, into the subterranean bowels of the Library.

"This is it," he said aloud, descending the stairs into a drafty underworld.

The room wasn't as secret as he had imagined. Neither was it so remote. In the back end of the Hall of Medicine the staircase plunged into a single, narrow hall of granite. The clay floor was cold beneath his sandaled feet. There was no light, and Thasos had to feel his way along the stonework until he reached a set of wooden doors, slightly open. When Thasos pushed, a soft lantern-light bled into the hall.

His pulse quickened at the thought that Hypatia might catch him here...indeed, that she might *be* in there. There was only one lantern on the red carpet, and by its dim light he could see a cedar desk stacked with papers and unwound scrolls, and the outline of a water-clock in the nearest corner. For a minute, he stayed like a statue in the doorway, expecting her to emerge from the shadows like a vengeful devil.

The water-clock trickled. The lantern's flame shivered in its glass prison.

Thasos removed his sandals and stepped inside. His bare soles relished the carpet's soft thickness.

I shouldn't be in here, he thought. Nonetheless, he moved to the desk and let his fingertips caress the cushioned chair. Then his hand opened the desk drawer and as he began to sort through a stack of envelopes and letters, he thought: Why am I doing this? I'm being a wretched snake!

Shame flooded his face, but his fingers continued flipping through the papers as if knowing the way. Suddenly his fingers stopped. With all the delicacy of plucking a blade of grass, Thasos lifted a folded sheet of inked parchment and held it to the light:

To my Philosopher, my Daughter, my Friend.

Instantly Thasos thought: Put it back! His heart thundered in rhythm to the nervous gyrations of the flame. The parchment yawned open in his hands. His eyes grew wide as he read what was penned there.

A cold draft touched him. Thasos nearly yelped in surprise. That's it, he thought. Put it back *now*, and get out of here. *Now.* He fixed everything as he had found it, withdrew into the hallway, and slid his feet into his sandals. Then he noticed a glowing light approaching him from the far end of the hall.

Like a cat, Thasos darted back into the room and closed the doors as he had found them. Footsteps padded closer, accompanied by two voices. His mind screamed an order at him: *Blow out the lantern!* Risking no hesitation, he obliged and the laboratory was engulfed in blackness. The doors swung inward while Thasos crouched in the corner across from the water-clock, and prayed.

"—the entire quarter was emptied," the first voice was saying. It was Hypatia's. She was suddenly standing in the doorway, illuminated from behind by someone's lantern.

She stepped in followed by a man Thasos had never seen before. The man was short, bald, and round, with a short grey beard on his chin. He was dressed in a purple toga, and by the light of the lantern he carried, his round face looked sunken and haunted.

"Surely the Governor can do something!?" the man shouted. Thasos removed his sandals again, his heart stammering with terror, and crept to the doorway as they passed. He heard Hypatia go to her darkened lantern. At the man's next words, Thasos slipped out.

Immediately, he cursed himself for being a fool and a spy. Idiot! What did you expect to find? Why risk everything like that? And was it even worth it, to see what Theon had written to her?

In the laboratory, Hypatia's voice carried: "I haven't spoken to Orestes about this yet. I'm sure he'll do something…and that's what has me concerned. He is not a subtle man."

"And what of us? We are teachers, we have influence! Surely there's something we can do! We all have a stake in what's happened!"

"Such as?"

The man's voice was strained and plaintive. "We are seekers of knowledge and through knowledge, truth. Shouldn't we be giving our students perspective on this tragedy? Before they hear it in the streets, why not prepare them? Use it to illustrate the evil that men do in God's name! Unmask this grudge-match between a Hebrew and Christian deity! Hypatia, if we don't…who will? As things stand now, the Archbishop is the only one speaking on matters of religion! We should state our piece to counter-balance his!"

For a long moment Hypatia was silent. Thasos held still, afraid that in the silence he might sneeze or pop a joint and be heard. Then he heard her voice: "Let Cyril hang himself with his own hypocrisies, Amedio. Now, what book did you want? Be quick; I have class in a few minutes."

Thasos began to breathe again. Still barefoot, he returned to the Main Hall, certain that Fortune had no more favors to bless him with.

CHAPTER 13

▼

When Synesius reached his home in Pentapolis later that night, he found a sealed letter tucked partway under his door. The Empire's postal service was reliable; horsemen would be sent along established routes where, at each rest-stop, a fresh rider and mount waited to take over. It was a service reserved for governmental dispatches or high-paying patrons, people who didn't trust their letters to the slow-moving Nile ferries that bore plebeian mail.

Synesius stooped and lifted the letter. On its papyrus Hypatia's neat handwriting was scrawled: *To Synesius, From the Philosopher.* The waxen seal was emblazoned with the colonnaded legend of the Great Library.

Pentapolis lay seventy miles south of Alexandria. It was a small community, green and wet in the autumn, built as a military outpost a century ago. Since then a community had grown up around it. The farming was good, and the surrounding Red Lands—that patch of desert known for its ruddy color—was the constant site for military training drills under General Simplicius.

The ferry trip had taken two days and he was tired and wanted a warm bath to ease the deep ache in his joints. The sight of the letter, however, quickened his heart. He eagerly broke the seal and, by silver moonlight, read:

Dearest Synesius,

You snuck out of Alexandria like a fox, so I thought I'd inform you that you can be found wherever you hide! Sincerely, I hope this message gladdens you. Your presence is already missed. Why do you stay there, old friend?

Presumably something very important called you back so soon. I had expected your company for weeks, not hours. Heliodorus had expected you to stay for good. When will you?

While you consider your answer, I have something to ask of you. Turn your gaze upwards the last day of the first week of November. Watch the night skies, my friend. We'll speak soon.

The evening air was moist and chilly and Synesius hugged himself for warmth as he pondered the letter's contents. He clutched it to his chest as if it were a talisman protecting him from the lonely streets. Finally, he retreated into his warm sandstone home.

She was right, of course. Alexandria owned his heart. Pentapolis was a chilly exile by comparison.

Why then, he thought, do I keep returning here?

He lit the candle on his desk and settled into his comfortable reed chair. His home was sparse, almost ascetic. The shelf above his desk supported three dozen theological scrolls, a leather-bound volume on philosophy, and two collections of astronomy. There was also a pile of blank parchment and several ink flasks. Synesius was one of the foremost letter-writers of his day.

By candlelight then, he reread Hypatia's letter and smiled at its mystery. He suddenly wanted her beside him. She was the greatest conversation partner he had ever known, and they had passed many nights in Alexandria with joyous hours of discussion and debate.

Why do I keep returning here, then? Why not move to where you're most happy? Am I afraid to tempt happiness again? Is that it?

He sighed, the force of his exhalation nearly snuffing out the candle's tiny flame. Yes, he thought. That's exactly why I stay here. God forgive me, but I'm afraid to tempt Fate.

Born in the North African city of Cyrene, Synesius had been raised by deeply Christian parents. He had gone to a religious school until he was seventeen. He was resolved, in fact, on pursuing a theological career until two things happened to him. The first was war. The second was love.

Cyrene was a small, isolated city not unlike Pentapolis. It lay far outside the Nile Delta facing the sea. Its remote location made it a favorite target for pirates and pillagers. In Synesius' youth, the worst of those raiders called themselves Set's Fury. Outlaws and outcastes the lot of them. They harassed the city's trade routes, killed travelers for sport. When Synesius was twenty-one word was circulating that Set's Fury had just recruited one thousand Arab mercenaries. The people of Cyrene despaired, fearing a direct invasion of their city. Synesius, thinking of his family's safety, joined the city militia. He took part in a preemptive strike against the would-be invaders. Victory was total.

A month later he met Myrrhine, a lovely Greek woman from Pentapolis who arrived in Cyrene with her family's merchant caravan. For five weeks they spent each day together. When she left, he was heartbroken and for six months, they exchanged letters until at last he worked up the resolve to move to Pentapolis to marry her.

Myrrhine bore him four sons. Synesius returned to his religious studies and became head of the local parish. And that might have been the story of his life had fate not intervened. In his fiftieth year, his reputation as a Christian preacher and scholar had reached the ears of several parishes in Alexandria. They invited him to visit as an honored guest. Flattered, he went. It was there that two new things happened to him, transforming his life yet again.

The first of these was his trip to see the esteemed Great Library. It had everything he could want to know, from original gospel texts to tantalizing glimpses of other faiths from around the world. Another man might have refused to acknowledge the exotic pages of foreign religious books; Synesius saw in them yet another manifestation of the God he had come to love. Who cared that God had revealed Himself to the people of India as Brahma? What did it matter that the people of Crete worshiped the ocean and all its life? Was not the ocean a product of the Lord, and so to revere it was to revere the Creator?

The second element of change was his meeting with a twenty-four-year-old woman named Hypatia, who at that time was teacher of mathematics and physics. Synesius was supposed to stay in Alexandria for a month; he wrote his wife and told her it would be two. He became a student of Hypatia's. In her, he had found a fierce intellect and passionate friend.

Yet once again, two major changes visited his life. This time, they weren't happy transformations. They were the lessons of death.

His own death he could have happily accepted. After all, he considered his life a richly diverse experience marked by a fine upbringing, a spiritual heart, an educated mind, and great friends. Death was not unwelcome for a man who had lived so fully. But no, with hideous prejudice death had spared him. Pentapolis had been threatened again with invasion. Synesius' four sons had enlisted in the army to repel them as their father had years before. The outcome was different. All his sons perished on the battlefield.

All of them! Would God have spared a single of his progeny? That unspeakable tragedy gave rise to the next. One year later his wife passed away in her sleep, almost on the very anniversary of their children's deaths. Synesius had awakened in the morning to find her a corpse, her soul departed without a farewell. Between sundown and sunrise, he had become an orphan in his own house.

The night after his wife's burial, Synesius had gone out into the desert and fought with God. "Why should we worship You?" he had challenged. "You, who never answers! You, who takes like a greedy child! You, who has never offered me a love that could match that of my wife or children! Was it jealousy, then, that You took them from me?"

The following days were black and hopeless. Then a letter arrived, sealed with red wax and written in black ink: TO SYNESIUS, FROM THE PHILOSO-PHER.

My friend Synesius,

There are no poems I can offer to console your grieving heart, nor flowers to lift your spirit. I will not pretend there was purpose in your loss. I can only offer you my friendship. You are missed here in Alexandria, and should you return I promise that your old friends await you...Heliodorus, Simplicius, and myself. We are here. You need not be alone in your grief.

Hypatia

Now Synesius winced at the painful brush of memories. He stared at his lonely home, remembering when Myrrhine and the boys had frequented its rooms. I'm living in a tomb, he thought. It's a tomb I'm afraid to leave.

He exhaled again, sharply, and the candle blew out. In the new dark Synesius folded Hypatia's letter and slipped it into the pocket of his toga. Enough of this self-indulgence, he thought angrily. Step out of your tomb. Go see a friend.

General Simplicius' home stood on the red perimeter of town. Synesius, wearing a wool cloak as shield against the cold, walked briskly to see him. They had left Alexandria together two days before, shortly after Hypatia's riverside lecture to the commoners.

"I'm awake," he heard Simplicius' voice through the door, responding to his knock. "Come in."

From the foyer Synesius went to the home's atrium, which had a large bath, wall-lanterns, and flowering plants. Simplicius was seated, reading. Two goblets were already out and filled with wine, anticipating his friend's visit.

"Do you know me that well?" Synesius joined him at the small corner table. Starlight poured in through the atrium's skylights.

"I knew you'd come once you saw Hypatia's letter. She meant to give it to you in person, but you vanished on her."

"I intend to see her again soon," Synesius replied, aware that it *had* been rude to duck away without saying goodbye. He hadn't meant to hurt anyone's feelings. "In a few weeks I'll return to stay the winter. I—" His voice trailed off. "She wrote you a letter as well?"

"About watching the skies, yes."

"What do you think it means?"

Simplicius shrugged and closed the book he had been reading, tossing it onto a pile of folded linens. "There must be a reason. We'll just have to see."

Synesius sipped his wine, swishing it around in his mouth to fill his palate with the bitter flavor. "It was nice in Alexandria, with all of us reunited. It was very nice."

The general nodded absently.

"Heliodorus looked well."

"Yes."

"Orestes, however, didn't."

"That," Simplicius said, his eyes glinting, "is what's on my mind. Not Orestes so much, but the Archbishop. You endorsed the man, didn't you?"

The lines on Synesius' forehead deepened. He sighed and regarded his goblet.

"Synesius?"

"I did endorse him." Synesius' voice was anxious. Archbishop Cyril had not been the favored choice for Patriarch. There was another man, a bishop named Timotheus, who was vying for the position. Timotheus was popular in Egypt, agreeable, a uniter rather than a divider.

Synesius sighed. "Cyril is passionate, educated. He believes very strongly in his causes."

"So might a thief. Or a murderer."

"But Cyril is neither. He will come around, Simplicius."

Simplicius showed his displeasure. "The man is ruining Alexandria. Why the hell didn't you support Timotheus instead?"

"Because Timotheus was a dotard! A grinning imbecile. I thought Cyril would be good for us. And I thought...in time, I thought I might shape him a bit, mold him. He worships me, you know. He has never forgotten how much my endorsement mattered. He calls me the True *Cathari*." Synesius wanted to smile. The expression wouldn't form.

"How would you have molded him?"

Synesius' bushy white eyebrows drew up sadly. "I would have taught Cyril the real nature of God."

"And when did God explain Himself to you?"

"A long time ago."

The general smiled, feeling sympathy and love for his friend. I know why you keep coming back here Synesius, he wanted to say. You're afraid to be happy. Alexandria lifts your spirits; you don't stay because you're afraid that fate will steal your joy as it did with your family. You're a superstitious fool! If Hypatia knew that you still secretly believed that things are fated to be, she'd give you such a tongue-lashing!

Rather than voice these thoughts, Simplicius said, "Okay. Tell me about the nature of God, as you'd tell Cyril."

"Good. Listen. Cyril hates the Jews—everyone knows that and he makes no secret about it. But why? You might say it's because he holds the Jews responsible for betraying Christ. But that's a feeble explanation. Do Egyptians still hate the Persians? Do Jews still hate the Egyptians? Do Persians hate Greeks?"

"Some do."

"Well…there will always be imbeciles who hold sons responsible for the father's deeds. But even Cyril can't hate the Jews for what they did four hundred years ago."

"Three hundred and eighty-two years, actually."

"Stop interrupting me. Cyril sees the Jews and Christians as worshipers of different gods, one named Yahweh and the other Jehovah. That's also the reason he, like his uncle, hates pagans. He considers them an affront to the One God because they have so many. But why does number matter? Why does name matter? It doesn't!"

Simplicius watched him, face stolid. "What matters, then?"

"What matters," Synesius said excitedly, "is the *actions* of any given people. Belief is irrelevant! Suppose you were Babylonian, and you worshiped Marduk, and the way you worshiped him was to dance around a fire, throwing spices into the flame."

"An interesting image."

"Or suppose you worshiped Dionysus, and your worship was to strip naked and frolic under the full moon."

"A more interesting image, to be sure."

"But suppose," Synesius continued, "that whoever you worshiped, you were kind to your neighbors, loving to your children, respectful of the elderly. It wouldn't matter what God or Gods you bow before!"

"I doubt the Church of Rome would endorse those words."

"I don't care. The Church is wrong about this. I believe in Jesus, the Son of God. I follow his lessons of love and forgiveness. But I refuse to believe the dogmatic approach to those lessons. Listen. There are Christians who perform evil deeds, Simplicius. Look at Hierax. Does it matter that he believes in Jesus Christ? Can that belief absolve him from raping a woman? It can't! Bring me a Babylonian who worships a hundred gods, and I'll tell you his gods don't matter…only *what he does in life matters.* Do you really think that our Creator would allow civilization to flourish for thousands of years and then, one day, call Moses up a hill and inform him that all those civilizations are worshiping false gods? Why not tell everyone at once? Why make a game of it?"

Simplicius imagined Cyril hearing blasphemous words such as these. "Okay…"

"I don't believe the Lord plays games. I believe different people of different faiths *do* worship the same God. They call him by various names and assign to him cultural values they know. At the Great Library, I studied other religions and yes, some were very violent. I don't believe in gods who demand human sacrifice! I don't believe in gods who call people to war! But the message of most deities is one of hope! And wasn't it hope that Jesus brought us? The Persians worship Ahura Mazda; they call him the Wise Lord and pray to him for protection from evil. Is that so different—at its core—from what Osiris was to the Egyptians? Or what Yahweh and Jehovah are to Jews and Christians?"

Simplicius peered at him skeptically from over the rim of his goblet. "And you really expect to say all this to Cyril? I don't think he'll worship you once he hears all that!"

"He shouldn't be worshiping me anyway. He—" Synesius' voice trailed off. "Did you hear that?"

"What?"

A loud knock came to Simplicius door. The general sprang up and went to the foyer, returning shortly with another letter.

"It's from Heliodorus," he said, hastily breaking the seal.

"What does it say?"

Simplicius' face darkened as he read the contents.

Synesius felt a twitch of tension. "What?"

"*What* is that Cyril has expelled the Jews from Alexandria!" Simplicius declared, his anger exploding. "The attack came last night. The synagogue is destroyed, homes wrecked. Families are leaving the city." When he saw Synesius' haunted eyes, he challenged, "I don't think Cyril shares your perceptions of God, Synesius. Here! Take the letter! The bottom half is for you."

With shaking hands Synesius accepted the parchment.

The general watched his old friend. "It looks like you'll be going to Alexandria sooner than you think."

CHAPTER 14

▼

Class didn't go as well as Thasos had hoped.

As promised, Hypatia called on him first. He stood calmly and began his prepared speech, the words flowing through his lips like fanciful tendrils of magician's smoke as his classmates sat, mesmerized. But it was Hypatia he was most concerned with, and her face was unreadable. He sweated, felt himself blushing. He pressed on with all the boldness he could muster. Finally he finished, and his classmates murmured approvingly while his desperate eyes went to his teacher.

"Very good, student," Hypatia said. Then she called on someone else.

That's it? he thought, wounded by her indifference. He sank into his seat numbly. Hypatia barely looked at him. She seemed unfazed by his hard work. In fact, she seemed distracted.

Or has she seen straight through me? His blush deepened. He didn't volunteer anything else during the entire class. When the three hours had passed, she dismissed them.

Thasos shuffled out the door in a fog of disappointment and self-loathing. Into the merciful privacy of the Library's manifold corridors he went, losing himself in the perfume of hallowed manuscripts. Sometimes he read. Often he sat, puzzled, in a lonely corner.

It was evening when he departed the building for his homeward trek.

Did I deserve such a cold reception? he thought angrily. Even if she perceived my soul, was there no worth in what I said?

He turned onto the Canopic Way. A dark shadow exploded at him from the corner of a building.

Thasos cried out, expecting Kapta. Then he recognized Arion's ungainly run.

"Have you gone mad?" Thasos hissed, heart pounding.

"I've been searching for you all day!"

"I was at the Library all day."

Arion's next words stuck in his throat as he noticed that Thasos was carrying a cylindrical leather casing. "Is that a Library scroll?"

"It is."

"You can't take that home!"

"I don't care. After the way Hypatia treated me today, I feel justified in *borrowing* this. I'll bring it back tomorrow."

"Thasos—"

"It's the transcript of a Dialogue from Athens," Thasos continued proudly. "It is twenty-five years old."

"Thasos, listen—"

"Let me finish. Each year in Athens, the instructors hold several Debates in which the students are urged to take part. Twenty-five years ago, there was a Schoolmaster named Tyndarus. Venture a guess as to who was a student during his tenure."

Arion held his breath and decided to let Thasos finish. He felt disgusted with his friend's self-preoccupation. It had been an unspoken strain on their friendship.

When Arion made no reply, Thasos continued. "Hypatia. She attended the University of Athens, Arion! And twenty-five years ago..." His voice trailed off as he saw his friend's impatience. "My story has a point to it, I assure you."

"Is it a point about the Jews?"

"What?"

"Have you heard about the Jews?"

"Yes. Once or twice, I've come across mention of their culture."

Arion was in no mood for amusement. "They're leaving, Thasos! Completely. Many have left already!"

Thasos' frown deepened, ruining the usual softness of his face. "What do you mean? Leaving...forever?"

"A mob attacked them last night. The Jews are departing the city in droves!"

Thasos felt as if he had been physically struck. "Arion..."

"Thasos, it happened. The whole city is talking about it. You must be the only soul who doesn't know!"

"Who attacked them?"

"We don't know...but people are whispering that it's the Archbishop's parishioners."

Thasos was silent. He knew that Jews and Christians had long been at odds. Of the little history he knew, he understood the fundamental division among their ranks. Yet many cultural groups had, throughout history, been at odds. There were still Egyptians who distrusted Persians on sight, remembering the way the Persians had so callously treated Egypt during the era of conquest. Even so, Thasos had never heard of a large-scale Egyptian-Persian riot.

"It's like Serapis," Arion said, trembling. "It's Serapis all over again. I never would have believed it could happen. Not again."

Thasos felt his coiled frustrations dissipating as he reflected on his friend's words. He knew, of course, about Serapis. All Alexandrians did. When King Ptolemy I chose Egypt as the ruling seat of his dynasty, he had popularized the Cult of Serapis—a god of unity—to unite the Greek and Egyptian peoples. The Temple of Serapis was built, glorious and beloved, a marble monument to the spectacular intercourse of two extraordinary civilizations.

When in 391 Emperor Theodosios banned all pagan religions, this temple became a battleground. The Edict had been read in the city's harbor. The pagans wept, the Christians cheered. Caught up in this spirit of religious victory, Patriarch Theophilus led the charge against Serapis' House. This attack was viciously repelled by pagan defenders. Soon, the streets surrounding the temple were literally running with blood. Governor Pentadius tried to quell the riots, but when Theophilus threatened to withhold communion from him, the prefect agreed to support his violent cause. Alexandria's militia was directed against the temple. Serapis was burned, its bare-chested idol dragged through the avenues by Theophilus' cheering mob.

"Doesn't this bother you?" Arion challenged, angry.

"It does!" Thasos finally raised his voice. "But it is beyond my control! This is a matter for government, not people like you and me."

An awkward silence settled between them. Arion panted, exhausted from the hours of searching for his friend and exasperated at the realization that the matter *was* beyond his control. He looked to his feet.

"Go ahead, tell me about the scroll you found," he said finally.

"It doesn't matter."

Thasos was bleakly silent during the remainder of his homeward stroll. The streets were filled with neighbors discussing the incident in the Hebrew District and Thasos listened to their whispers as he passed, forcing his way through their congested numbers to reach his home.

Demetria was seated at her workbench, adjacent to the kitchen, when he entered. She was running linen fibers through a ring cut in her terra-cotta bench, winding them around the rotating spindle. Her fingers worked with dextrous, spider-like expertise.

Thasos hung back in the doorway, imagining how conversation would proceed.

Mother?

A slow, brooding up-tilt of her head. *Have you cleared the yard of weeds?*

Yes. Before work this morning.

Silence.

Instead, Thasos crept by her, taking his sandals in hand so he could traverse the cool clay floor without making noise. He went to her bedroom. The wooden door was closed as usual, so Thasos carefully lifted the handle and pushed. A cool draft escaped into the hall.

The room's interior was an example of perfect order, with the pristine cleanliness of a Roman pool-house. Perfume bottles and cosmetic supplies were lined like soldiers atop her dresser; her clothes were neatly folded and stacked in a reed crate in the corner; her sewing supplies were delicately arranged in the walk-in closet. On the wall between the two windows, a painting of Demetria was hung.

Fearfully he moved to the closet. Two years after his father's death, Thasos had infiltrated this same closet and discovered Admetus' wooden Library chest. Thasos had thumbed through papers, vials, clay tablets, and scrolls, too young to know what to make of them, only aware that they held his father's scent. But then Demetria had caught him and went berserk. She had flown into a rage, striking him and demanding he never invade her privacy again.

It was the only time she had ever hit him. The episode had left him upset, confused, frightened. Why was the chest so dangerous? For years after, Thasos avoided it. Last week he had chanced to pry into it again…and from its contents had discovered Theon's prediction of falling stars.

Now he sought the chest again. He crouched, spotted the box beneath sheet piles and spools of cotton. He pulled it from its hiding place. It scraped lightly against the floor.

In his own room he carefully stored the box in the cool shadows beneath his bed. Then he stealthily returned to the foyer.

"Mother?" he said, approaching. "I thought you would be at the shop tonight."

"I wanted to work from home. My knees are hurting me this week."

"Do you need help with anything?"

"I want to you pick up some things at the market tomorrow morning."

"Of course. I meant, right now."

She shook her head, her blue eyes ensnared in her work. "In another hour you can help me by preparing dinner."

"Certainly," he said, feeling a familiar sadness welling in his chest.

He watched her work, fingers as dextrous as spider legs and spinnerets.

"My shop is getting ready for the winter shipment," he said at last. "The owners are like generals, barking orders and reminding us of our deadlines." He shrugged. "You know how managers are."

"Oh." Her fingers pulled a thread tightly.

"I am really enjoying the Library, too."

In a swift flash his mother produced a pair of shears and snipped two threads from the sheet she was making. They dangled in her other hand, their tautness broken. With a careless brush of her fingers they were tossed to the floor.

Silence.

"I have some reading to do," he said finally. He returned to his room, angry again, frustrated again. He pulled out the box and set it on his mattress.

It was three hands across in length, two in depth and width. It was made of a dark wood not native to Egypt, though the designs of the exterior were all Egyptian: sleek cats, crocodiles, falcons, the sun being devoured by a mighty serpent, triremes, scarab beetles, fish-headed men emerging from a lake, a bird engulfed in flames, and a man holding a single flame in the palm of his hand. The artistry was breathtaking.

The box had a bronze latch; Thasos lifted it and breathed in the sweet smell of old papyrus. There were several tightly-rolled scrolls, a rusted stylus, a copper model of planets orbiting the sun, and thick books stuffed with his father's notes. Thasos' fingers touched their binding, contemplating which one he wanted to read tonight. In the end, he closed the box and slid it back under his bed. Its contents had proved invaluable to him not only in learning about Hypatia, but also in making him appreciate his father's dedication to study. Admetus' notes referenced hundreds of books. Maybe thousands. It was an awe-inspiring discovery, but it also made Thasos burn with anguish.

I miss you, father. I was too young to understand you. I'm *still* too young to comprehend your depths. But you were right in sending me to the Library. I only wish you were here to heal our family. Only you can.

Thasos untucked the scroll he had borrowed from the Library. He flopped onto his back and unrolled it slowly, reading the debate between Schoolmaster Tyndarus and a certain female student named Hypatia. The paper was older than him yet was written at a time when Hypatia was roughly his age. It was an intriguing, comforting thought.

The document didn't explain why Hypatia had gone to Athens in the first place. It was written in the spring of her first year at the university.

Spring, and the annual Debates were initiated by Schoolmaster Tyndarus to a crowd of students who packed the university's coliseum, the document said. *Tyndarus, an expert on the philosophies of Paramenides, did lecture on the works of that philosopher and earned tremendous applause from his listeners.*

"'I declare that the universe is a static, unchanging place, and that change itself is impossible,'" stated the Schoolmaster. "'Would anyone care to challenge me on this?'" He then showed evident satisfaction when the female student Hypatia, daughter of Theon of Alexandria, raised her hand and stood.

Thasos wondered why Hypatia had so eagerly accepted his challenge. Had it been ego?

"The female student Hypatia claimed that Tyndarus and Paramenides were wrong and that the whole state of the universe was defined by change, the document continued. *Tyndarus, showing great pleasure, asked her to state her case."*

Thasos could picture the scene perfectly. He imagined a sunny day, when students gathered in the shade of trees which overhung the arena of debate. He pictured all eyes on young Hypatia, who was *"called down to the arena's center to stand before Tyndarus and her peers."*

"'It would be a pleasant concept if all was orderly in our world,'" Hypatia said, "'And yet that comfortable thought is no substitute for logic. There exists nothing static, nothing immutable, in the world around us. This is a truth as plain as day.'"

"'Day,'" Tyndarus interrupted, "'is just one item which makes my point, young student. The sun never fails to rise. Each night is followed by a day. Each day folds over into night! This is a cycle that is unchangeable, indeed, precisely immutable. Your own words, student Hypatia, oppose you.'"

"'When will the next rainstorm descend, Schoolmaster?'" the elegant lady-student countered. "'What is the precise level of water Egyptians can expect during the next flood season? You have said that the sun rises each day. I doubt anyone here would argue with that, except for me.'"

A great commotion, half of laughter, half whispers, exploded from the attending crowd. Tyndarus' face froze in an uncertain smirk.

"'Are you proposing that the sun might refuse to rise one day?'" he asked, incredulous. "'That one morning farmers will emerge to harvest their wheat and find that morning has simply forgotten to come?'" The audience laughed agreeably.

"*The sun does not rise, Schoolmaster,*" *Hypatia stated calmly.* "*The Earth turns, and as it does one side comes to face the sun.*"

The unnamed documenter of the debate had been an astute observer, for he had written that the Schoolmaster's face flashed in subtle anger at "*being so defied, by the young woman student.*" Perhaps it was this thinly-hidden anger that made Tyndarus utter his next words.

"*So the Earth turns, you are right! It turns immutably, unchanging, forever to be expected. To trip me on a detail is an unworthy tactic, yet I forgive it. Continue.*"

"*Let me try something more basic,*" *Hypatia said.* "*Like the fact that human beings are born, yet will die. The elements of the world wither them. As—*"

"*The fact that human beings die is a unchangeable law,*" *Tyndarus countered.* "*The life-and-death cycle is the rule of the cosmos.*"

"*The constructions of mankind,*" *Hypatia continued,* "*are subject to the environment. We build walls but walls crumble and—*"

"*The constructions of mankind are not important. What are such constructions made of? Stone. Marble. Gold. The elements themselves are important, for it is these things which are unchangeable. A tower may topple, yet from its stones a man might construct a bridge. The bridge may fall into a river, yet its stones might form a haven for fish.*" *His eyes glimmered with predatory smugness. His lips parted to say a single word to the young challenger:* "*Immutable.*"

Hypatia was then silent. The audience murmured. When a long silence had passed, Tyndarus' smile grew. The attendees applauded their Schoolmaster's success. Hands shot up to be the next challenger.

"*Thank you, Hypatia,*" *Tyndarus said in consolation. The audience hushed to listen to his post-Debate words.* "*But I would suggest that you temper your brazenness with a little more education. This is Athens, not Alexandria. We require more devotion to the art of Debate than is known in Egypt.*"

Tyndarus then picked another hand in the crowd, but suddenly Hypatia spoke in a loud voice that filled the arena.

"*I had not concluded my challenge, Schoolmaster Tyndarus,*" *Hypatia said.*

Tyndarus' eyes glimmered like a king puzzled by the remarks of his jester. "*It seems to me you had,*" *he said, earning more appraising laughter.* "*Yet I will grant you another opportunity to defend your position.*"

"*Thank you. Stones? The life-and-death cycle? The sun? Very well. Very well indeed. Stones are an element of Earth, but they are not immutable. Heated by the fires of mankind they become a metal that is malleable, shapeable, changeable. No stone could be a sword, no metal a stone. The chrysalis of an oven brings change to a world that had only known rocks. Life-and-death? Perhaps you can explain why some *infants die in their cribs, while others age to withered mummies? Is that predictable, Schoolmaster? As for the sun,'" Hypatia smiled. "'The sun exists on a calendar far older than the whole of human lives. Was there a sun when the world formed? Did the sun not form in the ways that suns do? If we were gifted with the eyes of Time, could we fail to realize that the static environment around us is actually changing at rates that no single lifetime can measure? Why do travelers find seashells on mountaintops? Why do we find bones of great dragons in the dirt, and where are the living examples of such beasts now? Did those beasts think that the sun would always rise for them? Did they have an endless calendar that failed to see the arrival of people? What you call static I call ignorance. I charge that the unchanging cycle of things you notice is like the world that a marsh-fly sees. If born at night, the fly will only live to see sunrise. If born during the day, it will see sunset. Should it write a book declaring one movement of the world, a creation and destruction of light, one time for all time? Do we, as people, have the patience of a tree that could bear witness to cities rising, fields irrigated, crops planted, harvested, blighted, planted again?'"*

Her words hushed the audience. No mouth quivered, all eyes were dazzled. Like men of caves who had seen the sun for the first time, a blanket of reverence had settled over all.

Except for Tyndarus.

"'Nonsense!'" he retorted, his smile a candle-wax that had melted off his face. "'The world is a stage set for mankind, with constants that ache to be recognized. Change is the illusion, Hypatia. It seems to happen but doesn't. Change is only order on a grander scale!'"

"'Order is exclusively a manmade invention!'" Hypatia replied. "'We build our values, our neat roads, our aqueducts, our symmetrical houses. We assign a handsome inventory of laws and rules and social mores! We made an orderly pantheon of deities who embody the aspects of a human mind! Yet despite our concept of order, the world is contrary. The waves of the ocean topple our ships, the earth breaks our homes, and mountains erupt to cover Roman cities with ash and lava—'"

"'Nonsense!'" the Schoolmaster shouted, angry and spitting. "'The universe does not operate that way!'"

"'What happened to Pompeii four hundred years ago,'" Hypatia continued as if he had never spoken, "'could have happened underwater. Had the hot molten rock cooled upon the waves and formed a new island to alter our precious maps, we might be privy to the creaks and moods of our planet! Our canvas of life is a dangerous, wild, and untamed papyrus. He who realizes this is better equipped to handle it. That is how the world is.'" She paused, and then her lips parted, and she spoke one word: "'Mutable.'"

Tyndarus shook his head rigorously. "'Nonsense. Ill-researched nonsense. You may return to your seat, Hypatia.'"

His words rang out and yet she continued to stand before him, with a cool defiance that brought gasps to the attendees.

"'I said,'" Tyndarus declared, "'that you may find your seat.'"

"'I am awaiting your counter-argument,'" she said quietly.

"'I voiced my counter-argument,'" he said. "'Which apparently you didn't hear.'"

Suddenly the Debate was interrupted by a voice from the back of the coliseum. "'For that matter, neither did I,'" the voice said. All heads turned to regard the University Elders, who had been hidden in the crowd, rising to their feet.

The Elders were an esteemed lot. Some of them had been Schoolmasters in the past. All of them were experts in philosophy and science.

The Elders had then cut through the crowd *"making room by their presence alone. They approached the Schoolmaster and his young challenger, greeted both, and took seats in the front row."*

"'Young lady,'" Elder Arkhippos said. "'Are you aware of the arguments of Thales and his contemporaries?'"

Very quietly, Hypatia replied, "'Yes.'"

"'The theories of universal substance?'"

"'Yes.'"

"'The questions of form and variety?'"

"'Yes.'"

"'Well,'" the Elder said, his wrinkled face stretching into a great smile, "'By all means, indulge me and accept my *challenge. Discuss these with your Schoolmaster. Debate them if you must.'" He folded his arms across his chest and waited expectantly.*

Hypatia had *"bowed politely and faced Tyndarus again."* She had discussed Thales. Heraclitus. Plato. *"She masterfully wove a tapestry of speculation that hovered in the minds of all present, like a quilt made from spools of thought. The students were her prisoners, and by the end of the Debate many dared to whisper that Tyndarus had been beaten. All the while, the eyes of the Elders never left the duel."*

Thasos finished the scroll breathless with excitement. Its words blazed vividly in his mind. The scroll ended by saying that the elders, satisfied with Hypatia's learning and powers of speech, were *"impressed enough to declare the young student the victor, and ask her to remain as student for another year. Hypatia accepted gratefully, though added, "One more year only, thank you."*

Thasos felt a smile form on his face. Quietly, he shook with light laughter, and in the depths of his heart he discovered a burning admiration for her—as bright as his desire.

"*You* really haven't changed, Hypatia," he said aloud, laughing heartily now. "You might have won a debate on mutability, but you haven't changed at all!"

CHAPTER 15

▼

Official Darius was walking home from the palace when he heard Marina's voice come suddenly from the high shrubbery of the roadside.

"For Orestes, that was an extremely brief meeting," she said. Marina stepped out from the flowering vegetation, looking pleased with herself. "How long was it? An hour? He must have been tired…he loves to hear himself speak!"

Darius stared at her, astonished at her audacity in coming to his home district. Persians and Arabs were the smallest ethnic group in Alexandria, thus their district was little more than four roads that cris-crossed. It was also arguably the most beautiful, aside from the riches of the royal district. Small waterways fed rows of sprouting rush, lotuses, dates, and hanging grapevines.

"He was hardly tired," Darius replied, sensing a strangeness to Marina's mood. "What are you doing here?"

She draped her arms over his neck. "I was waiting for you. I went to the Forum, and bought this scarf and this bracelet…and waited until I heard the meeting was over."

"How did you—"

Marina kissed him ruthlessly, her tongue forcing its way through his lips. Then, sensing his distance, she released him and gave an accusing stare. "Something wrong?"

"I was about to ask you the same thing. What are you doing in my home district, Marina?"

"Would you have preferred the palace?" She came at him again, hearing his anxiety but ignoring it.

"Marina," Darius said, trying to retreat. "Please, not here."

"Not here?" she taunted, raking her fingernails across the back of his neck and down his collarbones. "Why not?"

"Because I'm two blocks from my house, that's why!" He made a feeble attempt at wrenching free of her seductive grasp.

"Oh no you don't," she said in a child-like tease, hooking her fingernails into the back of his neck. "I want you right there, behind those date palms." With a nudge of her head, she indicated the cove of feathery-leaved trees that grew around the lesser canal's banks.

"Marina—"

"I want you inside me," she whispered. "Now."

Darius' member swelled into a throbbing erection. Immediately he felt drowned in her perfume, her touch, her whispers, her appearance. His eyes clouded over with urgency. Yes! he thought helplessly I need to be inside you, to feel your sex wrapped around mine! Even so close to my house where Kipa is eagerly waiting for me...

His flaring erection faltered, overtaken by shame.

Marina noted the change. "What's wrong?"

Darius shook his head. "I can't keep Kipa waiting. Not tonight."

"Is tonight a special holiday for you two?" Marina sneered. "An anniversary?"

"Marina—"

"Are you celebrating the day of your marriage, or of your infidelity?"

He was stricken silent. Marina's lips formed a cruel smirk. "I've waited all day and *now* I'm going to have you. Don't pretend you can say no, only to return to that idiot woman of yours!"

Anger flashed across Darius' face. "Kipa is no idiot."

"Kipa not idiot! Kipa not idiot!" Marina snapped, releasing her hold on his neck and turning away in a flourish of wrath. She pivoted, continued her verbal assault. "Kipa not speak like civilized person! Kipa need study much!"

"She loves me dearly!" Darius yelled in desperate defense. "And she *is* studying Greek, every night. I am there to help her."

"Get behind these trees," Marina commanded, "and get on your knees, lie on your back, and *get* inside me."

Darius trembled as his loins reacted to her words again. Marina saw his conflict and her own victory. His frustration delighted her appetites.

"Not here," Darius said with difficulty.

Marina stared coldly at him, knowing he could never look away from her. "I'm sure Kipa will wait up all night for you, Darius! Think of it as helping her.

As she waits for you to return like some dog awaiting its master, she'll have all that time to study!"

"And isn't your husband awaiting you?" Darius asked, his voice cracking as he tried to stall her. His erection had returned and was pulsating. He feared she would touch him again, and thereby shatter his resolve.

"Orestes doesn't care where I am!"

"He might care tonight after the meeting he just called," Darius said, hoping to change the course of conversation. "Your husband summoned every leader of the city to the palace. He's furious at the attack on the Hebrews. He spoke with such fire, such determination—"

"I don't care about the meeting."

"He made some powerful decisions tonight, and not one person questioned him. These next few weeks should be—"

"*I said I don't care about the meeting!*" Marina yelled, swept up by monstrous anger. "Go back to your idiot wife! Think of me when you're in bed with her tonight!"

Darius swallowed. Like a sulking, intimidated animal, he turned from her and headed down the road to his house. Marina watched him go.

"You always do!" she called after him. He didn't turn around.

She couldn't believe his refusal. Frantic, pulsing thoughts collided in her mind. She imagined herself following him home, knocking on his door and greeting Kipa when she answered. She could tell the woman everything about her husband's trysts, and watch as the hybrid wept at her lover's betrayal. Better yet would be the look on Darius' face.

Suddenly, Marina felt like screaming. Maybe laughing. Maybe pounding her fists against something. Her blood was like thunder and needed a release. *Go ahead, visit him!* she thought. *Make his little bitch wail! Make him weep!*

It would accomplish nothing, of course. If she went through with it she would lose him altogether and she wasn't anxious for that to happen.

"See you tomorrow, Darius," she said lustily, thinking of the ways she'd make him apologize for refusing her tonight. That alone would be worth the wait.

Marina returned to the palace.

When she arrived, the guards opened the iron gate for her and she passed them swiftly, glancing up at the palace windows to see each room dark. She entered, took off her scarf and threw it on a chair. She poured herself a glass of wine, fleetingly believing it would calm her riled emotions. When the last drop was gone, however, she was still restless and in need of release.

It was only a few hours after sundown, and she figured her husband would be awake, reading as he usually did by candlelight in the study. If she wasn't to have Darius, then a fight with Orestes could be a welcome catharsis, too, and so she ascended the stairs to look for him.

To her surprise, the study was dark. Marble statues stood like haunted forms in the room, silhouetted by the moonlight from the eastern window. She went to the bedroom, where to her astonishment she saw Orestes in bed...already asleep! He was half-concealed beneath the silken sheets, his muscular chest rising and falling.

Marina remained in the doorway, watching him. She couldn't deny that she was still attracted to him. The bed's pastel blue color seemed to swim around his sun-bronzed flesh. He was sleeping on his back, his right arm behind the pillow, his left over the sheets. He looked like a dark statue, carefully designed to depict a perfect masculine form.

Marina tried to dismiss her arousal. She stripped of her tunica and undergarments. In the bedroom mirror she regarded her naked body. Still beautiful, she told herself. Flat stomach and no trace of the fat that builds around older women. The fact that she had never bore a child helped. In the mirror, her eyes went to her sleeping husband.

How long has it been since we've coupled? she wondered. Four months? And even then, hadn't it been obligatory for him? Despite all his energy and stamina, she had been acutely aware that he wasn't thinking of her as he did it. It had been a horrible, lonely realization.

Marina sighed and let down her hair, keeping it tucked behind her ears. She went to the bed and joined him beneath the silken covers. Orestes didn't move.

Almost involuntarily, Marina touched his arm and traced her fingers up and down its length. Four months, she thought. What's wrong with breaking that drought? Feeling her energy mount, Marina leaned down and began kissing Orestes alongside his neck. She loved kissing Darius. He would moan so softly! In the bedroom shadows, Marina imagined that Darius was with her. Orestes could be her Darius tonight.

She bit softly into his collarbone, and was unexpectedly rewarded when Orestes groaned gently. His eyes were still closed but he shifted position so he faced her and ran his fingers through her hair. Pleased, Marina nibbled on his fingertips, losing herself in fantasy.

Then she was kissing him needfully. She tore back the sheets and found his member, long and hard like a stalk of oak. She carefully positioned above the rigid tip. He was almost too big to take, but her excitement made her slippery enough. She pressed down on him, impaling herself until it felt like it was in her stomach.

Remarkably, Orestes still seemed to be half-asleep. Even as his hands clutched her hips, his eyes had not opened. Could a person make love in their dreams, the way others sleepwalked?

It doesn't matter, Marina told herself. Eyes closed, she pictured Darius beneath her despite the vast difference in size. She imagined it was Darius' hands which held her. Marina rode her fantasy with bestial abandon. She thought of Darius, honey-skinned and black-haired, moaning in helpless surrender. Her body contracted in ecstasy as she felt Orestes' organ grow bigger still, filling her up. Then he pulsated in uncontrolled climax.

"Hypatia!" Orestes cried, eyes shut.

Marina's eyes snapped open. As if a blast of cold air had assaulted her, she froze atop her husband's throbbing organ.

If Orestes was awake he was not revealing it. As she watched, the pulse in his neck relaxed. He seemed to drift back to sleep.

Numbly, Marina dismounted him. She pulled the sheets up around herself. She tried to focus her thoughts. The room felt empty. For a moment, she considered leaping out of bed, shaking him awake and glaringly accuse him.

Of what? she thought. She watched him while he slept. His face was peaceful, and even his perennial frown had softened. He looked years younger. He looked...relaxed.

It was many hours before Marina was able to fall asleep. Rapid, vengeful thoughts flashed across the field of her mind.

PART II

▼

November 3, 414 A.D.

CHAPTER 16

▼

Hypatia awoke with a violent start, kicking an invisible opponent with a spastic, dream-driven shudder. She sat up at once, blind in the oily dark of predawn, and peeled her sheets off her nude body. The morning was chill. Hypatia hugged herself for warmth as she walked quickly to the washroom and lit the tinder of the water-heater. The washroom was sandstone, ruddy and rectangular, but the bath tub was in-ground and marble. Hypatia crouched by its edge, rubbed the goose-flesh that riddled her skin, and cried.

The tears came swiftly, and her sobbing gathered a deep echo in the room. It felt good to cry. She seated herself on the tub's edge, swung her legs into the basin, and shivered with cold and sorrow.

Too much is happening, she told herself. All this change is like a sandstorm, blowing into Alexandria with dark plumes of stinging grain. I can't handle it. I *can't.*

Four days had passed since the Governor's emergency session with the city officials, and though Hypatia hadn't been invited she had heard of the decisions Orestes had made. By the evening of the following day, notices started appearing on lampposts and walls. *"Any Malcontent who is seen Participating in a Religious Riot, or Speaking Words to fuel such a Riot, will be Arrested and Charged with Sedition against Alexandria,"* the posters declared. And arrests had already been made, owing to a fervent investigation into the attack on the Hebrews five days ago. More than three dozen men had been incarcerated. Yesterday, a mob of protesters opposing the arrests had taken to the streets. The city militia responded, smashing through their line and adding them to the imprisoned. It was the first time in twenty-three years that the militia had been used against Alexandrians.

Now fear and anger slithered through the streets. Soldiers ringed the jails and patrolled the residential districts for signs of trouble.

Then there was the matter of the Jews. Four hundred Hebrews, men and women, had fled the city. Hypatia hadn't visited their district in years but she pictured it now as a depleting well, silent and lightless. The synagogue, she'd been told, still stood like a blackened cinder, surrounded by empty homes. Hypatia had heard it all from her fellow professors and staff at the Library. The news had appalled and enraged her. Suddenly she found herself agreeing with Amedio. Shouldn't we do something? Shouldn't we, the intellectual elite of the city, raise our voices in protest?

By comparison, the frustration she felt over her manuscript seemed trivial. Her thoughts and ideas wouldn't gel, kept drying up whenever she tried to pluck them. She had since decided to move on to the construction of later chapters, but after hours of concentration and false starts she would find herself hopelessly lost in her creation's maze. There's no rush, she tried to console herself. The problem is you're such a damn perfectionist!

The long hiss from the water-heater rescued her from her sobbing. The bath water was ready. Hypatia turned the bronze nozzles of the tub. Steaming water burst from the faucet into the basin and she stepped in carefully, lay down, letting the water fill up around her. It was a wonderful sensation, her skin drowned by hot caresses. The tears on her face felt cool by comparison, but they kept coming, leaking from the corners of her eyes and joining the rising water. Her dark hair floated like a mane around her head.

Stop now, Hypatia told herself. You have class to teach in a few hours. Keep crying and the students will be able to tell. They'll see my puffy, red eyes. They'll see the anguish. They'll whisper: Hypatia...*crying?* Thinking that, her brow wrinkled in pain. The water's steam made a vaporous mist around her that was like the confusion she felt. She stared at the swirling patterns, watching them fold, unfold before her eyes.

Fine, she thought. If I'm going to feel sorry for myself and the rest of the world, then at least analyze *why* you're letting your self-control buckle with barely a complaint! I feel sick over what happened to the Jews...why? Because things like that shouldn't be happening anymore. Why else? Because this is a black stain on the city of tolerance. Anything else?

Because it reminds me of Serapis.

If nothing else, Hypatia thought, history is like a planet continually traversing the same path around a sun. Just when you think something's over, it comes looming back from the gloom on yet another pass.

She squeezed her eyes shut, tensing her fists and feet, then relaxing them. Yes, it does remind me of Serapis. Twenty-three years ago. Imbecile Theodosios and his Edict. The hideous melee at the harbor...and the streets...and the doomed defense at Serapis' Door.

She had been asked to join in that defense. When the first fighting erupted in the Great Harbor after the edict had been read there aloud, students had dashed to the Great Library to find her. They had pleaded with her to rally with them, to protect the seven-hundred-year-old pagan god. No, she had told them. I will not fight for any god. I believe in none. Man is more than a pawn for celestial idols! Don't sacrifice your lives in service of a statue!

Then so many had died. Good students, full of brilliance and convinced of their cause. And when Hypatia had seen their bodies being dragged away from the gutters of carnage, she had wept terribly and wondered if her advice had been true. I could have swayed the mob, couldn't I have? Most men didn't care one way or another about gods or temples. I could have stood with those defenders, and added my own supporters to the fight. But then wouldn't the temple have fallen anyway? Wasn't the Edict from a Roman Emperor, thus destroying any hope of opposing it? And in the end, wasn't the Temple of Serapis just a building—albeit a beautiful, ancient one?

Yes. Yes. And, yes.

Isn't the Great Library just a building, too?

Hypatia snapped her eyes open. The water had filled the tub half-way, and she twisted the nozzle with her toes to stop its flow. Anger overflowed her misery, and again the amorphous vapors seemed to symbolize her wrath.

The Great Library, she thought venomously, is *not* just a building. It is a storehouse of knowledge, a collection of minds dead and alive, a repository for civilization. Damn Serapis to hell, if I had to make a choice between a god and the Library! What is a temple, after all? Just a meeting place for people to bow before a mythical tyrant. What is the Library? A meeting place where people think, discover, educate, enhance, illustrate, create, forge, and uncover the intricacies of this life!

She smiled suddenly as the stone wall in her mind, the one inhibiting her writing, cracked and crumbled. *There's* a chapter all in itself! Teleology and religion! From the primitive worship of fire gods to the arrogant declaration of monotheism. Hypatia was tempted to fly from the tub, dripping water, and retreat to her bedroom where her manuscript awaited her. She was reminded of the tale of Archimedes, who had once leapt from a tub with the cry of "Eureka!" as the principle of displacement became fixed in his mind.

She resisted the temptation and asked the nebulous steam another question. What else is bothering me? Is it the loss of my father, his eternal absence, the way I imagine him with me?

Yes.

She allowed herself to fancy that he was standing outside the washroom door while she bathed, talking to her through the cedar. "Less than five days and the stars will fall!" he would say. "We'll watch them together, won't we?"

She smiled sadly. *Yes, father. And you'll be correct about it all, and I'll revise your astronomy book with a new chapter that includes this prediction, and future generations will know the name of Theon forever. I'm proud to call myself your daughter.*

"Have you told anyone? If I'm wrong, then I'll look like a fool—"

I've told my friends. A lawyer, a general, a theologian, and the governor. One of my students knows, also. His father was your friend Admetus.

"Admetus! And how does the son compare?"

He gave a presentation on Seneca last week. It was inspired—not quite as good as his ego believed it to be—but a worthy presentation regardless. He's a good boy. I feel honored to be teaching him...I think he's already found his father's footsteps.

The washroom's heat made a mask of moisture over her face. She felt herself wanting to sob again, but had no more tears.

"What's wrong, Hypatia?"

A lot, she answered. *A lot more than I can express right now. Not all of it has to do with religion or science, either. Some of it is baser than that.*

Hypatia closed her eyes again and surrendered to the warmth of the water.

The Kinaron District afforded one of the greatest views of the Nile River. Three miles from Hypatia's home, it lay on the western edge of the city. Its homes had been built on the high ground—from the western wall the Nile was visible as a flat ribbon winding across the farming Delta. As the black sky was glowing in the east, Archbishop Cyril was awake and pacing the streets of his home district when he saw a crocodile crossing his path.

He had almost walked right into it. The banks of the Kinaron canal were very dark and overshadowed by palm trees. The giant beast had padded out from the water and was crossing the street, its dragon-like tail swishing behind it, when Cyril nearly stumbled over it. Instantly, the prehistoric monster stopped and hissed, yawning a threatening signal. Cyril recoiled as if he'd been whipped in the face. Nile crocodiles were renowned for their aggression and appetites. They were also sinister creatures, slipping through the canals like assassins to nab livestock or, just as commonly, people.

The reptile hissed again, exuding a terribly rancid odor. Then it swung its triangular head and continued across the road until he could no longer see it. Cyril's heart stuttered painfully. He studied the darkness, fearing it would turn back for an open-mouthed lunge.

Cyril enjoyed walking before sunrise. He was not uncomfortable with solitude, and neither was intimidated by the demonic hours before God's light warmed the Earth's face. He was, however, terrified of reptiles. It took several minutes of listening to the dark before he was convinced the crocodile was really gone. The thing had been huge. Cyril sprinted down the road and turned east away from the canal, onto the old Kinaron Bridge. The sky was a band of gold there, heralding the start of a new day.

When Cyril had first come to Egypt, his uncle had warned him that the country belonged to the beasts. Black scorpions that could hide in a boot, ill-tempered baboons which plundered the refuse piles of men, asps and cobras which could invade a flowerpot, venomous puffer fish, and of course the timeless Nile dragons. "But those monsters serve as the backdrop for servants of older evils, Cyril. Egypt is a haven for the wicked, and the roots of its paganism run deep. Just as its deserts are inhospitable to life, so does Jesus' glory become a fragile flower assailed by heathen winds. Alexandria, with its mosaic of false faiths, is a harsh garden."

Cyril watched the night peel back from the sunrise. When he looked west again, he could see fishing boats dotting the mighty Nile. In the spring, the river levels would sink and leave behind black soil for farming; but in the wet autumn, farmers became fishermen.

A new day brings new hope, Cyril thought, and he knelt and offered a prayer to the God he loved. *I have struck a blow against the violators of Your Son, Lord. I am in Your humble service and ever shall be. Bless me with the strength to keep Your people united, to keep them strong, to make them see Your glory.*

A soft breeze touched his neck, a troublesome murmur on its wings. Then the breeze died, and all was silent until Cyril began the return jaunt to his church. When he reached the point in the road where he had seen the crocodile, he heard the murmur again, louder now, made of many voices. He quickened his pace and saw a large crowd of parishioners on the steps of the Caesarion, wailing and stomping their feet. Before he had gone walking, this same crowd had filed quietly into church for the morning's Mass, headed by Priest Tobias.

They saw him. "Archbishop!" In a flash he was surrounded, men and women throwing themselves to his feet, pounding the dirt.

"You must help us! Please, you must help us!" one woman screamed.

Before he could muster a response, a young man knelt and wrung his hands in despair. "How can they do this?" he demanded. He was bleeding from a wound to his forehead, the blood trickling down the length of his nose as if it were a red crack dividing his face in two.

Other faces, voices, stabbed at him in the maelstrom.

"They arrested Tobias, Archbishop! They marched up the aisles of the church—"

"—dragged him away, chained him—"

"—said he was inciting a riot—"

"How can we live like this, harassed—"

"Please! We appeal to you—"

"Be silent!" Cyril commanded. Their babble evaporated. He felt a terrible wave of anxiety as he asked them to explain what had driven them to such a desperate state.

"You mean you don't know?"

The question came from a familiar voice. Cyril saw Peter standing, slightly away from the crowd's periphery, on the outermost edge of the courtyard. He looked like a dark, sinister silhouette.

"If I knew, Peter, I wouldn't have asked," Cyril said in a hard voice.

But Peter would not be cowed. "The city military just arrested Priest Tobias *inside the Caesarion.* Add him to the eighty other Christian men this week who have been jailed by our Governor!" His voice became a panic-fringed screech. "Why, Archbishop? Is this our reward for expelling the Jews? *Is this what you promised us?*"

Cyril's stomach twisted into a painful knot. He fisted his hands, gouging his palms.

"Archbishop?" the woman asked.

He had expected the investigation into the attack on the synagogue. He had written the Regent Pulcheria with smooth diplomacy, claiming that the men who assaulted the Jews were not part of his parish but that Prefect Orestes would likely lump them all into one category. Predictably, Orestes was doing just that. But Cyril hadn't expected such a vicious, overpowering response. The past few days had seen incessant arrests. And now…a *priest* had been arrested, *in the middle of a sermon!?*

"Our Governor is blaming us all for the loss of the Jews," Cyril said, inwardly screaming at the chaos he felt. As he spoke, he recognized many faces in the crowd who had truly participated in that vengeful assault, and so he added, "He doesn't understand that what we did, we did to protect the True Faith!"

"He'll be feeding us to lions next!" Peter shouted.

The crowd tightened around Cyril, desperate to hear his words of solace. So he continued, seeing the opportunity to regain their confidence. "We will make it through this, I promise all of you. We will survive this storm, and emerge stronger and more united. We must stand together, tethered by love of our Savior. Do not fear soldiers or guards, for you are the soldiers of Christ and the guardians of His House on Earth."

Peter's voice soared above his: "And when the militia breaks down the doors to our own houses? What then?"

Cyril turned on Peter with explosive rage. "Be quiet, little boy!" But Peter did not heed the warning, and stood defiant on the steps of the rectory, so Cyril continued: "Is your faith so feeble? Do you fear jail more than damnation! Is that it, Peter? Will you be the first to betray us when the soldiers come?"

The crowd turned, slowly, to face Peter. Murder glimmered in their eyes.

"Archbishop!" Peter whispered, finally afraid of their reaction. "I would never betray you!"

Cyril wanted to laugh at his victory over this arrogant, impetuous little boy. The crowd was already surrounding him, ready to seize him, ready to silence him. "Then kneel, and beg forgiveness! Now!"

Peter shrank away from the crowd's simmering danger. On shaking knees, he complied with Cyril's command. The crowd looked to Cyril for guidance, as if to ask: Should we kill the blasphemer?

"Put your head in the dirt, Peter," Cyril said. Peter gave him a hurt, wretched look. He bent low, his forehead kissing the damp earth.

Cyril dismissed the crowd, telling them to be strong. Only when they were gone did Cyril look to Peter with deliberate coldness.

"Inside," he hissed.

Once he had closed the rectory door behind him, Cyril let his hand fly like a Pharaoh's whip and struck Peter in the face. The blow knocked him to one knee. Moving swiftly, Cyril placed one foot on Peter's side and pushed, rolling the boy over onto his back. Peter's head banged the clay floor and he yelped in pain.

"You are to never question me in front of others again," Cyril whispered, trembling. "Is this too complicated for a little boy like you to comprehend? Never speak against me again!"

Peter's eyes watered in a combination of pain, shame, and surprise. Cyril kept his foot on Peter's stomach, pressing firmly to pin him to the floor.

"Your archbishop is asking you, *now*, exactly what happened this morning," Cyril said.

Peter related the events of the last two hours. How Tobias had been giving the early Mass. How the man had praised the destruction of the Jewish temple. How he had promised future victories. Then how three men had suddenly stood in the church, revealed themselves as city guards, and arrested the priest, literally carrying him out while the parishioners cried and cursed.

Cyril listened with growing anxiety. When Peter had finished, he stepped off of him and turned away, not wanting Peter to see his face as he worried what to do.

If I hadn't gone walking this morning, he thought, then I might have been the one arrested instead of Tobias. They might have barged into my rectory and pulled me out of bed! But no…Orestes isn't a madman. He knows he can't arrest me. He sent those guards to Mass to enforce his foolish decree, but would never have authorized them to spirit *me* away if *I* had been giving the Mass. He picks on my subordinates, my followers. Never on me. Like a game of chess, the king can never be captured.

"The prefect is my newest opposition," Cyril said, more to himself than to Peter. Peter sat up, brushed off his tunic.

"He has never shown himself to be a Jew sympathizer," Peter chanced to say. "But neither is he an attendant at church, Archbishop."

"Are you a faithful servant, Peter?"

"Yes!" Peter cried, astonished at the implication. "Forgive me for speaking to you the way I did. I serve you, Cyril! I serve God!"

Cyril walked to his desk. Peter watched as he dipped a feather-pen in an ink jar and began writing a short letter. When the ink had dried, Cyril rolled the parchment tightly. He removed his bronze ring and slid the letter into the ring's embrace.

"I have a mission for you, Peter." Cyril looked ancient all of a sudden. The lines on his face seemed to delineate an antediluvian being who lived forever and only changed his name down through the centuries. His withered lips moved again: "I have a journey for you to undertake."

CHAPTER 17

▼

"Thasos!"

He turned at the sound of his name, gazing across the dining hall to see three of his classmates watching him from where they were seated at one of the tables. The hall was open, airy, and the scent of fresh grass swept through it pleasantly. Food was being prepared over a flame-pit and served steaming hot to the students.

"I've been a stranger, I apologize," Thasos said as he joined them, taking a spare seat. It was Karam who had spoken, dressed in an orange tunic and flanked by the blonde Celtic man—Thasos had learned his name was Torsten—and one of the two brother-types from class, named Basilio.

"You have," Karam agreed in a surreptitious tone. "You're not eating?"

"Not hungry," Thasos replied, though the sight of Karam's plate—porridge and a slice of herb-seasoned duck—looked delicious. Torsten, by contrast, was hungrily spooning thick clumps of food into his mouth. Thasos added, "I enjoyed your class presentations."

"And I enjoyed yours," Karam replied, his eyes merry and friendly. "On Seneca. It was inspiring."

"It was adequate, I hope."

"You're wondering if Hypatia enjoyed it?"

Thasos was taken aback by his peer's perceptiveness. "I don't require her enthusiasm. She holds us to a high standard, that's all, and I'm doing my best in meeting it." I *don't* require her enthusiasm, he thought. But this ache in my heart could certainly use some.

During the past few days Thasos had discovered an alarming increase in his feelings for her. She stayed with him, in memory, throughout each day. It's not just her body, he thought, but her smile, her energy, her passion, her words, her history. It's love.

For a moment, Thasos was tempted to spill Theon's secret prediction. He wanted to boast of his own privileged relationship with Hypatia…the woman every man wanted and none could have! The urge passed when he realized there was a strange, exotic intimacy in being one of the keepers of that secret. Thasos felt joined with her on a clandestine level, which no would-be suitor could ever attain. A man might touch Hypatia's hand in greeting, Thasos mused. Yet I have something better than that. I have a piece of her mind, her trust, and her faith.

In a way, we're already involved.

Basilio, in a squeaky voice that didn't seem to belong to him, said, "Thasos? Are you still with us?"

"Yes," Thasos said sheepishly.

Torsten grinned like a giddy Visigothic warrior. "A man only smiles like that when he has gone into the arms of a lovely woman."

"Does he?" Thasos challenged, embarrassed.

"He's blushing," Torsten observed.

"Certainly not."

"Look! He's as red as a tomato!"

Thasos shook his head, but his lips surrendered to a helpless smile.

"Only a woman," Torsten continued, undeterred, "could bring that kind of light to a man's face."

Karam regarded the Celt. "What would a man from Gaul know of that? I hear your homeland's women are indistinguishable from its men!"

"That comment," Torsten warned, "would get you killed where I'm from."

A playful banter erupted between the Arab and the Celt, for which Thasos was glad. But soon their attention returned to him.

"You've been mysterious, Thasos," Karam said with a glimmer in his dark eyes. "It is somewhat of a tradition, I hear, for men to confess their backgrounds when they become Library students. You haven't lingered long enough for us to ask. Come now, fill the pages for us."

Thasos shrugged. "There is not a single drop of mystery to me, I'm sorry to tell."

"You're Greek," Karam observed, to which Thasos nodded.

"And your father worked for the Library?"

"He was a scholar, yes."

"He must be proud of you then." Torsten studied his face.

"I don't know. He died when I was very young, but I know he was a student of Theon, Hypatia's father."

His words had an immediate effect on them.

"It looks like you're not quite so boring then, Greek," Karam said, pushing his plate of food away. "What about your father's father? Was he a scholar here, too? There are dynasties of philosophers at the Library, you know. Men whose ancestors were employed when Alexander still walked the Earth. Like Hypatia's family."

Thasos was startled. "You know her lineage? I only know about Theon."

"Theon comes from a long line of scientists, ask anyone. Her family dates back to the earliest Ptolemies. That's the case with most of the teachers here. Do you know Professor Amedio? He can supposedly trace his line to the old librarians of Babylon, two thousand years ago. What about you? Is Socrates or Pericles in your blood?"

"No," Thasos said flatly. "I come from a long line of craftsmen. We were carving stone, chopping wood, or blowing glass while others were conquering the world. Like I said, it's a boring tale."

Was that true? he wondered. Did my ancestors do nothing extraordinary? Or did they devote themselves to the mundane—building roads, digging canals, setting foundations—that allowed the extraordinary to live? Or was one of them a thinker, somewhere back in the mists of yesteryear? How much personal history is transmitted from one generation to the next? I have my father's build, my mother's skin…did I inherit my father's aptitude for study as well? How much of ourselves are we born with, and how much do we develop as we go along? After all, my grandfather who died before my birth was only a mason, from a long line of masons. How exactly did my father get started at the Great Library? It was a question Thasos was suddenly desperate to ask, though there was no one to answer him.

I miss you father, Thasos thought. I am reminded again of all that I lost when you passed on.

Another question, lifting out of his subconscious like a bird taking wing: What about my classmates and *their* families' histories? Were they the products of great traditions, or happenstance students like me?

"Tell me of yourselves," Thasos began. "Your own stories must be better than mine!"

They were. At least, Thasos was humbled by their unique origins. Torsten was the son of a Goth nobleman and heir to his clan. He had been sent by his father to study at the Great Library so he would become an enlightened ruler.

"It will break tradition," Torsten said quietly. "My clan has not been known for its intellectuals."

Indeed, Thasos thought with grim amusement. Your clan is part of the horde that swallowed the Roman Empire, isn't it? Should I hate you then, Torsten? Your roughly-drawn face, your golden hair tied in barbarian braids, your uncouth accent...are you the enemy of civilization or its newest inheritor?

Basilio spoke next. He and his brother were the product of spoiled wealth. Their families were in Constantinople, rich and noble. Thasos furtively glanced from Basilio to Torsten, comparing the two. Aren't you both equally capable of achieving in Hypatia's class? Does your blood really matter? I don't think so. Weren't all our ancestors hunters and gatherers at one time, in the mythic ages of prehistory?

Karam's tale was different from both. His stock had been fishermen in Persia, whose village was decimated by war. At a young age he had fled with his father and sister to find refuge in the Eastern Empire. Through Fate or Chance, a wealthy young man had fallen in love with Karam's sister, and the subsequent marriage had been a blessing to the family.

"My sister's husband takes care of us," Karam explained. "He was the one who noticed how good I was with numbers. Ever since I was a child, I had been able to do math in my head. Complex math, Thasos. I had thought everyone could do it, until my brother-in-law told me otherwise. He paid for my Library expenses and sent me here. He's a good man."

"I'm sure he is," Thasos said, and thought: This is my new circle of friends. Like Hypatia's, whoever those friends of hers are. Is *that* the magic of this place? Are lifelong friends made here, as surely as lifelong pursuits of knowledge are?

"The dining hall is beginning to clear," Basilio noted. "Class is starting."

They went together to the third chamber of the Hall of Astronomy, to find Hypatia waiting expectantly by the chalkboard.

"Good," Hypatia said as they walked in. Thasos apologized for their tardiness and was pleased when she smiled at him. *She smiled!* Dear Lord! My heart must sound like a legion of horses!

Hypatia dragged one of the empty stools to the front of the class and sat, facing them. She laced her hands in her lap, and sighed.

"You've come here to study astronomy, but for one hour I'd like to discuss a different subject. Are there any objections? Good. The stars can wait an hour. I want to talk to you about religion."

When class was over, Hypatia went briskly from the Library to the Canopic Way, intent on reaching the palace before her next class began. As she came within sight of its iron gates, she saw Heliodorus approaching from the opposite way.

"Good morning, Heliodorus."

"We shall soon see if it is," he said, and embraced her affectionately. "If a good morning is what you want, then perhaps you better see Orestes before I do."

Hypatia was puzzled by the comment. She tilted her head. "Are you the bearer of bad tidings?"

"I am the perpetrator of a conspiracy. I have already summoned the players."

"Players? What kind of game is this?"

By way of answer, Heliodorus reached into the pocket of his toga and retrieved a crumpled paper. He unraveled it for Hypatia.

"The Governor's decree." She nodded. "I've seen them everywhere. I wouldn't call Orestes' behavior a game."

"Neither would I. The game is of my own invention, Teacher, meant to return peace to Alexandria. The players are none other than your favorite students. Synesius, myself. Even Simplicius knows about it, though I don't have need of his help right now."

Hypatia saw the determination in his face. "You don't agree with how Orestes is responding to the attack on the Jews."

"I understand why he is doing it. But no, I don't agree with it...not with the way it's being done. This whole thing is volcanic; at any moment, we'll have blood drowning the streets, burying us alive. I have a plan, and now that Synesius is back I'm putting it into effect."

Hypatia finally understood his anxiety. "You don't expect Orestes to be receptive to this plan of yours?"

Heliodorus laughed. "I expect him to arrest *me* for even suggesting it."

Hypatia's lips formed a smile; she had witnessed Orestes' temper on a select few occasions. "Tell me your plan."

Heliodorus obliged. When he was finished, Hypatia shook her head.

"I don't know if I agree with you, either," she started. "But I suppose it deserves a chance."

"I'm an idealist. It's part of my charm."

She laughed, surprised by how quickly her chaotic emotions from the morning were now settling. The ease of her laughter surprised her. "I wish you luck."

He bowed to her, and went for the gates when Hypatia grabbed him by the cuff of his toga.

"Heliodorus?"

"Yes?"

"Can I play along?"

CHAPTER 18

▼

The palace conference hall was a high-domed room with six columns shaped like rigid papyrus buds that supported the ceiling. Through skylights in the dome, a welcome breeze invaded the chamber as Orestes, seated in a tall-backed chair behind a desk, listened to the Chief Magistrate, called the Expounder of the Law, give an arrest report.

That's more like it, Orestes thought happily as he felt the draft on his face. It smelled of the sea, and Orestes was momentarily distracted from the magistrate's words. He caught himself, however, and without effort focused on the joyous report he was hearing.

"Eighty-three arrests were made this week," the magistrate was saying. He was a lean, wiry man about fifty years old, dressed in a scarlet toga. He had lost a daughter in the street riots of 391, when Theodosios' decree had been announced in the harbor. The poor girl was reportedly innocent of the conflict—she was at the harbor that night to greet her cousins who had arrived from Constantinople aboard the same ship that delivered the edict. When the ensuing riot exploded, the girl had been caught in the fray and trampled to death.

Which makes him the perfect man for his position, Orestes thought in satisfaction. He cares about justice before anything else.

The magistrate continued, stone-faced and unemotional. For five days now, he said, the investigation into the attack on the Jews had resulted in a string of arrests. It hadn't been easy. The attackers, according to witnesses, had all been dressed in identical dark robes. But after the investigation's first day, one witness—a Jewish adolescent who said he was awakened by some fighting that had taken place right outside his window—had sworn he could identify two of the ones involved. Those two were arrested at the granary where they worked. They were pressed to name others. Further arrests were made. Now, the jail cells were overloaded with men—including those who had taken to violently protesting the arrests.

Six days now, Orestes thought, and not a single word of complaint from the Archbishop. He wasn't overly surprised; he figured that Cyril had already written to Pulcheria to complain of the massive arrests. But *I've* already written a rebuttal, Cyril. Every senator in Constantinople will be receiving it soon enough.

From the end of the hall, Servant Neith appeared and crossed the distance to him quickly. Orestes silenced the magistrate with a simple motion of his hand.

"Yes?"

Neith bowed apologetically. "Please excuse me, Governor. Hypatia insists on seeing you. I told her you were in conference, but she asked I inform you she is here."

"Send her in," Orestes said at once. He looked at the magistrate and said, "Your report is almost done, no?"

Neith went away, returning a few minutes later with Hypatia. Orestes struggled to keep the joy out of his face. She was like the sun spilling into the room.

Hypatia laced her hands in front of her and approached humbly. "I did not mean to interrupt, Governor."

Yes you did, he thought, noticing her playful smile. She's up to something. Yet his observation was engulfed by the pleasure of her presence. Just the sight of her triggered a flood of unexpected emotion. Orestes was alarmed at how quickly his eyes moistened.

With difficulty he forced himself to say, "You *are* interrupting, though. Most citizens make appointments to see their prefect."

"I will leave if you wish."

Her words caused pain to penetrate him like an arrow-shot. He suddenly wanted to stand up, brush past the magistrate, and embrace her. "You don't need to leave. Just wait." To the magistrate, he said, "Continue."

The magistrate nodded. "Per your orders, I've arranged for a slave-barge to be sent from up-river. It'll accommodate two hundred people…if necessary." Orestes could see that the magistrate, driven by his unbiased sense of justice, wanted to ask what the barge would be used for, as well as how much longer the arrests would continue. The investigation had already become a finger-pointing contest with no end in sight.

"Thank you for your report, Philippus. I know you feel the investigation has outlasted its usefulness." When Philippus made no reply, Orestes said, "End the investigation at once. Bring those arrested to trial. You may go."

The magistrate bowed, once to Orestes, once to Hypatia. When he was gone, Hypatia asked, "A slave-barge? For what, dare I ask?"

"To publicly humiliate the men guilty of rioting. They will be stripped, chained, and taken to every harbor from here to Memphis. They will be displayed as malcontents, dissidents, seditionists."

"They are all Cyril's parishioners?"

"Most of them. Some are Jews who participated in the fighting."

"Even though they were defending their homes?"

Orestes' eyes were piercing, watching her from across the desk. "I don't care. When that barge sets sail, I want all of Egypt to see that I make no distinction between a Christian and a Jew."

Hypatia found herself admiring his blunt philosophy. "And what will the Regent say, once she hears of it?"

"I can tell you what she'll hear. Cyril will presumably say that he was uninvolved in the attack, and that all his parishioners are being unfairly targeted by me. Anticipating that, I've defended the arrests with sworn statements from Philippus, Heliodorus, and others. 'I don't believe the Archbishop had anything to do with this atrocity,' I wrote. 'And most of his parishioners are good, decent people. Some are not.' What do you think?"

Hypatia smiled. "Direct."

Orestes stood and rounded the desk. The daylight flooding down from the skylights caught his eyes and made them shimmer like gold coins. He squinted while he moved to the shade of a column, and as he did Hypatia's eyes swept over his body in a sudden and shameful curiosity. He was dressed simply, in a dark blue, short-sleeve tunic that displayed his muscular arms.

"You've spoken to all the city officials about this, I presume?" she heard herself ask, alarmed at her rising temperature.

Orestes nodded. In the security of the shade he watched her.

"And are they all in agreement with your solution?"

Orestes held her stare. "Are you?"

Hypatia thought back to her conversation with Heliodorus moments earlier. Seeing her pensiveness, Orestes' pride faltered. He stepped forward as if to take her hands in his own, anxious suddenly. "Hypatia?"

"I do not disagree."

He laughed. "If I wanted to hear the double-talk of a diplomat, I'd have sent for one! Speak plain!"

"I have no better suggestion," she clarified. Isn't that true? she wondered. Do I agree entirely with Heliodorus? No. Why am I helping him, then? Because his suggestion is reasonable and should be given a chance to fail.

"I'm flattered!" Orestes replied. Hypatia smiled, surprised by the unusually affable tone in his voice.

Her smile only made her more beautiful to him, like the polished gleam on an extravagant treasure. She seemed even younger when she smiled, as if that simple movement of lips had shaved a decade off her life. It was tender, charming, innocent. Somehow, it gave Orestes hope.

"What brings you to me today?" he asked suddenly, his voice harder and more severe than he had intended.

That's the Orestes I know, Hypatia thought sadly. But his is a good question: Why am I here? I didn't expect to meet Heliodorus; I was coming to the palace on my own. Why?

"During a trying time like this I thought you might want a friend near," she said, wondering if it was true. "I wanted to tell you I support what you're doing...so long as it doesn't involve bartering criminals off to slave markets!"

Orestes stepped out of the shadow and into the sun again, and with a motion of his hand he invited Hypatia to walk with him down the length of the hall. When she joined him at his side, he continued: "Why else did you come?"

"Why else would I need to?"

"You're being coy," Orestes accused. "And evasive."

Am I? she wondered. I suppose I am, yes. I woke up today frustrated at the world and wanting to do something about it. That's why I talked to my students about religion. Amedio was right. We do have an obligation to address the disgusting horror that was levied against a population of this city. Maybe that's why I'm here...to see if there's more I can do.

They passed by a long wall-mirror as they went. Orestes glanced at their reflection and his heart lifted again at the prophecy in the glass. He suddenly pictured how life might have gone, had he *not* married Marina before his Egyptian campaign. Wasn't that why everything had changed? Wasn't my introduction to Hypatia during the inaugural ceremony the moment when my error became clear?

Certainly, he thought, there could be no couple more royal than he and Hypatia. The Governor Orestes, ruler of Alexandria and caretaker of its people. By his side, ageless Hypatia, greatest philosopher since the days of Plato. The city would throw rose petals upon them wherever they walked! *They are a model of beauty!* people would cry. And what children might such a union produce?

The mirror ended. Orestes was sad to see the fantasy terminate.

Above the room's door a fresco of Ptolemy I was illustrated. The general's lean jaw, cynical gaze, and the enigmatic smirk at his lips were rendered in faded paints. Hypatia traced her hand over the depiction. "Will you have *your* likeness painted here, Orestes? The latest in a line of great leaders?"

"History will tell me if I deserve that brand of immortality," he quipped.

"Or perhaps something as modest as the Alexander in the Great Library?"

Orestes grinned.

That's the Orestes I'd like to know, she thought. When he smiled his face brightened, his scowl-lines softened. Hypatia looked into his eyes, warmed by the intimacy of sharing his stare. "History will judge you well," she said.

"You flatter me," Orestes said uncomfortably.

"You are logical, rational, and strong. You are not governed by your emotions." She knew she *was* flattering him. Is it because I'm setting him up for his next visitor? Or because I like to flatter him, since he takes it so well? He absorbs compliments with grave seriousness. He relishes them humbly. And I like making him feel that way because of how he makes *me* feel.

Am I ready to admit that he stirs me?

Flushing with sudden lustfulness Hypatia said, "Do you intend to arrest the Archbishop too?"

"I intend to execute him," Orestes said. When he saw Hypatia's reaction, he laughed and said, "I'm joking. I will not arrest the Archbishop, lest the entire Empire condemn me for heresy."

"I am glad to hear that!"

"I thought you would be."

Silence fell, drifted lazily between them.

"How are you?" Hypatia asked, absorbed by his eyes. "Matters of state aside?"

"I am well," he said, absorbed by hers. "How are *you?*"

"Well."

He stood in awkward silence for a moment. "Thank you for your visit."

Hypatia stepped through the doorway. Orestes scolded himself for his callousness as he followed her. *She might have stayed longer had you not ended the conversation so abruptly!*

They exited the palace together and walked the stone path which led to the gates.

Say something!

"I am glad you came today," he managed. His voice was hollow and sad, for he realized how empty the palace would be once she left.

What if I never met Marina? What if I never accepted her invitation to dance? He did not believe in destiny. Life was about choices, and each choice opened up separate possibilities. A person could choose left as easily as right. Left...meet people, make friends or enemies, be a success or failure. Right...the same, just with a different cast of characters.

What if he had declined that dance in Greece?

Would you dance with me? he heard Marina ask him in memory.

Orestes imagined a new response: *No, thank you.*

Marina would then have turned away from him and found someone else, married someone else, come to live somewhere else. Orestes would still have gone on to become governor of Alexandria, and two months into his arrival, he would still have met Hypatia. He would have cultivated the same group of associates, from Heliodorus to Synesius to Simplicius. In that fanciful, alternate reality, he saw Hypatia as his wife. Palace parties would be nourished by Hypatia's philosophy instead of Marina's complaints. Certainly night hours would be different...if Hypatia had been willing.

The guards opened the gate. Hypatia hesitated.

"You are a reasonable man," she said again. "I trust that whatever comes this week, you will treat it with reason. Just like your muse."

"My muse?"

"Prometheus," Hypatia said with a smile. "I know how much you love that play!" Before Orestes could muster a reply, he saw Heliodorus behind the gates. The Philosopher and lawyer greeted each other.

I want you here with me, Orestes imagined telling her. Rather than risk her seeing his anguished expression, he pretended to inspect the peeling paint from the gate's bars.

"Governor?"

"Yes, Heliodorus, come in. Farewell, Hypatia."

CHAPTER 19

▼

Peter had been gone from the rectory three hours, and Cyril was relishing the moment of quietude when it was sharply broken by three knocks upon his door.

The Archbishop winced. He stared at his door from where he sat at his desk, his mind scrambling in fear. The knocks, after all, had been extremely loud. Three pounding explosions. Annoying, inflammatory, obnoxious.

Cyril stood up and faced the door warily. His typical confidence was melting like wax running swiftly down a candle's stalk. Were the soldiers here to make another arrest?

Impossible, he thought. If Regent Pulcheria heard that the Patriarch of Alexandria has been arrested, then Orestes would be deported to the fringe of the Empire. The Church of Rome would come down upon Alexandria like the wrath of God Himself. Surely the governor was not stupid.

Nonetheless, Cyril went timidly to the door. As he reached for the handle, the three knocks came again, the door vibrating. The hinges squealed in protest.

Cyril opened the door, and froze.

Synesius of Cyrene stood in the shade of the rectory's overhang, dressed in his plain pale toga, wearing an affable smile on his sunburnt face.

Synesius bowed in greeting. "Archbishop!"

Cyril blinked, shocked. Synesius brushed by him to enter the rectory and made a show of examining the small chamber. "I see little has changed in your tastes for decor."

Cyril shook his head as if casting off a dream. "Synesius? I haven't seen you in, I mean, you were last in…"

"Pentapolis," Synesius replied, and with cool self-assurance he sat down in the chair Cyril had occupied moments earlier. "But Alexandria is my home away from home."

A grin finally broke across Cyril's face, and his skin looked uncomfortable as it compensated for the expression, forced to stretch in a new way. "Please forgive me, Synesius! It is so good to see you! I am honored!"

"It has been a long time," Synesius admitted. "And you have done well for yourself."

"There has been much struggle attached to it." Cyril made a quick search for a jug of wine to offer his guest. Finding none, he apologized and said, "All triumph comes in the face of suffering."

"As a friend of mine would say, success is only possible on the road of challenge." Synesius stretched his legs, his joints crackling with the movement. "I have been walking for several hours. Did you ever complain about *walking* when you were a young man, Cyril?"

"Complain?"

"Was it ever a challenge? A difficulty to be applauded when surmounted?"

Cyril shrugged. "I don't recall it being a challenge, no."

"It wasn't!" Synesius chuckled. "The young have no destinations yet they run everywhere! Now I have many places to go, but lack the energy…it's a sad irony."

"Our energy simply transferred to our minds."

"Perhaps. But I am a good deal your senior, and would have happily settled for a compromise with the Lord. Give me a little more strength to my legs and feet, and I might sacrifice some of my mind!"

Cyril laughed. "It *is* good to see you! So many years, and I barely hear from you!"

"Life has been hard for me. I have been preoccupied."

"I didn't mean to imply—"

"It is quite all right," Synesius assured him.

Cyril felt an old strength returning to himself, rekindled by Synesius' presence. "Your support of me, when I needed it most, is not forgotten Synesius. Your petition to the Emperor was most appreciated."

Synesius saw his opening in the discussion. "I saw in you strength and courage, to tackle the questions and mysteries of our faith. Do you still consider yourself a man of strength?"

Cyril looked astonished. "Recent events can only attest to that!"

"Not just physical strength, as we've been discussing, but mental strength as well?"

"You doubt me?"

"I'll test you. There is a grave matter I need *your* help with. It concerns our prefect."

Cyril's eyes became inflamed boils. "I have already taken steps in addressing that problem."

"Then you'll help me?"

"Of course! You need only tell me what you want!"

"I want you to meet with the governor, and form a truce with him."

Cyril's gray eyes glimmered, half in confusion, half in suspicion. Not wishing to give the archbishop's temper a chance to ignite, Synesius continued. "God gave us reason, Cyril. You and Orestes are very reasonable. A truce would bring peace to Alexandria again."

"You would have me share the *same air* with the man who has ordered a city-wide harassment of Christians? Need I remind you that *you* are a Christian, Synesius?"

"You need *not*, Cyril," Synesius declared with authority. His wrinkled countenance shifted momentarily, as if the young man he had once been was straining to resurface in defiance of time. "But violence is *not* the Lord's way, for even when He was confronted with violence, He only spoke of love. The Governor feels injured by the departure of the Hebrews—"

"*I* was injured by their blindness!"

"Only the guiltless shall throw the first stones, Cyril."

Cyril's fingernails bit his skin. "You supported me."

"Yes," Synesius nodded. "But Cyril, the city does not belong to you. It does not belong to the prefect. The people perceive that you expelled a population of people—"

"A population of infidels!" Cyril hissed wrathfully.

"A *population* nevertheless!" Synesius said, and the extraordinary weight of his words, delivered in an even and unwavering voice, silenced the archbishop once again. "Make peace with the man you despise, and together forge a pact...not to benefit *your* people, nor *his* people, but *all* people. You must cooperate with the secular, as you preach for the holy."

"But what if he is unwilling to cooperate, Synesius?"

"You are both stubborn men," Synesius said, with an ease that was disarming.

"My stubbornness is for making the people see the glory and truth of God!"

Synesius decided to let that pass, but inwardly he replied to the archbishop: You don't see God, Cyril. You only see your reflection, and beyond it is a sea of people who can only be your parishioners or your enemies. You paint this world in such stark, unforgiving colors! When did you become so blind?

"The end of this week, Saturday, at sundown at the Great Harbor. The prefect Orestes will be waiting for you. You must do your part, Cyril. You must channel anger into peace, for they cannot exist simultaneously."

Cyril gave Synesius an accusatory scowl. "I do this for you, Synesius."

Synesius rose to his feet. "No. Do it for the city, and I will stand with you as I once did."

"I wasn't expecting you today," Orestes told Heliodorus, once Hypatia had vanished down the Canopic.

"I bring unexpected news from Synesius," the lawyer told him.

"Synesius? He is in Pentapolis, last I heard."

"He was in Pentapolis," Heliodorus admitted. "He recently returned."

"Why?"

Heliodorus paled slightly, his tanned pallor hiding his trepidation. "He heard of the expulsion of the Jews."

"Soon far-distant China will hear of it!"

"He came to offer his perspective."

"Perspective?" Orestes belted. "Is this a subject open to varying opinions? Get to the point Heliodorus. Right now."

"Synesius feels, as I do, that you should attempt a reconciliation with your enemy."

Orestes' eyes bulged. He cocked his head, as if seeking new meaning in Heliodorus' words. "Reconcile..." His voice trailed off. "Are you insane?"

Heliodorus sighed. "Synesius is talking to the archbishop even now. He feels, as I do and many in the city do, that the rivalry between the two of you should end in a treaty of compromise."

"Is this some political game to further your own ends, Heliodorus?" Orestes' voice was a scornful blast. "I should sooner embrace a Visigoth as my confidant!"

Maintaining the patient edge he had crafted long ago, Heliodorus would not allow himself to be riled. "The diplomat makes history as often as the warrior, just not in the same flash of fire and bronze."

Orestes tried his best to overcome his outrage. "With one population uprooted, *now* we talk peace?"

"The tide can turn in either direction for us, Orestes. Make the attempt. Meet with him, and afterwards it will be known that you met with him to try and quell this conflict. History will record it. People remember truces."

Orestes was silent in consideration. Hypatia's words returned to him like a dream: *You are logical, rational, and strong. You are not governed by your emotions.*

Heliodorus pressed his advantage. "Hatred of Jews is not Cyril's only policy. Like his uncle, Cyril considers pagans to be the enemies of God."

Orestes nodded vigorously. "Which applies to you, Egyptian. What does your quarter think of all this?"

"The Egyptians think of Cyril as the latest Set, trying to dethrone the true king. However, they will not take sides openly."

"Make your point."

"Meet with him and craft a treaty which will protect those you care about while staying out of the archbishop's way. He will not be anxious to cross you again, Orestes. The hippos share the same water with crocodiles, in an uneasy but resilient peace."

"Synesius stands by his faith, of course," Orestes said, disgusted.

"Synesius has no love for Cyril. He does this out of concern for another."

Orestes stared at Heliodorus a moment. Finally, he nodded in understanding.

"I suppose that the most *reasonable* thing for me to do would be to take part in this conspiracy."

"That would be akin to reason, Orestes."

Orestes sighed irritably. "Fine. I'll meet him next week, after the trial of his damn henchmen!" He spoke quickly, discarding unpalatable words.

"Governor? If I may, Cyril has been told you intend to meet him at the end of this week, by the harbor at sunset. He has no Mass that evening, and I believe that your own schedule is clear, too. In this matter, expedience is the most prudent art."

For a moment Heliodorus thought he had overstepped his bounds, that Orestes would explode in fiery wrath and revoke the lawyer's ambassadorial title. Anger steamed behind the prefect's eyes like rain water dancing on sun-baked earth. But all Orestes said was, "At sunset, then. Advise Cyril that I do not enjoy waiting."

Heliodorus sighed in quiet relief. "I certainly will."

CHAPTER 20

▼

Three days later on the rocky coastline of the Great Harbor, Orestes squinted into the wind and watched the sea break against the feet of the small island where the Pharos Lighthouse stood. The island was an oblong, unwelcoming formation a half mile north off the Alexandrian coast. The Lighthouse, by contrast, was the tallest manmade edifice on Earth and thus considered one of the Seven Wonders of the World by Herodotus. A towering limb of white marble ascending more than four hundred feet, the Pharos had been completed during the reign of Ptolemy II. Its base was square, its mid-section octagonal, its head rounded and bronze. Every night, a fire would blaze from this highest chamber, visible to sailors for more than forty miles like a smoldering red cloud hanging low in the heavens.

The sun was setting as Orestes stood gazing at the Pharos and the open sea beyond it. The top of the Lighthouse was still dark; its fire would not be lit until the first stars hatched in the black sky. Orestes' eyes went to the small cabin at the base of the Lighthouse, in which the Keepers of the Pharos lived. The Keepers were an ancient family line first appointed by Ptolemy II. Their devotion to the Lighthouse's upkeep was fanatical, and they lived on the island as voluntary recluses, exempt from taxation, rarely seen except when they rowed ashore for supplies or visits to the palace to deliver annual reports on the Pharos' condition.

What a strange life you people live, Orestes thought. You're like a pagan cult, I suppose, untouched by time. The world changes, yet you live on that tiny prison immune to all transformations. Rome rises, expands, falls, and you only learn about such things when you visit our world. Orestes couldn't decide if their life was idyllic or cowardly. He had visited them only once to watch how they worked, how they brandished brass keys and unlocked the Lighthouse door, ascended the dank staircase, and then like alchemists mixed the recipe for a fire that burned without wood. Polished mirrors amplified the flame's light.

He bristled suddenly as a stabbing cold wind leapt off the waves. The sensation jolted him from his thoughts and he felt a chill pass through him. A fine mist of seawater dampened the rocks at his feet.

"Archbishop, you are punctual," Orestes said when he heard the footsteps behind him. He did not turn, but waited until he could see Cyril in his peripheral vision. The man was dressed in a stoic's white tunic with a white sash tied at his waist. He stood left of Orestes, separated by several arms' lengths.

"And you," Cyril replied. He looked around, taking in the view. "An unusual location for our kind of meeting."

"I suppose our friends felt it was neutral ground. Neither a church, nor a palace."

Cyril considered that. He followed Orestes' gaze to the Pharos.

"It's beautiful structure," the prefect said. "I was just wondering what it must be like, for those people to live all alone on that isle in the shadow of such greatness."

When two more sets of waves had burst against the shore's rocks, Cyril answered, "It depends on one's definition of greatness, Governor. The Lighthouse is tall, to be sure."

Orestes turned to face Cyril, and the two beheld each other. The governor stood a full seven inches taller than the archbishop, and outweighed him by forty pounds of muscle; Cyril felt like a child staring into the face of an angry parent.

"*Our* people are great," Orestes said. "I have traveled throughout Greece and Rome, to islands and distant countries. There is no place on earth like Alexandria, Archbishop. It is a rare privilege that we both share a land such as this." He hesitated, the smell of seawater hovering in his nostrils. Then: "The time is long overdue for this talk between us."

Cyril was silent.

"It is an advantage that we share friends who believe in dialogue between men such as we," Orestes added.

Cyril remained silent. He watched the governor with hawk-like attentiveness. Let him make the first move, he thought.

Orestes noted his opponent's silence. He gave a humorless grin, as if having read his thoughts. "I have tolerated your parishioners so far because I believe that is the message of this city. Alexander's dream was to keep this a place of tolerance."

"Alexander thought he was God," Cyril retorted.

Orestes continued as if he hadn't heard him. "And yet a dark stain is spreading throughout my streets. A venom undoing the glue of our city. For centuries we have granted equality and respect to people of different faiths. Why is that changing now? It is no policy of mine that the tone of the city has begun to alter."

"There is only one faith, need I remind you? All others are false."

"I don't really care whose faith is right and whose is wrong. I care about peace and the comfort of my citizens."

"Your citizens," Cyril said, nearly hissing at Orestes' implication of ownership, "should be frightened of damnation."

Orestes didn't even blink. "And who damns them?"

"God."

"Pray-tell, when did God elect you to be his representative on Earth?"

Cyril held the governor's stare. "God teaches love and tolerance. He teaches peace, Governor. The Jews—"

"I didn't come here to discuss the Hebrews," Orestes interrupted.

"You didn't?" Cyril said, unable to hide his surprise.

"What is done is done," Orestes forced himself to say. "And what is done will not happen again. My decree has unanimous support, Archbishop. Anyone participating in a religious-driven riot will be subject to instant arrest."

"I am curious what Regent Pulcheria will think of this decree. Especially since it was passed without her knowledge or counsel."

"I am convinced she will do nothing but honor it."

Cyril felt his resolve buckle, hearing the certainty in Orestes' voice. How can he be so sure? he wondered. Numbly, he recalled the details of his own letter, sent to the child-ruler in anticipation of Orestes'. *Orestes is a fair and balanced man*, he had written, *and he believes he addresses all issues in such a manner. But the Jews of Egypt are crafty, and their tactics are atrocious. For example, My Lady, many in Egypt know that the greatest perpetrators of crimes against Jews are Jews themselves. Yet they will blame these offenses on Christians, my Christians. The case of Hierax which I have already written to you of is but one example. A woman is raped, and her family sees the benefits of blaming such an unspeakable act on their enemies instead of seeking out the true guilty. This violates a Commandment! I am anguished to write these words, but I believe Orestes has been tricked into taking sides.*

"We'll see in a few weeks," Cyril started diplomatically. "But I think Pulcheria will consider your decree to be a contradiction of the Edict of 391."

Orestes grinned, his eyes fierce. "I don't agree. I am not allowing pagan temples to operate. The Edict says nothing of granting people their own beliefs in their own homes."

"A technicality."

"An unenforceable reality," Orestes said, raising his voice slightly. "Constantinople's foremost concern is civic peace, particularly in our day and age."

"I know you've sent spies to listen to my recent sermons," Cyril said, glaring despite the tranquil smile he wore. "I have not violated your decree…though I disagree with it."

Orestes didn't take the bait. "I sent people to examine your conduct, yes. They told me you've found a new subject to screech about. They said you spoke about the evils of the Great Library."

"There was no decree against that," Cyril said, simmering.

Orestes felt his heart quicken. He suddenly thought back to his confrontation with his father after seeing his mother bloody on the kitchen floor. Old anger blossomed, and through clenched teeth he said, "And so we come to the subject I wanted to speak to you about. I want all riotous talk to cease, Archbishop. *All of it.* Is that clear?"

"I said that God speaks of love," Cyril said, noticing the fervor in Orestes' voice and sensing a vulnerable point. "Those pagan scrolls in that Library do not. Why study math? To count the eternities you'll spend in hell if God is not in your heart? Why study astronomy? To get a last glimpse of the heavens before you're assigned to the Pit? Why memorize the names of every animal on earth? Is it to try and mimic the knowledge of the all-knowing?"

"I was taught that it was to understand the world we live in," Orestes retorted.

Cyril's face changed. His memory kindled, and he saw a new evil more insidious than the Jews. That woman I saw weeks ago, preaching to the crowds by the canal! Peter's words came back to him: *I can only think it is Hypatia of whom you speak.* Hypatia. Daughter of the pagan Theon. A *teacher.*

"Ah," he said. "You were *taught.* Did this mysterious teacher also tell you to stay away from your church, after years of faithful attendance?"

Orestes knew it was inevitable that someone should bring that up. During his first year at Alexandria, Orestes went to church and even to temple. It was political, nothing more, for it put him in good graces with religious leaders, some of whom had helped him get elected. "No, Cyril. That was my decision."

Cyril gave him a cold stare, offended by the common use of his name. "I understand. The devil can assume a pleasing shape."

Something happened in Orestes' eyes. The dark color swirled, shifted. The man advanced a step, and said, "Church or no church you shall mind your tongue! Speak not of what you don't know! Do not forget who I am!"

That's it! Cyril thought triumphantly. *Draw him out!* But faced with Orestes' aggressive posture, Cyril couldn't remain dispassionate, couldn't calmly lead the man into tripping up on his anger. Before Cyril could help it, he blurted out, "Do not forget who *I* am!"

"And who are you, Cyril?" Orestes spat, drawing out his name like pronouncing an obscene pair of syllables. "An ambitious, hateful man who has long been battling me behind the faces of his sheep?"

"The Lord does not tolerate those who question his wisdom and mercy!"

"*Then the Lord has no place in Alexandria!*" Orestes declared and a sudden explosion of waves on the pier seemed to magnify his statement. "Is it the Lord's will to condemn others? Wasn't it your messiah who warned against violence? I see clear enough, Cyril! Your people are drunk on an alcohol that *you* provide!"

"My law comes from higher than yours!" Cyril retreated a step. He had never been so openly challenged. Not even by the Jews. Cyril was suddenly at a loss of how to deal with a man so far gone, so lost. *And yet he controls the city!*

"So you say! So you believe! I don't!"

Cyril's eyes grew wide. "You admit godlessness to me?"

"If disagreeing with you, Cyril, is godlessness, then let me bay at the moon!"

"I've heard of this woman. Heard how she drips sweet blasphemies to our youth in that pagan temple of hers. I understand she is quite beautiful, too."

"I want the riotous talk to stop." Orestes tried to steer the subject back to its original course. "If you bring violence to my people again, I will hunt you and your followers to the edge of the world. I will ensure that your poison does not infect the rest of civilization."

Now Cyril advanced, armed with new insight. "The poison, governor, is the shapely robed woman who draws so many people to her!"

Orestes shook his head, unexpectedly comforted by the thought of Hypatia and the memory of her last words to him. "The poison is your envy of her, that you can never have the respect that she commands. Your fellow Christians dislike you, Archbishop. Hypatia is respected by all."

Nonsense, Cyril thought, but said, "Which puts her in a powerful position."

Orestes said nothing.

"I can forgive what you did to Hierax. I can even forgive your defense of the Jews, though you fail to recognize that they had been harassing *my* people for longer than you know. But now I see that you have a witch as your advisor and confidant. That can only be forgiven by the Lord our God."

"I don't want His forgiveness, for I need it not."

"All people are in need of salvation—"

"All people are in need of education!" Orestes said, cutting the archbishop off. "It is so easy to control people when you tell them they are damned! It seems to me that you do the damning, like your uncle before you!"

"My uncle obviously didn't finish the job."

For a moment Orestes thought he was going to lose control. He saw himself striking Cyril, pummeling him as he had done to his own father long ago. With difficulty, he reigned in the violent impulse.

Cyril saw the battle in Orestes' eyes. "You really are corrupted," he said, believing it. "I will pray for you. I will ask the Lord to forgive all your sacrilege. But I fear we have nothing more to say to each other."

Orestes laughed without humor. "That has only now occurred to you?"

"May God be with you, Governor. I feel your soul will be in need of Him." He left Orestes standing on edge of the rocks.

Orestes watched him go.

A treaty? he thought, recalling Heliodorus' lofty ideal. A peace? A compromise? Let history record that we met. But let it also tell that I stand in the way of this man and the poison he spouts! If my life has prepared me for anything at all, then surely this battle is it.

CHAPTER 21

▼

Thasos bid farewell to his classmates Karam and Torsten and watched them go off on their separate ways as the afternoon was failing. Soon he was alone standing in the doorway of the Library, looking out on a the vacant hillside.

There had been no class for him that day, but Torsten and Karam had invited him, with their professor's permission, to sit in on their history class. He was glad he had accepted their offer. Hours after the class ended, Thasos was still exhilarated by the delicious flood of historical facts the professor had rattled off. In three hours, he felt he had witnessed the rise of Mesopotamia, met its kings, fought in its wars, and watched as the Persians ultimately conquered it. He was breathless by the end of the lecture.

Now, Thasos retired inside rather than go home. He lay down on one of the garden benches while he awaited Hypatia—she alone locked the building every night—and stared at the skylight, watching a spray of stars overtake the purple dusk. His clothes smelled like the Library, pungent oils from the swinging lamps, the scent of old parchment, the freshness of ink, the earthy smell of chalk, and he fancied himself a traveler returned from lands of exotic spices.

It wasn't long before Hypatia's slender figure emerged from the shadows of the Astronomy Hall. She was wearing a silver robe that covered her from neck to ankles, with only her hands and feet showing.

She saw him at once. "Thasos, you did not have class today."

He swung his legs around and stood. "I am well aware of that, Teacher."

"Come to admire the gardens?"

"Walk with me tonight."

At first Hypatia wasn't sure if she had heard him correctly. Thoughts of the Governor, Heliodorus, the city's strife, her father's prediction filled her head. But then Thasos' words penetrated. She frowned.

Is he still blind to my message? Had his recent enthusiasm for astronomy been an act? She felt the insult cut deep. A blush of anger crept into her face. Youth was not an excuse for such behavior, not when the teacher had made it very clear to the student what conduct was acceptable.

And what conduct was not.

Hypatia's eyes flashed a challenge. "I beg your pardon?"

Thasos approached, friendly and oblivious. "Walk with me. Around the campus. Tonight."

Worst of all was his feigned innocence, she thought, seeing his smile. She clearly recalled his first greeting to her: *May I request your company on a tour of this building?* Indeed. It was worse than insulting; it was tragic.

"The falling stars are twenty-four hours away, Thasos," she said carefully. "And I told you I would prefer to watch them from the security of my own yard."

"I know."

"Then there is little reason in continuing this path of discussion?"

"There are more reasons than I can list in a single afternoon, Teacher."

Hypatia scowled. "Young man, I am not available for a seduction. You certainly have your choice of sexual conquest in this city."

Thasos swallowed nervously, but stood his ground. "I was not speaking of seductions. Just a walk between two human beings beneath the canopy of stars. A walk, with you as my navigator and confidant and companion. That's all."

"And what would be the purpose of this nighttime stroll?"

"The pleasure of your company?"

"The purpose for me, Thasos?"

Thasos shrugged. "The pleasure of my company."

"And what makes you believe your company is so pleasurable?"

He was stung, believing that she *had* come to enjoy his presence. "Maybe because during the last few weeks I've proven myself? Maybe the fact that you're tolerating me now."

"*Tolerate* is a well-chosen word." Hypatia said, and turned away, walking briskly lest her anger get the better of her reason.

Thasos' voice echoed after her: "I thought we could talk about Hipparchus. I've formed some opinions you might want to hear, if only to laugh."

Hypatia stopped. She turned. A single shaft of starlight spilled down from above like a gossamer veil, turning her luminous as she crossed it, her robe shimmering magically, her skin becoming a smooth canvas for the light to cling to like mercury. She looked beautiful and frightening, a crystalline goddess or a ghostly Valkyrie.

"Over a glass of fine wine, perhaps?" Hypatia said, her face tightening. "Or maybe you intend to cook me a dinner, and serve it to me on the shore with a blanket shared between us? Then—" Her voice turned sultry, she stepped out of the light—"you could win me over the way so many have tried...and I could be your housewife, perhaps? You could tell me to put away the books and studies...I am a woman! I am a man's property! I am the object of his control and disciplining!"

Thasos' heart was impaled. "That's not what I mean!"

"Do you think you're the first would-be suitor to me?" Hypatia bellowed, causing him to shrink from her. "I have handled others in more dramatic ways! I'll not be an item to be packaged and told what to do, what to think, and what to love! This is the lesson I hoped you would have learned from our first encounter Thasos, native to Alexandria!"

"A walk, between two human beings...under the stars. That's all I want!"

Hypatia's eyes pinned him with scrutiny. "No, student. That's not all you want." And again she turned away.

His heart beat furiously as he sprang after her. "Everyone says that your father was a great man. Intelligent, driven, passionate about his work...much like you. I believe there is no woman like you in all the world. I believe that you have outdone your father's accomplishments. I am even reading one of your books. I'm...only on Page Nine, but it reads the way you talk. Exactly. For that alone, I know it will impress me, touch me, and teach me."

"Flattery is often a way to a woman's heart, Thasos. You're an accomplished tactician, I'll give you that."

"This isn't a tactic! We're not at war! I don't care that others have treated you as a lesser being. They were fools! Would you reject my friendship because of how some people treated you twenty-five years ago in *Athens?!*"

Hypatia spun around and said hotly, "You know *nothing* of me, and you are out of line, student!"

"I *would* like to know something of you!" he exclaimed, desperate. "I thought we were...I thought we were enjoying one another. I thought—"

"You thought you were netting me, Thasos." Hypatia said the words with disgust. She suddenly saw the past few classes as a string of attempts at earning her trust, like enticing an animal with breadcrumbs.

He flushed angrily. "You think I've been studying Seneca to net you? You think I'm playing some god-cursed game!" Aren't I? he thought crazily, his thoughts in turmoil. "I'm learning under your tutelage! I'm doing what my father wanted of me! And I enjoy your company, dammit! I don't come here to seduce you! I *don't!*"

Then he wondered: Don't I?

Hypatia saw how he was trying to convince himself more than her, but before she could reply he said, "I enjoy your lectures and our conversations! Is it so indelicate that I ask to enjoy your company? No wine! No food...I can't even cook that well! Just you and me and the stars! I didn't come here today to start a war with you! Some day all that will be left of you will be in your books and papers! Future audiences will read your words, and I can only hope they will be as touched by your mind as I am. But I have the chance to know *you*, as a person. Future people will never be able to walk with you. I ask for that privilege."

The words seemed to pour from somewhere deep inside him, as if they were pre-written and he were simply reciting them from a chalkboard in his heart.

Hypatia studied him. "I respectfully decline."

Thasos felt the pain of rejection like a lance in his chest. "Do you think me a liar?"

"I think you've convinced yourself that you want only my words."

He held out his arms helplessly. "Yes, Professor Hypatia, I find you more beautiful than Aphrodite! But tonight *is* about words! Would you feel more comfortable if we walked with a screen held between us, so I can only hear your voice?"

"I'm comfortable with our relationship in class. I have no interest in knowing you beyond that."

Thasos hardened his face, to avoid letting her see how much she had stung him. "You're a coward, Hypatia. You judge me so readily, when I think *you're* the one hiding from the possibility of a relationship with *anyone!*"

Now it was her whose face tightened, offended by the observation. "And so the truth comes out, Thasos. You *are* seeking a relationship, beyond that of a student and his teacher."

Thasos ground his teeth, shocked by the trap he had walked into. And why not? I *do* want a relationship with her! She's not wrong.

For a moment he recalled Theon's letter, the one he had discovered in her laboratory. Would it be a haughty tactic to paraphrase those words now?

"I am closing the Library for the night," Hypatia said firmly. "You have a home, Thasos. Go. If you want to plant your flag, find some willing whore!"

Thasos almost cried at the cruelty in her voice. *What would you know of physical affection?* he wanted to scream at her. Instead, he said, "If I wanted such things, dearest Teacher, then I wouldn't be devoting my days to your class. To this place. To you." He made for the doors, trying not to dash as tears spilled from his eyes. His heart ached like a festering wound.

Hypatia stared after him. She wandered to the gardens, trying to relax. She regarded her reflection in the garden water, watching it slide and shift like liquid glass.

After her Debate with Schoolmaster Tyndarus, the Elders of the school asked her to remain with them another year. At first, she wasn't sure. She wrote to her father for his opinion on the matter, and he responded with exploding enthusiasm. *Accept it!* he had written in his excited scribble. *Hypatia, I don't think you realize what an honor you have been given! You have the chance to showcase the strength of your mind to them! Accept it, my daughter, and know that you have done something to make yourself proud throughout all of your days!*

Yet what were such accomplishments, if she was always to be considered a game-animal to be hunted? She might as well take to teaching behind a brick wall so her students could indeed only hear her voice.

The Main Hall's silence was terrible after her fight. The omnipresent quietude seemed to chastize her for losing her temper.

And why did I lose my temper so fast? she wondered. I was harsh with him, but sometimes a dosage of pain forces maturity. Thasos needs to realize that he cannot be held hostage to his feelings. From somewhere else in her mind, a whispering voice taunted: The same way you're a hostage to your books and chastity?

"Nonsense," Hypatia told her reflection. She heard the lack of conviction in her voice. And then, as if the garden waters were clouding over by magic, she seemed to see in them an old letter her father had given her. It was a letter she kept in her laboratory desk:

Hypatia,

Today is your twentieth birthday. You have conquered Athens without need of an army! You have made me very proud, and I can already see that you will surpass your father in accomplishment and reputation. This, too, I admit with pride and joy. I haven't the words to elaborate on this feeling in my heart.

I understand, too, that you have learned difficult lessons in Athens. It is the way of society that you will be seen as a woman first, and thus will need to battle for respect because of it. Absurd? Indeed! Yet this is your challenge, just or unjust. You will surmount it. I often marvel at your strength of thought and of character. I can't say this power came from me or your mother; I think it is your own peculiar gift, Hypatia. I only taught you to recognize it, and you did the rest

What advice, then, can I give you on this day? Only this: Do not be too wary of companionship. That's a trapping many like us face; we forget that the heart is as important to nourish as the mind. I loved your mother, and would never have traded that love for the answer to all cosmic mysteries. Why? What is knowledge without someone to share it with? What are we if we have no one?

A most happy birthday, Hypatia.

Theon

Hypatia shook her head; the letter dissolved from her thoughts, and she saw her reflection staring up at her again. Its brow was dark with tension, its eyes brooding and afraid. She thought: Am I hiding?

Outside, she locked the Library doors. The grounds were vacant. The wind played like an invisible cat between the pillars of the peristyle, then dashed with unbridled freedom through the abandoned dining hall. A chill coiled around her spine at this implied extinction of students. For a moment, the loneliness was unbearable and Hypatia found herself fumbling for her key again, desperate to hide in the womb-like security of her laboratory.

She stopped, abruptly perceiving the irony. A sudden wind tousled her hair so that the dark strands gyrated like Medusa's snakes.

All right, she told her father's unseen ghost. I guess I *am* hiding. I guess I *am* afraid. I see that now...but it's my decision whether I do anything about it.

CHAPTER 22

▼

At long last Peter saw the dome of the Caesarion Church by moonlight and he spat into the dust with relief. His feet ached. An immense white callous had formed on the fourth toe of his right foot due to his long walk, and he was thirsty, hungry, and tired. *Three days* of walking! he thought angrily. I've done more than my share of penance for questioning the Archbishop.

At the edge of the Kinaron District's canal, he stopped, planted his rear in the dirt, and removed his sandal to massage his sore feet. The callous, he noticed with morbid intrigue, was hard and pointed, like an extra nail pushing its way out of the bottom of his toe. Then he resumed the final leg of his trek. He pulled himself up the rectory stairs and knocked, politely, on the door.

Cyril answered at once, looking stern and fatigued.

"I did as you asked," Peter said meekly.

"Tell me what happened."

Peter was burning up to ask for a drink of water, but he complied, sensing the man's irritable mood. Cyril had given him a special mission, complete with directions to a desert villa outside of Alexandria. By the end of the first day, Peter had holed up in a mildewy inn to sleep. At first light, he continued the trek and arrived at a community of sandstone hovels, little more than caves carved out of the red desert cliffs above the Nile's Delta.

It was badland country, unliveable, unfarmable. There was no soil, only hot rock and wind-driven sand and a natural amphitheater lying at the foot of the caves that pockmarked the low cliffs like dozens of black eyes, empty and soulless.

"You announced your presence?" Cyril said suddenly.

"I did," Peter replied. "I was careful not to approach the caves until I had let my voice carry, telling them who I was and who had sent me."

Once the last echoes of his voice had tumbled off the cliff-side, the first of the monks had appeared in one of the lower caves. Then two others, emerging from their primitive homes along the upper ridge of the cliff. What kind of men would live here? Peter had thought, chilled and frightened, acutely aware that he was an unwelcome trespasser.

The first of the monks approached him, clad in an earthy brown robe. His bare feet crossed the rocky ground without complaint. As he drew near, Peter felt that he was meeting with a reptile. The monk had a small face, round and wide like an asp's, with hard black eyes that squinted from a withered face as craggy as the landscape around it. His head was shaved like polished stone.

"I am Peter the Reader, assistant to the Patriarch of Alexandria," Peter had told him, disgusted by this aged fellow and the acrid smell of his breath. Trying not to recoil, he had added, "I was sent by the Patriarch, nephew of Theophilus, to deliver a message." He then produced the scroll Cyril had entrusted to him.

"I will hear the message from your lips," the monk had said, strangely offended.

Inwardly Peter had been annoyed. But he had dared not reveal this sentiment. The monk was old, maybe sixty, but there was a danger about him.

Cyril interrupted the memory with hasty words: "You told them everything? The Prefect's policies against Christians, the torture of Hierax, the sympathizing with Jews?"

"Everything. Then I read him the message, requesting the help of Nitria."

Cyril's face was fixed in a rictus of undisguised apprehension. "And?"

Peter's tongue felt like a stick in a parched well. "He said yes."

"Good!" Cyril exclaimed. He had been terrified that the reclusive monks of Nitria—the same people who had come to the aid of his uncle Theophilus in the anti-pagan campaign of 391—would refuse help. If *that* had happened…Cyril shivered, thankful he had allies at last.

"Archbishop?"

"What?"

"Some water, please?"

Cyril allowed the boy inside the rectory, where he poured him a cup of water from the amphora. Once Peter had greedily sucked down every drop, Cyril said, "What else happened?"

"What else? Nothing."

In fact, that wasn't true, but Peter didn't feel like describing the bizarre exchange which had transpired once the monk agreed to help.

"And how would *you* address this problem?" the monk had asked him. "How must one deal with the enemies to God?"

"By rooting them out like the weeds they are," Peter had replied. He hadn't been expecting to be thrust into an interrogation. "By sending every one of them to Judgement."

The monk had stared with what may have been approval. "Tell your master that in six days he will be as a general over an army of followers."

Peter had wondered what use these men could be. He had heard of the monks of Nitria. They were ascetics, forsaking all pleasure, living on scarce diets, spending each day and night in prayer and self-flagellation. They despised cities because cities were the invention of Cain, the murderer of Abel and the cursed of God.

"Six days," Peter had repeated, mostly to interrupt the awkward silence that had thickened during his contemplation. "I will tell the Archbishop." Eager to begin the journey home, Peter had turned to leave when the monk suddenly piped up behind him: "What do you read, Peter the Reader?"

"I read Scripture during Mass, between the sermons."

Again, the monk had nodded approvingly. Thinking there would be more to the monk's attempt at conversation, Peter had lingered until he realized the interview was over.

In the rectory, Cyril filled Peter's cup with more water and said, "I met with Governor Orestes while you were away. The light of God no longer shines in our prefect's heart; he's been diverted into shadows." He gave Peter a short summary of the argument.

"Is he possessed?" Peter cried. "His words sound atheist!"

"They did," Cyril agreed. "Yet I do not believe he is a corrupt soul."

"How can a man deny God and not be corrupt?"

"I believe that at one time, God looked favorably upon Orestes. I believe his heart was wrenched away from the truth."

"How?"

Cyril's voice thickened with subtle urgency. "You explain it, Peter. I know you have wisdom in your heart. Perception. Insight. What could possibly distract man's heart from the light of the Lord?"

Peter's lips quivered. "That's a question I would have asked you, Archbishop."

"Think, Peter. What could turn a man's eyes away from heaven? What could pervert a man's divinity? What could distract a man from God? You can figure it out."

The flattery was almost too much. Peter reeled from it, his heart rejoicing at this moment of trust. He almost embraced the Archbishop, desperate to be smothered by his incense-laden robe. Yet Cyril's question reverberated like an echo in his skull: *What could distract a man from God?*

The answer sprang from his mind like cobra striking from the underbrush. "Woman," Peter whispered. "A woman could do that."

Cyril's eyes flashed like grey stones burning in their sockets. "Two people then, in all of Alexandria, are aware of that truth."

Peter's face became both hopeful and cruel, and Cyril had a vision of the man he would one day become. "Two is a start."

CHAPTER 23

▼

I feel old, Heliodorus thought as he stood at the door to his house and hesitated, his hand resting on the bronze handle. He didn't turn it; his heart was sobbing and he couldn't bear for his beloved wife to see his anguish.

Twenty-four horrible hours had dragged by since Orestes and Cyril had met at the Great Harbor. Heliodorus had tried to see the Governor that same evening to learn of the encounter's outcome. For the first time ever, the guards had turned him away at the palace gates. All they would tell him was that Orestes would entertain no visitors.

Worse still was this morning, when he had tried a second time to gain admittance to the palace. Servant Neith had greeted him with downcast eyes. "Orestes does not wish to see you, Heliodorus. I am sorry." The lawyer had watched, sick, as Neith bowed apologetically and *closed the door* in his face.

The rest of the afternoon Heliodorus had walked to the harbor, sat on the pier, and blamed himself for the disastrous meeting between prefect and patriarch. There could be no other explanation for the dismissal. He blames me, Heliodorus thought. And he's right; I am to blame. As if to emphasize his feelings of self-deprecation, the children who met him when he returned home each evening were strangely absent tonight.

Enough self-pity. Heliodorus breathed deep and turned the handle. From the kitchen Nephthys peeked out, saw him, and smiled.

"I have a special recipe for us tonight," she said. "It's almost ready."

"It smells unique," he admitted, and walked with difficulty to the table. His joints, usually sprightly, ached like dull engineering. "I mean that in a flattering way, my love." He saw the porridge that was browning over the maw of the oven and added, "Have you raided the spice ports of Gaza?"

Nephthys hit him playfully. "I felt like preparing something different."

"Any occasion?"

She studied his eyes. "You're very preoccupied."

"You're changing the subject."

"What troubles you?"

His need to exorcize the demons of tension outweighed his pride in keeping them to himself, and he found himself telling her everything. When he was finished, he felt no catharsis; instead, his anxiety seemed to have sharpened, and with that newly-honed edge it jabbed his troubled heart.

Nephthys took his hands into her own and brought them up to her lips. She kissed each finger. "I am very proud of you."

"Proud?" he echoed in disbelief. "Nephthys, it was a disaster! I brought them together to reconcile, and all it did was get them to hate each other more! And I forced Orestes into this meeting! He'll hold me accountable."

"I thought you said no one could force him into anything he didn't choose?"

Her words silenced him. That much was true, he thought.

"Heliodorus? You set up the meeting. The fact that those two men botched the opportunity is not your fault."

"When I was younger," he whispered, "I used to think that man made his own destiny, the way a man can move a chess piece this way or that. I thought the law would be a weapon of peace and a tool of action, to chisel a future for me." He looked at her sadly. "For us."

Nephthys listened, unblinking.

"But it isn't that way," he said. "I wish it was."

"It *is* that way, and you're only saying this because you feel responsible for something you shouldn't feel responsible for. Heliodorus, our lives are not ruled by destiny or gods. You were the one to teach me that."

"I'm not saying destiny or gods," he said miserably. "I'm saying politics. Factions. Prejudices. It's all too much for any one man to combat. It's like trying to stop a sandstorm by blowing against it. It's—"

She put her finger against his lips. "Let's enjoy a dinner together, and then our bed together. You'll be thinking clearer in the morning."

He nodded with her finger still against his lips. In a desperate jolt of mood, he took it in her mouth and gently bit the tip.

"I meant *that* dinner, dear," Nephthys said, indicating the large bowl of porridge over the oven. "Oh, and don't forget you left this letter out from Hypatia. You said it was about tonight."

"Why the special meal?"

She tried hard to suppress a smile. "First tell me about the letter."

"Hypatia asked that you and I watch the skies tonight. No further explanation, just that it was important."

Nephthys shook her head. "Hypatia. Forever mysterious. Come, sit down. I have something to tell you."

CHAPTER 24

▼

The night sky above Thasos' house was filled with stars. They glittered like diamonds on black silk.

He lay atop his roof, hands laced behind his head. Hours earlier Demetria had retired to bed with barely a word as usual, and once he was sure she was asleep he had slipped out the back and climbed the roof, being careful not to dislodge the clay shingles. For the last hour now, he had concentrated on the sky while cursing himself for the opportunity he had spoiled.

He kept imagining Hypatia, lying on the grass of her yard, alone.

Why did I ask her for a walk yesterday? He repeated the silent question over and over in his mind. She told me I could watch the stars with her! I had forged so much progress! *Now I ruined it all!* The frustration was physical, the shame was worse. I *disappointed* her, he added miserably. I tried to seduce her and she rightfully rejected me. Wasn't that it? Wasn't seduction what I was attempting?

A sudden noise startled him. He looked to his neighbor's yard and saw a stray cat, black and sleek and thin, fleeing from the reed basket it had just toppled.

"A walk," Thasos whispered. His words were stolen by a sudden breeze. *That was truly all I wanted. Just to walk with her.*

He still wanted her…wanted her desperately, wanted to plunge between her legs. But that desire was tinged with other feelings, half-explored and hidden. He realized he didn't want to conquer her. He just…wanted to *be* with her. The fantasy flickered like an insubstantial dream: Hypatia and him, holding hands as they wandered the grounds of the Library. Talking.

In a way, *she* was inside *him*. There was a gentle sense of comfort in that thought and he absently placed his hands over his heart and closed his eyes.

Close your eyes, he heard her whisper in memory.

He suddenly remembered a parable from Plato known as the myth of the cave. Plato imagined a race of men born underground, chained to a bench all their lives, forced to stare at a blank wall on which shadows were being cast. These men, Plato said, would define their reality by what was being shown them…a bench and chains, a wall and shadows. But suppose one prisoner managed to get loose. He would stand, stretch, realize that shadows were being created for them. He would depart the bench and flee, finding a shaft that led to the upper world. He would climb, oblivious to the rocks that cut his hands, seeking only the brightening light above. Finally, he would emerge and witness the sun for the first time.

That's how I feel, so help me. Hypatia broke my chains.

A flash of white rippled behind Thasos' eyelids. Startled, he snapped his eyes open in time to see a second flash streak the sky. It was like a line of fizzling fire.

Another followed. Then another.

Wonderingly, he sat up.

Hypatia saw the first shooting star as she stood beside her sundial. The streaking light glittered in her eyes and she squealed in delight.

"Yes!" She clapped her hands together. Two more dazzling trails opened up the dark. Then a third, the brightest one yet, made her sundial cast a shadow that spun in a frantic half-circle across its polished face.

She laughed, giddy and possessed of wonder. *The falling stars are real.*

Inexplicable, otherworldly, but very, very real. Hypatia craned her neck until all she could see was the wondrous sky.

What were they?

No one knew, but explanations fired through her mind much like the celestial storm above. The planets whirl through space on their annual, elliptical routes around the sun. But space isn't empty. There are other things up there. Things like comets. Don't these shooting stars look like small comets, only moving far faster, like dragonflies through the heavens? If they're moving that fast, they must be close. *Very* close. What happens if a comet hits another comet? Certainly it must happen! If so there would be debris. Every so often a planet passes through that debris cloud and it's showered by little fragments…

How had Theon figured this out?

One thousand years ago, Hypatia thought, a Chinese scholar looked up into the night and saw a divine rain of fire. He wrote down his observation. Years passed. The Chinese province is conquered, looted, and destroyed, and the scholar's document is borne away by merchants. The plunder passes to India. Somewhere in Sogdiana, Alexander the Great intercepts a caravan and discovers the document, which has writing on it he has never seen before. Alexander sends the document to Babylon for examination. Years pass. One of Theon's students, Admetus, purchases several astronomical texts from a Persian merchant. Admetus brings them to Theon. Theon has it translated, compares it to Babylonian texts, does the math…makes the prediction.

Now, Hypatia thought, your daughter watches *your* brilliance light up the earth and sky. She smiled despite the tears streaking her face. Another shooting star flew by; her tear-stained vision splintered it into a thousand shards of white fire.

Now *I'm* a part of that history, she thought. From the notes of a Chinese priest all the way to me in Alexandria. It was an awe-inspiring connection. China, India, Babylon, Egypt…united in one mural across time. What of the future, now? What people, what nation, would look up and see these glittering storms? Paradoxically, it made her feel joyous and terribly alone.

Yet she wasn't alone. There were others who knew, others she had told. Surely they were watching the stars with her, experiencing the thrill of this magical night.

A voice intruded from memory.

Were you to keep to yourself the fact that in ten days there shall be a storm in the heavens, so great that even the stars will shake loose and drop into the desert?

I hope you're watching tonight, Thasos.

What is knowledge without someone to share it with?

What are we if we have no one?

Heliodorus called to his wife hurriedly, "Nephthys! Come here!"

She sat up in bed and leaned over his shoulder. Her liquid-dark gaze marveled at the celestial fireworks. "Great gods! What is it? What's happening?"

Heliodorus shook with silent, gleeful laughter. "Only Hypatia knows. By the morning, I will elicit an explanation from her!"

Nephthys kissed her husband's ear and, without taking her eyes off the remarkable event, whispered, "It is a good omen, Heliodorus. For us."

"Sir!"

"I know," General Simplicius told the sentry-guard as he watched the luminous sky from their military camp in Pentapolis.

"Witchery! A spell of the Devil!" The guard stammered with panic. At his words, more heads poked out from tents, more eyes were transfixed, more lips issued gasps of amazement. Shadows sprang out beneath their feet.

"There is no devil in what we are seeing tonight," Simplicius said with authoritative calm. The sentry was baffled by his commander's courage.

"What is it, then? Sir?"

"Something beyond my understanding," Simplicius admitted, "but something that is *capable of being understood* nonetheless." He looked out over the mass of pitched tents where his soldiers were emerging to view the night, and he shouted to them, "Do not be afraid! Fear is for the ignorant! It is a cave in which the unwise flee! We are seeing a marvel of the universe, my men! It is beautiful! It is a treasure for us to tell our future sons, of the night when we saw the sky open up and rain fire over the desert."

The men were hushed, hearing that. Their trembling ebbed, their fearful whispers died.

Simplicius was beaming with pride for Hypatia.

You asked me to watch the skies tonight, he imagined telling her. Dearest Teacher, I report to you that watch them I did, and had my eyes opened by you once again.

On the back porch of the inn he had been using since returning to Alexandria, Synesius sat with his legs folded under him, arms resting on his knees like an Eastern ascetic. The windows behind him were dark, the tavern quiet, the streets deserted at this late hour. By contrast, the heavens were extraordinary...and had just changed his life.

Precious seconds before the first shooting star, Synesius had decided to make a wager with himself. Since Hypatia obviously feels that something remarkable will happen tonight, he had thought, I'll play a little game with Fate. If nothing happens, then I'll return to Pentapolis in a few days. Otherwise...

"I'll move to Alexandria for good," he said aloud, the fireworks dancing in his gaze.

He laughed like a child. "I never break a wager. It's decided then. I will live out my final years where I am surrounded by friends. They will bury me. I will die happy."

CHAPTER 25

▼

Six days later, a gigantic snake slithered into Alexandria.

From the red deserts of Nitria it came, unwinding across the miles, sneaking down into the lush flood-plain and coiling its bulk at the gates of the city. Then it pressed its head against the gates and hissed. The guards unlocked the way, thinking of the large bribes they had been given to allow this creature inside.

It wound through the streets unseen. Its dark brown body rippled as it went— dark brown, because that was the color of the robes worn by the five hundred Nitrian monks who comprised its bulk. It found its way into the Kinaron District and splintered into individual homes for the night. Everything had been arranged.

In the days that followed, the snake crept into dusky back-alleys and gloomy taverns. It poked its head into churches, inns, and dockyards. It wormed into the marketplace and merchant pavilions. And everywhere it went, it whispered a gossip that spread like a true serpent's hiss.

There is a witch in the city! the hiss told every listener's ear. *There is a pagan sorceress at whose teat the young suckle!* The hiss seeped into private dining rooms. It was spoken behind closed doors, or among wives while they shopped at the Forum. It grew in volume until many homes were hissing in echo.

The native population of Alexandria came closest to recognizing the nature of the serpent, perhaps because their mythology offered a parallel. The Egyptians believed that as the sun god Ra soared through the sky each day, he was eternally pursued by a monstrous snake named Apophis. Should Apophis ever succeed in reaching Ra's blazing chariot, so the legend told, he would swallow the sun-god and the world would know only darkness, and the sun would never shine again.

CHAPTER 26

▼

The blasting heat of the oven blanketed Thasos' face as he pushed his breath through the blowpipe, watching the molten glass swell like an incandescent tick. Seven days had passed since the night of falling stars. It had been a festival week, and so most shops (but not his) were closed. There had been no classes at the Library, either. He had not seen or heard rumor of Hypatia since their last disastrous encounter. That was about to change. The festival was over...in three hours, he would be sitting in her class again. He looked forward to it with a mixture of hope and dread.

His glass shop had produced its quota for the large winter shipment. The finished inventory was being packaged neatly away in wooden crates and cushioned by straw so nothing would break. As Thasos labored, he considered the voyage those products would be taking. From Egypt, the vessel would go northward through the Mediterranean to Rome. Then the ship would hug the Italian peninsula and stop at Pisa despite the heavy barbarian presence there—Visigothic warlords had sent friendly letters to the shop promising profitable trade. From Pisa, the ship would go next to the port of Narbonne in Gaul, and finally to Spain.

As Thasos wiped his brow of sweat, he found himself thinking about that voyage. Where have *I* traveled to? The limits of my exploration are the Great Library!

For the first time in his life, he discovered a sudden desire to venture beyond Alexandria and wondered if it had to do with his study of Hypatia's Athenian adventure. Or was it the result of hearing his classmates' tales of origin? The purple vineyards of Constantinople, the gold mines of Persia, the fog-shrouded ice-bogs of Torsten's homeland. Thasos even imagined a voyage into the stars…en route to Red Mars, opulent Venus, distant Jupiter! Who peopled their shores?

From behind him, a familiar gruff voice intruded into his fantasy: "I went into the storeroom today."

"Really, Zeno?" Thasos replied without glancing at him. "A fascinating journey, to be sure."

Zeno did not smile. "The lid on the gold storage was partly open."

New perspiration broke across Thasos' forehead, and this time it wasn't from the heat. The shop kept barrels of metallic alloys for the purpose of making colored glass. Different metals when added to the oven's mixture would produce different hues. Tin made white glass. Cobalt made blue. And gold powder made red. It was one of the things Thasos found fascinating about his profession. Glass-making was a kind of alchemy, mixing the crushed lime and sand and feeding it to the fire. The result was the malleable glob that could be shaped, like Proteus, into anything. It could be made cloudy, invisible, or more reflective than the stillest pond.

"I sealed the gold jar myself last night," Zeno persisted, following him as he went to the marvering table to roll the bottom of the vase he was making. "And I know that you were the first one here today. The owners said they found you on the doorstep, beaming and ready for work!"

"Work makes me beam, Zeno."

Zeno leaned close. "Do you realize what would happen to you if I told the owners you were stealing gold from the storeroom?"

Thasos felt a bead of sweat run down his forehead and nestle in one of his eyebrows. He wiped it away with the back of his hand. He sighed. Turned to face his accuser. "What gripe do you have with me, Zeno?"

"Thieves have no place here, Thasos."

"I took a handful of gold powder," Thasos whispered, coming clean with the admission. "No more than we use to make red glass."

"Are you making red glass?"

"Yes."

Zeno's smile was cruel. "Then you *are* a thief. The owners would reward for that information." He made for the shop's office.

Thasos shouted after him: "Are you turning me in, or pressuring me into negotiations with you?"

Zeno stopped mid-stride. "Negotiations? What could a skinny boy like you possibly have to barter?"

"Knowledge," Thasos said.

"What kind of knowledge?"

"How to read, for one thing. And knowledge of who Seneca is."

Zeno remembered the odd name from his previous banter with Thasos. "And why should I care to read, or learn who Seneca is?"

Thasos grinned. "Not you, you barbarian. Your child."

Zeno bristled. His boy was of school age and was not doing well in classes. And everyone at the shop knew that he deeply loved his son and was concerned over his scholastic troubles.

"I could teach him," Thasos continued, pressing what he saw as his advantage, "to read as fluidly as the fish swims."

Zeno's eyes grew wide. He reddened about the face. Finally, a peculiar grin formed on his lips. "It seems you do have some goods worth bartering for. In exchange for my silence, you will tutor my child. We are agreed."

Three hours later, bathed and clad in a new tunic, Thasos sat in Hypatia's classroom and found that he dared not meet her eyes. He nestled in between Karam and Torsten as the former questioned their teacher on the text they had been discussing.

"Teacher," Karam said, "Hipparchus is proposing a chaotic universe. That seems contrary to what we see when we map the stars and planets. Venus always rises and sets, just as our calendars say it will. But Hipparchus implies that Venus could collide with something and be sent off course, perhaps even hurtling towards us!" He gave an uncertain laugh. "I can't say I like that possibility."

"Nor do I!" Hypatia responded. "But the universe is indifferent to us. Remember Pompeii? Today you hear people claim that Pompeii must have been evil; why else would God allow a volcano to destroy it? I say that had humans never existed, that volcano would still have erupted that August day in 79 A.D."

The oldest student in class nodded grimly. "We'll never know the truth."

"We do know the truth, Erasmus. Volcanos erupt. It's a natural inclination for people to assign divine properties to an eruption when a city or people are destroyed. Ignorance! The peak of bestial idiocy! There are physical properties at work behind a volcanic eruption, and one day we shall explain them."

"Maybe not," the student argued, visibly uncomfortable with Hypatia's fearless blasphemy. "You seem to make a lot of assumptions—"

"Do you know of Hippocrates?"

Erasmus scowled and said nothing. Hypatia recognized the fear in his eyes. It was the look of a man who believed that invisible judges were floating around him at all times, eager to deal out punishment.

"Well, Erasmus," she continued boldly, "Hippocrates is the father of medicine. We have his complete works here. In one of those works he tackled the subject of the falling sickness, or epilepsy as we call it now. You've heard of epilepsy?"

Erasmus nodded.

"When Hippocrates was alive, people thought epilepsy was divine punishment. He hated this belief, because even little children can be epileptic…and what kind of sin can a child have committed? Better, what kind of wicked God would punish children with a lifelong malady? Hippocrates studied the condition and said, 'People think epilepsy is divine because they don't understand it. But I propose that one day we'll learn what causes epilepsy, and at that moment it will cease being divine. So it is with everything in the universe.'" She saw Erasmus wince again. "*So it is*, Erasmus, *with everything in the universe.* One day our world will be explained. We need not resort to supernatural puppeteers."

"That's such a hopeless, soulless view!"

"Is it?" she countered. "Why? Erasmus, pay attention! Be comforted that we have each other to depend on! When waters rise and swallow crops, we count on one another to plant those crops again, to rebuild homes, to care for our sick! Some blame God and demand we make sacrifice to Him. If your village was being flooded would you, Erasmus, butcher your daughters like Abraham tried with Isaac, because some priest told you God demanded it? Or would you try to build canals to divert the water, understanding that there is a mechanism to why floods happen and no God has anything to do with it?"

Erasmus made no effort at replying. Anger and fear smoldered darkly in his eyes. He was flush from sagging throat to balding scalp.

Hypatia watched him. Do I push? she wondered. Like a splinter, his superstition needs to be dug out or it will forever limit him. He doesn't have to agree with me. But he mustn't balk so terribly at questioning!

The class was silent, sensing danger.

And then Thasos raised his hand. Hypatia jumped a little, surprised that he was willing to speak to her.

"Yes, Thasos?"

"I have a question."

Hypatia straightened, and all eyes swung away from Erasmus to him. "Please."

"I've read all of Hipparchus," Thasos said. "I think he's right; the universe *is* chaotic. Ultimately nothing we treasure is safe." He noted Erasmus' renewed expression of pain. "But if we learn enough, *we* could master that chaos. You talked about floods and how a skilled society can dig ditches to control them. Why not go further? If we learned why a volcano erupts, then might we not be able to control an eruption…or at least divert its lava flow away from cities? I suggest that with enough study a person can *be in control* of his own life."

"That's presumptuous," she said. "But possible."

Thasos didn't look away from her gaze. "If one man can predict a night of falling stars, is there no end to what man—or woman—can do?"

Hypatia felt a warm stirring in her heart. "Indeed, student. Indeed."

CHAPTER 27

▼

In his private study, Orestes glanced up from his reading as a strong breeze blew the curtains in and knocked a candle from its base. He caught the waxen cylinder before it could strike the floor, and imagined it as a fire-tipped dagger to be thrust into Archbishop Cyril's heart.

Yet as he returned the candle to its place he pushed the fantasy from his thoughts. I am not a murderer, he thought. But if I was he'd be the first person I'd kill.

Orestes sighed and found his place in the scroll he was reading, a treatise on famous voyages throughout time. But then a stronger breeze disturbed the curtains, and this time his candle was snuffed out without ever leaving its base. Orestes sprang to his feet in annoyance, tore the curtains from their hanging, and glared out at the palace pool as if to chastize the wind.

It's not the wind I'm angry at, he thought sheepishly.

Eighty-three men had been prosecuted during the past week. Twenty-nine of them had already been shipped out of Alexandria on a slave-barge to display them to every port along the Nile. There had been no arrests since, though seditious talk was still being overheard. It had been Heliodorus' suggestion to have guards *remind* people of the new decree, and if they still disobeyed, arrest them.

It's not his fault Cyril is a thug, he thought. The lawyer only meant well by arranging that meeting.

The week of festivities had gone well. There had been no riots, though seventeen people had been *reminded* to mind their tongues. According to guards, the people had taken the hint. The real trick, Orestes knew, was in surgically extracting the root of so much discontent.

Let Cyril make the next move. Allow yourself to relax…you need to. You're growing weary and irritable. Think of something pleasant.

Immediately he thought about Hypatia.

Alone in his study, he allowed himself to entertain a fantasy that had been building in his mind for the past several days. It was a fantasy of him being aboard his royal trireme, leaving Alexandria from the Great Harbor, pushing out into the open sea…with Hypatia by his side. He would stand on the upper deck, one hand on the rail and the other around Hypatia's waist. Together, they would watch the Pharos' flame dwindle into obscurity.

Where are we going? she might ask him.

To Greece, he would reply.

I've been there, Orestes.

And he would smile and retort: *Not where we're going, you haven't.*

Off the coast of mainland Greece were hundreds of islands. Some were green like emeralds. Others were grey with vicious rocks. Still others were hybrids of both. Yet *all* of them were tantalizing paradises where a couple might go to hide from the eyes of the world. They could step onto sands no human had ever set foot on before and claim it for themselves. After all, what more beautiful name for an island could there be than *Hypatia?* The fantasy brought a hopeful ache to his chest. But *what if Hypatia doesn't return my love?* he wondered. *What if we reached one of those isles only to confirm what everyone believes…that she wanted no husband?*

I'll take the chance.

A new gust of wind penetrated the study, scattering papers.

Orestes frowned as his nostrils filled with a strange new scent. When the breeze faltered the scent remained. It was pungent, earthy, and very close. It was as if someone had lit an incense bowl on the grounds of the palace.

Moved by curiosity and inexplicable dread, Orestes went to the audience chamber. There was no smell there, but when Orestes crossed the room and entered the dining hall he detected it again. He saw Neith dusting the candelabras. He called to her.

"Governor?"

Before he could ask, he spotted a small clay bowl on the floor beneath the doorway. It was a traditional Egyptian bowl, fired red-and-black. Hieroglyphics wound around its lip. A small flame danced in its center. The smell was very strong.

Neith followed his gaze. "Sorry Governor. The Lady returned from market early this morning and gave me the bowl. She ordered me to light it and put it there."

"Did she say *why?*"

The servant shook her head. "She only said we needed it for protection."

"Where the hell is she?"

Neith opened her mouth to reply when Marina stepped into the dining hall.

"Orestes!" she said sweetly. "I was just coming to fetch you!"

"What is the purpose for the spice bowl in the doorway?"

Marina was unsurprised by the question. "It's an incense bowl, Orestes."

"I know what it is," he snapped. Neith bowed and fled.

"Then you should know what it's for," Marina teased. She started to walk by him when he seized her by the arm and spun her towards him.

"I know you too well to think you've lost your mind," he said.

Marine laughed cruelly. "It's an Egyptian custom, Orestes! When there is an evil spirit near, strong incense should protect the household." She tried to pull away.

He held her fast. "Who is the evil spirit, Marina? What's this new game?"

"Haven't you heard?" She wanted to savor this moment, drinking in his panic. "Everyone at the marketplace was asking me if it was true!"

Rather than erupt, he gritted his teeth, forced to participate in whatever amusement she had planned.

"Aren't you curious?"

He said nothing. His hand released her.

Marina shrugged and walked away. "I suppose it isn't *that* important. After all, she's only a teacher at the Great Library."

"Unload your heart, Marina!"

She turned. "Not just any teacher. *Hypatia,* Orestes! It seems everyone thinks she is an evil, heathen sorceress! They've heard she secretly controls Alexandria! They think she boils potions and casts vile spells to turn officials against the church!"

Orestes' felt as if his blood was turning to ice. Marina perceived the terror in his eyes.

"Given these rumors," she continued cheerfully, "I thought it prudent to protect us, just in case the succubus tries invading *our* home!"

So Cyril had embarked on a new tactic, Orestes thought, clearly remembering the archbishop's statements about Hypatia during their meeting. He surely knows she is no witch. But he also knows that she is dear to me.

A moment later Orestes was at the palace stables, personally hitching two horses to his chariot to carry him to the Great Library as fast as they could manage.

The chariot driver was a young attendant who instantly perceived the governor's frantic mood as he climbed aboard the vehicle. Soon the carriage was jostling noisily along the cobbled palace road and swerving onto the Canopic Way while Orestes gripped the edge of the carriage and wished it could go faster still.

Inevitably, the sight of Orestes in his chariot caused a ruckus in the streets. People gawked at the gleaming carriage and white horses. At the bottom of the green hill on which the Library stood, he dismounted the vehicle and ordered the driver to wait for him.

From the street, two men dressed in thick brown robes watched the prefect sprint up the stairs. They looked at each other. They nodded conspiratorially.

"I will assign no reading today," Hypatia told her class as she dismissed them. "Instead, consider what we've discussed. We will continue tomorrow."

The students filed out into the hallway. Thasos was the last one to pass her, and he smiled gently as he went.

"Good day, Thasos."

"It was a good night, Teacher. A week ago."

"Yes."

Thasos noticed her turmoil. "I told no one."

"It was my pleasure to share it with you, Thasos."

"My pleasure was that you did." Thasos' heart erupted in despair and desire. "Good day, Teacher."

Thasos exited the classroom, blinded in the sudden shadow that existed between the lighted chamber behind him and the circuitous corridor. In that darkness, a shape moved at him with ferocious speed. Thasos felt it coming. He whirled into the wall to avoid the collision, nearly trampled by a tall, muscular figure going past him into the classroom.

Hypatia was looking at the doorway when Orestes strode in.

"Your timing is impressive," she admitted, immensely pleased to see him.

The governor regarded the outlay of the room without interest, trying to form the words he wanted to say. When he had first arrived in Alexandria, Hypatia had given him a tour of the Great Library. Since then, he visited it when he could…always on the pretense of listening to a lecture by one of the esteemed professors in the building's audience chamber, or to watch some inventor demonstrate a new device.

He quickly surveyed the empty stools and chalkboard. "I wish to speak with you."

"Please."

Orestes sighed inwardly. "How goes your research and writing?"

She saw through the small-talk; his energetic entrance and savage eyes belied a poorly-concealed agenda. "Today I feel inspired to work on my book at long last. The words of one of my students, in fact, provided the key."

"This is your calendar of days to come?"

"Yes."

"The cures to disease in some distant future?"

"Such are my hopes, among many."

Orestes stared at her fiercely. "What about the disease of fanaticism?"

For a moment Hypatia was silent, feeling his words over in her head. "What?"

"I would like to make a request."

"What is it you wish?" Hypatia asked cautiously.

"Not what I wish. What I *request*," Orestes said, his heart fluttering at the whimsical thought that on such a day as this, he need only speak his wish and have it come true. *I wish for you, Hypatia. For you alone.*

"I *request* that you accept passage on a ship to Athens."

She stared at him, uncomprehending. "For what purpose?"

"I recently received an Athenian emissary who mentioned, politely but sternly, that the Great Library was in possession of stolen manuscripts. I checked into the matter and he's right. Ptolemy III asked to borrow some original plays by Sophocles. He never gave them back."

"I know. No one ever asked for them back."

"Someone is asking now. Those plays are a national source of pride for the Athenians. They want them back."

"They can have them back," Hypatia said swiftly. "Send them with the next cargo ship; I don't need to go."

"Is it reason enough that your governor requests it?"

"No, it isn't."

Orestes shook his head. "You're a stubborn woman."

"And you are an irrational man."

"The request was made of me to have those documents returned. It is good policy to cooperate with our neighbors, and Athens will appreciate it."

"Why are you trying to get rid of me, Orestes?"

Orestes' gaze grew sterner. "You're smart enough to know why."

Hypatia allowed herself a slight smile. "I'm only a woman, Governor. Tell me why you want me to go."

"Because many hate you and what you stand for! Because Archbishop Cyril has many followers! Because each day his power grows stronger! Because rumors have begun, gaining the strength of a sandstorm. I command you to leave, Hypatia."

Hypatia's eyebrows raised. "Are you Alexander all of a sudden?"

Orestes' face was hard, threatening. "No, I am Orestes, prefect of Alexandria and not one to be disobeyed. When I command something of my subjects, they *comply*. I gave you an order."

"Am I subject or a friend?"

"Hypatia! Close the doors of the Library and wait until this hate-monger tires!"

She laughed without humor, crossing the room to him. "Cyril won't tire, Orestes. His thirst can never be satisfied."

Orestes wanted to grab her by the arm and forcibly drag her from the Library. *Let her beat at me in protest! I would do it because you are important to me!*

"People know how you stand on theology," Orestes challenged. "The entire world knows how you feel about that!"

"Do they?"

Orestes stepped back and adopted the posture of a public speaker addressing a crowd of multitudes. "'All dogmatic religions are fallacious and should never be accepted by self-respecting persons as final!' That, Hypatia, is an exact quote from you! And Cyril's followers will reply with stones, far heavier than words!"

"Words are heavier, Orestes," she countered with conviction. "Words will always be heavier than stones."

"I don't have time to indulge such sophistry! Words, stones! Do you wish to go the way of Socrates? Executed for your stubbornness?"

"I was not aware that my execution had been ordered."

Orestes started to pace the room, then broke off with a suddenness that made his cloak flow around him like an ocean wave. "Removing the Jews was only one step. Cyril is consolidating his power. He follows in his uncle's footsteps."

"As fanatics follow other fanatics, yes."

"People are sheep," Orestes said. "They cannot think for themselves. They—"

"They *can* think for themselves—"

"They *don't* think for themselves! People need to be shepherded, and they need a strong shepherd to do it. Cyril knows this as well as I do. He is in competition for the flock of Alexandrians."

"It was inevitable that knowledge and superstition should cross paths," Hypatia said, astonished at how open Orestes was being with his feelings. She could see his desire for her plainly. *And how much longer can I deny my attraction for him?* "I will not vacate my home city when this battle needs to be waged!"

Orestes looked disgusted. "Sophistry."

"If I were to keep silent then I surrender the Great Library to my enemies."

"I did not tell you to keep quiet. I only want you to leave Alexandria for a few months until I can handle Cyril."

Hypatia nodded. "I decline."

Again he considered grabbing her by the elbow. He changed the picture in his mind, and imagined lifting her up by her feet, draping her over his shoulder, and carrying her from the Library the way merchants hauled bags of grain.

"Then the Library will have guards," Orestes declared. "That is not negotiable. I would guard it myself if so asked. But even then I cannot be with you all the time."

"Orestes, I have many loyal friends. I trust in that."

"Strange how you call me by my name on some occasions, and my title on others," he noted.

"Aren't you both?"

"I am Governor to the people here. I am Orestes to you."

"Didn't you just order me to Greece as my Governor?"

Her playfulness, which he ordinarily found endearing, offended him now. "I'm sick of your games! If you had the insight you show about stars, you'd realize my orders were as me, Orestes. And you'd realize why I'm giving them to you! It's dangerous for you here. Cyril and his followers are going to continue to grow in power until they push you from this city like they did to the Hebrews."

"Let them try."

"Those who blindly believe will always outnumber those who question! It's a fact of life!"

"I'll change that, Governor."

"Are *you* Alexander all of a sudden?"

"No," she said, wanting him suddenly...so suddenly she felt it like fire between her legs. He looked so desperate, passionate, dangerous. She suddenly thought of that night in Athens, when the students had tried breaking into her room. She now imagined what Orestes would have done to those boys. "I'm just showing the self-confidence you instill in me."

Exasperated, Orestes shouted with waning strength, "Hypatia! You irritate me to no end, sometimes."

"You flatter me, Orestes." *And I want you*, she thought shamefully, *as much as you want me.* The lust was so powerful it scared her, bursting out of her like a possessing demon. Any moment, and she was going to fall into him.

"You…you…are too important to lose."

Free from confinement, the statement uncoiled awkwardly in the room and blotted out all other sound, real or imagined. And in that arena with all masks discarded, all shields and armor laid aside, Hypatia desperately fought two compulsions—the urge to fly from the room or straight into his arms.

A flustered reply was all she could manage.

"I will take care of my concerns. You take care of yours, Orestes."

That is precisely what I am trying to do! he wanted to shout. With simmering gaze and rigid voice, looking like one of Achilles' formidable warriors on the beaches of Troy, grim, beautiful, he said, "For now, Philosopher, I shall comply."

Her hand rested on his shoulder.

It had been an involuntary action, fluid and fast, and Orestes instantly reached up and touched her fingers.

"We must speak again," he said, his heart elated, thundering out an incredible pace.

"Athens never asked for me to bring back any plays, did they?"

Orestes' face went unreadable. "Good day, Hypatia."

He turned and left the classroom—indeed, *forced* himself to leave—still feeling her hand beneath his palm. And in the lonely room he'd left behind, Hypatia slumped against the nearest wall. Ashamed at her cowardice.

From atop the hill Orestes saw that the quiet street he had left minutes ago was now a thriving, rippling fray of bodies, as if an anthill had cracked open and insects were attacking the intruders. His chariot lay at the center of the throng. Men and women shook their fists at the terrified charioteer, yelling wordlessly. The usual pedestrian traffic of the Canopic were frozen, mesmerized by the tumultuous commotion.

He guessed there were one hundred people threatening his attendant, sixty of which were a type Orestes had never seen before. Clad in mud-brown robes, their heads shaven, they were the clear ring-leaders of the mob. The remainder was comprised of commonplace Alexandrians—commonplace if it wasn't for their fevered yelling.

The chariot attendant spotted Orestes as the governor descended the steps, and in the same instance the crowd did also. Their cries soared to a ferocious new cacophony.

Orestes' confusion folded into fear. Once in northern Greece, he had witnessed an angry mob rip apart a city official using nothing more than their hands and teeth; ordinary men and women degenerating into bloody vultures. The root of that murder had been taxes. What, he wondered, was *this* all about?

"We will not be ruled by a godless pagan!" one of the brown-robed crowd yelled to him.

"Orestes! How is your mistress?" another cried.

So that was it. Cyril's legions had spread word of the meeting at Great Harbor. The Archbishop had fed that information to his pack and they were rabid with it.

Orestes' attendant seized his chance and broke away from them, running to intercept the prefect. He shivered helplessly. "Governor, they came out in force. They're mad, all of them!"

Orestes deliberately looked away from the crowd and into the attendant's youthful face. He didn't want the mob to feel that he was intimidated by their numbers, and to acknowledge them with a continued stare would only encourage them. He would grant them no such advantage.

One hundred men constituted a formidable force, yet Orestes knew the equation was not based on visible numbers. Mobs were invariably built of cowards who rallied behind a select few leaders. If those leaders were felled, the mob would disintegrate. Even the most terrifying armies could be routed if their leader was dispatched for all to see; even the greatest of Earth's beasts would die if its heart was extracted.

"Is Cyril in the crowd?" Orestes asked the attendant.

"I…I don't know, governor! I—"

"Keep your voice down. Very well. You will march behind me and you will *not* look at the crowd. When we reach the chariot you will do the job I employed you to do, and that is to drive it. Is that clear?"

The attendant continued to tremble violently. Orestes was tempted to dismiss him. Yet that would only enforce the idea of weak leadership in the public's eyes.

From the hill, Thasos stood with a gathering of students frightened by the swelling numbers of rioters. Despite the distance, he had heard enough to know what the crowd was yelling about.

But why are they angry at the *Governor?* he wondered. Was it because he was rumored to be Hypatia's friend? And if that logic held true, won't I be equated with her soon enough?

Below, Orestes stalked to his chariot. Head held high.

"You spit on the Archbishop's truce?" screamed a man at the head of the crowd. "You deny the Savior's pledge of salvation?"

"Pagans are purified by fire!" a woman shrieked. There was something more unsettling in the voice of a woman making such a thinly-veiled threat, Orestes thought. Wasn't she someone's mother? How could she be the pedestal supporting a fine young son if she was capable of spewing such wrath?

Orestes reached the chariot, put his hand on its side, and began to hoist himself up. As he did so he singled out the nearest man in the crowd and said, as the crowd hushed, "Your crowd is stirring the anger of Regent Pulcheria! You threaten her rule, and the authority of the Empire! Tell your crowd to withdraw! Tell them!"

Not seeing a visible leader, Orestes decided to create one. And it worked: the stranger faltered, paling, at being the recipient of the Governor's accusation, while the crowd recoiled a step, confused or relieved at the displacement of blame.

But then, as Orestes was lifting himself into the vehicle, a brown-robed man burst from the crowd with one arm held high. In his contorted grip a jagged rock glistened like a black dagger. Orestes reacted swiftly, tried to turn out from the attack, but the assault was too sudden. The monk drove the rock into Orestes' skull with devastating power.

The pain was stunning. Orestes lost his balance and collapsed to his knees in the street. He was recovering from the initial shock when the second blow took him on the crown of his head. Time slowed. The monk raised his weapon a third time, while Orestes instinctively cradled his wounds, crippled with agony. The horses reared and screamed.

Blindly, Orestes struck his hands out in the hope of deflecting the next attack. He could see his attacker making another brutal arc with the rock, the crowd roaring. This time, the blow smashed into the back of his skull and Orestes hit the cobbled street face-first. Blood splattered into the stone crevices.

The sight galvanized Thasos, who even as the crowd cheered and the assailant held the glistening rock aloft in triumph, rushed down the stairs to the Governor's defense. He didn't even know why. The courage possessed him instantaneously. Yet as he reached the periphery of the mob he faltered, seeing the frenzied monks tearing one of the doors off the chariot while Orestes' head emptied at their feet.

As Thasos stood, frozen between decisions, a rock pelted him squarely in the chest. He saw the governor's attacker pointing at him.

"It is more than the Governor who is corrupted!" the man declared. The crowd paused in their vandalism and beheld Thasos. "It is the youth of this city! They are like an army of heathen soldiers! They will bring decay to all of you!"

A second rock, fired from the hand of another monk, struck him alongside his head.

Someone made a blind grab for him. Thasos was no warrior, but he saw that his would-be assailant had over-extended his reach. With a desperate shove, Thasos knocked him to the ground and looked once more to the fallen prefect, who was feebly trying to stand. But the crowd's rage burst to a new height when they saw Thasos push one of their own. Like blood-crazed sharks, they surged forward to seize him.

A hideous shriek erupted from behind the crowd. All heads turned. Like an angel dressed in silver armor, General Simplicius appeared and brandished a blunt iron club.

Simplicius let out a second eerie battle-cry and charged the crowd. Though they outnumbered him greatly, his gleaming fury and horrid ululation had an instant effect: The mob scattered in every direction but his. Simplicius batted his weapon into the nearest of the Nitrian monks. The club took him in the face, raining blood and teeth onto the street.

Orestes moaned helplessly.

"Be still Governor!" Simplicius cried. He looked at the fleeing crowd and shouted in rage, "Who wishes to be next?"

Seeing the dispersion, Thasos darted to Orestes' aid again. His sandals became soaked with the man's blood.

"Governor, let me help you," he said, cradling his head. Orestes began to crawl away. Hot blood spilled onto Thasos' arm.

As Simplicius watched the crowd evaporate, he spotted the Governor's attacker and did not hesitate. The monk paled and broke into a desperate run, but Simplicius, blazing with renewed wrath, threw his club like a spear into the man's legs. The man stumbled, tripped over his own legs, and in the next instant caught Simplicius' studded boot in his face.

With Thasos' help, Orestes managed to stand. Red crawled through his scalp and flowed in uneven rivers down his face. "Let me get Hypatia!"

Eyes glazed, Orestes managed a weak retort: "No."

The last fragments of the monks' numbers, seeing Simplicius occupied with his catch, began a verbal volley with the surrounding Alexandrians. Accusations, threats, and other oratory venom circulated through the heated air. The Alexandrians fought back, and a new fray seemed poised to erupt.

Simplicius ignored them. He dragged the semi-conscious assailant to Orestes as Thasos held the man steady. At the sight of the monk, Orestes' clouded eyes narrowed.

"Governor," Simplicius said, "This is the man who—"

"I know," Orestes said, wiping away the incessant flow of blood. The scarlet smear looked like war-paint. "Make him...look at...me."

Simplicius grasped the man's chin and wrenched him to face Orestes.

"You accuse pagans...of evil?" Orestes hissed with difficulty. His vision split, warbled, returned to normal. "There is no mirror wide enough for you to see the truth!"

The man managed a painful grimace. "God will forgive me but He won't forgive you!"

Suddenly new cries exploded from the crowd. Thasos, Orestes, and Simplicius turned to see the source. Halfway down the stairs Hypatia had appeared, staring in bewilderment at the scene below her.

"Witch!" Orestes' assailant screamed. "There's the sorceress now!"

Another replied, "She's the one responsible for this!"

Thasos spun around, blood boiling, and he charged the last man who had spoken. They collided, grappled, and fell, rolling over in the road.

"Get the little demon off me!" the man yelled as Thasos pummeled at him.

Hypatia sprang down the stairs when she saw the melee. Then her eyes noticed Orestes' horrid condition. She called to him.

Orestes paled at the sound of her voice. To Simplicius, he commanded, "Bring...your quarry to the...magistrate."

Orestes shuffled past Simplicius, nearly missing the chariot altogether as his sight swung out of balance. He bit the inside of his cheek, and the flash of pain reoriented him. He climbed aboard.

"Orestes!" Hypatia yelled again, but he had already taken the reigns of the horses in his hands and screamed a command to the beasts. The animals needed no further encouragement, and the mangled carriage squealed and scraped as it went careening down the Canopic.

Ten yards away, Thasos' fight ended as he was ripped off his victim by two monks. They held his arms. The other stood and grinned at him. "The Jews are gone and so a new vermin must be removed!"

"Release him!"

The voice froze the monk in his tracks.

"Hypatia!" Thasos yelled. "No!" He imagined her assaulted by the remaining monks, imagined blocks of stone turning her pale robe dark with bloodstains. He imagined her head being cracked open.

Yet Hypatia did not share his fear. She strode forward with a withering glare. They shrank back. Her face took on a vengeful countenance, her hands twisted into claws.

"Release him at once!" she commanded, bearing down. "You do not intimidate me. Neither will I allow you to intimidate one of my students. Release him now!" On she came, as if truly determined to rip the monks' eyes from their faces. The men holding Thasos let go and retreated a step. Hypatia snatched Thasos by the hand and pulled him away from them. Then she made for the stairs, holding Thasos in the vice-like grip of her right hand.

CHAPTER 28

▼

In the security of her classroom, Hypatia held the moistened cloth against Thasos' head. The impact of the rock hadn't even broken his skin, but a purplish-red lump had formed.

"You seem unharmed in physical terms," Hypatia told him.

Thasos shrugged. "The stone hit my head, Teacher. It had no chance against the thickness of my skull."

Hypatia couldn't stop the laugh. "Indeed. What of your spirit? Is that unfazed as well?"

She had seen everything, how he had run into the crowd to attack a man twice his size. It had been foolish and reproachful. She could not bring herself to chastize him, though, for she had also seen him rush to Orestes' aid when no other student or professor had dared.

Thasos took the cloth from her hand and patted it against the lump, to see if any blood was leaking. Satisfied, he tossed the cloth onto the nearest stool.

"My spirit is bruised but will heal, I assure you," he answered. She no longer looked like an avenging angel. She looked tired, anguished, and drawn, the lines of her face very visible, her age clearly showing.

"I should hate to lose a good student." Then: "How badly would you say the Governor was injured?"

Thasos shook his head. "He was bleeding horribly."

Hypatia stared at his blood-soaked sandals. She trembled.

Thasos read her desire to check on Orestes' condition. Alarmed at the notion of her traveling through the city alone, he said, "Please stay here, Teacher." He stared into her eyes, seeing himself reflected glossily. "You could have been killed, walking into the crowd like that."

"I protect my students. Especially the good ones."

Thasos could see nothing beyond her face and that penetrating gaze. "The good ones?"

A weakness began in Hypatia's knees and spread, rippling, throughout her body. It was the same as on the night of her confrontation with Schoolmaster Tyndarus in Athens. Courage was not the absence of fear; it was the armor one wore when confronting it. That armor now felt tattered and torn, and Hypatia feared she was going to fall. Thasos sensed this and reached out to catch her. For the first time, he cradled her in his arms.

The sensation was overwhelming. All at once, his nose was buried in her sweet-smelling hair and he could feel her warm body within the enclosure of his embrace. The line of her neck peeked through her curls.

"I'm fine," she said, embarrassed by her unsteadiness. Thasos released her. The loss of contact was devastating.

Heavy footsteps approached. General Simplicius entered the room.

Hypatia sprang upright. "Simplicius! Where did Orestes go?"

The general's face was grim. "I think he was heading to the palace."

"Then we must leave at once," Hypatia said, hastily fleeing from Thasos' side. "And we must find Setne. He is more skilled with the healing arts than anyone I've ever known."

Thasos was alone in the classroom.

Like the storm of falling stars, his thoughts streaked across his mind and gathered a thousand questions that whirled like a waterspout. Would the governor die? What would happen now? To the city? To the Christians? To the Empire? To the Library? How greatly would the world change by the light of tomorrow's sun?

I love Hypatia.

What a study in contrast! he thought. Should only a wall separate primal violence from surging love? Because I do love her, don't I?

Tears dripped from his eyes. He sobbed once and sank back to his stool.

"Yes," he said as the tears unloaded. "I do."

CHAPTER 29

▼

Lying on white sheets, his head wrapped in bloody bandages, Orestes lay still and silent. Crimson rags littered the floor of his bedroom. He perspired lightly. Dark shapes stood around his bed like underworld sentinels guarding a dead pharaoh.

The Physician Setne rinsed the last of his surgery tools—a pair of brass serrated tweezers—in a water bowl. Once cleaned, he placed it in his obsidian tray, a dark artist's palate where instead of colored paints there was papyrus gauze, glass vials of medicine, and a variety of metallic instruments.

Marina, Darius, and Hypatia stood around the governor, watching him sleep. Moments earlier they had waited fearfully in the dining room as Setne operated. Waiting for his voice to call them back.

Setne was an elderly Egyptian man with dark skin and skeletal hands. He had large, almond-shaped eyes and a beak-like nose. His lipless mouth turned down at the corners. He was bald but for a few grey strands sprouting dismally on the crown of his skull. Setne was the most respected physician in Egypt, a master of the old ways of healing and a student of the newest treatments, many of which he had pioneered. Before ever coming to Alexandria, he had studied Egyptian medicine in the now-forgotten cult of Imhotep in Upper Egypt. He brought that ancient knowledge with him when the Great Library employed him. Among the many tales which circulated about Setne, one of the most famous was how a Persian noble had sent for him to heal an ailing son. Arriving at the man's home, Setne had learned that the son was suffering from constant, horrid headaches. The boy had also gone blind four years earlier. Setne had listened to the patient's history. Then he explained to the father that he needed to open the boy's head or else the child would be dead within weeks. The father had agreed, and Setne put the boy into a thick opium trance and began his cutting. Seven hours later, Setne had emerged from the boy's bedroom with bloody hands. Seeing this, the father had screamed at Setne, called him a murderous demon, and rushed passed him to see his boy. He had expected to find his son dead, and was speechless when, instead, he discovered the child sitting up in bed. Still fogged from the opium, the boy had nonetheless grinned and said, "Your hair has gotten so grey, father!"

People called it a miracle. Setne ardently opposed such claims, explaining that a growth within the child's skull had been obstructing the boy's vision. If there *had* been a miracle associated with that surgery, it was that the child had not succumbed to the fevers that usually followed brain operations. They were almost always fatal, when they came. The boy had, thankfully, made a full recovery.

Those same fevers were now the immediate concern in Orestes' bedroom.

"The opium should be reaching its peak now," Setne told Marina. "He is feeling no more pain."

Marina nodded, staring at her injured husband. Her fingers brushed with Darius' in the gloom. Hypatia looked to Setne. "He should heal over the stitching?"

Setne's face was a solemn mask. "He will heal. It is not the wound itself which worries me, but the fevers which follow."

Hypatia swallowed anxiously. She had heard of these fevers, how a man might recover from an operation but succumb days later to life-shredding ills. No one knew why it happened.

A disturbance at the doorway of the room earned the attention of all. Neith entered, followed by Synesius and Simplicius.

"More visitors, my Lady," she told Marina.

Synesius approached the governor's bed like a wounded animal, his shoulders hunched in anxiety, his hands folded over his chest as if cradling a wound of his own. The general followed, removing the straps of his silver breastplate and laying them on the floor. In the gloom, Orestes seemed a dead man. His blood looked black, and the littered rags about him seemed the cerements of a corpse.

"Will he recover?" Synesius asked.

"It is the fevers I fear," the physician repeated, stone-faced and somber.

Marina could not take her eyes off Orestes' head bandage. Her life as a noblewoman had been sheltered from such realities. Only once, actually, had she seen a dead person. While a child in Greece, she had stumbled upon the body of a woman who had been torn apart by dogs. Yet the sight had not frightened her; it had been a neutral thing unto itself. A curiosity.

With the same curiosity, Marina stared at her husband's bloody bandages.

"What can we do in that event?" she asked Setne. "If the fevers get him?"

It was Hypatia who answered: "No physician has been able to treat that condition. We don't know why it happens."

Marina met Hypatia's glistening eyes. "A matter which eludes you, Hypatia? This is a grim situation indeed."

Suddenly Orestes' eyes fluttered open. The tiny movement brought all gazes to him, and his sharp intake of breath rang universally throughout the gathered company. He blinked, his eyes searching the shadows, and stopped on Synesius.

"Come close," he whispered in a voice barely audible. Flooded with compassion, Synesius obliged.

"Yes, Orestes. I am with you."

Orestes started to speak again, but Marina coldly overrode her husband and addressed the physician: "When will I have my bedroom back?"

Setne opened his mouth to speak when Hypatia's hand struck the woman across the mouth. Marina was so astonished she didn't know how to react. When she looked to her assailant, she was confronted with a pair of wrathful blue eyes.

"Your husband is trying to speak!" Hypatia hissed violently. "Be *silent!*"

Stunned, Marina's eyes opened like great sores. Her mouth moved, unable to settle on a response, while Orestes continued softly.

"Synesius…I…understand that…you and Heliodorus were…" He swallowed with difficulty. "…behind my meeting…with Cyril."

Synesius lowered his head sadly.

"I…chance to say…he and I…shall never…speak again." For an instant, Orestes' eyes registered their old strength despite his bedridden state. Then his head rolled to the side and he was motionless.

"He will not be able to stay awake," Setne said in a hollow voice.

Hypatia's voice cracked as she exclaimed, "Will he live?"

"His heart beats in his neck," Setne observed. "He still breathes. The opium is strong. The next few days are critical."

Marina's mouth was numb where Hypatia had struck her. Her mind raced with all kinds of responses, but she knew she had no allies in this bedroom. She tugged on Darius' hand and then fled the bedside, knowing he at least would follow.

When Marina was gone, Hypatia leaned very close to Orestes' ear. Close enough that her nose brushed against a stray strand of his hair.

"I will voyage with you to see the regent." Hypatia whispered so softly it seemed she mouthed the words. "We will set out together, and convince her to properly address the war in Alexandria."

"We should be here to guard him as he sleeps," Simplicius said. "A man can cling to life easier when he hears the voice of a friend."

Synesius closed his eyes tightly, new tears rolling down his face. *God*, he prayed in silent meditation. *You will hear me now, as I have been Your faithful and devoted servant. Save this man by keeping him here. The world is a better place with him in it.*

"What will happen with his attacker?" Hypatia whispered.

"He will not live to see tomorrow's sunset," Simplicius declared. "I was witness to the governor's attack. I will personally testify against the man."

What is happening to the world? Hypatia asked herself sorrowfully. What is happening to the city?

Orestes' lips quivered, and his voice came like a cracked breeze: "We can watch the Pharos as we leave."

The gathered people looked at each other in confusion, not comprehending his words. Hypatia understood, however. She came again to his ear.

"Yes," she whispered. "We will watch the Pharos as we go." New, hot tears ran down her face and clung to the edge of her jaw, shivered, and dripped onto the white bed-sheets. Orestes' hands tightened like a vice of steel around hers.

"Hypatia!" he cried.

"What?" she asked, rigid with attention. His sudden strength frightened her. Was he dying? Now?

"I..." his voice began to fail. "I want..."

"He cannot fight the opium," Setne said from the corner.

Orestes' face twisted in sadness. His breathing evened, becoming a long and gentle rhythm. He was motionless on the bed, the gentle rise and fall of his chest indicating that the flame of life had not yet extinguished from the shell of his body.

"You have to go," Marina told Darius at the top of the stairs. "They will want these moments alone with him."

Darius looked at his feet. In the gloom he appeared soft-faced and very young. "I know. Perhaps I should stay away for the next few days as well."

"It may not be that long."

Darius' frown deepened. "If he does recover..."

"*If* he recovers, he'll direct his energy into war with the Archbishop again. You and I will have more time, not less."

Darius didn't reply for a moment, though Marina could see that he was struggling to put his thoughts into words. She felt a pang of alarm shoot through her breast.

"I believe," Darius said finally, "that my days in coming here are over, Marina."

Marina felt as if she had swallowed acid. Keeping her voice level and in control, she asked, "Why?"

"It was not right what happened to him."

"I had nothing to do with it!" Marina exclaimed. "If anything I tried to discourage him from issuing that asinine decree!"

"The thrill has worn thin, Marina," Darius said guiltily.

Marina reeled back as if physically struck again. "You wound me such?"

"This has been a game for us both," Darius said, and to Marina's amazement an embarrassed smile formed on his lips. "I have grown tired."

"You *dare* to wound me such!"

"If he lives I'll not be the next man he has executed. If he dies, I'll not sleep with a widow." Darius nodded, satisfied with himself, and descended the stairs.

He'll return, she told herself numbly. He's upset, guilty, and confused. But he *will* be back.

For the rest of the night, those three words continuously paraded in her head like the end to a child's bed-time story:

He will return.

CHAPTER 30

▼

At first light Synesius departed the palace, marching through the blue chill of morning to the Caesarion Church. The night had passed like a slow madness. Every black hour had seen at least two friends by Orestes' bedside, and the palace servants hovered sleeplessly in the corridor just outside. Marina had vanished entirely. With her absence, Neith became the lady of the house. She ordered the other servants about as if conducting military drills, having them fetch fresh water for the governor, prepare breakfast for the guests, and rouse Setne (who had slept in the guestroom) whenever Orestes mumbled too much in his sleep. For his part, the governor slumbered deeply. Only once did he wake, to ask for opium. Then he perished into sleep again.

When Synesius crossed into the Kinaron District, he sourly observed that dozens of ascetic-looking men in brown robes had invaded it. With the fervent single-mindedness of ants, they were repairing fences, digging trenches, drawing water from the community wells, or sweeping the cobbled avenues free of sand. He approached the canal courtyard and they hesitated in their duties to watch him pass. A brooding hostility radiated from each sunburnt visage.

He did not recognize these people at first. In the earliest days of the Faith before Constantine even, Kinaron had been the city's sole bastion for Christians, an inconsequential ghetto, tight-knit and poor. As the Faith spread, competing churches hatched in the district—

Novations, Nestorians, others now forgotten—and the canal courtyard evolved into a lively debate center in which interpretations of Holy Scripture were thrashed about. It wasn't to last. Despising the divided condition of the Christian community, the then-Patriarch Theophilus had forbid the debates to take place, claiming that they endorsed dangerous heresies against the Church of Rome. Synesius' first visit to Alexandria took place before this prohibition, however, and he had happily participated in the energetic, round-table arguments.

Even then, he had never seen the particular breed of man he now saw in Kinaron. Then recognition fell into place. Nitrian fanatics, he thought disgustedly. The self-flagellating outcasts of civilization…inexplicably present in Alexandria!

When did this happen?

As he reached the steps of the rectory, two of the monks who had been scrubbing the church doors hurried to intercept him.

"You cannot see Cyril," one of them started, forming a barrier with his companion.

Synesius barely slackened his pace as he approached them, and his retort was hot. "In Alexandria the church is open to all. So are the streets and stairs! You will *stand aside*, as it is Synesius of Cyrene who comes calling. Stand aside *now!*"

He strode forth; the bigger of the monks recoiled a half-step and Synesius burst through the gap, glaring at the man who hadn't budged. He went up the stairs and pounded on its wooden frame. Three immense, hammer-like knocks.

Footsteps echoed behind the door. The bolt slid away. The door swung inward, and Peter the Reader peered out from the grey shadows within.

"Synesius!" Peter said, his eyes growing large. "You are unexpected!"

Synesius was not baited by the smile, and when Peter motioned for him to enter he made no effort at obliging the boy. "I am blessed, Peter. Where is Cyril?"

"He is holding a special morning Mass," Peter said carefully, looking suspiciously to the visitor's firmly-rooted feet. "You can come inside and wait for him, if you wish."

Synesius frowned as he considered that course of action. "No, but I ask that you bear a message to him from me." He reached into his robes and retrieved a yellowed scroll. He unraveled it gently, and held the curled document so Peter could see it. Without warning, he ripped it in two. He matched up the pieces and then tore it in four. He handed the tattered pieces to Peter.

Bewildered, Peter regarded the papers in his hands. "Is there a word to accompany this gift?"

"That gift," Synesius explained, "is a petition I drew up four years ago in support of Cyril's campaign. It offered words of welcome, of hope, and of good fortune at a time when most of the population was criticizing your master."

Peter glared coldly. "Is there anything else you would like me to say, Synesius?"

"Yes. Tell Cyril that Lucifer never betrayed God the way Cyril betrays the message of Christ. Tell him I will make certain the entire world knows it."

Synesius then turned his back on Peter. Five monks with shaven heads had gathered in a crescent formation at the bottom of the stairs. Synesius broke their line without any physical contact, marching through them as if they did not exist.

Two hours later, the fevers came to Governor Orestes.

He awoke flushed, sweating heavily and begging for water. Setne rushed to his bedside, and, with only a glance at Orestes' condition, ordered the servants to run cold water into the tub. Hypatia, Heliodorus, and Simplicius helped walk the governor to the washroom. Even sick, Orestes was ashamed of his weakened state, but the combination of weakness and opium inhibited his combative mood.

The cold water tortured him. Once he was bathed, Setne and Neith sponged down his body with a cool ointment that made him wince. He was then dressed in a loose-fitting tunic and walked back to bed.

The fever was relentless though. Soon his freshened body was acrid with sweat. His hair was plastered to his wet skin, his eyes wild and unfocused, while the servants kneaded new ointments into his flesh and mumbled ancient Persian prayers of healing.

"It can't hurt," Setne said of their prayers, and he himself muttered an antediluvian Egyptian hymn of protection as he poured a thick, putrid medicine down Orestes' throat. The governor tried to reject it, but was held steady by Hypatia and the general. In minutes, he was sleeping again. His sweat had formed a damp halo on the pillow around his head.

So many scholars and researchers, Hypatia thought. *We have an army of them in the Great Library, and still we lie helpless before a fever's tide! When will one of us spear new knowledge, carry it back, and cut it open to probe all it might yield?*

While Orestes slumbered, Hypatia sat in the corner of the room and pondered the problem. She recalled her conversation with Erasmus. *People think epilepsy is divine because we don't understand it,* she had said, quoting Hippocrates. *But I propose that one day we will know what causes epilepsy, and at that moment it will cease being divine.* Hypatia's heart sank as she meditated on the fact that, eight hundred years after Hippocrates had spoken those words, there was still no cure for epilepsy...and no cure for fever. But who could say when the discovery would come? Another eight hundred years? A mere century? Another year?

Tomorrow?

Orestes shifted violently in bed and his eyes opened. He begged weakly for more water, and when Setne brought the amphora to his lips he suckled it like an infant at his mother's breast. Then he was sleeping again, while Hypatia imagined she was running throughout the Library's vaults, shouting so that her voice swelled like rolling thunder in the building's belly: "The answer is here somewhere! A key, a map to the treasure of new understanding! Reveal yourself!" Perhaps because of her mathematician's background, she began to construct a blank equation in her head and wonder what values to juggle to divine an answer. What ingredients would turn fever to frost?

From the corner, she turned to Setne. "What do you think causes fever?"

The old Egyptian exhaled, his skeletal frame shrinking as he did until it looked like he might vanish. "If you leave a slab of meat outside, flies will lay their eggs in it. Those eggs will hatch, and the maggots will devour their fill. I think a fever is a kind of maggot. I think it gets into the body when the skin is breached."

Simplicius looked drawn and haggard by the lantern-light; the shades were closed. Hearing the physician's words, however, he looked thoughtful. "Is that why war-wounds turn bad if they're not washed? The flesh becomes poisoned; to save a soldier, sometimes the affected leg or arm needs to be cut away before the poison can spread."

"It has been proposed. But these maggots would have to be small…far smaller than the tiniest flea. Smaller than even Aristotle's eyes could tell."

Hypatia suddenly wished that her interests—astronomy, philosophy, mathematics—had encompassed medicine too. So much had been found already in that field. Men like Herophilus, a Library scholar who had distinguished the brain as a central point of command for the body and the heart as its director of blood; his successor Eristratos, who charted the digestive system and the effects of nutrition on the body; Galen, who had written a fifteen-volume set on human anatomy and the medicinal arts…and there were others, even now, enthusiastically striving to discover the great panacea.

But would any of it come in time to help Orestes? She realized how helpless she was. Her frustration coiled and knotted inside her. She looked at Orestes, and gasped when she saw he was staring at her.

"My assailant," Orestes whispered. "Who was he?"

Simplicius replied in a bristly voice, "A monk from Nitria, Governor. An unknown number of them infiltrated the city days ago. Heliodorus convened a meeting of the city councilmen and ordered all border guards interrogated. So far we've learned nothing."

"He…is…incarcerated?"

"In two hours, the trial will be held. I will testify, Governor."

Orestes tried to form a word. Abruptly he cried, softly, in pain. Setne scrambled to mix another dose of opium. New rivulets of sweat spilled down the governor's face, and with evident difficulty he managed to say, "Testify." He waited for the opium, and once he had drunk the partially-dissolved powder, he strained his next few words: "When…he is convicted…you have my decree that he is…to be executed."

Simplicius nodded grimly.

"Executed," Orestes repeated.

"Yes, Governor."

The trial was swift and saw Orestes' command carried out instantly when the conviction was rendered by the judges. The monk was named Ammonius, and he faced a panel of ten witnesses, including Simplicius, who had seen him attack the prefect. Heliodorus himself prosecuted Ammonius, and when the judgment was issued he led the monk to the execution platform—a raised wooden stage with a bench and bucket to catch decapitated heads.

The attending crowd condemned Ammonius as the executioner's axe swung, but there were many in the crowd who cheered their support. Most of these, Heliodorus noted dourly, were Ammonius' brown-robed peers. At the execution's conclusion, verbal sparring exploded amongst the two sides of the crowd.

"I was willing to testify," Hypatia told Heliodorus when the mob was forced by court guards to disperse, civil servants still scrubbing the blood from the platform. "I told you that before you started."

"I know." Heliodorus watched the monks exit the courtyard in single file. "And like before, I told you no. For one thing, you didn't witness the attack, just the aftermath. For another, I didn't want the record to show you testifying against this man. You are in enough danger as it is, Teacher."

His words troubled her, since they echoed what Orestes had said. She studied the retreating crowd as if with new eyes. She caught their shifty gazes and insidious gossip. *Am I overnight transformed into a demon?* she wondered. *How did this happen so quickly?*

Battling back her fear, she said, "If Orestes shows signs of weakening, fetch me at the Library at once."

Heliodorus looked pained. "You're walking to the Library alone?"

"Yes," Hypatia said. "It is two blocks away."

"Those monks are out there. Until I speak with Orestes, I can't do anything about them. Cyril's parishioners are out there too."

"And they would be lunatics to attack me in the open, in the wake of a trial such as this one. Besides, I have supporters in the crowd." *Don't I?* Weren't some of those faces the ones I see by the canal when I lecture to the commoners?

The evening air chilled her through her black gown, straight through to her bones, as she went on her way.

CHAPTER 31

▼

In the belly of the Caesarion Church, Archbishop Cyril found himself surrounded by four hundred hissing, yelling monks and he had to shout above their babble.

"Listen to me," Cyril said, his mouth going dry. "The last time the Governor harmed one of my people, I waited. The Lord is patient and so am I."

The church rang with the wails of their protests, and for the first time Cyril felt frightened of them. They grossly outnumbered him. In the darkened church, with their shaven heads and dark apparel, they looked like writing specters distilled from the very shadows.

"One of our own has been murdered!" a monk shrieked, shaking his fist. "What is the fifth commandment given to Moses, Archbishop?"

"Thou shalt not kill," Cyril answered without thinking.

"This Orestes admitted his godlessness to you?"

"He did."

"And so Ammonius goes into heaven as a martyr, killed by an atheist?"

Cyril realized he had entirely lost control of the discussion. Then he wondered if he had *ever* wielded control over these angry desert men; since their coming to Alexandria he had been answering their questions like a demeaned schoolboy. His frustration exploded. Out of habit he gouged his fingernails into his palms. Pain shot up his arms to his elbows.

"Our Ammonius," the monk said to his brothers. "Killed in this city named Alexandria. Killed by a new tyrant in a new Babylon!" His eyes blazed.

Cyril felt sudden wetness where his nails were pressing. "I am the Patriarch of Egypt, men from Nitria! Your man is indeed martyred by Orestes!"

"Then tell us what you intend to do, Cyril!" another demanded. "We served your uncle as devoted soldiers of the Lord. Yet your uncle was a man of *decisive* action!"

Cyril reeled from being openly challenged, like Peter's insubordination days ago. And unlike Peter he knew he couldn't reprimand the monk with a physical strike, for they were protective of their own, and to strike one was to strike all of them. Again, he felt very frightened. Blood dripped freely from his ruptured hands.

"Ammonius *is* martyred," Cyril repeated. The rectory door swung open and Peter himself entered. His presence sent an agitated ripple through the crowd. Peter halted in his tracks, sensing the threat, looking suddenly to Cyril for guidance.

"The silence that drips from your lips is most uninspiring," said a third monk.

Cyril could take it no longer. "It was not my order that you attack the prefect!" he yelled to his new challenger. "Pagan or atheist, *he* is not the source of rot in this city. If my uncle had gone after every pagan he would have died of exhaustion and accomplished nothing! Instead, he had the wisdom to realize that to stop a swarm of stinging insects, you must burn the hive! *So it was* that he leveled Serapis! Today we face a similar war! You have all done well in spreading the truth of Hypatia the Sorceress. *So it is* that Hypatia is our new Serapis."

"Her and her disciples," the first monk piped up. "Like that boy who tried protecting the Governor!"

"They are nothing but appendages, poisoned by her influence," Cyril persisted. "She carries on Eve's legacy of corruption."

The monks murmured in agreement at these words. Cyril was reminded of something his uncle had told him about these men. They hated women because they blamed her for the expulsion from Eden. Who had plucked knowledge from the Tree, and then shoved that fruit under Adam's nose despite the Law of the Lord? Therefore the Nitrians had sworn off women, vowing to never touch anything a woman had touched or drink from the same bowl.

Without warning, the window on the left side of the church exploded, showering the monks below it with glass. A stone struck the floor, bounced noisily, and rolled to the other side of the room.

"Beasts!" a male voice cried outside the shattered window. "You're nothing but beasts!"

A roar went up from the monks and the ones covered in glass charged the church doors to confront the voice. The door was wrenched open, revealing an enraged crowd of men and women.

"Beasts!" a woman cried. "Return to the desert where you belong!"

"You, too Cyril!" a young man shouted, seeing the archbishop. "You were never wanted here! *Never!*" Cyril was appalled. Fat droplets of blood spilled from his fingertips.

Peter had been silent during Cyril's discussion with the monks but he could not stand by while this new insult rang out. "Let us disperse them!" Peter cried. "Please, Archbishop! Don't let them talk to you this way! They are ignorant blasphemers!"

Another explosion, a musical ringing of glass on the floor. "Visigoths!" the crowd screamed.

The monks yelled at the crowd, though the words were lost in the angry cacophony of two mobs about to collide. Let it happen! Cyril thought. Let my soldiers stamp out this offense against the House of God! It worked against the Jews!

But then clarity returned. Despite the din of the riot, Cyril considered his own defense once Constantinople heard of the attack on the prefect.

I will deny ever summoning these men, he thought. He looked to the roaring fray.

No. I will admit to summoning them, because I needed to counter Orestes' militia against my parishioners. Ammonius got out of hand. The others are productive servants of the Faith.

"We don't want you here!" a woman screamed. A third window burst.

"Archbishop..." Peter pleaded, his eyes watering.

Cyril felt a sudden displacement of his mind, as if he were floating above the riot. The answer was perfectly clear.

These people were not responsible for their actions.

I forgive you, he said inwardly to the angered crowd. I forgive you all.

"Be calm, Peter." Cyril wiped away an itch on his forehead with his bloody hand. A crimson smear appeared. He flew forward with new confidence and the monks, turning and staring at him in wonder, parted like a curtain for him to reach the crowd.

"I forgive you," Cyril told them. "Each and every one of God's children are forgiven. You know not what you do."

"We don't want you here!" the woman repeated.

"I forgive you," Cyril told her. His confidence was nearly unbearable. The crowd's protests fell to a dull buzz. "All of you are forgiven!"

Hadn't that been Synesius' point? Cyril had been offended by Peter's report of the old man's visit, the shredded petition. The Archbishop had always considered him a pure child of God…but one who could not possibly lead the Christian religion or protect it from its enemies. Forgiveness didn't win wars. Cyril preferred *Revelations*, and how it described the King of kings riding out of heaven on a white horse to kill all nonbelievers.

Now, however, Cyril felt the strength of Synesius' conviction course through him like pleasurable shivers. These people have been corrupted, he thought again. Yes, Synesius, I will forgive them all.

Except for the one who has poisoned them.

The crowd sensed his surging confidence. They realized he would neither fight nor be cowed. Retreating, casting final insults and threats, they splintered away.

Cyril's palpable fervor crystallized into smug victory. He turned to the monks.

"You will not question me again," he told them. "Alexandria is my flock, which I've asked you to help me tend. Would you be wolves, gutting the very people we are supposed to be protecting? There is one serpent in Alexandria, and we will deal with her *when I command it!*"

Like a brown wave folding on a beach, the four hundred monks bowed to him. Cyril ordered them to return to their host families.

"You too, Peter," he added when they were gone. "I require solitude."

Peter was unable to take his eyes off the implied stigmata on Cyril's forehead or bloody hands. "Archbishop? Won't the Governor arrest all of us now?"

"Leave me be, Peter."

Peter bowed but didn't move. "I'm frightened."

For an instant, Cyril was furious that Peter was defying him again. His face twisted wrathfully, and in that moment he no longer seemed the image of Christ but rather, horridly, the figure of Cain—hands bloody from Abel's murder and the Mark of Sin branded on his forehead. Cyril moved to throttle the young boy. Before his fingers could close around his neck, he regained control.

"Go home. Now. I will handle everything as I always do."

Peter threw himself to Cyril's feet and kissed his toes. Then he scampered away. Cyril bolted the church doors. He felt exhausted. He retired to his washroom to rinse his hands. The blood continued leaking. Cyril grimaced at the irony of his wounds. He glanced into the mirror and held up his palms, watching the blood spread along the lines of his palm and trickle down his wrists. He saw the crimson smear on his forehead, and for several lengthy minutes he stared, as if magically compelled, to contemplate the man who looked back at him from the glass.

CHAPTER 32

▼

Demetria completed her sewing for the day. She folded the blankets she'd made and admired their arabesque patterns while packing them into a crate for delivery to the linen shop tomorrow.

Then she went for a walk.

She startled herself at how suddenly she decided. Wrapping a wool cloak over her blue tunica, slipping her feet into comfortable sandals, and rushing out into the cool air without looking back. The sun was dropping westward. Red, pink, purple, and yellow fought a war of colors on the canvas of the sky.

Demetria couldn't remember the last time she had gone for an evening stroll. Years, certainly. The night felt new. The brilliant firmament hurt to look at. The smell of sizzling meats from street-side vendors' ovens dominated the air, and she remembered how good that food tasted, drowned as it was in cooking oils and fats. Nearby, she saw one of those vendors laying seasoned strips of meat on his oven's grill while four lean boys waited in line, eyeing the food like starving cubs.

Her hand went to her deep tunica pocket. It was empty.

I can bring money tomorrow night, she told herself. Yes. I'll go for a walk tomorrow night, too!

Won't I?

Demetria swallowed anxiously, mindful of the pooling shadows spreading like oil across the tiles of the street. The air had icy fangs and it bit her ears, making her shudder. With difficulty, she forced her legs to keep moving.

Since the death of her husband, Demetria had shunned the idea of walking alone. Admetus had been irreplaceable company. She felt his absence even now, and the failing daylight seemed to mirror her faltering resolve to continue this stroll.

Death had never been easy for her. When she was a child, her parents had left her in the care of an aunt while they went traveling up-river. Two weeks into their journey, thieves killed them both. Demetria's aunt had been a frightful, unsympathetic woman abandoned by a husband years before. Long years of isolation were suffered in her custody. Demetria had no other family. Neither did she find friends to rescue her from her newfound prison.

It was Admetus who did. From their first encounter in her aunt's linen shop—him a customer and her the girl sweeping the floor, Demetria had felt a radiant warmth not known since her parents' departure. Admetus had been strikingly handsome, quick to laugh, possessed of a sharp wit and gentle temperament. He was also a bright man, a scholar employed by the Academy to convert old Egyptian literature into Latin and Greek. Admetus began finding excuses to visit her at the shop. When finally he asked for her hand in marriage, no day previous could equal her happiness…she had cried and told him, *"Yes! Yes, Admetus!"* And when soon into the marriage Admetus received word that the Great Library wished to employ his skills, the news had been joyous for the couple. It meant higher pay and more prestige.

It was also the beginning of the end.

At first, she paid little attention to the long hours he began keeping at the Library. She was pregnant with Thasos at the time, spurring her to visit the new mothers in the neighborhood for company. Even when Admetus missed dinner, Demetria never doubted his love. Each night he returned to her bed. She would cling to him then, falling asleep while intertwined with one of his sinewy arms.

When Thasos was born, she was enraptured by the miracle of life. Sometimes she was so overpowered by her good fortune that she cried with happiness. *My life*, she would think while little Thasos suckled at her breast and her husband held her hand, *is complete.*

Then the change began. It gathered momentum like a winter shadow growing long to herald the night. The Library began to devour more of Admetus' time. It returned with him when he came home. In bed after lovemaking, he mentally returned to those dusty aisles. She could feel him slipping away. It terrified her. Terrified her so greatly she couldn't speak of it. Her home became empty of his presence. It became cold.

Like her aunt's. Demetria felt the return of that old abandonment. Then one night Admetus was attacked by fever, and died the next day, and she was abandoned by him for good.

Demetria felt the memories shuffle by her like the autumnal wind that rustled her hair. She hesitated in her stroll. She glanced at the lengthy avenue behind her, wondering when Thasos would be home. He, too, was spending intractable hours at the Great Library. Demetria felt a blast of terror rip through her thoughts.

"I want to talk with you, Admetus," she whispered.

The wind died as she spoke. She gulped a deep breath, as if by doing so her resolve would harden. Then she went to see her husband.

Like Rome and other great cities of the world, Alexandria possessed its own necropolis. It was built on the sunken ground of the southeastern corner, a half-hour walk from Demetria's home. A wrought iron fence encircled it. Behind these cold bars, a darkly beautiful grid of mausoleums built to resemble houses clustered, complete with windows, red stucco roofs, and ornate front doors. They were called Burial Houses. Inside were rows of tombs and urns. Ivy was allowed to creep over the exteriors. Flowering plants were watered by the watchmen…little touches of life that did nothing to soften the maddening dread the necropolis conjured in Demetria's heart.

She descended the broken steps to the fence.

What am I doing? she screamed. Once a year she visited this place with her son. Now, alone, she felt defenseless. The necropolis was a maze. The Burial Houses watched her with dark-windowed eyes. She shuddered and pressed her face against the fence. As if by witchery, she found herself moving to the gate.

The gate's lock-hole was centered inside the etching of a starfish contained in a circle—the traditional Egyptian symbol for the otherworld. Seeing that, Demetria sighed in relief. She hadn't brought her key. All families with relatives in the necropolis were given a single iron key, designed to open the gate. Without the key, there was no getting in.

It was just as well, she thought. She was shivering and it wasn't from the cold. The anguish of Admetus' passing had shattered her, making her feel like a tree rotten away from the inside. Every visit reopened those wounds. She could not take another dose of that torture, not anymore.

Yet as Demetria drew her overcloak tighter and turned from the gate, she felt the key move in her pocket.

She stifled a scream of horror. How was this possible? A half hour ago, she had searched her pocket for coins to spend at the street vendor's cart!

No. Slowly, she realized the truth. Her tunica pocket *had* been empty…but her overcloak had a pocket of its own. She had not worn the woolen garment since last winter…the time of her last visit to the necropolis. With trembling fingers she withdrew the key from its hiding place. It was smooth and dull in her hand.

Did I know all along the key was in there? She struggled with the question, turning back to the gate and, to her alarm, inserting the key. The bolt retracted with a rusted squeal. Then Demetria became a sleepwalker, dreading each step that took her closer to Admetus' Burial House, unable to stop herself. The Houses studied her as she approached. Down an alley she went, crossing puddles of shadow, until she reached a smaller gate. She unlocked it, crossed a courtyard decorated with ferns and flowering plants, and stopped at his red Burial House door.

She turned the key in a final lock. She pushed the door open. A lightless, sandstone corridor stretched before her. The air inside was cool and dry, smelling of scented oils and stale flowers.

It was too dark to see within, but there was always a lantern hanging on the wall just inside. Demetria groped blindly in the dark, found it, lit the tinder. Then she thrust it in front of her and entered.

The chamber was tight, lined with walls of tombs on both sides of her. They were stacked from the floor to the low ceiling. Each sported a name chiseled into the rock. Above each name, a single fresco was painted to memorialize the deceased. Men hunted lions, sailed ships, laughed with their families, or were depicted in regal profile. In past years Demetria would stop to read the names and inscriptions on these tombs; now, she shambled by rote to her destination.

Admetus' tomb was at the far end of the House, three up from the ground. Demetria knelt, eye-level with his name-plate fresco. There, chiseled in the stone, she read by the lamp's scarlet glow: **ADMETUS, husband and father**, and below that was his epitaph: **JUST AS HE FOLLOWED ILLUMINATION, SO TOO DID HE ILLUMINATE**. Beneath the statement was a profile painting of him, a somewhat inaccurate rendering as it depicted his curly hair longer than he ever wore it. The nose, too, was flatter than his. Otherwise, it was a good likeness.

She set her lamp on the moldy floor. She folded her hands in her lap.

"Admetus," she cried helplessly, and the sound echoed like the ululation of a wraith in the Burial House.

Hypatia's trek up the Canopic to the Great Library was monitored by leering eyes of men and women, who grouped themselves into scattered islands of gossip along the road. Alexandrians were a typically friendly lot, seldom shy or wary of strangers. With an unaccountable but instantaneous certainty, Hypatia now sensed an ugly change in the dispositions of those surrounding her. Their conversations evaporated with her approach. Hypatia offered a smile to the nearest pack of men, but received silence in return.

It was with immeasurable relief that she reached the Library hill. Its slope was smooth and deserted. How ironic, she thought. *Now that I am alone, I feel safe.*

Not since her schooling in Athens had she experienced such fear in a crowd. Worse, many of the men and women she'd passed were *not* strangers to her. At her Academy lectures, by the canals, at the theater…she had seen them before. Where were their friendly greetings now? Where was their adoration?

Where was their love?

Hypatia was finally afraid, and when she reached the zenith of the stairs she hesitated, watching the courtyard for signs of danger. The peristyles were deserted—a disturbing image, suddenly, of how the Library might look in some future age when humanity was gone. The Library itself, with its unlit windows, stood like a massive sepulcher in the low moonlight.

No, I'm not afraid, she told herself. I'm terrified. Every shadow seems a killer tonight. How quickly I am transformed into a villain! I'd rather they worship me again, instead of displaying this inexplicable hostility.

She pushed herself onward, crossing the courtyard to the building's double doors. When she brandished her key, she had trouble inserting it. *Relax!* she told her trembling hands. The long brass key finally slipped into the mechanism. She pulled the doors open, slipped into the blackness of the Main Hall, and bolted the doors behind her.

Then she heard footsteps. Coming fast at her from the dark.

Nauseated with fear, Hypatia spun around, hands fisting, and roared, "*Reveal yourself, coward!*"

The footsteps halted. "My apologies," came the reply.

"Thasos?"

"It's me."

Hypatia's terror evaporated. "What are doing here this late?" The words barely left her mouth when she felt a stunning *deja vu.* She remembered locking up the Library for the night only to find Admetus still haunting the aisles.

Admetus? Were you intending on sleeping here tonight? The Library is closed!

Sorry, Philosopher! Admetus would chirp, laughing. *Never enough hours in a day!*

Thasos was entirely masked in shadow except for the top of his head, where his disheveled hair seemed to be attracting the silver starlight from the roof's oculus. "I fell asleep. I woke up this very instant."

He was relieved to see her. During the past few hours he had tucked himself away in a Library corner, reading to escape his anxiety over yesterday's drama. Gradually, his eyelids had grown heavy. He woke abruptly, finding the Library silent and empty.

"Go home, Thasos," Hypatia told him. "The Library is closed."

"The shadows are not our friends, tonight," he guessed, remembering the horrible panic in her voice a moment earlier. "Are you okay?"

Hypatia moved towards him, unused to speaking with a faceless blot of darkness. In the back-splash of light, she finally distinguished his eyes. The rest was fuzzy, indistinct. How easily this could be Admetus in front of me! she marveled. Life is so strange, so terrible, so sad.

"Hypatia?"

"I'm edgy," she told him. She sat down on the garden bench and invited him with a motion of her hand to join her. "I think our city is going mad."

He sat beside her. "Did the trial happen today?"

"It did. He was executed."

"And the Governor?"

"I don't know."

Thasos watched her face. He realized they had first met on this very spot. Back then, she had been illuminated by sunlight; now, it was the metallic luster of the night sky which gravitated to her eyes and hair. Illustrated by this ghostly luminosity, she looked unreal. A phantasm, too delightful to wear the robes of mortal flesh.

I want her, he thought again. His urge was savage and tender, obsessive and holy, springing from a host of irreconcilable appetites. He was desperate to console her, frantic to ravish her.

Then he caught himself, ashamed by the force of his desire. Hypatia will see it, he thought. She will see it in my face, and feel it in my eyes, and will again know that I am nothing but a slave chained to my hunger. And I can't seem to help it!

Hypatia, however, did not see or sense his frustration. She found herself thinking of Orestes' bedridden condition. Would he die? The question swelled in her mind. Setne had said that survival depended much on the individual, factoring in strength, will, and the body's capacity for healing. *Was Orestes strong?* Yes. *Was he of strong will?* Immeasurable stubbornness seemed more than an appropriate substitute. *What was his body's capacity for healing?* Hypatia had no idea. The blood of his parents could provide a hint. So might factors of his birth, sicknesses suffered as a child…but these were things unknown to her, and she figured that even if she possessed such quantitative data there was no equation known to make use of it. Like a looping road, her inner debate returned to square one.

"I wish I could have helped him," she heard Thasos say.

Hypatia was impressed by the sincerity of his confession. "You did help him, Thasos. But why? What did he mean to you, that you threw yourself to his defense so readily?"

Thasos considered the query. "He meant nothing to me, Teacher. I just could not stand by and watch the prefect of Egypt die at the hands of those monsters. What would I be to *not* stand against them? It could have been you lying there, in the street."

In the weeks she had known him, Thasos had managed to continually surprise her, changing from the silly would-be seducer to the young man who had rushed to Orestes' aid. Hypatia was moved by this newest evolution. It was something seldom seen in her students. It was something special.

She leaned towards him, one of her spiraling curls dislodging from her hairpin and falling over her chest. "I thank you. Orestes is a cherished friend of mine." Then she glanced at the Library's double doors, as if expecting a mob of torch-bearers gathering behind the windows, and added, "You should be careful going home tonight. Which reminds me…What kept you here so long today? I had canceled the class."

"I read. I was learning that planets cool from the same fire that suns are born out of. That a fragment of that ancient flame still burns at the center of every world. That's why volcanos spew molten blood; it's the blood of the Earth's core. And I learned that there are volcanos on the sun and maybe the moon."

"That sounds suspiciously like Democritus."

"It is Democritus…as understood by a local man."

Hypatia raised an eyebrow. "Really? And who would this scholar on his work be?"

"He's a student of the Library, young but full of perseverance. Greek by heritage."

"Alexandrian by country?"

"Yes. An astonishingly good-looking man, too, whose beauty is matched only by his resounding modesty."

"Is this Dionysus a student of mine?"

"Forever," Thasos said. "Forever your student."

Her smile faded, touched by his words.

Before the silence could deepen and become uncomfortable, he said, "Every-one says you're the wisest woman in the world, so I'm sure you see the wisdom in staying *here* tonight, Hypatia, where you're safe. You can't walk home tonight."

"Don't worry. I have a room in the dormitories."

"Then as long as I have your promise on that, I bid you goodnight."

"You have my promise, Thasos. And…thank you."

"Our son is doing as you wished him to," Demetria told her husband's tomb. "He is following in your steps, Admetus. He's a student at the Library. When he's not there, he reads its books on our roof. He never forgot what you told him: 'Give one year of yourself, Thasos!'" She paused, her eyes narrowing into a scowl. For a moment she thought she heard a shuffling sound behind her, at the entrance of the mausoleum, but dismissed it when it did not reappear.

Turning back to the painting, she screamed, "What was so magical about that place, that you abandoned me the way you did! *I loved you so much, Admetus!*" Her face was wet with hot, salty tears. "You threw me away, and for *what?* What did those books give you that I couldn't? Even in bed, I knew your mind was *still there!*" Her eyes blazed suddenly in insane anger. "It stole you from me! It stole you! *And now it's stealing Thasos!*"

Every time Thasos returned from the Library and told her some anecdote of his experiences there, she would cringe inwardly. She pictured him marrying a girl and then deserting her, seduced by a library…truly following his father's path.

For years Demetria had wondered if she had been at fault, somehow, in driving her husband away. But every time she considered that, she arrived at the same conclusion: It *wasn't* her fault. She had showered him with affection and love. She had labored over every meal, for the simple joy of seeing him smile when he ate it. Once at the marketplace together, Admetus had commented that he liked the perfume a woman was wearing. Demetria spent the next few days trying to find that perfume, just to surprise him. She wanted his happiness. She wanted to be a part of building him up, as he had been such a pillar to her.

"I loved you," she said, her voice cracking with helpless misery. "Lov*ed*. Wherever you are, know that I'm perfectly comfortable on my own now. I was on my own when we were together!" Her voice rang out through the mausoleum like the booming cry of a wounded goddess.

Through her anguish she kept thinking of Thasos. Day and night like an opium addict, he was in that place. What the hell could be so compelling, so unnaturally seductive, that a person might be lured there so constantly?

She had tried, when Admetus was alive, to understand the appeal of the Library. Once she went there in secret. She wandered, wide-eyed, through its mighty halls. She had glanced at its dusty scrolls and frowned at tedious reports on debates. Her confusion led to anger. Had she been exchanged for all *this*...a bizarre world of mildew and papyrus? If only he *had* been in love with someone else! A sufficient apology for that might have been forgiven! *But this?*

What had taken her husband?

It was customary for visitors to the necropolis to leave an offering. Demetria simply walked away, her heart relieved to have unburdened itself. She left the Burial House and closed the door behind her—

—and collided with another woman who had been standing outside the doorway; the impact made both women jump. Demetria, still clinging to the lamp, dropped it in surprise. The oil splattered and the fire spread.

"My apologies!" the stranger said.

Demetria cursed her, but seeing the fire she stalled her anger. With her wool overcloak she suffocated the flame before it could ignite the grass growing between the road's tiles. Crisis averted, she glared at the woman. "Fool!"

"I'm so sorry! Let me wash your cloak!"

The woman was a sweet-looking creature, perhaps fifty years old. She had sky-blue eyes of a dreamy, relaxed quality. Her skin was the color of cream, sagging around her throat, and sporting a rosy rouge too bright for her pallor. Most notably, however, was a streak of white hair that ran alongside her head, tucked behind her ear. The rest was brown, save for that spear of colorlessness.

Demetria sensed a confrontational element in the woman's delicate pleasantries. For several seconds, they beheld each other, scowl to smile.

Finally, Demetria said, "Do I know you?"

"No. But forgive me that I know something of *you*. Your words carried."

Immediately Demetria remembered the shuffling sound she had heard when in the mausoleum. She was outraged. "*You dare to interrupt another woman's mourning?*"

The venomous zeal of Demetria's voice should have been enough to send the woman running for her life. Instead, she held her ground and replied, "You are a person in pain, and I cannot help but listen when I hear torment."

"It wasn't torment!"

"*I've* suffered torment," the woman said, cooly unmoved by Demetria's anger. "But it is only natural that we should suffer."

"I—" Demetria stopped, perplexed by the statement. "Why is it natural?"

"We're surrounded by sin of our own making," the woman explained. "Even our rulers are agents against the Light. So I ask you, how can love triumph when so many are blind?"

Demetria stared, mute to respond to this sophistry, and felt the need to challenge it for no other reason than she had nothing else to do. Yet before she could muster a response, the woman continued.

"Egypt was born a pagan land, and simply tearing down the temples doesn't change that," the woman said. "People listen to actors instead of God's wisdom."

"I don't have time for—"

"They read scrolls of witchcraft instead of His Holy Word."

That stopped Demetria. Her words of rebuttal disintegrated in her mouth.

The woman with the white streak nodded, as if reading Demetria's thoughts. "I heard you mention the Library. Whoever you loved fell into it and never got out? Do you know what draws so many there?"

Demetria heard herself ask, in a voice like a child: "What?"

"It turns man's eyes to the ground so he can't look up at the glory of God. It seduces with spells and potions. I know all about it. I barely managed to save my own nephew from it."

Demetria felt pinned through the heart, affixed to an invisible wall. The mention of the woman's nephew conjured an image of her own son, and all she could imagine was that Thasos had not been saved, whatever "saved" meant.

"No," Demetria forced herself to say, shaking her head. "I've been there myself, and there's no witchcraft going on. Just a bunch of philosophic foolery, trying to sound important." Her husband had been neglectful, but not evil.

"Do you think the average Alexandrian would attend something that was blatantly sacrilegious?" the woman asked. Demetria noted that her sweet tone had turned accusatory. "How old?"

"What?"

"How old is your son, the one you were talking about?"

Again, Demetria felt irritated at the intrusion into her privacy. "Seventeen."

"Old enough to make up his own mind, to choose between right and wrong. Is he married?"

Demetria shook her head.

"Then dear woman, perhaps he is fallen to the sorceress that heads that dark school. Have you ever seen her?"

Demetria felt her mouth running dry. She tried to fish for the name of the woman teacher whom Thasos had mentioned after his first day of class, but couldn't remember it. Regardless, what woman would sacrifice marriage, children, and maturity to *teach*?

"Why else would so many young men go there," the woman asked, "leaving their wives and children behind? Why else?"

Demetria choked back a rise of tears. "I love my son."

"I believe you," the woman whispered. "Love defines human beings. Without it, we are lost, don't you think? How empty are lives are without love as our guiding light!"

"He loves *me*," Demetria insisted. "He helps support our household. He is…a good boy."

"I believe you. But for how much longer? When will he desert you the way your husband did?" The woman calmly imprisoned Demetria's hands in her own. "I felt much the way you do. I used to think nothing made sense, that the world was chaos. I thought the ground could fall away at any moment! But then I heard a man explain everything to me. He guides me, now. He teaches me to find others in need, and bring them…people like you, a caring mother who only wants the best for her son! I am going to hear this man speak tomorrow, an hour after sunrise. I would wait for you if you wish." When Demetria made no reaction—still astounded by the power this woman was wielding over her—she added, "I promise that your life will change…as mine did."

CHAPTER 33

▼

True to her word and mindful of her safety, Hypatia slept in the Great Library for the night, toiling at her manuscript in the snug security of her laboratory until her eyelids grew heavy and she retired to the dormitories to sleep. They were built at the back of the Library, containing a bedroom, washroom, and tiny study. Each room had a slit-like window.

She woke to see her window glowing with early daylight. Not bothering to shower, she hastily pinned up her hair, dressed into a fresh robe, and flew from the building to the palace. The day was warm. Dragonflies swarmed by her head as she hurried to discover how Orestes had fared during the night.

She reached the Royal District and encountered an unusually thick crowd near the courthouse and palace gates. She signaled the guards to let her in, and caught two words of a nearby conversation.

"He's dead."

Hypatia spun around at this news, paling and shuddering violently. The man who had spoken was a middle-aged noble with a receding hairline, speaking to a squat, fat-bellied man who, by the looks of his pristine toga, was also a noble. They both noticed Hypatia. They saw the agony in her eyes.

"Dead?" It was the only word she could manage, and her horror swallowed her like a maelstrom of black clouds. She was transported back to the day when she had discovered her father's death. His cold body. His lifeless stare, transfixed on the ceiling.

Then the balding man spoke again: "Yes, the monk named Ammonius is dead. He was executed last night."

"I know," Hypatia said, relieved by his words and friendliness towards her. Apparently, not everyone thought she was a monster. She thanked him, eager to see Orestes. Then she saw the palace doors open. Heliodorus came out, meeting her at the gate.

"Orestes is sleeping," he said. "He is still fighting the fevers, but he lives. For now."

Demetria left for market early, bent on beating the heavy crowds and getting the best selections. She was surprised, though, by the number of people already outside, filling the marketplace and adjacent roads. She could barely walk without brushing up against someone. Most Alexandrians woke before sunrise; few rushed to the market before first light, yet that was precisely what she found.

Swiftly, she bought the items she needed—fresh fruit, eggs, flour, and spices—and was returning home when she saw the route was completely strangled by a bigger crowd. Undulating walls of bodies, washed and unwashed, impeded her return jaunt.

Everywhere, voices buzzed like so many insects, and young boys darted like messenger-birds to spread the gossip. At last, Demetria couldn't help but be intrigued. She finally approached someone to ask what commotion had seized the city.

The man she addressed was surprised at her ignorance, but he happily indulged her. In a breathless gallop of gossip, he told her about the attack on the governor by a monk from Nitria, the execution of the guilty party last night, and a host of new arrests expected in coming days.

Demetria frowned at the news. Attacks? Executions? *Nitria?* As her neighbor turned away, she wondered what all this news meant.

"It is another sign of the darkness," a female voice said behind her.

When she looked she saw the woman from the necropolis. Demetria was angered at the sneaky intrusion. "Polite citizens introduce themselves," she barked.

The woman smiled like a sister patronizing her sibling's wrath. "I apologize, but I thought we were meeting there this morning." She pointed to the opposite side of the marketplace, where the canals of the Kinaron District glittered in the morning sun. Above the waterway residences stood the spires of the Caesarion Church.

The woman continued: "The archbishop is giving today's sermon, and I was hoping you'd join me in listening to him speak."

"I have things to do today," Demetria managed to say, but her voice was faltering. She weakly indicated her basket of produce and then, realizing her lack of conviction, looked helplessly at the woman.

The woman detected her dissolving will. She grasped Demetria's arm. "Come with me today. It was no accident we met yesterday. It was engineered by the Almighty that I should find you. Don't be afraid to walk these next few steps with me. If you don't want to do this for yourself, do it for your son."

CHAPTER 34

▼

Marina knocked insistently on the door to Darius' house. She knew he would be home, for the day had barely started and he was not an early riser. She also knew that his hybrid wife would be home, too, and this was just what she wanted.

The door yawned open, and Kipa appeared in the grey gloom of the foyer. Her brown face brightened. "Marina! You have visited us!"

"Yes!" Marina echoed, in parody of such cheerfulness. "I've come all this way to see *you*, Kipa!"

She had meant it as a sarcastic joke, but Kipa clearly didn't take it that way. The hybrid's smile widened like an earthquake fissure, and she clapped her hands together in unrestrained mirth. "I am glad! Please come in!"

Marina obliged. It was not the first time she had been in Darius' home. When Kipa was out shopping at the Forum, Marina had on half a dozen occasions come by. *That* had been a special thrill all its own, nearly as exquisite as making love to him in the palace. Knowing that she pleasured Kipa's husband on their very bed-sheets, that he would inevitably think of her when Kipa later crawled into bed with him, was deliciously intoxicating.

But those days were over now. Darius' unforgivable insult at the palace had decided her on confessing the affair, hurting him the way she had been hurt. She didn't care about consequences, for which Roman law was severe. I can always deny it, she thought. There's no proof, unless Darius himself publicly admits to it. Even then, I'll deny it. He means nothing to me anymore.

The thrill has worn thin!

"Darius!" Kipa called to the inner depths of the house. "We have company today!"

Marina sat on a sofa while she waited. The room was comfortable, filled with lots of traditional Egyptian furniture like the low, cedar table and tall-backed chairs which surrounded it. There were reed shelves affixed to the walls, holding glass dainties like perfume bottles and animal figurines. Some books, too, filled one row. A desk with lots of papyrus sheets and ink jars sat in the corner; Marina guessed it was where Kipa studied Greek. The rug was Persian; blue-and-gold arabesques interspersed with images of winged gods and ziggurats.

"May I get you some sweet-water?" Kipa's voice jarred her. Marina tore herself away from the lived-in scenery.

"No, thank you. Just sit with me. Talk with me."

At these words Kipa bubbled over with joy. Marina made the realization that the hybrid's life must have been a lonely one. She came from far up-river, after all. Darius had stolen her from those remote lands and deposited her in Alexandria, one of the largest cities on Earth. She spoke poor Greek and no Latin, so her social skills were stunted. She had no friends that Marina was aware of. Didn't that explain why she was fawning over this simple visit?

I know something of living an isolated life, Marina thought. As mortifying as it is, we apparently do share something in common, Kipa!

Just then Darius entered from the hallway. He saw Marina. His eyes grew in terror.

"Marina has come," Kipa chirped to him.

Darius became a statue. He perceived Marina's smirking lips. Without needing to speak, his thoughts were plain as day: *Please don't tell my wife! It would destroy her! I will go back with you, Marina! I will do whatever you want!*

But you've already injured me, Marina replied with her satisfied gaze. *You dared to wound me in my own home. This is only a returned favor.*

"Marina," Darius whispered helplessly.

Kipa turned to her guest. "My husband always so busy. We don't have time for guests, usually."

Marina did not look away from Darius' horror-stricken gaze as she replied. "Well, Kipa, I wanted to make you and your husband happy. That's why I've come to visit! In fact, I want to tell you some things that will make you even happier."

Darius shattered his paralysis and rushed to Marina's side. To Kipa, he said, "Beautiful, please get some sweet-water for us. Please."

"No," Marina said before Kipa could respond. "I can't stay long. The physician advised me to be at Orestes' bedside today."

Kipa lost her smile. "Your husband! Darius told me he is not good."

"Not well," Darius corrected her absently.

"Not well," Kipa replied.

Marina stiffened. "No, he is *not well*."

Please, Darius pleaded with his eyes. *Don't hurt Kipa like this!*

By way of reply Marina looked at his wife. "Do you always know where your husband is, Kipa?"

Kipa blinked. "He is working many times—" Darius interrupted quickly in Egyptian, saying something which was entirely foreign to Marina's ears.

"That's not very good etiquette!" Marina raised her voice. "Kipa, your husband shouldn't speak in heathen tongues when guests are present."

"My apologies, Marina," Kipa said, a worried frown marring her soft skin. "My husband was telling me—"

"Your husband comes to the palace many times, Kipa. When he's not at home, he's usually at the palace."

Darius looked like he was going to die. His skin had paled, softening its vital brown color to an anemic shade. His eyes filled with glassy, unutterable pain.

"My husband has very important work," Kipa continued, oblivious to the silent exchange. "Whole district comes to him for help. He is so patient." She smiled again, sadly, and put her hand on her husband's back in an affectionate caress. "To have me for wife, he is very patient."

A tear spilled from Darius' right eye. The way he had shifted himself to Marina, Kipa couldn't see it.

"You love your husband so much, don't you?"

"Very much. Extremely much."

Then this will shatter your illusions, Marina thought. "Your husband has been coming to see *me*, Kipa. What do you think of that?"

Kipa frowned again. She looked at Darius.

He was making a sound barely above a whisper. It was a silent sob that lightly shook in his throat. He closed his eyes and other tears escaped, trickling down his face.

"He knows you must be in pain, with your husband so sick," Kipa began. "He is always there for people in pain. I am very sorry for your husband's sick, Marina." She squeezed Marina's hands.

Realizing Kipa still didn't understand, Marina fixed her with an astonished gaze. Before she could elaborate, though, her voice stuck in her throat. *Didn't you hear me? Your husband has been coming to see me! He has been inside me! He has cried out as I control him! He cries* my *name! Didn't you hear me, you fool!*

Marina couldn't make her voice work. Her astonishment crumpled and was replaced by confusion. Was Kipa such a helpless innocent that she could sit there like a new flower, knowing only that she loved her husband? The observation touched a strange chord within her, and Marina felt her resolve dying.

"Does physician think your husband will be well?" Kipa asked.

Marina muttered in a hollow voice, "He has been fighting the fevers."

"I hope he is better soon. I should visit more. Just, I'm not familiar with city. Still, I should see you and your husband." She paused, nodded to herself, and continued with conviction: "I will see you tomorrow, Marina. I promise."

Abruptly, Marina felt herself break. It was as alarming as it was silent, but she knew instantly that she couldn't go through with the revelation. For reasons unknown to her, she found herself thinking back to the garden at her parent's house in Greece. As a little girl, the garden had been a source of joy, all the more since her mother had charged her with caring for it through the seasons. One morning, she had awakened to find its beautiful flowers and plants shriveled from a cold spell. Across the gulf of years, she remembered how devastated she had been.

Darius sensed the change in her. Marina stood up swiftly, overcome. She raced for the door.

Kipa moved faster, however. She intercepted Marina before she could exit and wrapped her in a tight embrace. "I'm sorry for your pain and your husband's sick! Your husband will be well! I will offer prayers!"

Marina shuddered in crippling anguish. The hybrid's embrace was the worst of all, for despite her frailty Kipa was nonetheless immobilizing Marina from a hasty departure. Darius looked on, helpless to understand what was happening.

When Marina was released she bolted from the house and was suddenly out in the hot afternoon air, running as if pursued. She thought of her husband, bloodied from surgery and motionless in coma-like helplessness.

Marina didn't look back as she fled the district.

In the dim bedroom of the palace, Orestes opened his eyes.

His first sensation was a dull pain that spider-cracked over the right side and back of his skull. There was also a throbbing behind his right eye. He licked his lips and tasted salty perspiration. When he tried to sit up, the pain forced him back down. He looked towards the window. Through the shades was dull blue light.

Morning light, he thought. How long since the attack? It was an unanswerable question, as time had melted for him in his fever's kiln. He examined his room. It was as vacant as a Pharaoh's tomb. He suddenly knew what the world would be like if he *had* died, or, if he would die yet. Another prefect would be appointed, another woman walking to and fro within these chambers. It was chilling how insignificant his moment of life was. A candle by the window, waiting to be snuffed out by the breeze: That was all it amounted to.

Though his head still throbbed Orestes resolved to sit up. He balanced his weight on his arms and stooped forward. Then, he brought his fingers up to feel the coarse bandages encircling his skull.

I must look so *royal*, he teased himself. Had the trial happened? Was that bastard executed?

Where was Hypatia?

The question floated above the rest. It hung like a halo of incense. Through his nightmare of pain and fever, he remembered Hypatia holding his hand. The memory was so vivid, in fact, that he could still feel a ghostly impression of her palm in his. He wasn't sure about the other memory, the one where she had been whispering lovingly in his ear. It seemed a dream, except for the sensation of her breath tickling his ear. What had she said?

His heart jumped with an eagerness to know. She *had* been by his side, holding his hand, whispering. Of those things, he was certain. But the specifics were lost to him. All he could remember was the tone of her voice. Softer than silk, cooler than autumn.

Loving.

It was a dream, he told himself. The fever obviously had boiled the lines of reality and wishful thinking. Orestes swung his legs over the side of the bed. Pushing Hypatia from his thoughts, he considered the ramifications of the monk's attack.

He smiled.

The tables were now turned on Patriarch Cyril. The Archbishop's arrogant little war had just tumbled into the wrong arena. The Empire, though infamous for backing church over state, would surely not tolerate civil unrest brought about by one man, Patriarch or not.

Yet as Orestes stared at the medicine-soaked rags littering the floor, he found his thoughts returning to Hypatia. He was gripped by a need to tell her how he felt. Nervous, anxious as he was about it, he *needed* to divulge his feelings. Withholding them was accomplishing nothing. But how would she take it? He had heard of her dramatics in turning down would-be suitors.

Orestes shrugged. Those other suitors weren't *me*.

He knew she had left Egypt only once. He, on the other hand, had traveled throughout a good portion of the Mediterranean. He had personally seen four of the Seven Wonders of the World, from the Statue of Zeus in his home city to the famed Mausoleum at Halicarnasus. Orestes couldn't offer poems, or paintings, or songs to Hypatia…but he could take her to the most magnificent sights the world had to offer. Then, to some tiny, unexplored isle. What better place for a relationship to take root? If she refused, what better place to lay the dream to rest?

Orestes' feet touched the floor. He tested his strength by trying to stand. The door yawned wide.

Like a specter from the grave, Setne was suddenly standing in the doorway. His eyes widened when he saw what Orestes was trying to do, and he shook his head in stern disapproval.

"Lie back in bed, governor."

"No."

Setne approached as nimbly and quickly as a bee. "I said lay back in bed."

Orestes regarded the man's severe expression. "I am the prefect of Egypt."

"And I am your physician," Setne said with equal force. "While you are under my care, you obey *my* words. Lay back down, governor, or I will forcibly encourage you to."

Orestes complied. He laughed at the absurdity of the situation.

"Here," Setne said, placing a child's rattle from his bag into Orestes' hand. "When you want to move, shake that. Then I will help you."

Orestes grasped the rattle between his fingers and shook it.

Setne smirked. "Fine. Sit up slowly and lean your weight against me."

"I am hungry."

"A breakfast is being prepared."

Orestes stood shakily. "Has everyone left me?"

"Everyone stayed by your bedside through your fevers," Setne said, helping Orestes to his feet. "Heliodorus and Simplicius should be returning within the hour. Your other friends are certain to stop back tonight."

"Hypatia?"

"Her too, I'm sure."

His legs felt unsteady beneath him. "How is my health?"

"You have much healing to do," Setne replied. "But the fevers have passed. Provided you obey me the next few days, I expect you to recover fully."

Pleasant news at last, he thought. He smiled at the thought of seeing his friends again. A weight seemed to lift from his chest, a warmth taking its place.

His friends.

The thought was as welcome as it was alien, but it nourished the new smile on his face. He repeated those two words silently, followed by the name of the woman he loved.

CHAPTER 35

▼

That night, the stars were as bright as lanterns hung from an onyx ceiling, and Thasos could read easily by their wintry glow. He was on his roof again, an illicitly-borrowed book in his hands. It was one of Hypatia's works; he had finished reading Democritus and was hungry for a taste of his beloved teacher's manuscripts, though this one was more about mathematics than straightforward astronomy, and consequently Thasos shuffled half-blind through its sections, turning the heavy papyrus sheets whether he comprehended the math or not.

I won't be a mathematician, he decided. Astronomy, however, was a delightful path to choose. Thasos unexpectedly made up his mind: He would pursue a career as scholar and astronomer. He would stay with the Library.

But how? Not anyone could join the Library's brotherhood. The resident scholars who resided in the dormitories were the intellectual resources of the Empire. The Library happily paid their salaries, knowing every spent coin was an investment in the future.

Thasos sighed, frustrated and feeling inadequate. So much had already been learned! After all, Eratosthenes had already measured the world and charted 44 constellations, Dionysus of Thrace had dissected language and labeled its parts, Heron had invented steam engines, Aristarchus had measured the sizes and distances of the sun and moon using trigonometry (which itself was developed at Alexandria,) Archimedes had discovered *pi* and crafted a host of mechanical inventions which had come to bear his name, Euclid wrote the book on geometry, Herophilus and Eristratos had documented the internal systems of the human body. What the hell was left?

Thasos knew he could give no company to the great scientists, nor to the philosophers, nor to the playwrights and poets of old. But every man couldn't be Socrates. Every woman couldn't be Hypatia. That didn't have to stop a person from aspiring to that end, did it? What had Hypatia said on the first day of class? Wasn't that advice worth following?

His thoughts swung back to his desire for Hypatia herself. What could he offer *her?* He was young, overly-virile, and belonged to the craftsman notch of society. He had *nothing* to offer her.

The sound of footsteps trampling the grass of his yard surprised him. He sprang up, fearful of violence, monks, riots. For an instant he imagined that they would fall upon his house with torches and stones.

Thasos leaned down from the roof and saw Arion's thickly-haired head.

"Thasos lives!" Arion exclaimed, catching sight of his friend. "He still breathes! By the gods I have found him!"

Thasos swung his legs over the roof's edge. "If any doubted it, now the entire neighborhood knows."

"Where have you been hiding?"

"Not hiding, Arion. Wandering, to find quiet places to read. Thinking. That's all."

Arion's eyes went to the book in Thasos' lap. "Come down here. What are you reading?"

Thasos swung down like a monkey, one hand still clutching the book. "Mathematics."

"Is it illustrated?"

"There are diagrams to promote comprehension."

Arion gave him a suspicious look. "What is Thasos doing reading a book without illustrations of shapely women in suggestive poses?" There was anger in his voice, and before Thasos could reply Arion plucked the work from his grasp. Thasos clawed for it, failed, while Arion tilted the spine to examine the author's name branded on the leather. "Ah-ha, now it becomes clear! I knew a woman had to fit into the picture! How interesting math becomes to a glass-worker...especially when it's taught by *Hy-pa-tia*, Thasos' favorite teacher! No wonder there are no illustrations! Her name alone keeps you at rigid attention!"

"Maybe I borrowed it because of that," Thasos said, making another flimsy grab for the book, failing again. "But there's more to it now."

Arion tossed the volume back to Thasos, who caught it, closed it, tucked it under his arm.

"There's more to *you* now, Thasos," Arion said, feeling a sadness inside. Tavern chases, jealousies, competitions, endless chatter about the feel of this one's skin and the taste of that one's lips had been irritating. But they also had sported their own legacy of familiarity, comfort, and amusement now sorely missed.

From an open window in Thasos' house, Demetria's voice piped sharply: "Thasos! Come in and eat now!"

"I'll be in momentarily!"

"What has gotten into you lately?" Arion persisted.

"I don't know, exactly."

"Well figure it out! I feel as if my best friend is deserting me for his teacher! And for what? What gold lies at the end of this quest? She will not comply with your carnal desires, Thasos. She won't take to your bed!"

"You know, I really don't care."

"You're not a mathematician."

"I'm not?"

"No, Thasos. You're fevered."

"Is the fevered mind better able to grasp certain levels of reality, which the healthy mind cannot?"

"*What?*"

Thasos struck his hands out to the stars like a god commanding them to shine. "Maybe my fever is that of a child who has just come into the world. For nine months he sleeps, blind to what exists around him. Then he's out! Then there's the sky, the wind, water and fire! He can touch grass for the first time! He can swim in the Nile or whatever rivers are near! Maybe mine is the fever of a man who realizes he's been sleeping for many years, and now he is truly awakened, able to think for himself! This is what my father wanted for me, Arion, I know that now."

"Thasos!" Demetria's voice issued again, shriller and more insistent. "Dinner is on the table!"

"Thank you!" Thasos shot back.

Arion recovered from his speechlessness. "There are other considerations, Thasos. I have heard people talking lately about the Library. Ever since the Jews were expelled there has been a growing rally against people who go there, people like us, and especially those near Hypatia. I fear for your safety."

A piercing cry came from inside the house, "*Thasos! Get inside now! I won't tell you again!*"

Thasos was stunned. "I have to eat dinner apparently, or there shall be a great earthquake. We will speak of this again soon."

Will we? Arion wondered, turning to leave.

Thasos regarded his house warily. Feeling very uncertain, he entered.

Demetria was at the counter, immobile, as he entered the kitchen. At the sound of his footsteps she sprang into action, setting a large pot in the basin to scrub later. As he seated himself at the table, she brought a plate of unleavened bread with dipping sauce.

"Tomorrow you are going to a carpenter who trains apprentices," Demetria said, setting the plate down.

Thasos looked at her. "I am?"

"Yes, Thasos, you are."

"Is the house in danger of collapse?"

"Your soul is in danger of collapse."

He sighed and rolled his eyes. "Yes, so I've heard."

With lightning speed she lashed out and struck his face. He was so startled by the blow that he dropped his bread into the dipping sauce.

Demetria spoke in an accusing, angry tone the likes of which he had never heard from her: "The sermon at the church today was delivered by the archbishop himself. He spoke of the evils which go on in your precious Library. Pagan scrolls! *My* son!"

The church? Thasos rubbed the red spot on his cheek. Since when did she go to church?

"You've never been to the Library, mother. You have to read books to be able to criticize them."

"I'll not read what the devil has scribed."

"The devil!" he exclaimed. "These books are written by the greatest minds that ever were. Ignorant attitudes like the words of the archbishop are what is holding us back!"

She slapped him again, harder.

"We were warned of this," she said, remembering the archbishop's words. "That those infected by that place would begin to question, would talk back! Would criticize him and the good he's doing, making mothers realize that to send their children to that witch is to send them to *hell!*"

Thasos leapt up and knocked over the table. "Hypatia is no witch! You don't even hear yourself! If there's anyone who sounds like a witch..." He didn't finish.

With more speed than he had ever seen, Demetria pounced him, grabbed hold of his arm and nearly took him off his feet.

"You'll not go there again!" she screamed, the cords on her neck as rigid as taut ropes. "I'll not be an agent to my son's damnation!"

"*There is no damnation!*" Thasos screamed back. "There is no hell! There is only the damnation we bring to each other! Devils are in human form, mother! They don't need cloven feet!"

A renewed surge of her fury pushed Thasos to the wall; he slammed into it and knocked a painting from where it was hanging. "Your mind is infected, Thasos!" She began to shiver violently. "I have much more experience with life than you do! You will obey my words!"

She seemed on the verge of tears or murder...the eruption terrified him. What was happening? He tried to speak but found himself overcome with emotion, nearly sobbing as he said, "And my father? What of his wishes?"

Admetus did this to you! Demetria thought, tears coming to her own eyes. Inwardly she wanted to hold Thasos, to cry into his shoulder, to tell him how much she missed his father...to tell him she didn't want to lose him too, her last-remaining family.

I can't be abandoned again!

"I knew your father was lost," she muttered, the words coming out in a manic stream, "lost to that place, lost to all of us, I just didn't realize the depth of his sin, his sorcery, Lord in heaven, we can pray for his soul, the both of us, Thasos! We can pray for his soul, but I'll not let you follow him down that path, I'll not let you go as well!"

I've always been here! Thasos wanted to cry. I've never abandoned you! *You* abandoned *me*, drawing up into an impervious shell!

"He died—"

"He gave himself to *sorcery*," Demetria repeated, remembering the archbishop's words. From memory she could hear his voice and see his intense grey eyes: *The devil has many guises, the devil calls to our loved ones with promises of delight, beckoning with sorcery and lust!*

"What defines the devil, mother?"

She snapped out of her contemplation. "That place defines—"

"What criteria define the devil? Violence? Evil? Victimizing the innocent?"

"Yes, Thasos. Yes."

"We are learning in *that place*, as you call it. This table—" He wrenched himself away from her and kicked the fallen furniture—"was built by men of knowledge. This house, our irrigation, our agriculture, all these are the results of knowledge! What is it mother? Is it too much of a strain to see the changes that knowledge has done for the world, for me as your son? Are you blind to my direction now? My thirst to understand this world I walk in?" His voice cracked, and he shouted his next words: "Some hateful old man with delusions of divinity tells you that something is evil, and you swallow it without question? *Is that truth?*"

She leapt upon him, pummeling her fists into his arms, chest, head.

"The devil won't corrupt my son!" she shrieked. "You will *never* go in that place again! Never! Let God be my witness!"

His next move was instinctive and horrible. His hands struck out, knocked her backwards where she stumbled over the table and hit the floor. She stared miserably from where she lay.

Shaking, he said, "What happened to my mother?"

"*What happened to my son?*"

"Your son?" Thasos repeated, and regarded the new rips and tears in his tunic, the red injuries on his arms. His body ached from her attack; a deeper agony clenched his heart. "Your son is obviously not wanted here anymore!" He turned and left the kitchen, passing through the foyer and out into the night.

"*No!*" Demetria cried, crazed with grief and confusion. She tried to stand but her legs buckled, and she could only scream his name with the last of her strength. The door slammed with the finality of a tomb.

CHAPTER 36

▼

Hypatia flew through the dark evening, her face pressed into the wind as she stood at her chariot's helm, reigns in hand, her two horses hastening from the palace grounds. She had gone to see the Governor only to find that he was sleeping again, but Setne gave her the happy news: Orestes had beaten the fevers. His chances of recovery were no longer in doubt.

For a selfish moment she had considered waking him. Of course Setne would never allow it, and besides, Orestes needed all the healing sleep he could get. For several minutes Hypatia had sat like a watchful spirit by his bedside. She wanted to talk to him, to watch his eyes, to hold his hand again. And when the temperature of the bedroom became unbearable for her, she had decided to leave…hoping a chariot ride on this chilly evening would cool the sordid, throbbing images in her head.

Now her silver carriage moved swiftly down the ancient Canopic avenue. The wind blew her hair back, her eyes squinted to the road ahead. Acting on impulse, she veered off the Canopic, yelling for more speed from Thoth and Minerva. They complied with noticeable pleasure, sensing the satisfaction this evening charge was giving their master. Side-by-side they raced, uncomplaining, looking splendid, their manes rippling like twin war-plumes.

The roads were deserted. A city of six hundred thousand souls, Hypatia thought, and I have only my steeds to share the night with. She crossed a canal bridge, the hooves of her horses rapidly thumping the planks beneath. Just as rapidly, images stormed her mind: her friends, Orestes, class, her manuscript, her father, Athens, Serapis, Cyril, her students, Thasos, the Library…all melting together in a stuttering mural.

The bridge ended. She steered into the deserted marketplace, seeing the empty kiosks, tents, and raised platforms. In eleven hours merchants and customers would bring it to life; now it seemed a ghastly netherworld.

Wasn't that what every city became, eventually? Hypatia's chariot rumbled beneath her, the wheels protesting her velocity, as she crossed the width of the open courtyard in nine seconds. How many cities had perished throughout time? Early in his career, Alexander had razed the proud Greek city of Thebes to punish a rebellion. Carthage, Troy, Persepolis, each vanishing in a flash of invaders' fire.

As these places fade from maps, she thought, so too do they fade from all memory save that of the wise.

She steered to West Harbor, startling four pier guards as she careened by them on the low road, and thought suddenly: Who will remember *me?* When the fire of my life has burned out, will I become a vestigial subject, too?

It doesn't matter, she thought. She firmly pulled one reign, changing direction again, leaving the harbor and climbing the high ground that overlooked the riverside homes of a lesser canal, the buildings crammed close, the windows dark. Beyond this congested region, she could see a wider canal that curled like a crescent moon to Kinaron, where by the bright stars she viewed the spires of the Caesarion. Her temper simmered, vengeful thoughts stewing as she gently tugged back on the reigns. Thoth and Minerva complied reluctantly. Her chariot wheels squealed on their axles, the vehicle slowing.

Then she heard the quiet thunder of another chariot.

Such vehicles were reserved for the social elite. The nobility had them. The occasional wealthy merchant. Hypatia's chariot was in fact property of the Library, though the mare and stallion belonged to her, passing into her keeping from the last Librarian at his retirement party.

The Patriarch used a chariot, too, she thought. How likely is it that he's out here now, unaware that his greatest enemy shares the night with him? But she knew it was more probable that a drunken nobleman was wheeling through Alexandria, wife or mistress beside him. How many cases had Heliodorus prosecuted in which a carousing noble had overturned his chariot in a seedy merchant district and was attacked, robbed, or raped?

From her vantage point on the high road she watched a tin carriage appear. Two black horses pulled it. Then she noticed the driver, tall against the dashboard.

"Don't," she told herself through gritted teeth. Her hands lifted the reigns.

Don't. Thoth and Minerva were rigid, sensing her renewed tension. The sound of the chariot on the main avenue below diminished as it continued to Kinaron.

For a moment she thought she might resist her fury's calling. Then she thought of Orestes and how his life had nearly been stolen, of the frenzied mob, of the Jews, of Serapis. Her self-control snapped. She bolted upright in her vehicle and shook the reigns. Her horses responded instantly.

She had no idea why she wanted to reach Cyril—it was plainly him—or what she wanted to say when she did. Reason had fled her. From the high ground she yelled her horses on, and they lurched over a hill, the chariot wheels striking a bump in the road, pitching her carriage airborne. It landed hard on the cobblestone.

The sound made the driver ahead turn, but at that moment she passed behind a series of buildings and was lost to his view. She drove expertly through a narrow back alley, reached a road parallel to his, and surged forward, intent on cutting him off at the Kinaron Bridge. She brought her chariot to a halt directly in Cyril's path.

He had to swerve, fighting for control of his panicking stallions. Once he had stayed the animals, his eyes blazed. "Maniac! You…"

His voice trailed off.

"Good evening, Archbishop," Hypatia replied, her face flush and dark with anger. With her wind-tossed hair and feral gaze, she looked dangerous.

And in that moment Cyril was truly afraid for his safety. *Was* she a demon? he wondered, intimidated by her maddened, turquoise eyes. He had never *believed* the gossip he had instructed the Nitrian monks to spread about her. That had been a tactic, designed to tarnish her crystal reputation and, just maybe, turn some of the city against her. Hypatia was cunning, a flagrant enemy to his cause, but Cyril didn't hold that she was a deadly, entrancing sorceress. Yet in the instant she had sprung from the adjacent road, dark hair wild, her control over the chariot almost supernatural, he reconsidered.

Hypatia did not wait for him to recover. "As you have not yet offered your condolences, I've come to solicit them."

Cyril blinked, bewildered. "My condolences?"

"Surely you have heard that Governor Orestes was attacked by a cowardly monk? Or are the walls of your church so thick that no news can penetrate them?"

Her challenging tone roused him. At last he smiled, eager to see if the stories of Hypatia's legendary debating prowess were true. He had learned much about her lately, questioning his parishioners, seeking more information on the Lady Philosopher. During that research she had grown in his mind, like a nightmare, dangerous, skillful, beguiling, tremendously influential. Now she stood before him, a woman of flesh, haughty, human, not the cosmic adversary he had fancied but just an aging beauty fallen from youth.

"There is no purpose in drawing treaties with Orestes when you are the source of his poisoning," Cyril replied. "How is the prefect?"

"Eager to deal out more punishment."

Cyril watched her carefully. He drew his chariot alongside hers, the four horses passing in edgy indifference. "Perhaps the walls of the Great Library are also thick, for I see plainly that news has not reached *you*. You are not wanted in Alexandria."

Hypatia smiled savagely. "Neither are you."

"We'll see who lasts," he said sourly. "The people will decide, Hypatia. I show them how to reach salvation. You keep them stuck here, in a maze of physical idolatry, worshiping Creation but not the Creator! Might not one of the scrolls in your Library be holy?"

"Archbishop, we're the reason you have a bible to read. We're the ones who had it translated and printed for the common people."

Coolly ignoring this, Cyril said, "There are people asking me why a prefect would refuse cooperation with the church, why a capable man like the governor would take arms against the faith of his righteous people. It was my error to address these concerns to the man himself."

"Ah," Hypatia said with a nod. "I understand clearly. It is me who is responsible for corrupting the governor. It is my evil wiles, learned from Lucifer himself."

"No. I'm sure you learned those wiles on your own. Tell me, I beg of you, what kind of world you think you're creating for the young of Alexandria?"

"A world where people use the full potential of their minds, where learning is the common appetite and knowledge the common food."

"And what do you feed the soul?"

Hypatia laughed, her anger dying quickly as she perceived his devices. "Not the nonsense you feed it, Cyril. About a year ago one of your former parishioners came to the Library and confessed what you'd been preaching. 'Sickness is handed out by the Devil on some occasions, by God on others! A couple who has lost their child must have sinned, and are thus being punished! God loves us but tortures us eternally in hell if we question Him!'" She flashed a humorless grin. "Do you recognize those teachings?"

"You wouldn't comprehend them, for all your learning," Cyril retorted thickly. "You need a soul to see the wisdom in such truths."

"And you are an expert on souls. I'm certain you can write a treatise on their weight, color, scent, volume, constitution, and degrees of radiance!"

"I recognize yours," he hissed. "Any man of the cloth knows the sight of damnation when he sees it."

Hypatia closed her eyes. "'Stop judging, that you may not be judged. For as you judge, so will you be judged, and the measure with which you measure will be measured out to you.'" She opened her eyes. "The Gospel of Matthew 7:1 and 7:2. Sound familiar, or do you not know the words of your own good book?"

Taken aback, hearing his source of study fired at him, Cyril bristled, stammered, panicked for a reply, and managed, "The unholy shall not speak His Word."

"Is that the eleventh commandment? Let us come to the point, Cyril! Leave my Library alone! Leave me alone in it! Leave my students alone! Crawl to your own church and stay there, preach to your people what you will, but trouble my students, my friends, the people of this city no more! Abide more closely to the words and deeds of your messiah!"

One of Cyril's horses neighed, kicked its hoof into the wooden bridge anxiously.

"You condemn yourself where you stand, dear woman."

"I'll not sweat over you, Cyril."

"You don't sweat at the fear of God's wrath, why should I expect you to fear me? But I know all about *you*, Hypatia of Alexandria. I know how you were shaped by your father, poisoned from birth."

"Educated from birth."

"Brought up to think you were a man."

"No, just an individual."

Yelling, spit flying from his teeth, Cyril exclaimed, "Once again Eve plucks from the tree of knowledge!"

"While Adam prefers the bliss of oxen!"

"He should have cut out her tongue." Cyril's blood was pounding as he switched to Latin. "*Deo favente.*"

"*Beati pacifici,*" Hypatia countered. In sensing his showmanship of a second language, she laughed and introduced a third. "*Yewem sesh, Imakhu Cyril!*"

Cyril scowled at the ancient Egyptian syllables, forced to acknowledge his ignorance of them. This arrogant bitch! He imagined her stripped, bound, beaten into submission. "I can see how easily you seduce our young men. You prey upon them."

"You can't perceive me any other way. If not just a pagan, then a pagan temptress! Will you describe me next as sporting horns which break through my scalp?"

"But people will see the light," he promised desperately. "The Bible says—"

Finally losing her cool, Hypatia shouted, "Whatever you want it to say! You wave it in front of your parishioners like a golden idol and tell them that their unhappiness in life is caused by whoever disagrees with it! You tell them it talks about love while you speak in a voice twisted by power! What an opiate your position must be! What control! Like a master puppeteer you have your followers charmed by you, the mighty Cyril on his pulpit! You tell them that the Library causes them grief, that I am the latest incarnation of evil in this world! And what do they do, Cyril? Like starving dogs they come barking at my door, threatening me and my students. You are the accomplished animal-trainer, the king with the unquestioning subjects! You offer your people a drink that is hard to refuse! You provide neat answers that are like sugar. You deny them responsibility for their actions by blaming it on anything and everything you can. I call you the latest court magician, the latest charlatan, the jester who has his eye on the throne! And you have a legion of followers who whimper at your heals and would *kill* for you because you tell them they are damned, cursed, stained with original sin and the only way to wash it out is to obey, without question, what you require of them. Oh, Cyril, how gratifying for you! How seductive! And how *corruptive!*"

Hypatia gave a caustic laugh and shook the reigns on her horses, dismissing him with a wave of her hand like brushing away an annoying fly. If her words had stricken him into silence, that dismissal, *that* absent wave, drove him mad. Cyril's fury exploded and he bounded from his chariot with an agility that surprised even him. He landed on the foot-rail of her chariot, his hands clamping down on her neck.

He wanted to kill her right then, to shake her, choke her, silence her, to throw her disused body into the stream beneath. Hypatia beheld a rage she had never seen before. Her Schoolmaster in Athens had been wrathful from wounded pride and closeted lust; Cyril, however, was acutely suffering from terrible needs, or for want of something which didn't exist. And she was finally afraid, knowing that Cyril could harm her if he wished right there, his fingers hooking into her neck like iron prongs.

Rather than recoil, Hypatia leaned into his face even as he strangled her.

She hissed.

The expression was terrible. The Patriarch, horrified, withdrew and slipped from the foot-rail. He landed hard against his chariot's wheel.

"How true evil shows its colors," she said, and a shake of her reigns sent Thoth and Minerva trotting away.

The soft flesh of her neck ached as she drove home. She steered the vehicle into her yard, passed the sundial and approached the small stable.

She unhitched her animals from the carriage. She led them into their private stalls, stroked their hair, and closed their doors for the night.

Footsteps rushed up rapidly behind her.

CHAPTER 37

▼

Thoth stamped one hoof in agitation, his immense black eyes glancing fearfully to the stable entrance. How many have come for me? Hypatia wondered, aware that she was cornered and weaponless. There is nothing I can do but face my assailants.

Then she turned and saw Thasos at the doorway's edge, looking weary and haunted. "I did not mean to startle you, Teacher."

"Then never do it again!" she commanded, but relief softened her anger and there was comfort in seeing him. "Thasos, I don't give lectures from my home."

He trembled where he stood. "No lecture, Teacher."

"You don't look well."

"Am I disturbing you here, on your property?"

The question was asked with such innocence that Hypatia could not bring herself to chastise him. She sighed. "No, Thasos. You're not disturbing me." Given recent events, the challenge of warding off his naive infatuation was welcome.

Hypatia closed the gap between them. "Why are you here, student?"

Thasos retreated so she could join him in the starlight. Then he carefully produced something from his tunic pocket. Hypatia saw a glass angel sitting in the palm of his hand.

It glittered as if still molten, like crystal ichor. The head was a little sphere set atop a bell-shaped body, rippled to imitate wearing robes. It had slender arms that reached up, as if holding the universe in its wide embrace. From its back sprouted bird-like wings, textured like true feathers.

Yet the glass angel was not transparent, not entirely. Hues of soft, undulating color distinguished its elements. The head and hands were milky-white. The robes were emerald-green. The wings glinted in varying hues of red. The miniature seraph sat in Thasos' palm and, although lacking facial features, expressed a whimsical joy for having been given form.

Hypatia regarded it in silence.

"I made it," Thasos said. "For you."

Hypatia touched the angel, lifting it from the platform of his hand. She placed it in her own, studying the details in wonderment. "How?"

"Mathematics is your sphere of power. Glass-working is mine."

Hypatia ran her finger down the angel's robes. "How did you make the colors?"

"I added certain alloys to the mix. Tin gives the milky hue."

"And the red wings?"

"Gold," Thasos breathed. "Like the color of sunlight reflected in Nile waters."

The statue *was* adorable. And there was something magical about it, this little *ushabti* as the Egyptians would call it. Venus had sprouted fully-formed from the head of Zeus but what Thasos had done was more impressive, for unlike the gods he had labored, with skillful hands, to birth this image into permanence.

"Glass-working is not your only sphere of power Thasos."

"Hypatia—"

"I am proud of you. Your father—I knew your father well, Thasos—he would be so very proud of you."

"I am flattered Philosopher, but—"

"I don't love you Thasos," Hypatia said.

Thasos steadied his breathing, coping with the flash of pain those five words sent through him like a javelin strike. He swallowed. "I know."

Hypatia waited.

Thasos managed a weak smile. "But I love you, Philosopher."

She heard the sincerity in his voice. Men had professed love for her before, wielding the word as a key with which they hoped to open passage to her body. What did such men love? The animal, throbbing moment of sex alone? Like a flag planted in fertile soil, how they might boast of their triumph! *I owned the Philosopher for a night! How she cried! How she moaned! How she wrapped her legs around me and bent to my will!*

Thasos shook his head as if reading her thoughts and disagreeing with them. "I came here tonight to tell you that."

Hypatia frowned and walked past him, out into her yard and night air. "This is hardly an appropriate night for this revelation, Thasos. I am very tired and the day has been longer than you imagine."

He laughed, a short humorless laughter that folded into lonesome sorrow. "You misunderstand me. I don't seek your love in return."

"What, then?"

"A walk, Hypatia. For all the reasons I've already given. A walk between two human beings—"

She spun around, the quickness of her movement making her robe twist so that, for an instant, it mirrored the rippled texture of the glass angel. "And if I should refuse you? Will your love turn to hate, and betray its possessiveness?"

"Whether you refuse me or not," he replied slowly, "It's all I...will ever ask of you. Aside from the privilege of being your student forever."

He looked so vibrant, passionate in a way she had never seen in him before. It occurred to her that she could refuse him, and that he would honor his declaration. But she knew she didn't love him. There in the yard, she realized who had captured her heart.

"Thasos...please go home. You flatter me, and I *am* flattered, but you—"

"I can't honor your request, only because I have no home to go to right now."

"What?"

Thasos let out a deep breath. "It has been a long night for me as well, Hypatia. I thought we might enjoy what remains of it before the sun breaks over the horizon. I promise no juvenile poetry."

She smiled. She couldn't help it.

"Or haughty games of a young man," he continued. "Just a walk, with mutual conversation and an appreciation for the stars, for they are out in force tonight, like a thousand Lighthouses to drive away the night. I—"

He stopped. Her hand was held out to him.

The sight elated and terrified him. He was stunned at how much courage it took to respond, to lift his hand in reply and lace his fingers with hers.

"I will walk with you, Thasos. One walk, but then we must return, for there are classes in the morning."

The ache in his heart cried happily. *One walk. If that's all you ever allow me, I will cherish it for as long as I exist.*

"We do have class," he agreed. "In the morning, Teacher, and for many mornings to come."

Not once did she release his hand.

Together they took a leisurely route through the Royal Square, and up into the deserted marketplace where they sat at a table and discussed the heavens and the earth. They wandered to the Great Harbor, lazily passing anchored ships and discussing the promise of other lands. The Pharos burned red in the night.

It is said, she told him, *that the Tomb of Alexander is buried beneath the Lighthouse.*

I think I'd like my tomb to be beneath the Restless Jackal, he responded. She laughed and squeezed his hand.

On the rocky shoreline, they sat and studied the brightening sky, mighty Ra emerging from his watery sepulcher.

The sun was the original god for people, she told him. *Why do people pray to the sky? Because the sky captivates us. It instills our wonder. Its thunderstorms become our angry deities, its rain is the manna that sustains us…and the sun lights our way.*

In the blushing dawn, they even walked to the necropolis and peered through its iron fence.

My father is here, Thasos told her. *In a hall with other scholars, he sleeps eternally.*

My father as well, Hypatia said. *There is a special house here where the Library stores its great thinkers. Someday, me as well.*

A cheerful thought, Teacher.

A realistic thought, she replied. *Not worth dwelling on, but certainly deserving of the occasional reflection. Someday, foreign people will enter the streets of the necropolis and run their hands across our tombs and brush dust from our name-plates.*

And after death?

Worry about life, Thasos, she told him. *Leave a legacy for people to follow…like that which our fathers left to us. Make a difference while you're alive.*

Yes, Teacher.

The day hatched in a golden glow. Alexandria awoke as they ended their walk in the green cove at the feet of the Library's hill.

You have class in a few hours, she told him.

Of that I am aware, he said.

I will call on you to discuss Democritus.

Putting my legendary modesty aside, I am quite ready, Teacher.

Good day Thasos, she said to him.

He touched his forehead to the back of her hand. He wanted to kiss her. He wanted to tell her how much it hurt to release her hand.

"Good day, Professor Hypatia," he said. He watched her vanish from the cove, climbing the long stairs to the Great Library. And then he cried, not in sorrow or happiness but rather in fear, haunted by the knowledge that one day she would be gone forever.

CHAPTER 38

▼

Sunrise brightened the Egyptian District, and when Heliodorus answered a knock at his door he found Synesius waiting on the stoop.

"I hope I am not disturbing your breakfast," Synesius started.

"Nonsense," Heliodorus declared, showing his friend in. "Sit down and eat with us, fool. We want the company." As he spoke, Nephthys peeked around the corner and smiled warmly at their visitor.

"Nephthys, you grow more beautiful each revolution of the sun," Synesius told her, and tried to smile, but the weight of his recent fears—particularly those revolving around the governor—inhibited the expression and brought new creases of worry to his face. Heliodorus read the expression and immediately set about quelling it.

"Orestes will live," he said, guiding him to a seat in the bright atrium of the house where a table of figs, grapes, steamed catfish, and tea waited for him, Nephthys sipping from her cup. "I just came from the palace an hour ago. Setne said the governor is not taking any visitors, but that he will live." He gave a hearty laugh. "Orestes' head must be made of Damascus steel!"

Synesius sighed so deeply it seemed his entire frame might collapse beneath his white robes. He slumped in his chair, as limp as a deflated waterskin. He buried his face in his hands. "That news sustains my heart, Heliodorus!"

The lawyer walked behind his wife's seat, slipping his arms around her waist. "I have other news to tell you as well, my friend."

Synesius was still recovering from the good news about Orestes; he barely heard Heliodorus' words. "With all that has happened, I nearly forgot about Hypatia's prediction of falling stars! Did you watch them?"

"I did. The event was well-timed for Nephthys and I." He placed his hand on her stomach. "In the wake of those stars, the glow of life has come to this household once again."

Synesius blinked, not understanding.

"A baby, Synesius!" Nephthys said, smiling broadly. "A baby has begun again!"

His reaction was not what they had been expecting. His mouth opened, his eyes stared. His breathing came in fast, frantic inhalations.

"Synesius?"

He tried to speak. Instead, tears spilled down his time-beaten face. His two friends were suddenly at his side.

"I am fine," Synesius managed, hastily wiping his eyes and nose. "I'm sorry, I couldn't help that, I'm sorry." Heliodorus placed his hand on his friend's shoulder. Beneath his touch, Synesius seemed frail and vulnerable. "I cannot express how happy I am for the both of you! And it means so much more, so much more to me."

Heliodorus gave him a puzzled look.

Synesius wiped his eyes again. "I have been in a crisis lately, Heliodorus. I have looked into the future afraid at the changes happening. Your child," he smiled at Nephthys, "is unexpected news, but news I cherish. Before I die, I wanted one piece of good fortune to befall the people I love."

"Die?" Heliodorus said in alarm. "What are you talking about?"

"I am not immortal, Heliodorus! I am an old man! Older than the rest of you. It may not be tomorrow, but it's coming."

"Stop," Nephthys interrupted. "Sit down and be with us!"

Synesius reached for the tea when suddenly a new thought sprang to his mind, and he sputtered excitedly, "We must tell Hypatia!" He began to cry again.

Laughing softly, yet deeply moved by Synesius' outpouring feelings, Heliodorus offered him a hand-towel. Synesius chuckled when he saw it, and he dried his eyes sheepishly. "I really am an old fool!"

Heliodorus said, "Speak no more of endings! But I ask that you keep our secret until our group is reassembled. I want to tell them all myself."

Synesius hid behind the hand-towel as he feebly tried to suppress the continued flow of tears. The picture Heliodorus had painted was unbearably poignant. He imagined it with a vividness that rivaled an actual memory: Orestes, newly recovered from his wounds, and Simplicius returned from the fields of war, and Hypatia, and himself, and Heliodorus and his wife…gathered again on the patio of the palace, to toast to a future they would craft together, to pass the torch on to a new generation that even now was taking form and shape.

"Have you seen Hypatia?" Synesius asked suddenly. "Is she well?"

"I'm sure she's fine. She'll be at the palace tonight, once her classes are finished."

CHAPTER 39

▼

Evening came to Alexandria and as the Great Library emptied of its students, Hypatia retired to the building's deepest chamber where, by the yellow glow of a lantern, she regarded the scroll in front of her.

Though her lengthy desk lay nearby, she sat as always on the red-carpeted floor with her bare feet drawn under her. She twirled her feather pen in hand, considering the next lines to write. Four finished chapters so far, she thought proudly. And it's good.

Her earlier books would, perhaps, be of more value to future scholars. But her seventh was becoming special to her...though she could already imagine the dormitory arguments it would incite. Like a favorite child, it held unique promise...because it dared to imagine the future.

I should feel tired, she thought, remembering her night-long walk with Thasos. In the middle of the afternoon grogginess had crept into her. But then the feeling passed and she was filled with sudden energy, inexplicably galvanized to work on her book. The writing of it was proceeding swiftly...her pen could barely keep pace with her stream of thoughts. Now her fingers ached, and the page was filled with ink that needed to dry. She stood at last, stretching, her back cracking as she did.

On the edge of her desk, Thasos' glass angel glinted in the soft light. Hypatia noticed it and smiled.

"All right," she told the tiny statue. "I'll write the letter."

Since separating from Thasos at the end of their walk, she had been thinking of the letter she should write to him. Even during class—while he spoke impressively on Democritus—she was mentally composing what she wanted to say. Now as her book's ink was drying, she had the time to set her feelings down.

Hypatia gently pushed her work-in-progress aside. She plucked a blank leaf of parchment from the darkness, refreshed her pen, and started a new composition. Her thoughts came effortlessly, growing from word to sentence to paragraph.

Most of her friendships had matured through letters. Synesius, Simplicius, Heliodorus. Orestes was an exception, would always be an exception. *Orestes*, Setne had told her, *would recover.*

He *will* recover, she told herself as she finished the letter. And he'll bring order to Alexandria again...and then he and I will speak.

She hesitated, reflecting on her plan.

No. Orestes and I will speak *tonight*. I've waited long enough; two years of feeling this way and condemning myself for those feelings. Just as Thasos overcame fear to speak to me, I'll summon whatever courage is necessary to tell Orestes...to tell him what I need to say.

The letter dried. She folded the page twice, slipped it into an envelope, and addressed it to her student. Then she stood and reached for the lantern.

The thought occurred of walking by Thasos' house and leaving the envelope under his door, but she had no idea where he lived. He said he worked at a glass shop, but she didn't know which one. Just before turning out the light, she saw a bound volume she had taken out for reference and, on impulse, she slid the envelope behind its front cover. Tomorrow, she decided, I'll give it to him.

Hypatia lifted the glass angel and slipped it into a pocket of her robe. Leaning over the desk, the cuffs of her robe dangling, she extinguished the lantern and the room went dark as if it had never existed at all.

Outside, Hypatia shut the Library's doors. The grounds were vacant at this late hour save for a lone professor hurrying to the dormitories. She hurried faster, anxious and excited and eager to see Orestes. At the Library stables, she procured her chariot and rode out, taking the rutted, steep vehicle path that snaked down the hill and joined the road parallel to the Canopic. The night was overcast but the moon ripped through the clouds, an albino eye observing her as she went.

They attacked her at the bottom of the hill. Bursting from the shadows and shrubbery like ravens, thirty robed men with shaved heads fell upon her chariot. Minerva went berserk, stomping in wild terror and nearly capsizing the carriage. Thoth stood his ground and reared, his legs threatening the men in front.

"*Go!*" Hypatia screamed, partly to galvanize her steeds, partly to draw the attention of city guards, wherever they were. Three monks flung themselves onto the chariot, grabbing for her where she sat behind the dashboard.

It happened so fast Hypatia felt she was watching someone else. Her right arm was seized; she tried to jerk it away but then someone snatched a fistful of her hair, yanking and snapping her head back. She was wrenched out of the seat. As her feet came last, she kicked blindly, feeling her sandal connect with someone's face. The carriage jostled under her, her panicking horses fighting the crowd. Then she heard a sickening *whack!* as a weapon—probably a club of some kind—struck Minerva on the face. The creature's cry was pitiable.

Hypatia felt a dozen hands on her, cruelly pulling at her robe, grabbing a foot, throwing her to the street. As she landed, she heard rapid blows raining upon her steeds; in the gap between two monks, she watched Thoth collapse onto his side, a robed attacker leaping like a baboon into the air above him, club raised, eyes crazed with battle-lust. Then the gap closed. She heard, didn't see, the death-blow.

Hypatia scrambled to her feet, shaking. The nearest monk shoved her into the pulsing wall of bodies. She didn't fight the momentum. Rather, she threw herself into it, hoping to break their line. She was caught. Shoved back.

With more luck than judgment, Hypatia avoided the first fist being swung for her nose. But the reflex disrupted her balance and she stumbled, tripped over someone's feet, and fell. A thick-sandaled foot connected with her head. The force of impact spun her around as the next kick connected with her mouth. Her teeth rattled, salty blood squirting onto her tongue.

No! she panicked, replaying the sight of the monk killing her horse. Instinctively, she held up her hands to protect her head. Two monks imprisoned her flailing arms, pinning them to the street and snapping two of her fingers in the process. A howl of agony gathered in her throat. Like a hammer, a fist came down on her nose. The gristle exploded, hot blood spouting from her nostrils. For an instant, the world disappeared.

When she recovered Hypatia realized she was being dragged by her hair, her robe shredding roughly beneath her. *Think!* she cried silently, feeling rivulets of blood run off her face. I'm being dragged by my hair.

Only by the hair!

Surrounded as she was, she realized the attack had ceased except for the one man who was pulling her, the others running alongside, cheering. Hypatia took the chance. She seized a fistful of her hair, intent on ripping it free. Before she could achieve her purpose a wooden club came down across her forearm, and she screeched wildly in pain.

Peter the Reader hit her with the club a second time. The blow took her in the stomach, and he saw the pagan woman's eyes roll back to show their whites. "Get the chariot!" he screamed. "Hurry, get the chariot!" The crowd responded with explosive enthusiasm.

The monk dragging her tugged roughly. Too roughly. Her hair ripped free and her head fell to the street with a meaty thud. Hypatia moaned. New men came around, grabbing her. Two clutched her arms, while a third went for one of her legs. Seizing the opportunity, Hypatia used the immobilized foot as leverage and kicked her other foot straight into the man's mouth. He choked on his own teeth, falling backwards into the stormy sea of brown robes.

She tried twisting out of their grip as they dragged her again, the skin peeling off her legs from the merciless friction. *Guards will hear me!* she thought, blind with terror. *They'll respond!*

Then Peter's club landed on the side of her neck. The impact sounded like an explosion to her ears and the world seemed to slow down for a moment. As if in a dream she watched herself lifted above the mob, each limb captured.

They dumped her into a tin chariot, concealed in a grove of canal-side palms. Three men, including Peter, squeezed in with her. She was face-first with the floor, watching a scarlet pool pour from her ruined nose. The chariot lurched forward, horses galloping.

"You look good down there," Peter said, aroused at the sight of her rear's two bloodied crescents peeking through her tattered robe.

When they reached the Kinaron courtyard, the church parishioners were waiting. Peter stood, looking for Cyril in the crowd and disappointed when he didn't see him. You ordered this! he thought, puzzled. We have her, Archbishop! She's groveling at my feet!

The Caesarion's doors yawned like a crocodilian maw.

"We have her!" Peter proudly told the crowd. With the other monks, he lifted Hypatia's slumped body from the chariot. Men and women cried exultantly, surging forward. "Stop!" he said aghast. "Not here!" He kicked at the crowd and lost his grip on the pagan's arms. Her upper half struck the ground. Instantly she kicked her legs free, too.

But when she tried to hoist herself up she inevitably put pressure on her injured arm and the pain exploded, knocking her back to the ground. It's broken! My arm is broken…but Setne is my friend, he'll fix it, he'll fix *me*…

Peter couldn't stop the crowd. They fell upon Hypatia, pulled her to her feet, and pushed her inside the church. She spilled onto the unforgiving floor.

Hypatia had never been in the Caesarion before; its interior was dark but she could tell the chamber was very large. She heard the footsteps of two hundred people streaming in behind her.

"I'm not your enemy!" Hypatia shouted, facing the parishioners. "No God gives you the right to—"

A woman flew forward, shrieking wordlessly. She was about the same age as Hypatia but far more withered looking, loose skin jiggling at her throat, a single streak of white in her hair.

"*A pit of sulfur forever and ever!*" the woman cried, and sprang upon Hypatia. The philosopher twisted her body and the woman was shunted to the floor. Seeing their comrade downed, the parishioners dashed forward, their numbers devouring Hypatia, fists pummeling with merciless abandon.

"Kill the witch!"

To kill is prohibited by your own commandments! Hypatia wanted to shout, but she needed all her breath. A blow took her in the head and her vision was temporarily swamped by dancing red lights. In the maelstrom of pain and panic, Hypatia heard her clothes being torn away from her body. Cold air beset her skin. She was turned over like a doll and the last of her garments plucked away. The glass angel Thasos had given her was launched out of her robe's pocket by the force of the crowd, and it went careening over their heads like a true spirit. It struck the nearest wall and exploded.

Hypatia saw blood leaking from dozens of wounds across her body. It was thick and slippery like oil; her attackers' fists splashed in the crimson gore, sliding over the wet surface. At the height of her horror, Hypatia heard her ribs cracking from the merciless pressure of the attack.

This is where I die, she thought. Through blurred eyes she watched the fanatic faces of the mob. *Packs. See, Schoolmaster? I was right...the packs followed me here to Egypt. They got me.*

The savage pounding of flesh became distant to her ears.

Heliodorus? she cried silently. *Simplicius?*

"Stop!"

The crowd obeyed, backing away. Peter strode forward, treasuring the control he had been given. He halted before Hypatia, a reed basket in his hands.

He had never seen a naked woman before, and his eyes glimmered with triumphant lust, mesmerized by her writhing breasts and convulsing torment. Hypatia flopped onto her stomach, then rolled again to her side, trying to find a position that didn't hurt too much. Every which way she turned, a moan of torment escaped her.

That's it, Peter thought. Moan for me.

Die for me.

"See what happens to the enemies of God?" he asked the crowd. Then he emptied the reed basket of its contents. Shattered bits of pottery and sea shells clattered to the floor. The crowd greedily grabbed the pieces, passed them about like unholy eucharist.

Hypatia couldn't lie still. The pain was so excruciating that her body spasmed uncontrollably. She forced herself to stand on shaky legs.

Orestes? she thought helplessly. *Synesius?*

Peter brandished a shard of pottery. "What's wrong, Hypatia? Stand up, that's it! Give us a lecture!"

The parishioners echoed his request: "Lecture! Yes, witch! Give us a final lecture!"

Hypatia knew what they wanted. They had broken her body. Now they wanted her spirit. And if I give them what they want, will they let me live?

No.

They're here to kill me. To ruin me, cripple me, end me.

She was surprised by the calmness that found her. Her pain didn't lessen, but it seemed to move out of her, like another person's pain. She found herself thinking of the Pharos. She thought of the halls in the Library. She thought of her six books.

Almost seven.

Orestes. Heliodorus. Synesius. Simplicius. They would remember her. They would cherish her teachings. Thasos...he would remember her too. Especially when he received her letter. Despite her tortured body, she nearly smiled as she imagined his reaction when he read it:

Dear Thasos,

I enjoyed our walk last night. I enjoyed our conversation, learning about you and your dreams. I'm sorry I can't give you what you want, Thasos, and perhaps my friendship will never be 'fair compensation' as you once put it.

I offer that friendship, regardless. I look at you and feel incredible pride in being able to call myself your teacher. You honor your father's memory,

Thasos. I never told you how easily he absorbed whatever he read. His fluency in subjects would have made him a great teacher, too. You have this same gift; Democritus would have applauded your presentation today. You were passionate about what you were saying. You strode from the classroom eager to learn more.

Last night you told me that you wish to remain with the Library longer than the year your father's funds permit. If after a year you still feel that way, then I can arrange it.

Friendships sometimes begin in interesting ways. Someday I will have to tell you the story of how I met my circle of friends. One day, I will introduce you to them.

Good day, student.

My last letter, she thought. *My life's over now.*

She regarded the crowd with a surge of new strength. She forced herself to stand as tall as she could, the blood running over her sleek body. She grinned.

Peter froze. What's happening? Cyril! I know you're watching from somewhere! *Why is she smiling?*

"Learning...will go on," Hypatia struggled to say. She coughed, twisted violently from the pain that tore through her, fighting back the vomit in her throat. "You can't...cripple it. One day all...of you...will...be forgotten...I promise that!" Chills raced over her body. Resilient, facing her fate, she said, "One day no...self-respecting person will dare...to stand...in the pool of...*murder that you have made!*"

Enraged beyond endurance, Peter cried, "By God this woman shall be silent!"

He leaped and drove the shard into her neck, and the crowd followed suit, tearing her flesh, cleaning the bone of muscle. Hypatia stumbled from one attacker to another. For a miraculous instant, she saw an opening between the bodies, and she limped for it. Then her right arm was caught, her left, her hair, and she was pulled back into the fray.

Her final scream was hideous.

Thasos awoke with a start.

His heart was beating fearfully in the darkness of Arion's bedroom. He bolted upright, shivering.

Slowly, his eyes adjusted to the inky spirals of shadow that swam before his blurred vision. The room began to form out of the gloom, and he could see Arion bundled under the sheets of the opposite cot.

Panic swirled in his chest. Thasos slid his legs over the bedside and slipped his feet into sandals. He crossed the room and reached the hallway. It looked grey and dull, with feeble moonlight cascading through the window at the corridor's end.

It was the same window that, two months ago, robbers had used to get inside his friend's house. There was no glass—in Egypt, the need for free-flowing ventilation prohibited most homes from using anything more than wooden lattice-work to fill a frame—and Thasos tensed, moving stealthily towards it. The living room lay off the corridor. Reaching the corner, Thasos listened for the tell-tale signs of an intruder.

Silence.

Then, the sound of glassware clinking against glassware.

There was someone in the house.

Thasos would gladly have embraced the catharsis that a brawl could supply, had a robber dared to bother him after the fight he'd had with his mother. But yesterday had been wonderful—his hand still smelled of Hypatia's jasmine perfume—and he had spent the hours after her class reading, excitedly ploughing through more chapters of Democritus' last manuscript. He didn't have the heart for a fight...not now.

He peeked into the room. He saw Arion's sofa, glass table, and two reed chairs. A disarrayed game of Senet. Bamboo bridge designs, miniature in scale, on the floor near a flower vase. A painting of the pyramids on the clay walls. Shelves, lined with pottery...and slinking at the feet of the shelves, a grey cat.

Thasos exhaled, immensely relieved. It gazed at him in alarm.

Could have been worse, he thought, shooing the creature out the window. In some parts of the city, baboons were as likely an intruder as cats...and getting rid of *them* wasn't nearly as easy.

At the window, Thasos surveyed the darkened neighborhood.

Was it the cat that woke me? Or a dream?

Yes, he thought. I think it was a dream. He strained to recall its details, failing. From where he stood, he could see three homes...all silent as Burial Houses, black windows cold. He felt beset by uncharacteristic superstition. Like an Assyrian priest reading cracks in oracle bones, Thasos was certain that tonight was ominous. He turned away from the window and regarded the living room once more. Its corners were cloaked in gloom, empty and uninteresting. Thasos frowned. Reluctantly, he returned to bed.

Under the covers, he soothed himself to sleep by replaying the memory of Hypatia walking beside him, holding his hand. He smiled knowing that Hypatia was asleep in her house, dreaming the dreams that inspired her.

The darkened streets intruded into his thoughts. Cold, empty, and heartless.

Thasos exhaled slowly, to exorcize his strangely persistent dread. He drew the sheets up to his neck. He pretended he was hugging her in the blackness.

Just before he succumbed to sleep, he remembered his nightmare. In it he had been blind, a prisoner of eternal shadows, alone in a vast echo chamber until the sound of exploding glass had startled him awake.

CHAPTER 40

▼

In the days that followed, no one could remember how Governor Orestes learned of Hypatia's murder. On the evening of November 21, however, he left the palace and went directly to the Great Harbor.

Hours later, his royal trireme pulled away from Alexandria. The double-decked ship looked like a toy against the dark sea. Its mighty oars dipped into the water, the galley-slaves' muscular bodies glistening, the sails deployed to catch a midnight wind.

On the upper deck, Governor Orestes leaned against the rails and didn't look back at the land he was leaving. He had stepped onto the vessel as if in a daze, barely noticing that although night had fallen the Great Lighthouse was unlit. No Keeper stood on the shore of the island. No brass key was unlocking the door at its base. No light was sundering the darkness as he departed the mighty city of Alexandria.

In past days he might have been enraged by the failure of the Pharos' flame. He might have summoned the Keeper and demanded to know why the fire remained unlit.

Instead, he stared at the open sea with a gaze that never registered anything he was seeing. Beyond the bow of the ship lay a vast, uninterrupted horizon of water.

Orestes pressed himself into the rails, one hand feebly clutching the wooden bar, the other held over his heart as if nursing a wound. Yet no tears fell from his eyes. No cry issued from his throat. His eyes finally settled on the most distant point of the horizon, and he found himself imagining what it might be like to reach that dreary edge of the world.

There is no edge of the world, he heard Hypatia say in memory. *The world is a sphere, orbiting the larger sphere of the sun.*

Yet that shrouded horizon really did look like a great cliff, the world flat. Orestes wanted to reach that faraway perimeter. He wanted to order the slaves to continue rowing, the ship tilting as it encountered the world's edge. The bow would dip lower than the ocean floor as it crossed the threshold. Then the vessel would slide off the Earth. A white waterfall of mist would be their only company as they plummeted to eternity. No crash, no splintering of mastheads, no watery doom. Just an endless fall, forever, into grey oblivion.

Behind him, the Great Lighthouse was a dead tower.

Waves broke against the ship's hull. Droplets sprayed over him, but Orestes made no move to wipe the shivering beads from his face. He only licked his lips, marveling at how the ocean tasted like tears.

And blood.

What would it be like, Orestes mused again, *to keep going, out and out, across the gulf of sea and time?*

The wind and water were cold. The air stung his vision. The droplets of sea-spray trickled down his face, making watery trails just below his eyes.

CHAPTER 41

▼

The sun was setting behind Thasos on the last evening of his lectures. He stood beneath a palm tree with the Nile flowing behind him, a large crowd gathered at his feet. For one hour he had been speaking; now, suddenly, his voice was strangled by emotion. He hesitated, turned his head so his listeners wouldn't see the anguish on his face. While he fought to suppress the pain, he pretended to be watching the crimson sun dying on the horizon.

The silent crowd waited, anxious for him to continue. When he looked back he saw their desperate faces.

Two years had passed since Hypatia's murder. In that time, a new governor, an additional church, and a selective exodus had descended on Alexandria in turn. No secular authority ever challenged the city's Patriarch again.

Two years, Thasos thought, feeling the weight of those words in his mind. In space, the Earth has twice slipped around the sun. *On* Earth, a new age has risen. An age of shadows.

"She had so many friends," the forlorn voice of a woman from his audience said. "What happened to them?"

"I met General Simplicius only once," Thasos replied. "During a riot outside the Library when the Governor was attacked. Following Hypatia's funeral, he returned to the city of Pentapolis where he had been conducting some kind of military reform. However, I hear he returned only to request a transfer. Rumors place him on the eastern edge of the Empire, as far from Alexandria as he could manage.

"Another friend of Hypatia's, a lawyer, departed the city with his wife two months later, resigning from the Royal Court. He currently lives with his wife in

Memphis, the city of old Egypt. It took four letters before he finally replied to me, and then only to say that he was not ready for a correspondence. I hear that he recently had a daughter, and that his attention has been going to raising her."

Raising her properly, the letter had said. Thasos often ruminated on that statement from Heliodorus. The man hadn't even told Thasos what the little girl's name was, but Thasos had his own theories and hoped one day the lawyer would accept a correspondence, if only to clear up that mystery.

"The man known as Synesius of Cyrene died the evening of her funeral," Thasos continued. "He was found by his friends on the floor of an old inn. Archbishop Cyril held a massive funeral for him, a parade that filled the Canopic Way.

"Cyril," Thasos said, the name hissing off his tongue, "Cyril is applauded as a champion of his Faith. His followers burned the Library a few months later. I hear that some of its halls are still intact, that some scrolls escaped the flames. I don't know...I haven't been to Alexandria in almost two years."

But wasn't anything done to Hypatia's murderers? the pained faces asked him without words. *Did no one mourn? Did no soldier of courage stand up to the new tyranny?*

But the city *did* mourn for Hypatia, Thasos remembered. They mourned beyond words. He remembered the public funeral, when men and women alike had wailed in the streets as the Library Council spoke a eulogy for the Philosopher. He remembered seeing her closest friends standing at the head of the procession, white-faced and visibly broken. And he remembered his own unutterable agony when he first heard the news.

Two years now, and that agony continued to sit in the center of his chest like a boil that never died.

"I hear that Regent Pulcheria was outraged when this news reached her. I hear she ordered an investigation into the murder." Thasos paused. "That is the last I hear of it. I have written to her myself, but she apparently deems herself above correspondence with a simple boy from Egypt."

"What of Orestes?" the same woman asked. "Has anyone heard from him?"

"No. When news of her death reached him, he vanished. One vessel in the Great Harbor went missing, and neither ship nor governor was seen again."

Again, the crowd was reflective. Many were Alexandrians and remembered Hypatia well. Others were from surrounding villas and had come to listen to this wandering scholar.

Alexandria! Thasos' heart shouted, longing for the sight of its streets and canals again. After Hypatia's funeral, Thasos had gone directly to the Great

Library and stole several manuscripts, packing them into a satchel, not trusting the Council to keep them safe since they had failed at protecting their most treasured teacher. Then he left a note for Arion, bidding him farewell. He walked out of Alexandria that night, following the Nile south into upper Egypt. He had slept in seedy inns or, when no rooms were available, in anchored ships unbeknownst to the crews who had come ashore. He walked for one year. The sun blistered his skin, the desert cracked his lips, yet he had continued as if a sleepwalker, clutching the sacred remains of the Library close to his breast.

Into the old lands he had gone, the sun-beaten ruins of a lost age his only companions. He went to Giza and gazed upon the Great Pyramid and the enigmatic Sphinx, and had cried that he could not share these sights with his beloved Hypatia. Then onward, deeper into Egypt, to Karnak's decaying obelisks and crumbling valley of ram-headed guardians. His journey had ended in Thebes. There, watching the sun rise over the city's avenue of sphinxes, Thasos had decided to turn around. He had decided to go home.

Along the way, he also decided to give voice to his tortured thoughts and memories. On the brown sand dunes of Thebes, he had given his very first lecture to a crowd of three hundred Egyptians. He had told them what had happened down-river. He had taught them about Hypatia of Alexandria.

For another year he walked, north, as if a new man who tread over the corpse of his earlier self. Each stop along the way, he spoke to ever-increasing gatherings. Some accused him of being a pagan, to which Thasos replied with the story of Serapis. Others accused him of sowing seeds of dissent in the new order, to which Thasos replied with the words of Socrates. Others asked him for answers to their questions of meaning and mystery, to which Thasos replied with the teachings of Hypatia.

Two years, and he was finally returning to Alexandria. Word of his lectures had spread. There were those who knew he was coming, a fact Thasos could not deny when he noticed, among his listeners, several men in brown robes.

It was one of these men who raised his hand suddenly, and stood, and addressed Thasos: "Forgive me young man, but it sounds as if you challenge the wisdom of God's Word and the Word of the Church. What you speak of is a holy execution, not a murder."

Anger flashed in Thasos' heart. He stared at the monk's smiling countenance. The audience was deathly still.

He thought of his second day at Hypatia's class.

Socrates' convictions were his murderers.

No, Hypatia said in memory. *His fellow men were his murderers. Be sure to understand that distinction.*

I understand now, Teacher.

"No," Thasos said with conviction. "Hypatia was murdered by men who have raped and slain our world, whose hands drip with blood. She was destroyed by people who kill, allegedly in the name of love! By people who silence those who disagree with them. Who stamp out the freedom to think. By people who are the jagged rocks on the seas of discovery."

The monk lost his complacent smile.

"Tonight," Thasos told his listeners, "The sky will glimmer with stars. Watch them. Realize they are *something we can understand.* You must be an observer of this world! Gather facts and formulate opinions, then test those opinions. Build on the work of others, and expand our understanding of the universe. Because that's our purpose." His voice quivered, a tear spilled. "That's our future."

And then one day, he thought, *some of you may discover the books I buried in a little box in Thebes. I dug for hours, and then placed Hypatia's works in a bronze chest, and covered that chest with earth. Now those books sleep until they are found again...in some distant age when the world has changed.*

The sun set behind him, turning the Nile into a scarlet ribbon that slithered down the valley. Alexandria lay ahead.

The heat of the flames began to sear his skin. Thasos swallowed and searched the black sky for star or moon. He found none. Overcast clouds strangled the heavens, low and ominous. The tears on his face became hot as the fire approached.

No constellation looks down upon this, he thought solemnly. No wandering planet. Even the silver moon averts its gaze. Once more, Thasos looked to the envelope at his feet.

"I love you, Hypatia," he whispered, the words cleaving his heart. "I love you so much!"

The heat of the flames delivered its first wave of blistering pain. Thasos winced, caught a cry of fear in his throat, choked it back.

How I wish we could have explored the stars together! He watched the envelope blacken and crumple. How I miss the feel of you in my arms and your whisper at my ear! Oh Hypatia!

The fire reached him. The crowd cheered.

"Know that I love you forever!"

After the murder of Hypatia, the classical age of learning came to a crashing, dismal end. Countless "pagan" books which contradicted the Roman Church's view of the cosmos were destroyed, never to be recovered. Civilization plummeted into the Dark Ages, where it remained for one thousand years.

In 646 A.D., Muslim forces conquered Alexandria and completed the destruction of the Great Library, using the remaining "infidel" texts as fuel to heat their bath water. Several volumes survived in Constantinople until the Turkish invasion of 1453. Several books went with the escapees to Italy where they helped spark the Italian Renaissance. The books left behind were destroyed.

Archbishop Cyril was subsequently declared a Christian Saint, a title he continues to hold today.

In 1563, the Spanish missionary Diego de Landa felt that his attempt at converting the Mayan people of South America was being thwarted by their devotion to an ancient library of native literature. He had the irreplaceable books gathered and burned in the public square.

October, 2001. Egyptian President Hosni Mubarak unveiled the newly-created Bibliotheca Alexandrina, a recreation of the Ptolemaic-era Great Library. It houses an estimated four million books, covering an astounding range of subjects and civilizations.

The future remains unknown.

0-595-34252-3

JUN - 8 2006

Printed in the United States
46492LVS00008B/45